Kate Hardy has always loved books, and could read before she went to school. She discovered Mills & Boon books when she was twelve, and decided that this was what she wanted to do. When she isn't writing Kate enjoys reading, cinema, ballroom dancing and the gym. You can contact her via her website: katehardy.com.

Michelle Major grew up in Ohio but dreamed of living in the mountains. Soon after graduating with a degree in journalism, she pointed her car west and settled in Colorado. Her life and house are filled with one great husband, two beautiful kids, a few furry pets and several well-behaved reptiles. She's grateful to have found her passion writing stories with happy endings. Michelle loves to hear from her readers at michellemajor.com.

D1442675

KU-632-438

Also by Kate Hardy

Her Festive Doorstep Baby
His Shy Cinderella
The Runaway Bride and the Billionaire
Christmas Bride for the Boss
Unlocking the Italian Doc's Heart
Reunited at the Altar
Carrying the Single Dad's Baby

Miracles at Muswell Hill Hospital miniseries
Christmas with Her Daredevil Doc
Their Pregnancy Gift

Also by Michelle Major

Falling for the Wrong Brother
Coming Home to Crimson
Sleigh Bells in Crimson
Romancing the Wallflower
Christmas on Crimson Mountain
Always the Best Man
Her Soldier of Fortune
A Fortune in Waiting
Secrets of the A-List

Discover more at millsandboon.co.uk

A DIAMOND IN THE SNOW

KATE HARDY

SECOND CHANCE IN STONECREEK

MICHELLE MAJOR

MILLS & BOON

First Published in Great Britain 2018
by Mills & Boon, an imprint of HarperCollinsPublishers,
1 London Bridge Street, London, SE1 9GF

A Diamond in the Snow © 2018 Pamela Brooks
Second Chance in Stonecreek © 2018 Michelle Major

ISBN: 978-0-263-26534-7

1018

MIX
Paper from
responsible sources
FSC™ C007454

This book is produced from independently certified FSC™ paper to ensure responsible forest management.

For more information visit: www.harpercollins.co.uk/green

Printed and bound in Spain
by CPI, Barcelona

A DIAMOND IN THE SNOW

KATE HARDY

For Jo Rendell-Dodd, with love and thanks for coming on my research trip, and Megan, with love and thanks for putting up with a recalcitrant author! xxx

CHAPTER ONE

'VICTORIA?' FELICITY, THE textile conservation expert who was doing the annual survey of the displays at Chiverton Hall, stood awkwardly in the office doorway. 'Could I have a quick word?'

Victoria's heart sank. Felicity and her team were checking for anything that might need conservation work over the winter. The fact that she wanted a word must mean she'd found something. 'Bad news?'

'It's not *all* bad,' Felicity said brightly. 'There are a couple of rooms where you need to lower the light levels a bit more, to limit the fade damage, but those moth traps have worked brilliantly and there's no evidence of silverfish or death watch beetle—all the holes in the wood are the same as they were last time round and there's no evidence of frazz.'

Frazz, Victoria knew, were the little shavings of wood caused by beetles chomping through it. And that would've meant major structural repairs to whatever was affected, anything from a chair to floorboards to oak panelling. 'I'm glad to hear that.' Though she knew Felicity wouldn't have come to talk about something minor. 'But?'

Felicity sighed. 'I was checking the gilt on a mirror and I found mould behind it.'

'*Mould?*' Victoria looked at her in shock. 'But we keep

an eye on the humidity levels and we've installed conservation heating.' The type that switched on according to the relative humidity in a room, not the temperature. 'How can we have mould?' A nasty thought struck her. 'Oh, no. Is there a leak somewhere that's caused dampness in a wall?' Though Victoria walked through the rooms every day. Surely she should've spotted any signs of water damage?

Felicity shook her head. 'I think it probably started before you put in the heating, when the humidity wasn't quite right, and we didn't spot it at the last survey because it was behind the mirror and it's only just grown out to the edge. Unless we're doing a full clean of the wall coverings—' something that they only did every five years '—we don't take the mirrors and paintings down.'

'Sorry.' Victoria bit her lip. 'I didn't mean it to sound as if I was having a go at you.'

'I know. It's the sort of news that'd upset anyone.'

Victoria smiled, relieved that the conservation expert hadn't taken offence. 'Which room?'

'The ballroom.'

Victoria's favourite room in the house; she loved the way the silk damask wall hangings literally glowed in the light. As children, she and Lizzie had imagined Regency balls taking place there; they'd dressed up and pretended to be one of their ancestors. Well, Lizzie's ancestors, really, as Victoria was adopted; though Patrick and Diana Hamilton had never treated her as if she were anything other than their biological and much-loved daughter.

'I guess behind the mirror is the obvious place for mould to start,' Victoria said. 'We don't use the fireplaces, so there's cold, damp air in the chimney breast, and the dampness would be trapped between the wall and the mirror.'

'Exactly that,' Felicity said. 'You know, if you ever get bored running this place, I'd be more than happy to poach you as a senior member of my team.'

Victoria summoned a smile, though she felt like bawling her eyes out. Mould wasn't good in any building, but it was especially problematic when it came to heritage buildings. 'Thanks, but I'm never going to get bored here.' Though if Lizzie, the true heir to Chiverton Hall, had lived, she would've been the one taking over from their parents. Victoria probably would've ended up working in either food history or conservation but with books, rather than with textiles. 'How bad is it?'

'Bad enough that we'll need to take the hangings down to dry them out. We can't fix it in situ. Hopefully a thorough clean with the conservation vac and a soft brush will get out most of the damage, but if the material's been weakened too much we'll have to put a backing on it.'

'Worst-case?' Victoria asked.

'The silk will be too fragile to go back, and we'll need a specialist weaving company to produce a reproduction for us.'

Victoria dragged in a breath. 'The whole room?'

'Hopefully we can get away with one wall,' Felicity said.

Even one wall would be costly and time-consuming. 'I know the actual cost and time to fix it will depend on what the damage looks like on the reverse side, and the wall might need work as well,' Victoria said. 'I'm not going to hold you to an exact figure but, just so I can get a handle on this, can you give me a ballpark figure for the worst-case scenario?'

Felicity named a figure that made Victoria wince. It was way over the sum she'd allocated for maintenance in the annual budget. And she knew the insurance wouldn't cover it because mould counted as a gradually operating cause. She'd have to find the money for the restoration from somewhere. But where?

'Short of a lottery win or me marrying a millionaire—' which absolutely wasn't going to happen because, apart from the fact she didn't actually know any millionaires, she wasn't even dating anyone, and her exes had made it very clear that she wasn't desirable enough for marriage '—I'm going to have to work out how to fund this.'

'Start with heritage grants,' Felicity advised. 'You'll have a better case if you can show that whatever you're doing will help with education.'

'Like we did when we installed the conservation heating—putting up information boards for the visitors and a blog on the website giving regular updates, with photographs as well as text,' Victoria said promptly.

'And, if we pick the team carefully, we can have students learning conservation skills under our supervision,' Felicity said. 'The ballroom is a perfect example of a Regency interior, so it's important enough to merit conservation.'

Victoria lifted her chin. 'Right. I'd better face the damage.'

Felicity patted her shoulder. 'I know, love. I could've cried when I saw it, and it's not even mine.'

It wasn't really Victoria's, either. Even though her father had sorted out the entail years ago, so the house would pass to her rather than to some distant male relative, she wasn't a Hamilton by birth. Her parents loved her dearly, just as she loved them; but she was still very aware that their real daughter lay in the churchyard next door. And right now Victoria felt as if she'd let them all down. She was supposed to be taking care of her parents and the house, for Lizzie's sake, and she'd failed.

Actually seeing the damage made it feel worse.

Without the mirror over the mantelpiece to reflect light back from the windows opposite, the room seemed darker and smaller. And when Felicity turned off the overhead light and shone her UV torch on the wall, the mould growth glowed luminescent.

'The hangings from that whole wall are going to have to come down,' Felicity said. 'With polythene sheeting over it, to stop the spores spreading.'

'And everyone needs to be wearing protective equipment while they do it,' Victoria said. 'And we'll have to measure the mould spores in the air. If it's bad, then we'll have to keep visitors out of the room completely.'

Felicity patted her shoulder. 'Don't worry. We'll get this fixed so the ballroom shines again.'

Victoria was prepared to do whatever it took. Fill out endless forms, beg every institution going for a loan. Or find a millionaire and talk him into marrying her and saving the ballroom. After her ex had been so forthcoming about where she fell short, Victoria was under no illusions that she was attractive enough for an ordinary man, let alone a millionaire who could have his pick of women; but she knew from past experience that the house was a real draw for potential suitors. All she needed was a millionaire instead of a gold-digger to fall in love with it. Which kind of made her a gold-digger, but she'd live with that. She'd be the perfect wife, for the house's sake.

When Felicity and her team had left for the day, Victoria walked up and down the Long Gallery with her dog at her heels, just as countless Hamilton women had done over the centuries, not seeing the ancient oil paintings or the view over the formal knot gardens. All she could think about was what a mess she'd made. She wasn't a coward—she'd tell her parents the news today—but she wasn't going to tell them until she'd worked out a solution.

Pacing cleared her head enough for her to spend half an hour on the Internet, checking things. And finally she went to her parents' apartment.

'Hello, darling. You're late tonight. Are you eating with us? I've made chicken cacciatore—your favourite,' her mother said.

'You might not want to feed me when you hear the news,' Victoria said with a sigh. She wasn't sure she was up to eating, either. She still felt too sick. 'Felicity found a problem.'

'Bad?' Patrick Hamilton asked.

She nodded. 'Mould in the ballroom, behind the mirror. They found it when they were checking the gilt. Best-case scenario, they'll take the hangings down on that wall, dry them out, remove the mould and put backing on the weak areas of silk. Worst-case, we'll have to get reproduction hangings made for that whole wall. We won't know until the hangings come down.' She dragged in a breath. 'Hopefully we can get a heritage grant. If they turn us down because they've already allocated the funds for the year, then we'll have to raise the money ourselves. We'll have to raise a bit of it in any case.' And she had ideas about that. It'd be a lot of work, but she didn't mind.

'Firstly,' Patrick said, 'you can stop beating yourself up, darling.'

'But I should ha—' she began.

'It was behind the mirror, you said, so nobody would've known it was there until it reached the edge,' Patrick pointed out gently. 'If I'd still been running the house, the mould would still have been there.' He narrowed his eyes at her. 'You're too hard on yourself, Victoria. You're doing a brilliant job. This year has been our best ever for visitor numbers, and your mother and I are incredibly proud of you.' She could hear the worry and the warmth in her father's voice and she knew he meant what he said. But why couldn't she let herself believe it? Why couldn't she feel as if she was *enough*? 'Lizzie would be proud of you, too,' Patrick continued.

At the mention of her little sister, Victoria's throat felt thick and her eyes prickled with tears.

'It'll work out, darling,' Diana said, enveloping her in a hug. 'These things always do.'

'I've been thinking about how we can raise the money. I know we usually close from half-term so we have a chance to do the conservation work before the visitor season starts again, but maybe we could open the house at Christmas this year. Just some of the rooms,' Victoria said. 'We could trim them up for Christmas as it would've been in Regency times, and hold workshops teaching people how to make Christmas wreaths and stained-glass ornaments and old-fashioned confectionery. And we could hold a proper Regency ball, with everyone in Regency dress and supper served exactly as it would've been two hundred years ago.'

'Just like you and Lizzie used to pretend, when you were little and you'd just discovered Jane Austen.' Diana ruffled her hair. 'That's a splendid idea. But it'll be a lot of extra work, darling.'

'I don't mind.' It wasn't a job to her: she loved what she did. It was her *life*.

'We can hire in some help to support you,' Patrick said.

Victoria shook her head. 'We can't afford it, Dad. The cost of fixing the ballroom is going to be astronomical.'

'Then we can try and find a volunteer to help you,' Patrick said.

'Yes—I can ask around,' Diana added. 'There's bound

to be someone we know whose son or daughter is taking a gap year and would leap at the chance to get experience like this. We could offer bed and board here, if that would help.'

'Maybe this could be the start of a new Chiverton tradition,' Patrick said. 'The annual Christmas ball. In years to come, your grandchildren will still be talking about how you saved the ballroom.'

Grandchildren.

Victoria knew how much her parents wanted grandchildren—and she knew she was letting them down there, too.

The problem was, she'd never met the man who made her want to get married, much less have children. Her relationships had all fizzled out—mainly when she'd discovered that the men she'd dated hadn't wanted her, they'd wanted the house and the lifestyle they thought went with it. Once they'd discovered the lifestyle didn't match their dreams, she hadn't seen them for dust. And she'd been stupid enough to be fooled three times, now. Never again.

She'd fallen back on the excuse of being too busy to date, which meant her parents had taken to inviting eligible men over for dinner. Every couple of weeks they'd surprise her with someone who'd just dropped in to say hello. It drove her crazy; but how could she complain when she was so hopeless and couldn't seem to find someone for herself?

Maybe the one good thing about the ballroom restoration was that it might distract her parents from matchmaking. Just for a little while.

'A new tradition sounds lovely,' she said, and forced herself to smile.

'That's my girl,' Patrick said, and patted her on the shoulder. 'We'll find you some help. And we'll get that mould sorted. Together.'

* * *

Sam felt a twinge of guilt as he parked on the gravel outside his parents' house. He really ought to come home more often. It wasn't that far from London to Cambridge, and he was their only child. He really ought to make more of an effort.

His first inkling that something might be wrong was when he walked into the house with a large bouquet of flowers for his mother and a bottle of wine for his father, and his mother started crying.

He put everything he was carrying onto the kitchen table and hugged her. 'If I'd known you were allergic to lilies, Mum, I would've brought you chocolate instead.'

'It's not that. I love the flowers.' She sniffed.

He narrowed his eyes. 'What, then?' Please, not the unthinkable. Several of his friends had recently discovered that their parents were splitting up and were having a hard time dealing with it. But his parents' marriage was rock-solid, he was sure.

'It's your dad. He had a TIA on Wednesday night—a mini-stroke.'

'What?' Wednesday was three days ago. He stared at her in horror. 'Mum, why on earth didn't you call me? I would've come straight to the hospital. You know that.'

She didn't meet his eye. 'You're busy at work, sweetie.'

'Dad's more important than work, and so are you.' He blew out a breath. 'Is he still in hospital? Is he all right? And how are *you* doing?'

'He's recuperating at home, and I'm fine.'

The first bit might be true, but the second definitely wasn't. 'Mum, I hate that you went through this on your own.' On Wednesday night, he'd been out partying. Without a clue that his father was in the emergency department with a potentially life-changing illness. 'What did the doctors say?'

'That if he wants to avoid having another one, or even a full-blown stroke, he needs to take it easier. Maybe think about retiring.'

Which was Sam's cue to come back to Cambridge and take over Patrick's place as the head of the family firm of stockbrokers. Leave the fast-paced, high-octane job he loved in the buzzing, vibrant capital for a staid, quiet job in an equally staid, quiet city.

He pushed the thought aside. Of course he'd do the right thing by his family. He wasn't *that* shallow and self-ish, whatever his girlfriends liked to claim. There was a good reason why he kept all his relationships light. He'd learned the hard way that women saw him as a golden ticket to their future. Which wasn't what he wanted.

'And he needs to cut down on alcohol, stop smoking the cigars he thinks I don't know about, eat more health-ily and take more exercise,' Denise added.

Sam glanced at the wine: his father's favourite. 'So this was the worst thing I could've brought him.'

'It's not your fault, love.'

'So, what—porridge rather than bacon for breakfast, no salt, and no butter on his vegetables?' Which meant his father wasn't going to be happy.

Denise nodded. 'But they've given him medication to thin his blood and stop another clot forming.' She bit her lip. 'Next time, it might be a full-blown stroke.'

Which might affect his father's speech, his mobility and his ability to think clearly. Sam's duty was very clear. 'I'll call my boss tonight and hand in my notice. I'm com-ing home to support you.'

'We can't ask you to do that, Sammy.'

'You're not asking. I'm offering,' he pointed out, and

hugged her again. 'Mum, I want you to promise me you'll never deal with anything like this on your own again. You call me. It doesn't matter what time of day or night. You and Dad come first.'

She blinked away tears. 'Oh, Sammy. I know you've got a busy life in London. I didn't want to bother you.'

'It bothers me a lot more that you didn't tell me,' he said grimly. 'Promise me.'

'I promise,' she said.

'Good. Put the wine in the rack, and I'll think of something else to give Dad. Where is he?'

'In the living room. He's, um, not in the best of moods.'

Sam could imagine. 'I'll get him smiling, Mum.'

Alan Weatherby was sitting in an armchair with a rug over his knees and a scowl on his face.

'Hey, Dad.' Sam patted his father's shoulder. 'On a scale of one to ten of boredom, you're at eleven, right?'

'Your mother fusses and won't let me do anything. She says I have to rest.'

But his father wasn't known for sitting still. Resting would be incredibly frustrating for him. 'Maybe we could go to the golf club and shoot a couple of holes,' Sam suggested.

Alan rolled his eyes. 'It's play, not shoot. Which just shows you're a complete rookie and you'll hack divots out of the green and embarrass me.'

Sam didn't take offence. He knew how he'd feel in his father's shoes: cooped up, miserable and at odds with the world. 'A walk, then,' he suggested. 'I could take you both to the university botanical gardens.' A place he knew his mother loved. 'And we could have a cup of tea in the café.' Though without the scones and clotted cream he knew his father would like. 'A change of scenery might help.'

'Hmm,' Alan said.

'In your shoes, I'd be bored and grumpy, too,' Sam said. 'But your health's important, Dad. You need to look after yourself, especially as you're—'

'I'm not old, before you say it,' Alan cut in. 'Sixty-three isn't old. There's plenty of life in me yet.'

'And I want it to stay that way,' Sam said. 'The medics told you to take things easier, eat well, take a bit of exercise and reduce your stress.'

'Your mother's trying to make me eat lentils. *Lentils.*' Alan looked disgusted.

Sam couldn't hide a grin. 'They're not as bad as you think.'

'Don't *you* start. I thought you'd bring me contraband.'

He had. But only because he hadn't known the situation. 'No chance. I want you about for a lot longer.'

'Is that why you're dragging your feet about settling down and having children?'

If only his father knew. But Sam hadn't told any of his family why he'd broken his engagement to Olivia, two years before. Or why he'd got engaged to her in the first place. Even now it left a nasty taste in his mouth. Nowadays he made sure his girlfriends knew that he was looking for fun and not for for ever. Olivia had broken his ability to trust, and he wasn't sure he wanted to take another risk with his heart.

'No,' he said. 'Dad, there's an easy solution to all this.'

Alan frowned. 'What?'

'Let me take over Weatherby's from you,' Sam said. 'You've more than earned some time off to play golf and have weekends away with Mum. And I've spent the last six years in the City, learning the ropes. You'll be leaving the business in safe hands.'

Alan shook his head. 'The fund you manage is high

risk. It's extreme. Half of our clients would look at your record, panic, and find themselves another stockbroker.'

'Apart from the fact that any strategy I recommended to a client would depend on the client's attitude towards risk,' Sam said dryly, 'I'm good at my job, Dad. That's why they promoted me.'

'You take risks,' Alan repeated.

'Calculated ones.'

'You're still young and reckless.'

'I'm twenty-seven,' Sam said, 'and I'm not reckless.'

'Prove it.'

Sam frowned. 'How?'

'Take an ordinary job for three months.'

'How's that going to prove anything?' Sam asked, mystified.

'It'll show me that you can connect to people in the real word. That you can see that actions have consequences.'

'Dad, I already do connect to people in the real world, and of course I know that actions have consequences,' Sam said, frowning.

'Take an ordinary job,' Alan repeated. 'Show me that you can take directions and listen to other people.'

Which had absolutely nothing to do with running a firm of stockbrokers, Sam thought.

Either he'd accidentally spoken aloud, or his doubts showed on his face, because Alan said softly, 'It's got everything to do with running the firm. It's about listening and relating to people—staff as well as clients. In London, you live in a bubble. You're insulated from your investors and everyone you mix with is like you—young, well-off and living in the fast lane.'

Most people would consider that Samuel Weatherby had made a success of his career. He'd got a job on his own merits after university rather than expecting to be a shoo-in at his father's business, he'd shown an aptitude for fund management and he'd been promoted quickly. But it sounded as if his father thought his job was worthless, and that hurt.

'Not all,' he said. 'There's Jude.' His best friend was an actor with a growing reputation on the stage, and people were talking about him in terms of being the Olivier of his generation.

'Right now,' Alan said, 'I don't think you're settled enough to work at Weatherby's. If I let you take over from me now, it'd be more stressful than running it myself.'

Sam reminded himself that his father had had a rough week—a mini-stroke that had brought him face to face with the idea of getting old or even dying, the prospect of having to change all the things he liked most about his lifestyle and feeling stuck at home when he wanted to be doing what he always did. Right now, Alan was simply lashing out at the nearest target—his son.

'Take an ordinary job for three months, and if you can do that then I'll be happy that I'm leaving the family business in safe hands,' Alan said.

Sam could tell his father to forget it and stomp off back to London in a huff. But the fear he'd seen in his mother's eyes stopped him. Alan was at risk of another mini-stroke or even a full-blown one. Sam couldn't stand by and watch his father drive himself into an early grave. 'So what sort of job do you have in mind, Dad?' he asked.

'Actually, now you mention it, there is one,' Alan said. 'Working for one of my clients. Nice chap. He owns a stately home. A building problem's cropped up in the last week or so and they need to raise some money. He was talking to me about cashing in some investments, but as the market's just dipped I think now's not a good time.'

Raising money. Sam was very, very good at turning

small funds into big ones. But he had a feeling that this particular client wouldn't be comfortable with the high-risk strategy he'd need to adopt to do that.

'The job would be voluntary,' Alan continued, 'because they can't afford to pay anyone. You'd be helping to organise the fundraising events.'

Sam couldn't help smiling.

'What's so funny?' Alan demanded.

'You wanted me to get an ordinary job. I thought you meant something in retail or a call centre. Ordinary people don't own stately homes, Dad.'

'No,' Alan said crisply, 'but their visitors and staff are ordinary and you'll be interacting with them.'

'A voluntary job.' Three months with no salary. But he'd be on garden leave; and even if that didn't work out, he'd managed his personal investments well enough that he could easily afford to take a sabbatical. Jude was coming back from a tour in rep to a three-month run in the West End and could stay at Sam's flat; it would save Jude having to find a landlady who was happy to have a theatrical lodger, and in return Sam would know that his flat was in safe hands. 'OK. I'll talk to him and see if I'll be a good fit.'

'Good.' Alan paused. 'The botanical gardens and afternoon tea, you said.'

'One scone, no cream, and no sugar in your tea,' Sam said.

Alan rolled his eyes. 'You're as bossy as your mother.'

Sam grinned. 'More like I'm as bossy as you, Dad.'

'You might have a point,' Alan allowed. 'Go and tell your mother to get ready. I'll have a word with Patrick and see if we can line up a chat for tomorrow.'

And Sam would have a quiet chat with his boss. This was time for payback. He wasn't thrilled with the idea of working in a stately home for three months, but if that was what it took to make sure his father stayed healthy and happy, he'd do it.

CHAPTER TWO

'So what do you actually know about this man who wants to come and help us, Dad?' Victoria asked.

'He's my stockbroker's son,' Patrick said.

'So is he taking a gap year? Is his degree going to be in history?'

'I don't know,' Patrick said, 'but Alan said he's very keen.'

He must be, Victoria thought, to arrange an interview for nine o'clock on a Sunday morning. 'Did you want to interview him, then, as you know his father?'

Patrick smiled and patted her shoulder. 'Absolutely not, darling. You're the one he's going to be working with. It needs to be your decision.'

'If you change your mind, we'll be in the office,' Victoria said.

It was a shame her father had been so vague about the details; he hadn't even asked for a rudimentary CV. Then again, her father came from the era of the gentleman's agreement and he didn't like paperwork. Hopefully the lad would bring his exam certificates with him and she'd be able to get an idea of his education so far and his interests, and whether he'd be the right one to help her.

Part of her thought there was something rude and arrogant about interviewing a volunteer for a job you weren't actually paying them to do; on the other hand, if he was hopeless, he'd be more of a hindrance than a help because she'd have to double-check everything he did. Plus, even though he wasn't being paid, he was getting valuable experience that might help him with applications for further study or a job in the heritage sector.

'Come on, Humphrey,' she said to her fox-red Labrador, who was curled up on the chair where he knew he wasn't supposed to be. 'Let's go for a walk.' It was more to clear her head before the interview than anything else. It felt as if she'd spent weeks wrestling with forms.

At the W-word, the Labrador sprang off the chair, wagged his tail and followed her into the garden.

Growing up at Chiverton had been such a privilege. Victoria loved everything about the place, from the mellow golden stone it was built from, through to the big sash windows that surrounded the huge Venetian window at the back of the house, through to the pedimented portico at the front. She loved the gardens that sprawled around the house and were full of daffodils and bluebells in the spring, the way the sunrise was reflected in the lake, and the formal knot garden at the side full of box and lavender. And most of all she loved the ballroom.

Her plans were going to require a lot of organisational skills. But hopefully Samuel Weatherby would fall in love with the place, too, and support her fundraising effort.

Humphrey headed straight for the lake as soon as they were outside and was already swimming after the ducks before she had a chance to call him back.

'I'm banishing you to the kitchen,' she said when he finally came out of the lake and shook the water from his coat. 'I don't want you scaring off our volunteer.' Unless he was unsuitable—and then perhaps she could offer him a coffee in the kitchen, and Humphrey would leap all over their volunteer and make him withdraw his offer of help.

She could imagine Lizzie's soft giggle and, 'But, Tori, that's so *naughty*!' Lizzie was one of the two people Victoria had ever allowed to shorten her name.

She shook herself. She didn't have time for sentiment right now. She needed to be businesslike and sort out her questions for her impending visitor to make sure he had the qualities she needed. Someone efficient and calm, who could use his initiative, drive a hard bargain, and not mind mucking in and getting his hands dirty. And definitely not someone clumsy.

In return, he'd get experience on his CV. She tried not to feel guilty about the lack of a salary. So many internships nowadays were unpaid. Besides, as her mother had suggested, they could offer him accommodation and meals; and Victoria could always buy him some books for his course. Textbooks cost an arm and a leg.

She changed into her business suit and had just finished dealing with an email when the landline in her office shrilled. She picked up the phone. 'Victoria Hamilton.'

'May I speak to Mr Hamilton, please? It's Samuel Weatherby. I believe he's expecting me.'

He sounded confident, which was probably a good thing. 'Actually,' she said, 'you're seeing me. I'm his daughter and I run the house.' She wasn't going to give him a hard time about asking for the wrong person. The message had probably become garbled between their fathers.

'My apologies, Ms Hamilton,' he said.

He was quick to recover, at any rate, she thought. 'I assume, as you're ringing me, you're at the gate?'

'Yes. I parked in the visitor car park. Is that OK, or do I need to move my car?'

'It's fine. I'll come and let you in,' she said.

Humphrey whined at the door as she walked past.

'You are not coming with me and jumping all over our poor student,' Victoria told him, but her tone was soft. 'I'll take you for another run later.'

The house was gorgeous, Samuel thought as he walked down the gravelled drive. The equal of any London townhouse, with those huge windows and perfect proportions. The house was clearly well cared for; there was no evidence of it being some mouldering pile with broken windows and damaged stonework, and what he could see of the gardens was neat and tidy.

He paused to read the visitor information board. So the Hamilton family had lived here for two hundred and fifty years. From the woodcut on the board, the place had barely changed in that time—at least, on the outside. Obviously running water, electricity and some form of heating had been installed.

Despite the fact that the house was in the middle of nowhere and he was used to living and working in the centre of London, a few minutes away from everything, there was something about the place that drew him. He could definitely work here for three months, if it would help keep his father happy and healthy.

All he had to do was to convince Patrick Hamilton that he was the man for the job. It would've been helpful if his father had given him a bit more information about what the job actually entailed, so he could've crafted a CV to suit. As it was, he'd have to make do with his current CV—and hope that Patrick didn't look too closely at it or panic about the hedge fund management stuff.

He glanced at his watch. Five minutes early. He could

either kick his heels out here, on the wrong side of a locked gate, or he could get this thing started.

He took his phone from his pocket. Despite this place being in the middle of nowhere, it had a decent signal, to his relief. He called the number his father had given him.

'Victoria Hamilton,' a crisp voice said.

Patrick's wife or daughter, Sam presumed. He couldn't quite gauge her age from her voice. 'May I speak to Mr Hamilton, please? It's Samuel Weatherby. I believe he's expecting me.'

'Actually,' she corrected, 'you're seeing me. I'm his daughter and I run the house.'

Something his father had definitely neglected to tell him. Alarm bells rang in Sam's head. Please don't let this be some elaborate ruse on his father's part to fix him up with someone he considered a suitable partner. Sam didn't *want* a partner. He was quite happy with his life just the way it was, thank you.

Then again, brooding over your own mortality probably meant you didn't pay as much attention to detail as usual. And Sam wanted this job. He'd give his father the benefit of the doubt. 'My apologies, Ms Hamilton.'

'I assume, as you're ringing me, you're at the gate?'

'Yes. I parked in the visitor car park. Is that OK, or do I need to move my car?'

'It's fine. I'll come and let you in,' she said.

He ended the call, and a couple of minutes later a woman came walking round the corner.

She was wearing a well-cut dark business suit and low-heeled shoes. Her dark hair was woven into a severe French pleat, and she wore the bare minimum of make-up. Sam couldn't quite sum her up: she dressed like a woman in her forties, but her skin was unlined enough for her to be around his own age.

'Sorry to keep you waiting, Mr Weatherby.' She tapped a code into the keypad, opened the gate and held out her hand to shake his.

Formal, too. OK. He'd let himself be guided by her.

Her handshake was completely businesslike, firm enough to warn him that she wasn't a pushover and yet she wasn't trying to prove that she was physically as strong as a man.

'Welcome to Chiverton Hall, Mr Weatherby.'

'Sam,' he said. Though he noticed that she didn't ask him to call her by her own first name.

'I'm afraid my father hasn't told me much about you, other than that you're interested in a voluntary job here for the next three months—so I assume that either you're a mature student, or you're changing career and you're looking for some experience to help with that.'

She thought he was a student? Then again, he'd been expecting to deal with her father. There had definitely been some crossed wires. 'I'm changing career,' he said. Which was true: just not the whole truth.

'Did you bring your CV with you?'

'No.' Which had been stupid of him. 'But I can access it on my phone and email it over to you.'

'Thank you. That would be useful.' Her smile was kind, and made it clear she thought he wasn't up to the job.

This was ridiculous. Why should he have to prove himself to a woman he'd never met before, for a temporary *and* voluntary post?

Though, according to his father, they needed help. Having someone clueless who'd need to take up lots of her time for training was the last thing she needed. In her shoes, he'd be the same—wanting someone capable.

'Let me show you round the house,' she said, 'and you

can tell me what you want to get out of a three-month placement.'

Proof for his father that he could take direction and deal with ordinary people. If he told her that, she'd run a mile. And he needed to get this job, so he could stay here to keep an eye on his parents. 'Experience,' he said instead.

'Of conservation work or management?'

'Possibly both.' He felt ridiculously underprepared. He'd expected a casual chat with a friend of his father's, and an immediate offer to start work there the next week. What an arrogant idiot he was. Maybe his father had a point. To give himself thinking time, he asked, 'What does the job actually entail?'

She blew out a breath. 'Background: we do an annual survey to check on the condition of our textiles and see what work we need to do over the winter.'

He assumed this was standard practice in the heritage sector.

'My surveyor found mould in the silk hangings in the ballroom. It's going to cost a lot to fix, so we're applying for heritage grants and we're also running some fundraising events.'

'So where do I come in?' he asked.

'That depends on your skill set.'

Good answer. Victoria Hamilton was definitely one of the sharper tools in the box.

'If you're good at website design, I need to update our website with information about the ballroom restoration and its progress. If you're good at figures, then budgeting and cost control would be a help. If you've managed events, then I'd want you to help to set up the programme and run them.'

Help to, he noticed. She clearly had no intention of giving up control. 'Who fills the gaps?' he asked.

'Me.'

'That's quite a wide range of skills.'

She shrugged. 'I started helping with the house as soon as I was old enough. And Dad's gradually been passing his responsibilities to me. I've been in charge of running the house for two years. You have to be adaptable so you can meet any challenge life throws up. In the heritage sector, every day is different.'

Her father believed in her, whereas his didn't trust him. Part of him envied her. But that wasn't why he was here.

'I'll give you the short version of the house tour,' she said.

Stately homes had never really been Sam's thing. He remembered being taken to them when he was young, but he'd been bored and restless until it was time to run around in the parkland or, even better, a children's play area. But he needed to look enthusiastic right now, if he was to stand any chance of getting this job. 'I'd love to see around,' he fibbed.

She led him round to the front. 'The entrance hall is the first room people would see when they visited, so it needed to look impressive.'

Hence the chandelier, the stunning black and white marble floor, the artwork and the huge curving double staircase. He could imagine women walking down the staircase, with the trains of their dresses sweeping down behind them; and he made a mental note to ask Victoria whether any of her events involved people in period dress—because that *was* something he could help with, through Jude.

There were plenty of portraits on the walls; he assumed most of them were of Hamilton ancestors.

'Once they'd been impressed by the entrance hall—and obviously they'd focus on the plasterwork on the ceiling, not the chandelier—visitors would go up the staircase and into the salon,' she said.

Again, the room was lavishly decorated, with rich carpets and gilt-framed paintings.

'If you were close to the family, you'd go into the withdrawing room,' she said.

Another sumptuous room.

'Closer still, and you'd be invited to the bedroom.'

He couldn't help raising his eyebrows at her.

She didn't even crack a smile, just earnestly explained to him, 'They didn't just dress and sleep here. A lot of business was conducted in the private rooms.'

'Uh-huh.' It was all about money, not sex, then.

'And if you were really, really close, you'd be invited into the closet. This one was remodelled as a dressing room in the mid-eighteen-hundreds, but originally it was the closet.' She indicated a small, plain room.

He managed to stop himself making a witty remark about closets. Mainly because he didn't think she'd find it funny. Victoria Hamilton was the most serious and earnest woman he'd ever met. 'Surely the more important your guest, the posher the room you'd use?'

'No. The public rooms meant everyone could hear what you were talking about. Nowadays it'd be the equivalent of, say, video-calling your bank manager about your overdraft on speakerphone in the middle of a crowded coffee shop. The more privacy you wanted, the smaller the room and the smaller the number of people who could overhear you and gossip. Even the servants couldn't overhear things in the closet.'

'Got you. So that's where you'd plot your business deals?'

'Or revolutions, or marriage-brokering.'

He followed her back to the salon.

'Then we have the Long Gallery—it runs the whole length of the house. When it was too cold and wet to walk in the gardens, they'd walk here. Mainly just promenading up and down, looking at the pictures or through the windows at the garden. It's a good place to think.'

She flushed slightly then, and Sam realised she'd accidentally told him something personal. When Victoria Hamilton needed to think, she paced. Here.

'Next door, in the ballroom, they'd hold musical soirées. Sometimes it was a piano recital, sometimes there would be singing, and sometimes they'd have a string quartet for a ball.'

'The room where you have the mould problem,' he remembered. Was she blinking away tears? Crying over a *room*?

'We've tested the air and it's safe for visitors—you don't need a mask or anything,' she said.

He wasn't going to pretend he knew much about mould, other than the black stuff that had crept across the ceiling of his friends' houses during his student days. So he simply followed her through.

'Oh.' It wasn't quite what he'd expected. The walls, curtains and upholstery were all cream and duck-egg-blue; there was a thick rug in the centre of the room, a grand piano, and chairs and chaises-longue laid out along the walls. There were mirrors on all the walls, reflecting the light from the windows and the chandelier.

'It's not a huge ballroom,' she said. 'Big enough for about fifty, and they'd have supper downstairs in the dining room or they'd lay out a standing supper in the Long Gallery.'

'Is it ever used as a ballroom now?' he asked, intrigued.

'Not for years, but I'm planning to use it as part of the fundraising. It'll be a Christmas ball, with everyone wearing Regency dress, and dinner will be a proper Regency ball supper.'

Her dark eyes were bright, and it was the first time Sam had seen her really animated. It shocked him to realise how gorgeous she was, when she wasn't being earnest. When she was talking about something she really loved, she *glowed*.

'That all sounds fun.'

'We'll attract fans of Austen and the Regency,' she said. 'And that'll be the theme for the week. Craft workshops and decking the house out for Christmas, so visitors can feel part of the past.'

Feel part of the past. Now Sam understood her. This was clearly her favourite room in the house, and she must be devastated by the fact that this was the room with the problem. Now he could see why she'd blinked away tears.

'Forgive me for being dense, but I can't see any signs of mould,' he said. 'Isn't it usually black and on the ceiling?'

'This is white and it's behind the mirror that usually goes over the mantelpiece, but it's just come to the edge. You can see it under ultraviolet light.' She sighed. 'We'll have to take the hangings down to dry them out and then make sure we get all the spores.'

He walked over to the mantelpiece and put his fingers to the wall, and she winced visibly.

'Don't touch because of the mould?' he asked.

'Don't touch because of the oils on your fingertips, which will damage the silk,' she corrected.

'So this isn't wallpaper?'

'It's silk,' she said, 'though it's hung as wallpaper.'

'Pasted to the wall?'

'Hung on wooden battens,' she said. 'I'm guessing you haven't covered the care of textiles or paper on your course, then.'

He was going to have to come clean about this—at least partially. 'Now you've shown me round, why don't we talk about the job?' he asked.

'OK.' She led him through the house without commenting, but he could tell that she didn't take her surroundings for granted, she loved the place. It was her passion—just as he'd thought that fund management was his, but meeting Victoria had shown him that his feelings didn't even come close. Otherwise why would he feel perfectly fine about dropping everything to take over from his father?

Stockbroking wasn't his passion, either. He was doing this to make sure his father had a lot less stress in his life.

Did he even have a passion? he wondered. His best friend, Jude, lit up whenever Shakespeare was mentioned. Whereas Sam... He enjoyed the fast pace of his life, but there wasn't anything that really moved him or drove him. Since Olivia, he'd shut off from everything, lived just for the moment. He'd thought he was happy. But now he was starting to wonder. Was his father right and he was living in a useless bubble?

He shook himself and followed Victoria through a door in the panelling, and then down a narrow staircase.

'Shortcut—the former servants' corridors,' she said, and ushered him into a room that was clearly her office.

Everything was neat and tidy. Obviously she had a clear desk policy, because the only things on the gleaming wood were a laptop computer, a photograph, and a pot of pens. The walls were lined with shelves, and the box files on them were all neatly labelled.

'May I offer you some coffee?' she asked.

Right now he could kill for coffee. It might help him get his brain back into some semblance of order. 'Yes, please.'

'Are you a dog person or a cat person?' she asked.

That was a bit out of left field. Would it affect a potential job offer? 'I didn't grow up with either,' he said carefully, 'so I'd say I'm neutral. Though I'd certainly never hurt an animal.'

'OK. Wait here and I'll bring the coffee back. My dog's a bit over-friendly and he's wet—which is why he's in the kitchen,' she explained. 'How do you take your coffee?'

'Black, no sugar, thanks.'

'Two minutes,' she said. 'And perhaps you can email me your CV while I'm sorting coffee.' She took a business card from the top drawer of her desk and handed it to him. 'My email address is here.'

'Sure,' he said.

Samuel Weatherby was nothing like Victoria had been expecting. He was older, for a start—about her own age, rather than being an undergraduate or just applying for his second degree—and much more polished. Urbane. Although she wasn't one for fashion, she could tell that his suit and shoes were both expensively cut. Way outside the budget of the nerdy young student she'd thought he'd be.

So who exactly was Samuel Weatherby, and why had he come for this job?

She put the kettle on, shook grounds into the cafetière and made a fuss over Humphrey, who was still wet and muddy from the lake. While the coffee was brewing, she slipped her phone from the pocket of her jacket and checked her email. Samuel had sent over his CV—and it was nothing like what she'd expected. She was right in that he was her own age, but there was nothing even vaguely historical or PR-based on his CV. His degree was in economics and he worked as a hedge fund manager. Why would someone who worked in high finance, with a huge salary, want to take three months' work as an unpaid intern in a country house? It didn't make sense.

Frowning, she poured two mugs of coffee, added milk to her own mug, and was in the process of juggling them while trying to close the kitchen door when Humphrey burst past her.

'No, Humph—' she began, but she was much too late.

Judging by the 'oof' from her office, thirty kilograms of muddy Labrador had just landed on Samuel Weatherby's lap. Wincing, she hurried to the office and put the mugs on her desk. There were muddy paw prints all over Samuel's trousers and hair all over his jacket, and Humphrey was wagging his tail, completely unrepentant and pleased with himself for making a new friend.

'I'm so sorry,' she said. 'He's young—fifteen months—and his manners aren't quite there yet. He didn't mean any harm, and I'll pay your dry-cleaning bill.'

'It's fine.' Though Samuel made no move towards the dog. Definitely not a dog person, then, she thought. 'Thank you for the coffee.'

'Pleasure. I'm going to put this monster back in the kitchen.' She held Humphrey's collar firmly and took him back down the corridor to the kitchen. 'You are *so* bad,' she whispered. 'But you might have done me a favour—put him off working here, so I won't have to ask difficult questions.'

But, when she got back to her office, Samuel was the picture of equanimity. He wasn't on his feet, ready to make an excuse to leave; he looked perfectly comfortable in his chair.

She was going to have to ask the difficult questions, then.

'I read your CV while I made the coffee,' she said. 'And I'm confused. You're a hedge fund manager. A successful one, judging by your career history.' There had been a series of rapid promotions. 'Why on earth would you want to give up a career like that to do voluntary work?'

'A change of heart from a greedy banker?' he suggested.

Victoria wasn't quite sure whether he was teasing or telling the truth. Everyone always told her she was too serious, but she just wasn't any good at working out when people were teasing. Just as she'd proved hopeless at telling who really liked her for herself and who had their eyes on the money.

She played it safe and went for serious. 'You're not into historical stuff. You were surprised by some of the things I told you, which anyone who'd studied social history would've taken for granted; and I took you past artwork and furniture in the public rooms that would've made anyone who worked in the heritage sector quiver, stop me and ask more.'

Busted. Sam had just seen them as pretty pictures and nice furnishings.

Which meant he had nothing left to lose, because she obviously thought he wouldn't be right for the job. The truth it was. 'Do you want to know why I really want this job?' he asked.

She just looked at him, her dark eyes wary.

'OK. My dad really is your dad's stockbroker, and he talked to your dad to set up an interview for me.'

'But why? Is it some kind of weird bet among your hedge fund manager friends?'

That stung, but he knew she had a point. People in his world didn't exactly have great PR among the rest of the population, who thought they were all spoiled and overpaid and had a warped sense of humour. 'No. They're all going to think I'm insane, and so is my boss.' He sighed. 'This whole interview is confidential, yes?'

'Of course.'

'Good. Bottom line—and I need to ask you not to tell anyone this.' He paused. At her nod, he continued, 'My dad's not in the best of health right now. I offered to resign and take over the family business, so he can retire and relax a bit.'

'That's more logical than working here. Fund management and stockbroking have a lot in common.' Her eyes narrowed. 'Obviously he said no, or you wouldn't be here. Why do you want to be my intern?'

He might as well tell her the truth. 'Because Dad thinks I live in a bubble and doing this job for three months will prove to him that I can relate to ordinary people.'

'I'd say you're switching one bubble for another.' And, to her credit, her mouth was twitching slightly. So maybe she did have a sense of humour under all that earnestness and could also see the funny side of the situation. 'I've never met your dad, because my dad still handles the investment side of things here.' She looked straight at him. 'Does your dad think you can't take directions from a woman?'

'Possibly. To be fair, neither can he. I think he'll be driving my mum insane,' he said. 'Which is the other reason I want to come back to Cambridge. Dad has a low boredom threshold and I think she'll need help to get him to be sensible and follow the doctor's orders.'

'That,' she said, 'does you a lot of credit. But I'm not sure this is the right job for you, Samuel. You're way over-qualified to be my intern, and frankly your salary is a lot more than mine. Even if you earn the average salary for your job—and from your CV I'm guessing you're at the higher end—your annual salary, pre-tax, would keep this house going for six months.'

It took him seconds to do the maths. It cost that much to run an estate? Staff, maintenance, insurance, taxes... Maybe he could help there and look at her budget, see if the income streams worked hard enough. 'Take my salary out of the equation. It's not relevant. What attributes do you need in your intern?'

'I want someone who can work on their own initiative but who's not too proud to ask questions.'

'I tick both boxes,' he said.

'Someone who understands figures, which obviously you do. Someone who's good with people.'

'I'm good with people,' he said. 'I have project management skills. I know how to work to a budget and a timeframe. I admit I know next to nothing about history or conservation, but I'm a fast learner.'

'I think,' she said, 'you'd be bored. You're used to living in the middle of London, with an insanely fast-paced job. Here, life's much slower. If I gave you the job, you'd be unhappy—and that's not fair on you, or on the rest of my team.'

'If you don't give me the job, I'll be unhappy,' he countered. 'I want to be able to keep an eye on my dad. He's not going to retire until I prove myself to him. The longer it takes me to find a job where I can do that—even though, frankly, it's insulting—the longer he'll keep pushing himself too hard, and the more likely it is he'll have a full-blown stroke. This is about damage limitation. I have most of the skills you need and I can learn the rest. And I have contacts in London who can help with other things—publicity, website design, that sort of thing.'

She shook her head. 'I don't have the budget for provincial consultancy fees, let alone London ones.'

'You won't need it. I can call in favours,' he said. 'Give me the job, Ms Hamilton. Please.'

CHAPTER THREE

IN THE HALF-HOUR since they'd first met, Victoria had worked out that she and Samuel had next to nothing in common. He was all about figures and she was about words. He lived in the fast lane and she was more than happy to spend her life here in the country house where she'd grown up, curating the past.

But she needed help to raise funds, and he needed a job to make his father believe in him. As long as they could work together, giving him this job could solve a problem for both of them.

'Let's say a week's trial,' she said. 'See if we can work together.'

'Thank you,' he said.

'If you hate it here, that still gives me enough time to find another intern before things get really hectic.'

He inclined his head. 'And if you can't stand me, then you only have to put up with me for a week.'

'I wasn't going to be rude enough to say that.' But she'd thought it, and she could feel the guilty colour bursting into her cheeks.

'Lighten up. I was teasing, Vicky.'

'Victoria,' she corrected. Not that she'd offered to be on first name terms with him.

As if he'd read her mind, he asked, 'Do your staff normally call you Ms Hamilton?'

'No,' she admitted.

'But you prefer formality.'

'Nobody shortens my name. Why are you making it a problem?'

'I'm not.' He looked at her. 'I need to make friends with your dog and meet the rest of your team. At work tomorrow, would you prefer me to wear a suit or casual clothes?'

'The house is open for visitors tomorrow afternoon,' she said. 'But if you're meeting Humphrey...' She winced, seeing the mud smeared over his expensive suit.

'How about,' he said, 'I wear jeans in the morning so it doesn't matter if the dog covers me with mud, but I bring a suit for when the house is open? Or do your house stewards wear period costume?'

'You'll need training before you can be a steward. And we don't usually wear period dress. But I was thinking about it for the events on the Christmas week,' she added.

'Good idea,' he said. 'It would be an additional visitor attraction.'

She had a sudden vision of him in Regency dress and went hot all over. Samuel Wetherby could *definitely* be a visitor attraction. He looked good enough in modern dress; in Regency dress, he'd be stunning. She shook herself. 'Yes,' she said, striving to keep her voice cool and calm. 'OK. I'll see you tomorrow at nine. If you can give me your registration number, I'll make the sure the stewards know you're staff so they won't ask you to pay for parking.'

'Sure. Do you have paper and a pen?'

She took a notepad from her drawer and passed it to him. He scribbled the number down for her. 'Nine o'clock, then.'

'Nine o'clock—and welcome to the team.' She held out her hand to shake his, and when his skin touched hers it felt almost like an electric shock.

How ridiculous. She never reacted to anyone like this. And it was completely inappropriate to have the hots for her intern. Even if he was really easy on the eye—tall, with neatly cut dark hair, green eyes and a killer smile. To give herself a tiny bit of breathing space and remind herself that she was his boss for the next week, at the bare minimum, so she had to keep this professional, she took a copy of the house guide book from the shelf behind her and handed it to him.

'Bedtime reading?' he asked.

Bedtime. There was a hint of sultriness in his tone. Was he doing this deliberately? A twinkle in his eye made her think that he might be teasing her. And now she felt tongue-tied and stupid. 'I thought it might be useful background,' she mumbled.

'It will be.' He smiled at her. 'Thank you for giving me a chance.'

Honestly. He could have charmed his way into any job, not just this one. Part of her wondered if it was some elaborate plot between her parents and his to set them up together; but of course not. A man as gorgeous as Samuel Weatherby had probably been snapped up years ago. Not that she was going to ask if accepting this job would cause a problem with his partner. She didn't want him to think she was fishing for information. 'See you tomorrow,' she said, hating that she didn't sound anywhere near as businesslike as she should.

From hedge fund manager to intern. This next bit of his life was going to be like the ancient Chinese curse, Sam thought: *interesting.* He sent a quick text to his mother to tell her he'd got the job and was just nipping back to London to sort out a few things but would be back later that evening. Then he hooked his phone up to the hands-free system in his car and headed back to London.

His first call was to his best friend.

'Bit early for you on a Sunday, isn't it, Sammy?' Jude asked.

'I'm in Cambridge, so I had an early Saturday night,' Sam explained.

'Is everything okay?'

'I'm not sure.' Sam filled him in on the situation.

'Oh, my God. I'm so sorry. How is your dad?'

'Grumpy. Worried sick and not admitting it. And I think Mum's patience with him is going to wear thin pretty quickly.' Sam paused. 'You'd do the same, wouldn't you?'

'Give up my career and move back home to keep an eye on my parents, you mean?' Jude asked.

'I was always going to come back to Cambridge and take over the firm from Dad,' Sam reminded him. 'It's just happening a bit sooner than I expected.'

'In your shoes, I'd do the same,' Jude said.

Which made Sam feel slightly better about his decision. 'I'm not putting the flat on the market until the spring, so I can rescue you from the dragon landladies and give you a key so you've got somewhere to stay for your West End run, if you like.'

'Are you sure?'

''Course I'm sure.'

'I can only afford to give you the going landlady rent towards the mortgage,' Jude warned.

Sam knew that theatre actors didn't have the massive salary everyone thought they did. 'That's not necessary. I'll know the flat is being looked after rather than being left empty, and that's worth more than any rent. But I'm very happy for you to dedicate your first award win to me.'

Jude laughed. 'You could be waiting a while. Thanks. I accept. And you've more than earned that dedication.'

'I'm heading to London now, to pack. Come and pick up the keys at lunchtime.'

'Will do. And thanks again.' Jude paused. 'Have you told your boss?'

'Not yet. That's the next call.'

'Good luck with that.'

'It'll be fine,' Sam said, with a confidence he didn't quite feel.

'Are you *insane*?' was his boss's reaction when Sam told him he was resigning.

'No.'

'You were supposed to be visiting your parents for the weekend. And I know you haven't been headhunted, because that kind of news never stays secret for long. Why the hell are you resigning?'

'Confidentially, Nigel?' Sam asked. 'And I mean it. Not a word to anyone.'

Nigel sighed. 'All right. Tell me.'

'Dad was rushed into hospital this week. Mum didn't tell me until I got home. It was a mini-stroke and he seems OK now, but if he doesn't slow down he could have a full-blown stroke. I need to be here to keep an eye on them both.'

'Fine—then take a sabbatical until your father's well again.'

'I can't do that. It's permanent. I'm not coming back,' Sam said. 'If I'd been headhunted, I'd be on three months of garden leave with immediate effect, according to my contract.' Which gave him the three months in which he needed to convince his father that he wasn't reckless.

Then it hit him. Of course, his father would know about the clause giving three months' garden leave; that was obviously why Alan had specified three months working in an 'ordinary' job.

'You haven't been headhunted,' Nigel pointed out.

'But I'm going to take over the family business from Dad,' Sam said, 'so that counts as working in the same area and it's the same thing. I'm pretty sure HR will have me locked out of the computer system at work as soon as you tell them.'

'What do you want—a pay rise or more responsibility?' Nigel asked.

'Neither. This isn't a ruse to get more money or a promotion. I really do want to keep an eye on my parents.' The way both of them seemed to have aged twenty years overnight had shocked Sam. As their only child, he knew it was his responsibility to look after them—and, more than that, he *wanted* to take care of them. They'd always supported him. Now it was his turn to be supportive.

'You're serious, aren't you?' Nigel asked.

'Completely.' Sam knew that people in his world had a reputation for being shallow, but any decent person would do what he was doing. Wouldn't they?

Nigel coughed. 'Well, if things change, you'll always be welcomed back. And I hope everything goes all right with your dad.'

'Thanks. Do you need me to do any paperwork?'

'I'll sort it out with HR. Email me the address where you're staying so I can get the paper copies to you.'

'I will do. And thanks, Nigel. I know I'm dropping you in it and I appreciate it.'

'I guess at least you're not going to a competitor. And, as you said, you'd be on garden leave anyway.'

'If whoever takes over from me needs any advice or information, I'll be available,' Sam said.

'That's fair. All right. Well, good luck.'

'Thanks, Nigel.'

All bridges fully burned, Sam thought. He'd agreed a week's trial with Victoria; now he'd officially resigned, he needed to make sure the trial worked out so she let him stay on at Chiverton until his dad was ready for him to take over.

He stopped off at a supermarket to buy a box of nice biscuits and some fruit as a welcome for his new colleagues. Then he browsed in the pet section and bought a squeaky toy, tennis balls, and a bag of dog treats.

Back at his flat, he packed a suitcase and his laptop. The rest of the contents, once Jude had finished his West End run and was back in rep, could either go with the flat or to charity. Funny how little sentiment Sam had for his belongings. Then again, he really only used his flat as a place to sleep. He didn't have the same connection to the building that Victoria Hamilton had to Chiverton Hall.

When Jude arrived to collect the key, he insisted on taking Sam for lunch. And then Sam drove back to Cambridge. To his new life. And hopefully he could help keep his father in good health.

The next morning, at exactly five minutes to nine, the phone on Victoria's desk shrilled.

'Victoria Hamilton.'

'Samuel Weatherby, reporting for duty, ma'am.'

'I'll come and let you in,' she said. Humphrey trotted along beside her to the gate, his nose just ahead of her knee; she'd given up trying to make him walk to heel. 'I want you on your best behaviour,' she warned. 'If Samuel's a good intern, I want to keep him until after the ball.'

Humphrey gave her a look as if to say, 'And if he's not?'

'If he's not, you can run off with all his things and make him chase you right to the end of the park—and then do some judicious chewing,' Victoria said.

And oh, Samuel *would* have to look good in jeans. Faded jeans that fitted him perfectly, teamed with a mustard-coloured sweater she suspected might be cashmere and brown suede boots. His coat was expensively cut, and he was carrying a battered leather satchel and a carrier bag from a high-end supermarket.

'I left my suit and shoes in the car,' he said with a smile.

'I can sort out a locker for you, if you like,' she said.

'It's fine.' He eyed the Labrador. 'Right. First off, dog, you and I need to make friends.'

'His name is Humphrey,' she supplied.

'As in Bogart?'

She nodded. 'When he was a tiny pup, he looked like Bogart, all droopy jowls.'

'Humphrey, I come bearing gifts,' Samuel said. 'May I?' He produced a tennis ball from the carrier bag. 'Sit, and I'll throw it for you.'

'Better go further back in the grounds before you throw it for him,' Victoria said. 'The garden team has enough to do without Humphrey running across the flower beds and squishing the new plants.'

'Oh.' Samuel gave her a sheepish grin, and it made her tingle all over. 'I didn't think of that.' He glanced in the bag. 'What about a squeaky toy?'

She wrinkled her nose. 'That's really kind of you, but it'll take him less than three minutes to unpick all the stitching, unstuff it, and get the squeaker out. Then he'll shred what's left and spread it over three rooms.'

He grimaced. 'You can tell I know nothing about dogs. I bought him some treats as well, but I guess you'd better check they're suitable. Though I did buy organic ones with no preservatives or gluten.'

He'd tried so hard. Victoria's heart melted. 'Thank you. I'm sure he'll love them.' She took pity on him. 'The way to make friends with him is to ignore him and let him come to you. No sudden movements, let him sniff you, and if he rolls over onto his back it means he likes you and he's expecting a tummy rub.'

Two minutes later, Humphrey was enjoying a thorough fuss. When Samuel stopped, Humphrey gave him an indignant look and waved his paw imperiously.

Sam grinned. 'You know what he's saying, don't you? "Play it again, Sam,"' he said in his best Bogart drawl.

Victoria didn't quite have the heart to correct him on the misquote. He was making such an effort. And his smile was so cute...

Not that she should be noticing how cute Samuel was. This was strictly business.

'OK. We've established you and Humphrey are going to get on.' Which was a big hurdle for her. If her dog didn't like her intern, it would make things really difficult. 'Just don't leave your lunchtime sandwich within his reach and unguarded, because Labradors are horribly greedy,' she warned. 'Coffee?'

'Yes, please. So what's the agenda for this morning?'

'I want to finalise what we're doing for Christmas week, then do a project plan for each event, costings and an overall critical path analysis.'

He looked at her as if she'd just grown two heads.

'What?' she asked.

'I wasn't expect—' He stopped himself.

'You weren't expecting me to be in the slightest bit businesslike?'

He winced. 'To be fair, when you showed me round

yesterday it was clear how much you love this place. And in my experience that kind of feeling tends to blind people to financial practicalities.'

'Sadly, you can't run a house like this on love. You have to learn to juggle things—and you need to keep an eye on costs, without making the sort of false economies that'll cause you problems in the future.'

'Noted,' he said. 'So, your timeline. Do you already have a list of events?'

'Yes and no. I brainstormed a few things with my parents.'

'It might,' he said, 'be worth brainstorming with a complete outsider. Someone who doesn't know the limitations and might come up with something totally impractical that will spark off a more practical idea.'

'Is that your way of telling me you want to brainstorm with me?'

He smiled. 'Why don't I make the coffee? By the way, I brought a box of biscuits and some fruit to say hello to the rest of the team. And I picked up some biscotti this morning from the bakery round the corner from my parents, as it's my first day working here and I need to make a good impression on the boss.'

She wasn't sure whether he was teasing her or not. 'Thank you,' she said warily.

'It's an intern's duty to make coffee, so point me in the direction of the kitchen and I'll make it. Milk and sugar?'

'Just a splash of milk, please.' She showed him the kitchen and where everything was kept, then headed back to her office with Humphrey by her side.

Samuel came back with coffee and a plate of biscotti and retrieved the dog treats from his satchel. 'Are these OK?' he asked, handing her the packet.

'They're his favourites. He'll be your friend for life.'

She looked at the dog, who was wagging his tail hopefully. 'Humphrey, sit.'

Humphrey sat.

'Paw,' she said.

Humphrey lifted one paw and gave Samuel a soulful look.

'Do I throw it to him?' Samuel asked.

'Yes, or you can leave it in your hand and he'll take it—though he might need reminding to be gentle.'

'I'm not scared of dogs. I know I sound stupid, asking, but none of my friends had dogs when I was growing up so I don't actually know how to act around them.'

The fact that he was admitting where he didn't have experience boded well for him working here and it reassured her. 'Would you say that to your dad?' she asked.

'If he asked me.'

She frowned. 'Then why does your dad think you're reckless?'

'Because my particular fund deals in high-risk investments.' He looked at her, his green eyes wide with sincerity. 'Which I wouldn't recommend to a client who wants a low-risk investment.' He shrugged. 'But I guess Dad's view of me might be a bit biased.'

'What did you do?' she asked, expecting him to say that he'd had a few speeding fines.

'I applied only to one university,' he said. 'Dad thought I was being stupid, not having a backup. But I didn't need a plan B because I knew I'd get my grades.'

She wasn't sure if she found his confidence more scary or sexy.

'And there's my car. Dad would prefer me to have a big four-by-four or a saloon car. Probably a grey one.'

'Don't tell me—yours is a red two-seater, low-slung and fast?'

'And convertible,' he said. 'And, yes, before you ask, I've had two speeding fines. But the last one was three years ago and it wasn't in this car. I've learned from my mistakes.'

Clever, capable, and charming. And the tiniest bit of a rogue, she thought. Women must fall for Samuel Weatherby in droves. She'd better make sure she wasn't one of them. Apart from the fact that her judgement in men was hopeless, she didn't have the time or the emotional space for it. She needed to concentrate on raising money for the ballroom restoration.

'Right. Brainstorm,' she said brusquely. 'We normally close the house to visitors from the middle of October through to February half-term, so we can clean properly and do any restoration work. But this year I want to open the house for the whole week before Christmas, maybe just the main rooms, and deck it out as it would've been in Regency times. I want to hold workshops for Christmas crafts, a dance class before the ball, and then a Regency costumed ball on the Saturday night with the kind of supper that would've been served during the Regency period.'

'Don't forget Santa for the little ones,' Samuel said.

She shook her head. 'If you mean Santa with his red suit and beard and ho-ho-ho, that's an American tradition and it didn't appear in England until the eighteen-fifties—which is way later than the Regency.'

'But if you're trying to attract family visitors, you know that the children will expect to see Santa,' he pointed out.

'This is a Regency Christmas,' she said, 'to go with the Regency ballroom.'

'So no Father Christmas.' He frowned. 'But you will at least have Christmas trees?'

She winced. 'In Regency times, Christmas trees were pretty much limited to the Royal family, after Queen

Charlotte introduced her yew tree decked with almonds, raisins and candles in eighteen hundred. They didn't become popular among ordinary people until after a magazine drawing of Victoria and Albert's tree in 1848.'

'No Father Christmas and no Christmas trees. It doesn't sound like much fun. What did they actually do to decorate the house in Regency times, then?' he asked.

'Greenery and garlands.'

'Dull,' Samuel said. 'People will look at it and see what they're missing from today—proper Christmas trees and Santa.'

'Which are anachronistic,' she protested.

'Who cares?'

'I do, actually.' She frowned at him. 'Attention to detail is important.'

'OK, I get that you're a history fiend, but normal people don't really care if you're a few years out on a tradition,' he said. 'Isn't Christmas meant to be about fun?'

'Ye-es,' she said warily.

'Then ignore the fact that they're a few years out and use Santa and the Christmas trees,' he said. 'You already have things in the house that are modern—electric light and running water, for starters. You don't light the house with candles any more, do you?'

'Only because the insurance company would have a hissy fit.'

'Well, then. What's the problem with having modern Christmas traditions as well?'

Because then it wouldn't be a Regency Christmas.

Her dismay must have shown in her face, because he said, 'Lighten up a bit, Vicky.'

'My name is Victoria.'

He raised an eyebrow. '"Plain Victoria, and bonny Vic, and sometimes Tori the curst…"'

It was so out of left field that she wasn't sure she was hearing him correctly. Was he quoting Petruchio's speech at her, but substituting every variety of her own name instead of Kate?

He continued, "'Queen of Plum Hall, my super-dainty Vicky...'"

He *was*. Her eyes narrowed. 'Are you calling me a shrew?'

'Just trying a few different names,' he said, though his expression said that he knew perfectly well what he was doing.

'*Shrew* was one of my A-level texts. You didn't do English A level—' according to his CV, she remembered, he'd studied maths, further maths, economics and law '—but you're the same age as me. Did your girlfriend take English and make you test her on quotes or something?'

'No. I tested my best friend on his lines when he was at RADA.'

She ignored the fact that his best friend was an actor. So he *had* been calling her a shrew. 'I'm not difficult.' Though there were parallels between herself and Katherine: she was the elder daughter, and Lizzie had been so beautiful. And she was unmarriageable without the house as a dowry.

'You can call me a stool, if it makes you feel better.'

He clearly understood all the nuances of the phrase. 'It doesn't. I'm trying to take things seriously.'

'Maybe too seriously,' he said.

That stung, because she knew it was true. But why couldn't he understand how important this was to her? 'It's not a game. Do you have any idea how serious mould is in heritage settings? Fabric is incredibly vulnerable to damage.'

'And it's being fixed.'

'We're taking the wall hangings down this week to dry them.' She was dreading what else they might find.

'Can't you leave them where they are and just put more heating in the room to dry it out?'

'No. If you just add heat, the mould will grow like mad and feed off the fabric. It's humidity that we need to deal with,' she explained.

'OK. I promise to take this seriously,' he said. 'But I still think you need Santa and Christmas trees. They might be anachronistically wrong, but not to have them would be commercially wrong—and this is about raising money.' He paused. 'What else?'

'In Regency times they'd have a kissing ball.'

His eyes gleamed slightly. 'Ball as in dance?'

'Ball as in greenery,' she said. 'It's made from holly, ivy, rosemary and mistletoe.'

'Hence the kissing.' The gleam intensified, making her feel hot all over.

'Hence the kissing.' And how bad was it that she found herself wondering what it would be like to kiss Samuel Weatherby? To cover how flustered she felt, she buried herself back in historical detail. 'It'd be decorated with spices, apples, oranges, ribbons and candles.'

'Spices?'

'Cinnamon sticks, most likely,' she said. 'Maybe nutmeg. And they'd keep a Yule log burning—which we obviously can't do, for insurance reasons. And there would be sprigs of holly in every jug and spread across every windowsill.'

'No tinsel, then.'

'Absolutely no tinsel. And no Christmas cards—the first ones were Victorian, they weren't in colour and they didn't really become popular until the Penny Post was introduced.'

'Victorian.' He looked thoughtful. 'Why don't you make it a Victorian Christmas week, then? It'd be easier.'

'Because Regency costume is nicer than Victorian,' she said, 'and the ballroom furnishings are Regency.'

'And you're going to get everyone to dress up in Regency costume for the ball?'

She nodded. 'I need to think about whether to do the food as standing tables—a buffet, in modern terms—or seated tables in the dining room. I think tables would be nice, and we can have them set out in the Regency way—though I'm not going quite as far as the Prince of Wales and having a stream of fish swimming down the room.'

'Fish?' He sounded mystified.

'The Prince wanted to be known as the grandest host of all time. When he became Prince Regent, he held a ball for two thousand guests; there was a table in the middle of the room, two hundred feet long, with a stream, banks lined with flowers, and real fish swimming in it. There were sixty waiters—one of them in a full suit of armour—and the banquet went on until dawn.' She spread her hands. 'And two years later he had another ball where they served more than nine hundred different dishes.'

'That,' he said, 'is showing off and disgustingly extravagant.'

'Exactly. So mine's going to be more sensible. I'll still serve it *à la française*, so all the dishes will be laid out on the table and you tell the servers what you'd like. Soup and fish for the first course, meats and vegetables and custards and jellies for the second, and then the wafers and sponge biscuits with dessert wine, fresh fruit and sweetmeats. Actually, the Victoria Hamilton who lived here in the Regency era kept a very detailed diary, and I was planning on using things from her menus.'

* * *

The woman she was named after, perhaps? Sam looked at her. When she was talking about historic food like this, she *glowed*. This was clearly her passion. And it drew him.

'Is that what you would have done if you hadn't taken over from your dad?' he asked. 'Food history?'

'That or book conservation,' she said.

He could definitely see her among rare old books, all quiet and serious.

'What's so different about historical food?' he asked.

'The taste,' she said. 'As a student, I did a seminar in food in history, and our tutor did a workshop where we made Tudor sweetmeats. We made candied roses, marchpane and these Portuguese oranges—basically filled with a kind of marmalade—and the flavours were so intense.'

'Could you run a workshop like that, as part of Christmas events?' he asked.

'It's on my list of possibles. I thought people might like to make Georgian stamped biscuits and sugar mice,' she said. 'And maybe violet and orange cachous.'

'Sounds good,' he said. 'What about outside? I know fairy lights aren't historical, but they'd mean you could open in the evenings, show people the garden as a kind of winter wonderland thing, and you could maybe have a kind of pop-up café offering mulled wine, hot chocolate, and hot snacks—say paninis and doughnuts. Oh, and definitely hot chestnuts as it's Christmas.'

'Cost it for me,' she said, 'and we'll discuss it.'

He blinked. 'Just like that?'

She shrugged. 'You're sensible. You know we're on a budget so it won't be all-singing, all-dancing and fireworks.'

'Fireworks?' He grinned. 'We *could...*'

'Cost it,' she said, rather than taking the bait and telling him they didn't have fireworks in Regency times. Or maybe they did. Not that he was going to ask her, right now.

She was clearly throwing him in at the deep end. That was fine by him. This was going to be a challenge—and he'd make sure it was also going to be fun. 'Do you have a list of approved suppliers, or can I just go wild?'

'I have a database,' she said. 'It's searchable by name, location and goods or service. And I've included ones we won't ever use again, with a note as to why.'

'Did you design the database yourself?' he asked, suddenly curious.

'Yes.' She shrugged off the achievement. 'It was a bit quicker than our old index cards.'

A woman not to underestimate, then. 'OK. Do you want me to work in here with you?'

'If you don't mind sharing my desk,' she said.

Her desk was an ancient table, easily big enough for them to share. 'That's fine.'

'I'll just move some of my stuff, to give you some room,' she said.

Given that he'd noticed her clear desk policy yesterday, she hardly had to move a thing. But she did move a photograph of herself as a teenager, standing with another teen; it looked as if the picture had been taken in the grounds here.

'Who's this?' he asked, picking it up from the mantelpiece where she'd put it and looking more closely. 'Your best friend?'

'My little sister, Lizzie,' she said.

But there didn't seem to be a more recent photograph of them in the room. They didn't look much alike, either; Lizzie was several inches taller than Victoria, with a mop of blonde curls and blue eyes rather than dark hair and dark eyes like her sister's. Yet the way they were posing together, their arms wrapped around each other and clearly laughing, made it obvious that they were close.

'So Lizzie doesn't help to run the house or the garden?' he asked. 'Or is she still a student, off somewhere working on her PhD?'

Victoria sucked in a breath. 'No. She died six months after this picture was taken. Leukaemia.'

Sam flinched. He'd had no idea. Why hadn't his father warned him? 'I'm sorry. That must've been hard for you.'

'For all of us, especially Mum and Dad. But you were sort of right. Lizzie was my best friend as well as my sister.'

And now he had an inkling why she was so serious. Losing your younger sibling would be hard at any age, but especially so in your teens. 'How old were you?' he asked.

'I was fifteen and she was thirteen. Twelve years ago, now.' She looked straight at him. 'Lizzie loved Jane Austen and the Regency. The ballroom was her favourite room, too.'

So Victoria wasn't just saving the room for the house's sake: it was in memory of her beloved little sister.

No wonder she was so serious about it.

'The restoration—and the ball—will be a nice testimonial to her, then,' he said.

She nodded. 'And it's why I can't just be frivolous and fluffy about it. It needs to be *right*.'

'I get that, now,' he said. 'Though Lizzie doesn't look the type who'd want you to be all doom and gloom.'

'No. Lizzie was one of these really sunny people who always saw the sparkle. She'd love the idea of planning a Regency ball and a historical supper, based on the diary of the Victoria Hamilton who lived here in Regency times.'

'Life's short,' he said. 'You learned that with your sister. I'm learning that with my dad. And maybe we need to make the most of it and find the fun.'

'Gather ye rosebuds?' she asked dryly.

'Perhaps.' He looked at her. 'OK. I'll make a start on the costings for the trees and Santa, if you can log me into your database.'

'Thanks. Actually, I've already added you to the intranet. Your password's valid for this week.' She wrote it down for him. 'Let me know if you need any extra information.'

Even though he was busy making lists of what he needed and companies that could quote for the work, Sam found himself watching Victoria covertly. She absolutely wasn't his type. The women he dated were glamorous and high-maintenance, and they were all very clear that he was looking for fun and not to settle down. Victoria was reserved and didn't seem in the slightest bit bothered that there was dog hair over her clothes, and she was definitely not the frivolous type. He had a feeling that it was a long, long time since Victoria Hamilton had had fun.

And there was definitely something about her. Something that drew him, that intrigued him and made him want to know more.

But he couldn't act on that attraction or on the urge to get to know her better and teach her to lighten up. This was only a temporary post and he was supposed to be her intern. He needed to concentrate on that and on proving himself to his father, he reminded himself sharply. OK, she wasn't like Olivia—but he still couldn't let himself get involved. For both their sakes.

CHAPTER FOUR

IT WAS WEIRD, sharing her office, Victoria thought. She was quite used to people popping in to see her or to make a fuss of Humphrey but having someone in her space all the time that morning felt odd.

She tried not to eavesdrop on Samuel's calls; she didn't want him to think she was a micromanager, and besides they both knew that he was way overqualified to be her intern. He'd spent years working in finance, so getting quotes and working out costings would be practically second nature to him. If he wanted her input, he'd ask for it.

She'd sent a note round to her team to let them know that Samuel was working with them for a week, possibly longer, to help with the ballroom fundraising. So of course everyone dropped in to her office to meet him and say hello.

Samuel charmed every single one of them, even the older and more guarded members of the team. 'I brought biscuits and fruit as a way of saying hello to everyone and I've put them in the kitchen, so please help yourself,' he said.

Watching him with everyone, Victoria had to admit that his people skills were excellent. He listened: he paid attention and he made everyone feel important.

He charmed her parents, too, when they dropped by

to say hello. Though she noticed that he didn't mention his father's health, so clearly her own father wasn't aware of the situation with his stockbroker. Maybe Samuel was worried that it would be bad for business if anyone knew about his father's mini-stroke, though she rather thought that her father would be more concerned about an old friend than panicking about the safety of his investments.

By the end of the morning, she still hadn't worked Samuel out. He was a mass of contradictions. His father thought him reckless; yet he was prepared to give up a high-profile job and a massive salary so he could come home to keep an eye on his parents. He was an only child, yet he'd empathised with the loss of her sister. His working life had been all about figures and predicting the future, yet he could quote obscure bits of Shakespeare.

He still hadn't mentioned a partner, so was he single? Was he a workaholic like herself, too busy to bother with dating? But she couldn't ask, because that would mean he could ask her personal questions, too—and she had a feeling that if she gave her stock answers he'd see right through them. She didn't want his pity. Didn't need it. She was quite happy with her life just the way it was.

All the same, she was glad when Nicola, the senior room manager in her team, offered to take him to work with the room stewards for the afternoon. Just so she could get her equilibrium back.

'See you tomorrow, boss,' Samuel said at the end of the day, after he'd helped the stewards to close up the house.

'Sure.' She smiled at him. 'Thanks for your help. And for the biscotti and Humphrey's treats.'

'Pleasure.' He raised an eyebrow. 'I'm beginning to get why this place is special.'

'Good.' If he fell in love with the house, then he'd go above and beyond to save the ballroom.

* * *

The tough day of the week was Tuesday: the day the hangings were coming down from the ballroom. Victoria was awake at stupid o'clock and walked through the ballroom, Humphrey at her side, before the sun rose. This was Lizzie's heritage, and she hadn't taken enough care of it. 'I'm sorry, Lizzie,' she whispered, feeling sick. 'I've let you down. And I've let Mum and Dad down.'

Humphrey whined and pushed his nose into her hand to comfort her.

'I'll fix it. Whatever it takes,' she said softly.

Felicity's team wore protective clothing and masks so they wouldn't breathe in the mould spores, and the ballroom was going to be out of bounds to everyone for a couple of days, to make sure there weren't mould spores in the air. On Friday morning, the room would get a thorough vacuuming—and she'd be the one to do it.

'You're going to need pictures of the hangings coming down for the website page,' Samuel said. 'Do you want me to take them for you?'

So she wouldn't have to face her favourite room being dismantled? 'Thank you,' she said, 'for being kind. But I need to face this. Humphrey, stay here, and don't chew anything,' she added to the dog.

'He'll be fine with me,' Samuel said.

The Labrador had taken a real shine to Samuel. Part of Victoria felt a bit miffed that her dog had seemed to switch his loyalties so fast; but then again it was good that Humphrey was behaving well and not chewing Samuel's laces or his car key.

'Thanks,' she said, and headed for the ballroom. Once in her protective clothing and mask, she went in to the ballroom.

Bereft of furniture, the carpet, the paintings and the

mirrors, the room looked forlorn. And the bare wall over the mantelpiece where the first strip of silk was coming down made her feel sick. It felt as if part of her childhood had been stripped away with the hangings—the part she'd loved so much with her sister. Misery flooded through her.

'OK, sweetie?' Felicity asked, patting her arm.

'Yes.' It was a big fat lie, and they both knew it.

'The good news is that you don't have a problem with the wall, so you're not going to have to get a builder in.'

Building work in heritage properties was always super-slow and super-costly, because there were so many reg-ulations. She was glad that was one burden she didn't have to face.

'If we can't repair it well enough once it's properly dry and we've got rid of the mould, we've got the spe-cialist weaving company on standby,' Felicity said. 'It's going to be fine.'

'Of course.' Victoria did her best to look and sound professional. And she took photographs of the wall as each strip came down, as well as photographing the silk itself, until the whole wall was bare.

When she got back down to her office, intending to make a start on the restoration project page for the web-site, Samuel stood up.

'You wanted an intern who uses his initiative, you said.'

She frowned. 'Yes.'

'Good. I'm taking you out to lunch,' he said.

She shook her head. 'That's kind, but I have a lot to do.' And burying herself in work had always helped in the past, when she was miserable.

'Delegate some of it to me,' he said, 'and let's get out of here. Just for an hour or so. Felicity's team has every-thing under control upstairs; the house isn't open this af-ternoon, so you can justify a lunch break.'

'I—'

'No arguments,' he said, not letting her even get the beginnings of an excuse out.

The fight went out of her. He was right. At this point, she could do with being away from here so she could get herself back under control.

'I'm driving,' he added. 'Get whatever you need. We're going out.'

There was no bossiness in his tone, just decisiveness. And a hint of sympathy. She picked up her handbag, put her phone in it, and grabbed her jacket. 'I'm guessing you're not planning on going somewhere dog-friendly?'

'No, but I'll scrounge some leftovers for Humphrey.'

'I'll go and leave him in my flat, then. Back in a tick.'

She settled the dog in his bed, then went back to the office and followed Samuel out to his car.

'Keep your coat on. It's cold, but the sun's shining. Roof down,' Samuel said.

Showing off?

But she had to admit that it was fun, driving with the cold air on her face while her feet were still warm. And he was a much more sensible driver than she'd expected.

'Lunch,' he said, parking at a country pub. 'I'm buying. No arguments.' He shepherded her inside, completely oblivious to the way every female head swivelled in his direction and then gave her a surprised look, as if wondering what someone as gorgeous as him was doing with someone as plain and ordinary as her.

Then he charmed the waitress into giving them a table near the open fire and perused the menu. 'Comfort food. Chicken Dijon with mashed potatoes and buttered kale sounds good to me. And don't tell me you don't feel like eating. Of course you don't. But this will help. Promise.'

She ordered the same as him. He didn't push her to

talk, but the food was fabulous and he was right about lunch making her feel better.

'Thank you,' she said.

He tipped his head slightly to one side. 'My pleasure. I know this ballroom thing's hard for you, but the silk's being looked after and today's going to be the worst day.'

'Unless I fail to get anything at all from the heritage fund,' she said, 'and the damage is worse than Felicity thinks it is, in which case we'll have to sell artwork. Which will break Dad's heart, because he loves every single painting in the house.'

'You've got costings for the worst-case scenario. And you're not the sort to give up. You're not going to have to sell any artwork. You'll get funding—plus there's the fundraising stuff we're working on.'

Strange how much it warmed her when he said 'we're'.

'I guess,' she said. 'I have a lot of memories of Lizzie in that room. We both loved it.'

'The memories will always be there,' he reminded her. 'And, OK, the room's going to look weird for a while, but in three months' time this will all be over and it'll look just as it always did. Plus you get to hold your costumed ball in there, just in time for Christmas.'

Without Lizzie. Every so often, something came out of left field to make Victoria miss her little sister dreadfully. This was just one of those moments. Lizzie would've loved all the dressing up and the music and the dancing. She would've enjoyed helping to choose the food, too. And Victoria would've enjoyed sharing it with her sister.

Her thoughts were clearly written over her face, because he said softly, 'Your sister will be there in spirit.'

'Yes. She will.'

Samuel made her eat pudding, too. Treacle sponge with custard. She was going to have to take Humphrey for a longer run than usual every day for the next week, to burn off all the extra calories—but Samuel was right. This helped.

'Better?' he asked when she'd finished her coffee.

She nodded. 'Thank you. Much. But I should pay for lunch. I mean, you're my intern.'

'Doesn't matter. My old salary—which I'm still being paid, by the way, as I'm officially on garden leave—is a lot more than yours. Plus this was my idea, so it's my bill.' His gaze met hers, and suddenly there was an odd feeling in the pit of her stomach.

'Tell you what—you can buy me lunch later in the week, if it makes you feel better.'

Which felt like planning a date, and it sent her into a spin. 'Won't your partner mind?' The words were out before she could stop them. How horrific. Now he'd think she was fishing—either for information about his private life, or for confirmation that this was an actual date, and she wasn't sure which one was the most embarrassing.

'No partner,' he said easily. 'And if yours minds, tell him it's a business lunch.'

Not a date.

Not that a man as stunningly beautiful as Samuel Weatherby would want to date her. He must have women falling at his feet every single day. A plain, over-serious woman like her—well, Paul had made it clear that the only reason a man would be attracted to her was Chiverton Hall.

Her tongue felt as if it was glued to the roof of her mouth. 'Uh-huh,' was about all she could manage to say.

Great. Now he'd think she had the hots for him.

Maybe she should invent a partner.

But then he might mention her 'boyfriend' to her parents, and things would get way too complicated. Better to keep it simple. 'No partner, and this is a business lunch.'

'Indeed,' he said.

And how bad was it that his smile made her knees go weak?

To her relief, he didn't push her to talk while he drove her back to Chiverton. Humphrey was thrilled to see them, and Felicity's team had left; but Felicity had left a note on Victoria's desk, together with a box file.

Found these behind the hangings. Thought you might enjoy them.

She opened the box file, glanced through the contents and exclaimed in delight. 'Look at this! We already know when the room was turned into a ballroom, because we have Victoria Hamilton's diary. But here's a dance card, and some sheet music. I wonder how they got behind the hangings?'

'No idea,' he said. 'But I'd say it's worth photographing for your restoration page.'

She nodded. 'And maybe a display case, later on.'

'What's a dance card?' he asked.

'A booklet, really, where ladies could record who they were dancing with for each dance. Before Regency times, dancing was super-formal and one couple had to go all the way down the set and back again, so it could take half an hour for just one dance. And there was a really strict hierarchy as well—but things became a bit more fluid in Regency times and the dances were shorter. People brought dance cards back from Vienna and they became really fashionable,' she explained. 'Some of them were really pretty—they looked like fans, and there might be a ribbon to attach it to your wrist.' She examined the sheet music again. 'This is in three-four time. Waltz.' She grinned. 'So our Victoria was a little bit fast, then.'

He blinked. 'Fast?'

'Not quite Lady Emma Hamilton,' she said. 'No relation, either. But the waltz was considered a bit indecorous. Even Byron wrote a poem against waltzing.' She shrugged. 'But it was super-fashionable.'

Victoria was glowing again and she'd lost that hunted look she'd had earlier, Sam thought.

He'd suggested getting away while the silk was being taken out of the house because he could see how much she hated the situation. He'd intended to be kind; but it had turned into something more than that. He'd been so aware of her—how her dark eyes had golden highlights in them when she was interested about something, and how her mouth had a perfect Cupid's bow.

Which was ridiculous.

Victoria Hamilton wasn't his type. She was way too earnest and serious. She was the sort of woman who'd expect for ever, not just for fun.

Yet she'd asked him about his partner.

Their relationship was strictly business, so if he *had* been dating someone he couldn't see how having lunch with Victoria would be a problem. And she'd looked surprised when she'd asked him. Had her question been inadvertent, then? And did that mean she was interested in him?

Though she'd neatly sidestepped his own question at first. It made him wonder why; but if he asked her then it might become an issue.

Instead, he made a fuss of the dog. 'Well, that all sounds good. Something to put in a press release, anyway.' He smiled at her. 'I'm going to talk to the garden team.' He wanted to find out their views about lighting up the grounds, what was practical and how he could organise the power supply. And also it would put enough distance between himself and Victoria so he could remind himself that she was absolutely out of bounds.

On Friday, Samuel presented Victoria with a folder. 'Costings and project outlines,' he said.

'OK. Talk me through them.'

'Christmas trees,' he said. 'We want a huge one in the courtyard and several in the house. I've got a deal with a local supplier. He gives us a very nice discount, and we allow him to mention that he's our official supplier this year in his promotional material.'

'Uh-huh.'

'Obviously we need lights, and I'm assuming you can't do traditional candles because of the fire risk. I did start researching Christmas decorations, but I thought that's more your thing so I haven't included costings or suggestions.'

'OK,' she said.

'Give me a list of what you want, and I'll sort out the sources and costings,' he said.

'I'll do that for this afternoon,' she said.

'Good. Next, staff,' he said. 'Obviously you have the house stewards, the ones with all the knowledge. But, if you want to make this real for people, you need staff in Regency dress. Tableaux. I was thinking six footmen and six maids should be enough, and they'll also be able to act as waiting staff at the ball.'

'It sounds wonderful,' she said, 'but I don't have the budget to hire actors. Even if we can talk volunteers into it, we'd still need costumes.'

'No budget needed,' he said. 'I'm calling in favours,

remember? They'll all bring their own costumes; in return, the people who make the costumes get photographs on their website and yours, with credit, and the actors can include this on their CVs and use photographs on their own social media.'

'You've talked actors into doing this for nothing?'

He nodded. 'They're all willing to learn any lines you might want, or to improvise.'

'How did you manage this?' she asked, astonished.

'It's a quid pro quo,' he said. 'They get experience of working in Regency costume, which they can use if they're auditioning for costume dramas or films. They're all people who trained with my best friend.'

She remembered him talking about his best friend learning lines from Shakespeare. 'So is your best friend well-known?'

'In theatrical circles, yes. He's going to be huge. Jude Lindsey.'

It wasn't a name she recognised, but she didn't get to the theatre in London very often nowadays. Though she was impressed by Samuel's clear loyalty towards his friend. 'OK.'

'Outside lights, I've talked to the garden team, and we've come up with a lighting plan. I can walk you through it outside, if you like. I've sourced lights we can hire at a very cheap rate for up to a fortnight, and it's the same deal as the Christmas trees—they get to mention that they're our official sponsors, and we name-check them on our website and on all publicity material.'

He had far more chutzpah than she did; it was hardly surprising that he'd done so well. She would've struggled. 'That's all great. Thank you.' She paused. 'Did you go for fireworks in the end?'

'Sadly, they're out of budget,' he said. 'But maybe you

could hold a concert in the grounds in the summer, with fireworks at the end—they'd look great reflected in the lake. And you could have pop-up food stalls.'

'It's a good thought,' she said. 'That's all really useful. And I owe you lunch and a quick chat.'

'An appraisal?' he asked.

'Something like that. Though it goes both ways. Do you like Italian food?'

'Yes.'

'Good. And I'm driving. Give me twenty minutes to assimilate this.'

'OK. I'll go and annoy the garden team,' he said. 'I'm scrounging cuttings and advice for my mum. I hope that's OK?'

'Of course,' she said with a smile.

His paperwork was impeccable. She didn't need him to walk her through the outdoor lighting scheme, because he'd mocked up photographs and marked up a copy of the visitor map. No wonder he'd been promoted so quickly as a hedge fund manager. He thought on his feet.

Once they were settled at their table in the Italian restaurant in the next village and they'd ordered lunch, she looked at him. 'First of all, your ideas are excellent. I have no idea how you sweet-talked everyone into offering you such amazing deals, but I'm very grateful. From my point of view, you've been a brilliant intern and frankly I think you're more than capable of doing *my* job, let alone the intern's.'

He inclined his head. 'Thank you.'

'I can't afford you as a consultant and I feel horrible about asking you to stay on until after the ball, without paying you anything.'

'So does that mean I don't get the job?'

'No. It means I feel guilty.'

He spread his hands. 'I knew the score when I accepted the week's trial.'

'So,' she said. 'The appraisal goes both ways. Your turn.'

'From my point of view, running events in a country house is nothing like what I do. It's like stepping into a different world. There are restrictions—which obviously there are in finance as well, but I'm surprised everything is so hidebound.'

Including the person who managed the house, who wanted everything to be as historically accurate as possible—except he was too polite to say so, she thought.

'But I'm enjoying it,' he said. 'We're talking until Christmas, right?'

'Three months' voluntary work,' she confirmed.

'I'm on three months' garden leave,' he said. 'Which means I can't take a job in any kind of financial services, including my dad's company. And I'm still being paid. So it's not as if I'm a starving student who has to rely on his parents' support. Working for you means I have a valid excuse for living with my parents and keeping an eye on them—but it also means I'm not with them twenty-four-seven, which I think would end up with all of us wanting to murder each other. And it also means I'm proving myself to my dad.'

'Carry on like this, and your reference will be glowing so much they'll see it from the space station,' she said.

'Thank you.' He smiled at her.

She had a feeling there was something more. 'But?'

'Can I be honest?'

He was going to turn her down. She ignored the sinking feeling of disappointment. 'Of course.'

'You need to lighten up,' he said. 'Worry less.'

She'd heard that before. 'It's who I am,' she said.

'Here's the deal. I work with you on the Christmas week events, and you let me teach you how to have fun.'

'That,' she said, 'sounds just a bit worrying. Especially when you told me that your own father thinks you're reckless.'

'Was I reckless when I drove you or when I put together the garden plan?'

'No.'

'Well, then. Those are my terms.'

'So that makes me your pet project?'

He shrugged. 'Take it or leave it.'

Even though she thought he was being a tiny bit patronising, she needed his help with the restoration funding. Without him on board, she might not get the deals he'd negotiated. She certainly wouldn't get the servants in Regency livery. She didn't really have a choice. And she wasn't going to admit to herself that she was rather enjoying having him around.

'I'll take it,' she said. 'Welcome to the team.'

'Thank you.' He raised his glass of water. 'So here's to having fun.'

'Here's to restoring the ballroom,' she said.

'And having fun.'

He'd left her no way out. 'And having fun.'

CHAPTER FIVE

'FUN,' VICTORIA SAID on Monday morning. 'That's what this week will be about.'

Samuel gave her a suspicious look. 'Define fun.'

'Christmas decorations,' she said.

'You've already told me about those,' he said with a sigh. 'They're not fun in the slightest. Greenery, holly and a mistletoe ball. No sparkle, no ho-ho-ho, no nothing.'

'As we're having semi-anachronistic Christmas trees,' she said, 'we need decorations for them.'

'Tinsel!'

She narrowed her eyes at him. 'You know perfectly well tinsel's ana—'

'—chronistic,' he finished with a grin.

She ignored him. 'I think they need to match the decor of the room they're in. So we'll have red baubles and taffeta ribbons in the dining room. The one by the staircase needs to be all gold—we can gather pine cones from the estate and dried allium heads, which we can spray-paint gold.'

'Because of course spray paint was available in Regency times,' he said dryly.

'You're the one who's all about anachronism,' she reminded him. 'Dried alliums and peacock feathers will make stunning centrepieces for the mantels or the table.'

'Aren't peacock feathers supposed to be unlucky?'

She shrugged. 'We have a late Victorian bedroom here with original wallpaper—the famous Liberty peacock one,' she said.

'Famous?'

'Sometimes I feel as if I'm fifty years older than you.' She sighed. 'Come with me and I'll show you. Humphrey, stay, because I don't want muddy paw prints on the counterpane. It's an original, which is way too fragile to go in the washing machine.' She showed Samuel up to the small bedroom with its glorious turquoise, gold and navy wallpaper. The same print was on the counterpane on the wrought iron bed, the drapes were plain blue to match the background of the wallpaper, and the wooden shutters were painted the same turquoise as the wallpaper.

'Wow,' he said. 'I wasn't expecting this. It looks almost modern.'

'Timeless elegance,' she said. The wrought iron bedframe had been painted ivory and gold, the lamps on the chests of drawers next to the bed had cream silk shades, and next to the fireplace was a wooden trolley containing a cream washstand set. The fireplace was black leaded and had a set of fire irons beside it.

'You can really imagine a guest at a house party staying here,' he said.

She nodded. 'It's my favourite room in the main house, after the ballroom and the library. I love the peacock feathers.'

'And that's why you're having them in the centrepieces.' He frowned. 'How do you even get peacock feathers? I haven't seen any peacocks in the ground.'

'Florist suppliers,' she said. 'The feathers are steam-cleaned. We have a rota of volunteers who do the floral arrangements in the house—in exchange, they get flowers from our garden to use at home. One of them's bound to know who to contact, and I'm hoping I can talk them into running a couple of workshops on Christmas wreaths and arrangements.'

'Sounds good,' he said. 'What other workshops are you planning?'

'There's a local artist who sells her stained glass in our shop,' she said. 'I'm hoping she'll run a couple of workshops on making a stained-glass tree ornament. Plus the Regency Christmas sweetmeats—the local sweet maker who supplies our shop will hopefully agree to do that. Then there's the Regency dance class and the ball.'

'If you're recreating the ball from Victoria's diary, maybe you should publish a transcription of the diary,' he said thoughtfully.

'I'd love to do an edition,' she admitted. 'But I don't have the time right now.'

'Delegate more to me to give you some time,' he suggested.

She smiled. 'That's nice of you to offer, but I think Victoria's diary could be my research rabbit hole. Once I start, you might not see me again for months.'

What did it feel like to be so passionate about something? Sam wondered. Part of him envied her. Keeping everything light meant he never really connected with anything.

'OK. So this week we're planning Christmas decorations,' he said.

'And a couple of trial runs, so we can see how long it takes to make them. We need to dry orange slices and either source or make snowflakes, plus dry the alliums and spray-paint them and the pine cones.' She gave him a wry look. 'You're the one who was on about fun. Don't back out on me now.'

'I'm not backing out. Though I probably haven't done anything artistic since infant school,' he warned.

'That's OK. And it might impress your dad.'

Sam wasn't convinced. 'Uh-huh. What else?'

'The ball. We need to book someone to run a Regency dance class—the steps aren't the same as modern ballroom dancing—and call the dances in the evening,' she said. 'Plus a string quartet. As you have contacts in the acting world, do you have musician friends as well?'

He shook his head. 'The dance teacher will probably know someone. Or it might be worth talking to the university.'

She looked thoughtful. 'That's a good idea. My old college had a really strong music department. I could call them.'

'You were at Cambridge?' Though he didn't know why he was so surprised. He already knew she was bright. 'What made you choose Cambridge over Oxford?'

She shrugged. 'It meant I could live here and keep an eye on Mum and Dad.'

So she hadn't had the full student experience, the way he had, living away from home and having the space to find out who you were. He didn't have to ask why she'd felt she needed to look after her parents; it had been only a few years after her sister's death. Now he knew why she'd been so understanding about why he wanted to keep an eye on his own parents. She'd already been there. 'Call them,' he said. 'What else?'

'Food. I've been working on the menu, based on Victoria's diary. My best friend, Jaz, is a food historian, so I'm hoping to get her students involved.'

'You could get a lot of interest from magazines if you wrote an article about a Regency Christmas dinner. They'll be planning the Christmas issue about now,' he said.

'Planned them already and putting them to bed, more like,' she said. 'Anyway, it's not a Christmas dinner. It's a ball supper.'

'Even so. You'll need to do a trial run on the food, so you could set up a table here. If we're careful with the angle, it won't matter if there isn't a Christmas tree in shot.'

'Do you have any magazine contacts?' she asked.

'No.' He shrugged. 'OK. So that's decorations, workshops, food and the ball itself. What about costume? Do you have a Regency dress?'

'I do, but it's a day dress rather than a ball gown. Meaning it's lawn rather than silk,' she explained.

He grinned. 'I would say, Cinderella, that you shall go to the ball—except obviously you're organising it so of course you'll be there, plus you're the daughter of the house rather than the one who'd been forced to be a skivvy.'

'Watch who you're calling an ugly sister,' she said. Her tone was light, but Sam had noticed her flinch.

'What did I say?' he asked.

'Nothing.'

'Victoria.' He took her hand. 'I was teasing. In my hamfisted way, I was trying to say I thought it might be nice to sort out our costumes together. If you don't mind me going to the ball with you, and obviously I'll buy a ticket.'

'Uh-huh.'

He sighed. 'Tell me. Please. So I don't put my foot in it again.'

The thing that gnawed away at her, the thing that pushed her to try harder and harder.

'Tell me,' he said softly.

He was still holding her hand.

Her voice felt cracked as she whispered, 'I kind of am Cinderella. I'm adopted.'

He looked at her. 'You're still the daughter of the house. From what I can see, you parents adore you. Your dad spent ages in the garden with me last week, singing your praises.'

'It's not…' She dragged in a breath. 'Mum and Dad didn't think they could have children. They tried IVF, but it didn't work out. So they adopted me—and then Mum fell pregnant with Lizzie. They've never, ever made me feel less than theirs or less important than Lizzie; but I've always thought that if they had to lose a daughter, it should've been me, not her, because she was their real daughter.'

'That's survivor guilt talking,' he said. 'And you're not being fair to yourself.'

'I promised Lizzie when she was dying that I'd look after them. Look after the house. Be the Hamilton daughter.' She swallowed hard. 'The house would've gone to Lizzie, because she was Mum and Dad's biological daughter, and I was fine with that. But then…' She closed her eyes for a moment and looked away, unable to bear the pity in his face. 'Lizzie died. Which left us all in limbo. Dad unpicked all the legal stuff so the house would go to me rather than to the nearest male relative, but it's not really mine. I'm the custodian.'

'Listen to me.' His voice was very soft. 'You are most definitely the heir to the house and it definitely belongs to you. You're the heart of this place. It doesn't matter about biology. You love this place and this family, and that's what's important.'

'Uh-huh.' She blew out a breath. 'But that's why…'

'Why you're so serious and earnest all the time, because you feel you owe your parents a debt and you have to work three times as hard as anyone else, to prove you're worthy of the Hamilton name.'

She stared at him, shocked that he'd understood without her having to explain. 'Yes.'

'Newsflash,' he said. 'You *are* worthy. And if your little sister loved you even ten per cent as much as you clearly loved her, she would've hated to see you beating yourself up like this.'

Humphrey chose that moment to bark.

'Even your dog agrees with me,' he said. 'You're more than good enough to do this.'

And he was still holding her hand.

This time, she met his gaze head-on. His green eyes were filled with sincerity—and something else she couldn't quite put her finger on. Shockingly, she found herself leaning towards him and her lips parting slightly. He was leaning towards her, too. For a second, she thought he was actually going to kiss her. And oh, how much she wanted this.

But then Humphrey barked. Samuel dropped her hand as if he'd just been scalded and took a backward step.

Two seconds later, there was a rap on her open door. 'Victoria?'

She forced a smile. She liked the senior room manager very much, but right now she felt as if she'd just made a fool of herself. And she was grateful that Nicola hadn't witnessed it. 'Hi, Nicola. What can I do for you?' she asked rather more brightly than she felt.

'Just checking that you're happy with the steward rota for this week.' Nicola smiled at her.

She hadn't had time to look at it. But Nicola knew what she was doing. 'It's fine.'

'Good. Sam, are you joining us at all this week? I

haven't put you in the rota, but I can fit you in anywhere you like.'

Samuel gave her his most charming smile. 'Although I'd love to, I think the boss has plans for me, this week— something to do with alliums, pine cones and spray paint.'

'Shame. You had all the ladies eating out of your hand—he hand-sold a dozen cream teas the other day, you know,' Nicola added to Victoria.

'Good for the café, then,' Victoria said, making an effort to recover her equilibrium.

'One thing, though. I didn't like to correct you in front of visitors, Sam, but I'm not sure our scone recipe really is originally from Chiverton,' Nicola confided.

'Maybe,' Victoria said, 'I should take a look at Victoria's diary and see if there's anything there. I was planning on using some of her recipes for the ball, anyway.'

'On behalf of the stewards,' Nicola said, 'we'd be very happy to be guinea pigs for anything you want to try making beforehand.'

'Sounds like fun,' Samuel said. 'We could have a Georgian lunch party, maybe. Or an early dinner after the garden closes, so the garden team can be part of it, too.'

'What a good idea,' Nicola said.

The idea was gathering momentum; although Victoria could say no, she didn't want to sour the atmosphere. 'Thursday next week, then,' she said. 'Though I need a sous-chef.' She gave Samuel a pointed look.

'My cooking skills aren't advanced enough.' He held up both hands in a gesture of surrender. 'When I hold dinner parties, it's either out at a restaurant or I get caterers in.'

'Time you broadened your skill set, then, young man,' Nicola said with a grin. 'Anything we need to know about, Victoria?'

'The information boards for the ballroom should be arriving at some point today. And I've checked the mould levels in the room—it's all fine.'

'Grand. I'll see you later,' Nicola said with a smile, and disappeared.

'I really don't cook,' Samuel said. 'Unless you count shoving something into the microwave.'

'You're the one who suggested holding a trial run of the supper,' she reminded him. 'And didn't you tell me to delegate stuff to you?'

'Not cooking. Unless you want to go down with food-poisoning,' he retorted.

'Microwave meals,' she said, rolling her eyes.

'There's nothing wrong with them. Anyway, you still live with your parents. Does your mum cook for you?'

'Sometimes; and sometimes I cook for my parents. Technically, right now you're living with yours,' she pointed out, 'so you're not in a position to criticise.'

'I'm not criticising.' He looked at her. 'Really. I don't cook.'

'We'll do it Regency style,' she said. 'Though I'll use a modern oven, the rest of it will be by hand.'

His eyes glittered. 'You said this week's going to be about fun.'

'It is.'

'Hmm. I bet Mr Darcy never had to cook anything.'

'You,' she said, 'are not Mr Darcy.' Though she had a feeling that he'd look absolutely stunning in Regency costume. To get her wayward thoughts under control, she resorted to briskness. 'Right. Jaz gave me the name of a woman who makes period costumes—Mrs Prinks—and the costumes on her website look really good, so I'd like to make an appointment with her to organise a dress.'

'Does she do men's costumes as well?'

'Yes.'

'Then we should go together,' he suggested. 'Is Mrs Prinks her real name?'

'I'd guess it was her business name,' Victoria said. 'If you can organise an appointment with her, I'll contact the man who teaches Regency dance in Cambridge and see if Jaz can fit us in this week. And, after we've organised all that, we're going to make Georgian biscuits.'

'Right.' His eyes narrowed. 'And I get decent coffee for being a kitchen serf?'

'Decent coffee,' she promised. 'And you also get to charm the stewards this afternoon by offering them something to have with their cup of tea that you made with your own fair hands.'

It didn't take long to sort out all the meetings. 'It's a pity that we couldn't have done both London trips on the same day,' she said.

'We could stay in London on the night between,' he said. 'At my flat.'

'Your flat.' She thought of that almost-kiss and went hot all over.

'I have a spare bedroom,' he said, 'so that wasn't a proposition.'

And how embarrassing that she'd thought that—albeit only for a nanosecond. 'It's a sensible suggestion. Thank you. I accept,' she said briskly. 'Right. I'll divert the office phone to my mobile. My kitchen awaits.'

'How do you know you've got the ingredients?' he asked.

'Shortbread biscuits and the like have been around for more than a thousand years,' she said. 'The recipes haven't changed that much over the years.'

'Are you telling me you've got a recipe for biscuits made a thousand years ago?'

'Not exactly, but I can make you fourteenth-century gingerbread from *The Forme of Cury*.'

'Curry?' He looked mystified.

'*Cury*. From the French *cuire*, to cook,' she said. 'Though it's not quite like the cakey gingerbread you get today.' She was glad of the safety of historical research. Where she wouldn't have to think about Samuel Weatherby and what it would be like if he kissed her. 'Think yourself lucky I'm not suggesting you make Roman honey cakes with a hand whisk. Jaz and I did that as undergraduates and you wouldn't believe how long it took to get the honey and eggs to the right texture.'

Sam was intrigued. What would Victoria's flat be like? He was guessing it would be as neat and tidy as she kept the office, but would it be as impersonal? Or would it give him more of a clue to the woman who'd surprised him earlier by her lack of confidence?

She led him through one of the servants' corridors—clearly this was a shortcut she'd been using for a long time—and then into her flat. Like the rest of the house, the rooms had high ceilings and large sash windows. The living room was almost entirely given over to books, though there was a comfortable-looking sofa and a small television in the corner. 'My room,' she said, indicating a closed door. 'Bathroom, if you need it. And the kitchen.'

The layout was incredibly old-fashioned—a butler's sink, which overlooked the lake, open shelving full of Kilner jars, a dresser with what he guessed were antique china plates, a scrubbed pine table with four chairs—but with a very modern oven. He blinked at it. 'Shouldn't you have an Aga or something?'

'Nope. Mum doesn't, either. I like the open, old-fashioned kitchen layout, like the nineteenth-century one we have on show downstairs, but I also love my modern oven.' She opened a drawer, took out an apron and handed it to him.

'You seriously expect me to wear a floral pinny?'

'If you're as much of a novice in the kitchen as you claim to be, you'll end up covered in flour without it.'

'As long as you don't take photographs and stick them on your website,' he grumbled.

She looked thoughtful. 'Experiments in Georgian cooking... Actually, you're pretty enough to get us a lot of hits.'

'Pretty?' This was outrageous.

And then he realised that the most earnest and serious woman he'd ever met was teasing him. And that he was more than tempted to extract a forfeit in the form of a kiss.

Which wasn't a good idea.

He needed to focus.

'Right.' He put the apron on.

'If you dressed as Mr Darcy, we could pose this in the kitchen downstairs,' she said. 'And then it could go on the website. Floral pinny being optional.'

'No,' he said.

'Fine.' She took some old-fashioned scales from the dresser, a large earthenware bowl from the cupboard, and grabbed a wooden spoon and rolling pin. Then she took her phone from her pocket and flicked into the Internet. 'Here we go. One historical biscuit recipe.'

It appeared to be a photograph of a page in a book. A very old printed page. 'Is that an F?' he asked, squinting at it.

'It's a long S,' she said.

'China oranges—does that say "rasp"?'

'Yes. Meaning you grate the rind,' she explained.

'OK.' He peered at the page. 'I don't know a lot about cooking, but six pounds of flour sounds a lot.'

'We'll divide the recipe by four, just to make it manageable. A pound and a half of flour, half a pound of butter, four ounces of granulated sugar—and you're lucky I'm not making you prepare loaf sugar—and enough milk to make it into a dough.'

'What's volatile?' he asked as he rolled up his sleeves.

'Ammonium bicarbonate. We'll use baking powder instead,' she said.

'OK.' He washed his hands while she took the ingredients from her store cupboards, then read the recipe again. 'Rub the butter into the flour.' He didn't have a clue what that meant, and it must've been obvious because she smiled and demonstrated. 'It needs to look like sand. Quite fine.'

Once he'd done that to her satisfaction, he grated orange rind and added it to the mixture, stirred in the sugar and baking powder, then poured in the milk and stirred it until a dough formed.

She'd already floured a marble pastry board for him.

'Is this an antique?' he asked.

'No. You get to play with the antique in a minute.'

'Seriously? I'm actually cooking with something antique? But shouldn't it be in a display case or something?'

'No. It was made to be used,' she said. 'I'd use a quarter of the dough at a time. Roll it once, turn it, and roll again.' She showed him.

'How thin?'

'Half a centimetre—or, in Regency terms, a quarter of an inch.'

He did so.

'And then you cut the dough into strips, using the rolling pin as a guide.'

'Lay the strips on top of each other in a pile to prevent the face drying,' he read.

'Don't worry too much about that. They won't dry out in the quantities we're making,' she said.

He cut the strips.

'And now for the fun bit.' She gave him a wooden block with a handle. 'This is an antique biscuit stamp, made of boxwood so it's durable and it won't taint the food.'

'Regency?'

'Regency,' she confirmed. 'Two hundred years old, so if we say each generation is twenty-five years, your five-times great-grandmother would've been a baby when this was first used.'

He handled the block reverently. The knob acting as the handle was worn smooth, but he could make out the pattern on the bottom of the block: a crown and a border of leaves. And six nails. 'What are the nails for?' he asked.

'Docking,' she said. 'The nails prick the biscuits to make sure the dough doesn't bubble up in the oven. It's old tech, but it works beautifully.'

'Like the old nursery rhyme. "Pat it and prick it and mark it with B,"' he said.

'Exactly.'

He pressed the stamp on to one of the strips of dough.

'Cut alongside the edge of the stamp, and that's your biscuit made,' she said.

It was amazing how quickly the pile of biscuits grew. And how much fun it was. Victoria transferred them to a baking tray lined with paper, and Sam realised she must have preheated the oven.

'Ten minutes,' she said. 'They would've used wire racks, possibly lining them with paper, but we'll do it the modern way.'

Within a few moments, the kitchen was filled with a faint scent of orange.

'We dunk our biscuits in tea,' she said, 'but in Regency times you'd dip them in dessert wine at the end of a meal.'

'I can't believe you just made me bake cookies. Or that you actually use an antique in your kitchen.'

She smiled. 'I like the connection to the kitchen here from centuries ago.'

He had the strongest feeling that she used history as a protective layer. Just as he used his fast lifestyle to protect him from getting involved.

What if…?

He shook himself. OK, she wasn't like Olivia, but how did he know he could trust her?

Once the biscuits were out of the oven and cooling, she looked at him. 'So do you want me to get you a coffee of your choice from the café?'

'No. I'm happy with whatever you have here,' he said. 'As you have a modern oven, do I assume you have a modern coffee machine hidden away?'

'Using pods that will take quite a few decades to disintegrate in a landfill site?' She shook her head. 'I use a cafetière. In Regency times they would've boiled the coffee in a pot, added isinglass to clarify it, then set it by the fire until the grounds had sunk to the bottom of the pot.'

Trust her to know that.

'Have you thought about running regular workshops here about Regency cookery? I think you'd get a lot of takers,' he said. 'You know your stuff. Although I'm not a cook or a history buff, I've really enjoyed doing this.'

She went pink. 'Thanks. Maybe I should think about it.'

'You'd be really good.'

She looked away, not quite able to accept the compliment. From what she'd let slip earlier, he understood why;

but at the same time surely she could see how much her parents valued her? The only person who didn't value Victoria Hamilton, he thought, was herself.

'I'll make coffee,' she said.

By the time she'd made the coffee, the biscuits were ready and cool enough to handle. He tried one. 'Wow. You can actually taste the orange. This is nicer than I thought it'd be.'

'I've always liked that recipe. You can tweak it a bit to suit the circumstances—add lemon rind instead of orange, or other spices. Cinnamon's nice at Christmas.' She fed Humphrey a corner of a biscuit. 'You've done well.'

He'd risen to her challenge. Now it was his turn to challenge her. 'So do I get to see these ancient recipes of yours?'

Her eyes narrowed for a moment, as if she was making a decision. 'OK. But unless your hands are scrupulously clean, I'd ask you not to touch pages of the older books—and don't touch the print. The oils on your fingers will damage it.'

'Right.' He'd put up with her being super-serious about that. This was what mattered to her—and she was sharing it with him. Trusting him. Funny how it made him feel so warm inside.

She showed him the modern edition of the medieval cookbook she'd talked about earlier. And then he discovered that some of her collection really was old. No wonder she'd been a bit wary about letting him handle it. It must be worth a fortune. He blinked at the frontispiece of one. 'That's getting on for two hundred and fifty years old. Is it from the library here?'

'No. It was my twenty-first present from Mum and Dad.'

'Most women would've asked for jewellery.'

He realised he'd spoken aloud when she shrugged. 'So I'm weird.'

'No… Just different.' And, the more time he spent with her, the more she intrigued him. Even though he'd told himself she wasn't his type, he was beginning to think that maybe she was. Victoria Hamilton was like no other woman he'd ever met. And, if her senior room manager hadn't knocked on the door this morning, he would've kissed her.

He still wanted to kiss her. Very much. Although it also scared the hell out of him, he had a nasty feeling that, if he let her, Victoria Hamilton could really matter to him.

He distracted himself by looking at the photographs on her mantelpiece. Pictures of herself and Lizzie and their parents, as she'd expected. Her graduation. And one on graduation day, with another woman. 'Who's this?' he asked.

'Jaz. My best friend.'

The food historian, he remembered. In the photograph, Victoria was smiling and relaxed. And, for once, her hair was down. 'Are you going to wear your hair like that for the ball?'

'Regency women always had their hair up for formal occasions—usually in a bun at the back, sometimes with flowers or jewellery wound in it, and with little ringlets in the front. Which is probably how I'll do mine for the ball, though I'll use modern curling tongs rather than Regency ones.'

Trust her to know that. And she'd look beautiful.

'Right. Have you finished your coffee? The house will be open for visitors soon, and it'd be nice to give the biscuits to the stewards before we open,' she said brightly.

In other words, she wasn't comfortable with him being in her space. She was putting distance between them. Which was probably a very good idea.

CHAPTER SIX

PREDICTABLY, ALL THE stewards were thrilled by the biscuits. So were Victoria's parents. And Samuel insisted on taking samples to everyone they spoke to connected with the ball during the week, basking in all the praise.

'I could be your official biscuit-maker for the ball,' he said. 'They should go on the menu as Weatherby's Wonders.'

She groaned. 'I've created a monster.'

'Call me Frankenstein,' he said with a grin; then, before she could protest, he added, 'And yes, I know Frankenstein's the doctor, not the creature.'

'You've read it?' she asked, slightly surprised.

'No, but Jude acted in a performance,' he said. 'And he's determined that I shouldn't ever become a boring financier with no culture, so he made sure I knew the important bits.'

She couldn't help smiling at that. 'Indeed.'

'My dad,' Samuel said, breathing on his nails and polishing them ostentatiously on his cashmere sweater, 'was so impressed with the biscuits last night that he would like to know who I am and what you've done with his son.'

She laughed. 'You're incorrigible.'

When they went to London on the following Tuesday, Jaz adored Samuel from the second he offered her a biscuit. 'It's made from a two-hundred-year-old recipe and stamped with a block that was used when my five-times great-grandmother was a baby. *And* they're my first ever attempt at baking,' he said, fluttering his eyelashes at her.

'I'll make coffee to go with them,' Jaz said, and tried a biscuit. 'Well, now. It looks as if we might have another sous-chef to add to my third-year tutorial group,' she said with a smile. 'My second years want to know if you'll do another ball next year, Tori, so they get the same experience. My third years don't care that it's the week before Christmas and technically it's out of term-time, because they're all thrilled at having the chance to cook a historical banquet for fifty people—and even more thrilled that you're letting them stay at Chiverton.'

'I can't afford to pay them,' Victoria said, 'so the least I can do is give them a bed and their food.'

'The experience is going to be so good for them. They've all been sketching layouts and suggesting menus—even though I warned them you're probably going to use recipes from the house rather than ones from Hannah Glasse or Frederick Nutt.'

'I'm very happy to have their input,' Victoria said. 'It can be a joint thing.'

'Here you go. Six lots of suggestions,' Jaz said, handing her a file, 'and I'm pleased to say they're all original and nothing's copied from source material.'

Samuel pored over the layouts with Victoria. 'I'm assuming that's a separate layout for each course, but... I don't quite get it. They've got puddings on the table at the same time as roast meat and vegetables.'

'It's how things were served at the time. Nowadays we serve *à la russe*,' Jaz said, 'which means one course after the other. In Regency times it was *à la française*, so all the dishes were set out at the same time and you served yourself and the people round you with the dishes you wanted. Or, if what you really wanted was at the other side of the table, a footman would bring it round.'

'Right.' He still looked confused.

'Presentation was really important,' Victoria said. 'Everything needs to be symmetrical.'

'But no stream in the middle of the table with fish swimming in it, right?' he asked.

'You've obviously been talking about *that* ball,' Jaz said with a smile. 'It also has to be practical. So, right, no fish. And we're going to do this as a buffet.'

'So if you've got blancmange and jelly on the table at the same time as a game pie and vegetables,' Samuel said, 'then do people go up for a second time to make it two courses?'

'No. We start with soup and fish on a white tablecloth,' Victoria said, 'and then the table's cleared away and the next course is laid out. The tablecloths are layered over each other, so the servants can clear things away quickly.'

'A lot of the ball-goers will be Austen fans,' Jaz said. 'So you absolutely have to include white soup.'

'What's that?' Samuel asked.

'It's a sort of cream of chicken soup, made with almonds,' Victoria explained. 'Agreed, Jaz. And artichoke soup for a vegetarian option.'

'Were people vegetarian in Regency times?' Samuel looked surprised,

'Yes. They called it the Pythagorean system,' Victoria said. 'Mary Shelley was a veggie. As was her husband—and even a barbarian like you must've heard of Percy Bysshe Shelley.'

'*Ozymandias,*' he said. 'Jude used to declaim it a lot in sixth form.'

'Jude?' Jaz asked.

'Jude Lindsey. My best friend,' Samuel said.

'As in the actor?' At Samuel's nod, she said, 'I saw him in *Twelfth Night* last year and he was amazing. Usually I think Sebastian's a selfish opportunist, but your friend actually made me sympathise with him.'

'I'll tell him,' Samuel said. 'He'll be pleased.' He looked at the table plan again. 'So how much of this is vegetarian? You can't just feed them side dishes.'

'Absolutely,' Victoria said.

'What about something with tofu?' he asked. Then he wrinkled his nose. 'No, they wouldn't have had tofu in Regency England.'

'Actually, Benjamin Franklin wrote a letter from London to a friend in Philadelphia in 1770, talking about tofu,' Jaz said. 'So we could mould tofu into a fish shape, colour it with paprika, and carve cucumber scales. Call it mock salmon. We could make two smaller ones to flank the salmon centrepiece. Are we doing notes with the menu, Tori?'

'To give the historical perspective? I think we should,' Victoria said. 'And maybe include some of Victoria's recipes from her diary.'

'Two soups, salmon, mock salmon, and salads,' Jaz said.

'When everyone had finished the first course, the dishes would go back to the kitchen and the footmen would take off the white tablecloth to reveal a green one,' Victoria said to Samuel. 'What's the consensus for the second course, Jaz?'

'My students think two roast meats—chicken and beef—plus a raised game pie, with a vegetable fricassee and maccheroni for the vegetarian options,' Jaz said promptly.

'Macaroni?' Samuel blinked. 'It's not just a nineteen-fifties thing?'

'It's been about since at least the fourteenth century,' Jaz said.

'Though the Regency version would've had a béchamel sauce with lemon and nutmeg rather than cheese,' Victoria said. 'They ate cauliflower cheese, too—they called it cauliflower *à la Flamand*.'

'We can have that as a side,' Jaz said. 'My students also suggest celery stewed in broth, haricot beans *lyonnaise*, and carrots.'

'Perfect,' Victoria said. 'Maybe lentil cutlets or a mushroom pudding as another vegetarian option.'

'Done,' Jaz said, adding it to her list.

'Puddings?'

'And they're really going to be served at the same time as the mains?' Samuel asked. 'Won't they get cold?'

'Yes and yes,' Victoria said. 'We're going to cheat and use cold puddings, so it won't matter.' She looked at the file the students had put together. 'Blancmange, apple tart, lemon jelly—plus raspberry cream, because we can use one of Victoria's recipes. I'll photograph that one for you and send it over with a transcription.'

'Fantastic. So that leaves us with the sweetmeats,' Jaz said.

Samuel coughed. 'Weatherby's Wonders.'

Jaz patted his arm. 'Yes, sweetie. You can show off your biscuits. Though my students have been studying Nutt and they're dying to try out his orange, ground almond and egg white biscuits.'

'Sounds good to me,' Victoria said. 'So at this point, Samuel, the footmen take away the cloth to reveal bare wood, and dessert is laid out. Wafers, biscuits and fresh fruit.'

'Definitely including a pineapple—that would impress the guests in Regency times. You needed a hothouse to grow pineapples, meaning you'd spent a lot of money on your garden,' Jaz explained. 'And I think prawlongs.'

'That's pralines, to you,' Victoria added in a stage whisper to Samuel. 'Almonds and pistachios browned in a sugar syrup.'

'Chocolates?' he asked hopefully.

'Anachronistic,' Victoria said. 'It'd be another forty years before dipped chocolates were produced.'

'But your modern audience will expect them.'

'No, they won't. The ball audience will be mainly history buffs. They'll *know*,' Victoria countered.

Jaz raised an eyebrow. 'This sounds like an ongoing fight.'

'It is. He wants Christmas trees and *Santa*,' Victoria said, rolling her eyes.

'You try telling a four-year-old why the mean lady in the house won't let her see Santa,' Samuel retorted.

Jaz laughed. 'You have a point. Probably with the Christmas trees as well, even though the Hamiltons weren't close to George III. But I agree with Tori over the chocolates. Best stick to fruit, wafers and sweetmeats.'

'You're ganging up on me,' Samuel complained, but he was smiling. And it was hard to take her eyes off him.

'I think that's it,' Victoria said. 'I'll make sure we have rooms ready for the students, and I'll give them a personal tour of the house. We don't usually have stuff that people can handle in the kitchen, but I'll make an exception for your students, plus I'll let them play with my collection. And I'll pick up the transport bill.'

'That'll be a minibus with me driving,' Jaz said.

'Perfect. Thanks.'

Jaz smiled at her. 'I know technically we could've done all this over the phone.'

'But it was a good excuse to come and see you,' Victoria said.

'I've managed to move a meeting so we can do lunch, if you have time?'

'Definitely.' Victoria looked at Samuel. 'Would you like to join us, or would you prefer some time to yourself?'

'How could I refuse two such charming companions?' he asked. 'Plus, as your intern, I'm supposed to be shadowing you.'

'Overqualified intern,' she corrected.

'Still your intern,' he said with a grin, nudging her. 'You don't get rid of me that easily.'

Jaz found them a table at a nearby Greek restaurant which she said served amazing *meze,* and they spent the next hour talking. When Victoria excused herself to go to the Ladies, Jaz said, 'I'll come with you.'

Victoria knew she was in for a grilling.

'Just imagine him dressed as Darcy,' Jaz said. 'You've got to do that for the promotional material for the ball. You'll sell out in *seconds.*'

'Don't say that in front of him,' Victoria begged. 'His head's big enough already. All the stewards are eating out of his hand—and even Bob the gardener has taken to dropping in to my office every morning to say hello to "his boy". Normally I have to go and find Bob for an update.'

Jaz whistled. 'Impressive. Seriously, though, Sam's adorable. I know you said you're doing each other a favour with this intern thing, but are you an item?'

Victoria felt a wave of heat spread through her. 'No. He's my intern.'

'You don't look at each other as if he's just your intern,' Jaz said thoughtfully. 'So what's the problem? He's already seeing someone?'

'No. Don't read anything into it. He's just a born flirt and a charmer, and I'm responding to that.'

'On the surface, maybe. I think there's more to him than that. Otherwise he'd be too selfish to come home and keep an eye on his parents,' Jaz pointed out.

'He's nice,' Victoria admitted. 'His dad doesn't give him enough credit. But…' She wrinkled her nose. 'I don't think he's the settling type. Plus he's already told me he thinks I'm too serious.'

'Well, you know you are,' Jaz said, giving her a hug. 'Though he's definitely a good influence on you. It's great to see you laughing.'

Victoria ignored the compliment. 'And he's way out of my league.'

Jaz scoffed. 'Of course he isn't.'

'Come on, Jaz. The last three men who dated me saw me as the heir to Chiverton, not as me. And I was too stupid to see that they were all gold-diggers who wanted what they thought was the big stately home and tons of money.' Whereas the reality was that stately homes were massive money-pits.

'They were the stupid ones, not you,' Jaz said loyally. 'I love Chiverton, but you're worth way more than the house.'

'That's because you're my best friend. Paul made it very clear that nobody would want to date me for my own sake.' And Victoria hadn't let herself get involved since.

'Paul,' Jaz said firmly, 'was a liar and a slimeball. He wasn't good enough for you. And I think Samuel likes you.'

'As a colleague.'

'No, I mean *like* likes.'

'He doesn't.' Victoria was really glad that she hadn't confessed to her best friend about that almost-kiss. 'Nothing's going to happen. He's negotiated some brilliant deals for me with suppliers and I won't do anything to jeopardise that. I need the fundraising to work, Jaz.'

'I know.' Jaz hugged her again. 'Make a move on him after the ball, then.'

'Maybe,' Victoria said, to stop her friend arguing. Nothing was going to happen between her and a man as gorgeous—and as unserious—as Samuel Weatherby. They absolutely weren't suitable. Chalk and cheese. She'd be stupid to let herself hope for anything more than their business arrangement.

Jaz had a tutorial after lunch, so Samuel looked at Victoria. 'Your choice. Exhibition, museum, art gallery, or back to my flat? Jude's in rehearsal today but he'll be around this evening so you'll get to meet him then.'

'Your flat sounds good,' she said. And then, while his heart was halfway through skipping a beat, she added, 'Would you mind if I did a bit of work?'

'Sure,' he said easily. He'd pretty much expected that to be her reaction. She'd clearly enjoyed seeing Jaz, but even then she'd been focused on the task in hand, finalising the menu for the ball.

Though he'd also noticed something else. 'You said nobody ever shortened your first name,' he said. 'Jaz did.'

'I've known her for nearly ten years.'

'So she's the only one allowed to call you Tori?'

'And Lizzie.'

He frowned, remembering that she'd told him about being adopted. Had her parents been more formal and reserved with her than with their biological daughter? 'Did your parents call her Lizzie?'

'No. They called her Elizabeth,' she said. 'Which isn't to say they weren't close. Just they grew up in a more formal family atmosphere.'

'Dad only calls me Samuel when he's angry.' He looked at her. 'You always call me Samuel.'

'Not because I'm angry with you. Because I guess I'm like my parents,' she said. 'More formal.'

Except with her sister and her best friend, he thought. 'And Jaz?'

'Nobody ever calls her Jasmine. She says it's too much like "jazz hands".'

He couldn't help laughing. 'I liked her.'

'Good. Because you'll be making Weatherby's Wonders under her supervision.'

'Can't I make them under yours?'

She shook her head. 'I'm going to be running around with a clipboard and a pile of lists, making sure everything's been done.'

At his flat, he opened the front door. Funny, he'd been away for less than a month, but he could barely remember how the place felt.

Jude had thankfully left the place tidy.

'Right. Grand tour. Bathroom—there are clean towels in the linen cupboard, so help yourself to whatever you need.' He opened the next door. 'Bedroom. Make yourself comfortable.'

'Thank you.' She placed her bag neatly in the room.

'Jude's room.' He gestured to another door. 'I think I told you he's looking after the place for me for the next couple of months.'

'So where are you sleeping?' she asked.

'The sofa.'

'But—'

'But nothing. You're my guest and my sofa's comfortable enough for me,' he cut in. 'Kitchen.'

She peered in. 'Either Jude is even tidier than I am, or this room never gets used.'

'Apart from making cups of tea and toast,' he admitted, 'it probably doesn't. Jude normally sweet-talks other people into making him dinner and he'll either pay his share of dinner or bring the wine.'

'Got you.' She tipped her head to one side. 'Though, now you know how to make Weatherby's Wonders…'

He laughed. 'I don't possess a set of scales and I'm pretty sure Jude doesn't. If it doesn't come out of a tin to serve on toast or out of a supermarket chiller cabinet to go in the microwave, it won't be in this room.'

'Shame,' she said, wandering over to the dining table by the window. 'You've got an amazing view here. Right over the river.'

He had a sudden vision of her in his kitchen, pottering around and creating historical dishes. A dinner party where her academic friends mingled with his City friends, where the wine was good and the conversation was even better…

He shook himself. That was *so* not happening. He didn't live here any more and he couldn't imagine anything that would make her move from Chiverton. Plus they weren't an item. He wasn't looking for a girlfriend.

'It's the same as the view from the living room,' he said, ushering her into the next room and trying to get that weird image out of his head. If he ever did settle down, it would be with someone much less earnest than Victoria Hamilton.

And he wasn't going to let himself think about what it might be like to kiss her.

She was off limits.

'This is a lovely room,' she said, walking over to the French doors in the living room. 'And you've got a balcony.'

'It's nice in the summer, sitting with a glass of wine and watching the river,' he said. Though he was aware of how different his living room was from hers. No walls lined with books. No dog asleep on a chair. A much, much larger television with a state-of-the-art games console.

'It's lovely,' she said.

But he'd seen her apartment at Chiverton. A place that was much smaller than his but was definitely home. A living room that was practically a library, but also was a place where friends would squash up together on the sofa, or where she'd sprawl out on the sofa with a book, and Humphrey would be curled up next to her. A kitchen that was used every day, where she'd cook for friends or for her parents.

And he absolutely wasn't going to wonder if her bedroom was anything like that old-fashioned room she'd shown him in the main part of the house, with a cast-iron Victorian bedstead; or how she'd look with her hair loose and spread over her pillow...

'Do you mind if I do some work?' she asked, clearly oblivious to what was going on in his head.

'Sure. When I brought work home, I'd work on the table in the kitchen. Is that OK for you?'

'It'll be lovely, thanks.'

He didn't want her to be polite and businesslike. He wanted those barriers down.

But that wasn't fair. He wasn't offering a future, and Victoria Hamilton wasn't the sort who'd live in the moment or have a fling just for fun.

'I'll make coffee,' he said. 'I'll check with Jude to see

if he's going to be home for dinner. Would you rather I ordered a takeaway or would you like to go out for dinner?'

'Provided I pay, I don't mind which,' she said.

Weird how he couldn't settle to anything. Once he'd made coffee and Victoria had thanked him politely, she busied herself on her laptop. He went into the living room to give her a quiet space to work in. Flicking channels used up some time, but there wasn't anything he wanted to watch. He was bored within ten minutes of switching on the games console. Even sitting watching the river had lost its appeal.

He texted Jude, who replied that he'd be back for dinner. And then Sam lasted for as long as it took to finish his coffee before he went back to where Victoria was sitting. 'More coffee?' he asked.

'No, thanks.'

Why did he have to notice how cute her smile was?

He realised he must've been staring at her, because she tipped her head to one side. 'Sorry. Am I in your way?'

'No, of course not.'

'Something you wanted?'

Yes, but he couldn't ask. 'No.'

'Bored?'

He wrinkled his nose. 'I never used to spend enough time here to get bored.'

'In work at the crack of dawn so you were ready for the opening of trading, then out partying afterwards until late?'

Why did that suddenly sound so shallow—and, worse still, uninviting? 'Yes.'

Was that pity he saw in her eyes? 'You probably work longer hours than I do,' he said. Well, *did*. Since he'd been working at Chiverton, she'd sent him home dead on five o'clock. He'd spent more time with his parents in the last two weeks than he had in the whole of the previous year. The strain on both their faces was easing, convincing him that he was doing the right thing by moving back to Cambridge.

Today offered more proof, because he didn't feel as if he belonged here any more. He'd lived in London since his first term at university, when he was eighteen, and had loved every second of it. But he hadn't thought about the city once since being back in Cambridge. He hadn't missed it at all.

'If you're really bored and none of your friends are available,' she said, 'you could make a start on drafting the programme for our Christmas week.'

'OK,' he said. 'Mind if I sit with you?'

There was a glint of amusement in her eyes. 'We've been here before. Except your table is a bit newer than mine.'

'I guess.' Sharing his space instead of hers.

And her smile warmed him all the way through.

Predictably, Jude swept in later and charmed Victoria by wanting to know all about the house and quoting Shakespeare and Austen at her. She absolutely bloomed under his attention, still her usual earnest self but there was a sparkle about her. Sam was shocked to realise that the weird, unsettling feeling in his stomach was jealousy.

For pity's sake.

He'd never been jealous before, and he had no grounds to be jealous now. He wasn't in the market for a relationship, he had absolutely no claims on Victoria, and Jude was his best friend. Why the hell should he be jealous?

But he was.

And he didn't trust himself not to snap, particularly when Victoria—who'd refused to let him buy her dinner—accepted Jude's offer of buying them all the best pizza in London.

'Pizza's hardly Regency food,' Sam said.

'Ah, but the lady's off duty right now, so she can eat modern stuff,' Jude said with a smile.

'Plus, I hate to tell you this, but Neapolitan pizza's been around since the eighteenth century, and a kind of version of it—basically flatbread—has been around since Roman times,' Victoria added.

'Know-all,' Sam muttered, annoyed by Jude and frustrated that Victoria seemed to be blossoming so much under his best friend's attentions.

Jude and Victoria shared a glance. '"Why, he is the Prince's jester, a very dull fool; only his gift is in devising impossible slanders,"' Jude said.

'Yeah, yeah. I know. *Shakespeare*,' Sam said and scowled, even more irritated.

Jude clapped his shoulder. 'Cheer up, mate.'

'Mmm,' Sam said, knowing he was being an idiot and not having a clue how to stop himself.

'Worrying about your dad?' Victoria asked.

And now he had guilt to add to the jealousy. He hadn't even called his parents today.

This was stupid. He'd met Victoria's best friend and liked her; and he'd wanted Victoria to like Jude. The fact that she did ought to make him happy, not foul-tempered. 'I'll go and call home,' he said. 'Excuse me.'

Jude topped up Victoria's wine. 'He's not usually grumpy like this. He must be really worried about his dad.' He looked at her. 'So he's really going to stay in Cambridge?'

'You know the situation. He's doing an excellent job— obviously he's way overqualified to be my intern—and I think his dad's completely out of order with all this stuff about Samuel being reckless, because he isn't.'

'Sam parties hard,' Jude said. 'But he works harder.'

'So you've known him since university?' Victoria asked.

'Since we were toddlers,' Jude said. 'And it didn't matter that he was this maths genius and I always had my nose in Shakespeare. We understood each other.'

'He said he used to help you learn your lines.' She gave him a rueful smile. 'I'm assuming you played Petruchio at some point.'

'He quoted Petruchio at you?' Jude winced. 'I know we've only just met, but you're no Katherine. I'd say you were Beatrice, if anything.'

'Thank you for the compliment. But he might have a point.'

'So you're a Shakespeare fan?'

'*Shrew* was my A-level text. But, yes, Jaz and I used to go to all the student productions. She saw you in *Twelfth Night*, by the way, and loved you.'

He rolled his eyes. 'Sebastian's a selfish idiot. I tried to make him decent.'

'She noticed,' Victoria said. And it occurred to her how well Jude and Jaz would get on together. Maybe she could introduce them. 'So you always wanted to act?'

Jude nodded. 'Sam bought me champagne when I got a place at RADA. Just as I bought him champagne when he got his first job—and his first promotion. Not that there was ever any doubt he'd do well.'

It was pretty clear that Jude and Sam loved each other like brothers.

'He's one of the good guys,' Victoria said. 'And he's been amazing with the restoration project. He's called in all kinds of favours I wouldn't have been able to do.'

'I think it's good for him to be out of London for a bit,' Jude said. 'And I can't believe you've got him baking.' He smiled. 'Sadly, I'm performing in the matinee and the evening show that day, or I'd so buy a ticket to the ball.'

'You're welcome at Chiverton any time,' she said. 'If you have a day off, come down and we'll cook you a trial run of some of the dishes.'

'So I get to see Sam in a pinny?' Jude grinned. 'I'll definitely give you a donation for the restoration, for that.'

'I heard that,' Sam said, walking into the room. 'If the pinny makes an appearance, there are strict rules. Very, very *strict* rules. No photographs and no video calls.'

'Spoilsport.' Jude laughed.

'How was your dad?' Victoria asked.

'Fine.'

'Good.'

Whatever dark mood he'd been in seemed to have lifted, and the conversation for the rest of the evening was much lighter. Victoria excused herself to go to bed relatively early, presuming that Sam and Jude would want some time together to catch up. But when she went to get herself a glass of water from the kitchen, half an hour later, she could hear them talking in the living room. And then she heard her name.

'I like her,' Jude said. 'And I think you do, too.'

'Don't try to matchmake,' Sam warned. 'You know I'm not looking for a relationship.'

Exactly as she'd guessed. There was no way she'd consider making a move now. She was done with making a fool of herself.

'Yes, and I know why.' Jude sighed. 'Does she know about Olivia?'

Olivia? He'd never mentioned the name before. Victoria felt sick. He'd said he didn't have a partner. Had he been lying to her?

'I haven't told her. I don't want her to know what a gullible idiot I was.'

Gullible idiot? The words were spiked with hurt. It sounded as if Olivia was his ex and she'd hurt him. Badly. Victoria knew how that felt. She'd made that mistake herself, falling for someone who had a different agenda from her own. Worse still, it had been more than once. But now she knew that her judgement in men couldn't be trusted. It sounded as if Sam felt the same way about his judgement in women. That he, too, had huge trust issues.

'Anyway, we're not dating. I'm her intern. End of.'

'That's not the way you look at her,' Jude said. 'Or the way she looks at you.'

'Still not happening,' Sam said. 'Don't interfere.'

'It's been two years,' Jude said. 'Maybe—'

'No. I don't do serious. I'm looking for fun, not for for ever.'

And then it sounded as if one of them was getting up—maybe heading for the kitchen to replenish their glasses or something. Not wanting to be caught eavesdropping, Victoria fled.

Back in her bedroom—Sam's bedroom—her mind was whirling. Who was Olivia, and what had she done to hurt Sam so much that he didn't want to get involved with anyone?

Not that she could ask him. And it was none of her business.

But it was clear to her that he didn't want to act on any attraction he might feel towards her. So she was going to have to squash any feelings she had, too, and keep things strictly business between them.

CHAPTER SEVEN

THE NEXT MORNING, Sam noticed that Victoria was very quiet over breakfast.

'Everything OK?' he asked.

'Fine, thanks.' But her smile didn't quite reach her eyes. She was quiet on the way to Mrs Prinks the costume-maker, too, whereas Sam had expected her to be lit up, talking about patterns and fabrics and design.

'So what do I need for a Regency ball outfit?' he asked.

'Breeches, shirt, cravat, waistcoat, tailcoat, white stockings, and pumps,' she said.

Nothing about colours or materials. Weird. The Victoria he knew was all about details. He tried another tack. 'I'd like to buy your dress.'

'There's no need.'

'I know, but I'd like to.' He paused. 'And then I can choose the material.'

'OK.'

What? Now he knew there was definitely something wrong. 'The Victoria Hamilton I've got to know would've given me a lecture about authentic styles, colours and fabrics. You just told me I could deck you out in lime-green polyester with purple spots if I wanted to.'

'Sorry,' she said. 'Just a bit of a headache.'

He wasn't sure she was telling the truth. It felt as if

she'd gone back into her shell. The woman who'd taught him how to make Regency biscuits and shyly tried to tease him was nowhere in evidence. And he missed her.

It wasn't until they were actually in the costume workshop and she was discussing bias cut with Mrs Prinks that the bright, sparkling academic he knew made an appearance.

'Red,' he said. 'You need a red ball gown. Bright scarlet.'

She shook her head. 'Something a bit plainer.'

'Beige?' He scoffed. 'It's your ball, Victoria. Your ballroom. And you've put a lot of work in. You should be the belle of the ball.'

'I'd rather be in the background. Red's too bright.'

'Actually he's got a point. With your colouring, it would look stunning.' Mrs Prinks took a bolt of silk from her shelf, unwrapped a few turns and held the silk up against Victoria.

The colour definitely suited her. For a moment, their gazes met, and his heart actually skipped a beat. Not good. He'd been frank with Jude last night after Victoria had gone to bed. He liked her. A lot. But he couldn't offer her for ever, he had his parents to think about, and she had Chiverton Hall to think about. He knew she was nothing like Olivia, but his ex had destroyed his trust in love.

He couldn't see how they could get over the obstacles.

There was the slightest, slightest wash of colour in her face.

'I'll take it,' she said.

Within half an hour, everything was wrapped up. They'd come back for a final fitting in a few weeks, and their costumes would be ready before the ball.

They headed back to Cambridge, grabbing a sandwich from a deli on the way to the station to eat on the train.

As Sam had half expected, Victoria worked on the train. He wasn't sure if it was just her work ethic kicking in, or if she was trying to avoid him.

Just before they reached Cambridge, he sent her a text.

Have I done something to upset you? If so, I apologise, and please tell me what I've done so I don't repeat it.

She looked up from her phone. 'You're sitting opposite me, Samuel. You could've just spoken to me.'

Not when she was this remote. 'That doesn't answer my question.'

She shook her head. 'You haven't done anything. I'm just tired.'

He was still pretty sure she wasn't telling the whole truth, but he'd also worked out that Victoria Hamilton was stubborn. Pushing her now would end up with her backing further away.

He'd let it drop for today, and maybe tomorrow would be better.

'You can go straight to your parents', if you like,' Victoria said when their train pulled into the station.

'I need a quick word with Bob about the outdoor stuff,' Samuel said. 'So if you don't mind me sharing a taxi with you, I'll come back to Chiverton.'

What she really wanted was time on her own so she could get it through her thick skull once and for all that Samuel Weatherby was off limits. But he already thought he'd upset her, so she also needed to play nice—because she definitely didn't want to tell him what was going on in her head. 'Sure,' she said.

But when they got back to Chiverton, they didn't even make it to her office before her parents intercepted them.

'Darling, did you have a nice time? How's Jaz?' Diana asked.

'Yes, thanks,' Victoria fibbed slightly, 'and Jaz is fine. She sends her love.'

'Good, good.'

Why were her parents looking so shifty? she wondered.

'You remember Donald Freeman, don't you, darling?' Patrick asked genially. 'He just popped over to say hello, so we've asked him to stay for dinner.'

Oh, no. Now she recognised that shifty look for what it was. Her parents had just found her yet another suitable man to date. They'd invited him to dinner, so then he'd feel obliged to ask Victoria out to dinner.

Maybe she really was tired, or maybe she'd gone temporarily insane, because she found herself saying, 'Well, it'll be nice for him to meet my fiancé.'

'Fiancé?' Diana stared at her in shock. 'You're engaged?'

Oh, no. Saying she was dating would've been enough. She really shouldn't have panicked and made up an engagement, of all things, but when she opened her mouth to backtrack, the lie decided to make itself that little bit more tangled. 'Yes, I know it's ridiculously fast, but you know when you meet The One, don't you, Mum?' She gave Samuel a sidelong glance.

'You mean, you and Samuel?' Patrick asked, his jaw dropping.

'Yes.' She took Samuel's hand and squeezed it, sending him a silent plea to run with this for now and she'd explain and fix things later.

'Oh, my dear boy. I'm so pleased.' Patrick took Samuel's free hand and shook it warmly.

'One thing,' Samuel said. 'This isn't common knowledge, and I need it to remain that way, but Dad's not in the best of health right now. So we weren't planning to announce anything officially until he's better.'

He was thinking on his feet faster than she was, Victoria thought. And she was so grateful that he wasn't exposing her for the liar she was.

'Of course we'll keep it to ourselves—about your father's health and about the engagement.' Diana hugged him warmly. 'I'm so sorry to hear your father's poorly, Samuel, but how lovely about you and Victoria. You know, the news might well cheer him up.'

'To be on the safe side,' Samuel said, 'I'd rather keep this between us.'

'Of course, of course,' Patrick said.

'A whirlwind romance.' Diana's face was wreathed in smiles. 'Every cloud *does* have a silver lining. If we hadn't had that problem in the ballroom, you wouldn't have needed an intern, Victoria, and you would never have met Samuel.'

'No. Just let us put our things in the office,' Victoria said brightly, not daring to look at Samuel's face. He'd sounded neutral rather than furious at the stunt she'd just pulled, and she hoped he'd hear her out and let her explain. 'We'll come up and see Donald in a moment.'

'Of course, darling.' Patrick hugged her. 'We're so pleased.'

She'd think of a way to 'break' the engagement nicely, with the minimum of hurt to her parents. But in the meantime she really needed to concentrate on the fundraising. Having to deal with her parents' matchmaking was just too much right now.

Samuel didn't say anything until they got to the office. Then he closed the door behind them. 'Right,' he said, his voice still neutral and his face completely unreadable. 'Care to tell me what that was all about?'

'Firstly, thank you for going along with it—at least for now. And I'm sorry I've dragged you into this.' She took a deep breath. 'Basically, my parents are desperate for me to find Mr Right, settle down and produce grandchildren.'

'Uh-huh.'

'Because I haven't met anyone, they've taken to parading suitable men in front of me—the sons of family friends, mainly. Donald's just one more in a long, long line. And right now I could do with not having to deal with men who don't really fancy me and are trying to be polite to my parents for their own parents' sake. I want to concentrate on the fundraising. I guess I panicked and said the first thing that came into my head to put them off—that I was already seeing someone.'

'Engaged, you said,' he corrected. 'The One.'

She squirmed. 'Again, I apologise. I panicked and they were the first words out of my mouth. I know I shouldn't have said it and I hope I haven't done any harm. You did say you weren't seeing anyone.'

'As long as your parents don't take out an ad in *The Times* or something.'

'They're not going to make any announcements without our permission,' she said. 'You heard my mum. They'll keep the news to themselves.'

'So why,' he asked, 'don't you date?'

She definitely wasn't telling him the real reason. She didn't want him to know how stupid and hopeless and worthless she was—or see any pity in his eyes when he looked at her. 'I just haven't met anyone I really want to date.' Except Samuel himself, and he didn't count. She looked at him. 'And you don't date, either. Why not?' She held her breath. Would he tell her about the mysterious Olivia?

'I want to concentrate on supporting my parents.'

In a situation he'd only known about for a couple of weeks. What about before then? Not that she wanted to risk alienating him by asking awkward questions. She needed him to support her. Just for a little while. 'I know it's a bit of a cheek,' she said, 'but would you mind going along with this, just until after the ball?'

'Let me get this straight,' Sam said. 'You want me to pretend to be your fiancé for the next couple of months—and then you're going to break it off with me at Christmas?'

She winced. 'We might have to finesse the timing a little bit, but basically yes. It'll stop my parents trying to find me a suitable husband and give me the space to concentrate on the fundraising.'

'My parents do that every so often, too,' he said. 'They invite suitable women over for dinner parties.' It was one of the reasons he hadn't come home often enough.

'So, as you know exactly what it's like, maybe we can be each other's dating decoys?' she said.

'Lying doesn't sit well with me.' He blew out a breath. 'Going along with this means lying to your parents.'

'I know, and I feel bad about that, but it's for a good cause. And it's not a lie that will hurt them.'

'What about when we break up?' he pointed out.

'I'll think up a good reason. And I'll take the blame—I'm not going to paint you as a heartless cad or anything,' she said.

Her fake fiancé.

Then again, his last engagement had been even more fake. At least Victoria was being honest and not pretending to be in love with him, the way Olivia had. Maybe there were degrees of lying. 'What about an engagement ring?' he asked.

'We don't need one. We can say we're waiting until your dad's better.'

'And you're absolutely sure my parents aren't going to hear anything about this?'

'If we let people here know that it's a big secret, they'll all be thrilled that they've been taken into our confidence,' she said. 'And we can get them to promise to keep it secret.'

'If we're engaged, people are going to expect us to kiss.' A wave of heat spread through him at the idea. The thing he'd wanted to do almost since he'd first met her— the thing he'd almost done recently—except his common sense had held him back.

Kiss the girl.

'No, they're not. They know I'm—well, a bit formal and not demonstrative.'

'But I am,' he said. 'Maybe meeting me is what changed you. Because I'm The One.'

Her eyes narrowed. 'Are you saying you're expecting benefits?'

'I'm saying,' he said, 'that people are going to expect to catch us holding hands and kissing. Otherwise, they're not going to believe that we've had a whirlwind romance and we're engaged within a couple of weeks of first meeting.'

Her eyes widened again. 'I…'

'So,' he said. 'If I go along with this pretend fiancé thing, what's in it for me?'

'Not a reference for your dad,' she said promptly. 'I wouldn't insult you like that. You'll earn your reference.'

She might be lying about their relationship, but otherwise he knew she was scrupulously honest. 'Noted. And thank you.'

'You could,' she said, 'have a sense of doing something kind and helpful. That's what's in it for you.'

'Uh-huh.'

She sighed, as if realising that it wasn't enough. 'Or I could owe you a favour.'

'Of my choice, to be taken at a time of my choosing.'

She looked at him for a long, long while. Then she nodded. 'I forgot you're a hotshot negotiator. And I'm not in a place to argue with you right now. OK. A favour, to be taken at the time of your choosing.'

'And now we seal the deal,' he said. 'As an engaged couple would.'

Her eyes were huge and full of panic.

'It's not going to hurt, I promise,' he said, and brushed his mouth very lightly against hers. Once, twice.

'Oh! Sorry,' a voice said behind them.

'Mum!' Victoria flushed to the roots of her hair.

'I was just coming to see… Well. Come up when you're ready,' Diana said, and backed out of the office.

'Your mum's just caught me kissing you. Mission accomplished, I think,' Sam said.

'Uh-huh.' Victoria looked slightly dazed.

'Last thing. I need a pet name for you,' he said. 'I can't call you Ms Hamilton. And I'm not calling you Victoria.'

'You've only known me for a couple of weeks,' she said.

'But I'm your fiancé. Which means I get to call you a pet name.'

She shook her head. 'All my boyfriends called me Victoria.'

'A fiancé is one step closer than a boyfriend.'

'Don't push it,' she warned.

'Victoria. Vicky. Vickster. The V-woman.'

Her eyes narrowed. 'I'm no Katherine, but you could definitely be Petruchio right now.'

'Kiss me, Vicky,' he said with a grin. At her rolled eyes, he said, 'You *so* set that up.'

'Not funny.'

Just to show her that it was, he stole a kiss.

But then it suddenly wasn't funny any more, because his mouth was tingling where it touched hers.

He hadn't reacted to anyone like that since Olivia—or even with her, if he was honest. He'd asked Olivia to marry him out of a sense of duty, knowing it wasn't what he wanted but knowing he had to do the right thing.

He pulled back. Victoria's face was flushed and there was a glitter in her eyes that told him she felt this weird sensation, too.

This was *dangerous*.

'We'd better go and see your parents,' he said.

Donald Freeman turned out to be a nice enough man, but he definitely wasn't right for Victoria, Samuel thought. Thankfully, after he'd congratulated them on their engagement, he excused himself from dinner, having suddenly remembered a previous appointment. And that meant Samuel could excuse himself, too, on the grounds of wanting to check on his dad.

Victoria drove him back to his parents' place. 'Thank you,' she said.

'OK. I'll see you tomorrow. And thanks for the lift.'

'I'm doing the meal for the stewards tomorrow,' she said. 'You could ask your parents if they'd like to come.'

He sucked in a breath. 'And then yours will think they know about the engagement, and things will start to get *really* complicated. No.'

'OK. Perhaps you can take some dishes home for them, then.' She gave him a smile. 'In anachronistic plastic tubs.'

'They'll appreciate that. And I'll take some photographs for the website,' he said. 'Without any anachronistic plastic tubs in sight.'

Part of him wanted to kiss her goodnight. He'd liked the feel of her mouth against his. But that wasn't part of the rules of their fake engagement.

'See you tomorrow,' he said.

Victoria told her parents another white lie, that night: that she was tired, and could do with an early night. She sat up to make her lists of what she was going to cook tomorrow, the prep plan and the timings; but she was still wide awake at stupid o'clock, guilt weighing heavily on her. Samuel was right. When she broke the engagement, her parents would be so hurt. She should've just steeled herself and told them gently that she didn't want them to keep trying to fix her up with suitable men. It would've upset them, yes, but not nearly as much as learning the truth was going to upset them.

What an idiot she was.

She couldn't even talk this over with Jaz, because she knew what her best friend would say: that Victoria was attracted to Samuel, and her subconscious had seen this as a chance to get together with him, which was why she'd said they were engaged rather than dating.

She was horribly aware that was very near the truth. And she just hoped that Samuel hadn't worked that out for himself.

She was up at the crack of dawn and headed for the supermarket, armed with a list of groceries she needed for the trial run of the ball supper. At least she'd be so busy cooking this morning that she wouldn't have time to think. She'd left a note for Samuel, saying that she'd switched the office phone through to her mobile and was working in the café kitchen this morning; but what she hadn't expected was for him to come over to the kitchen before anyone had even started in the café that morning.

'Good morning.' She eyed him warily.

'Sous-chef reporting for duty,' he said. 'What do you need me to do? Even if it's just washing up or keeping an eye on a pot for you—you can't cook for twenty people single-handed. And I assume you're cooking with modern equipment, as you're in the kitchens here.'

'I need more oven space than I have in my flat,' she said. 'I'm sure the kitchen team won't mind giving me some help.'

'But I'm your intern. I'm meant to be helping you.'

She looked at him. 'OK. If you don't mind topping-and-tailing the French beans and peeling the carrots, that would be great.'

'Good.' He smiled at her. 'Where's Humphrey?'

'With Mum and Dad. He loves roast chicken so he's on a promise of leftovers.'

He smiled. 'And a good run, after the meal.'

'Absolutely.'

'So are we cooking the meal that you planned out with Jaz?'

'Not the whole thing,' she said. 'I'm just doing the white soup and the artichoke soup for the first course, roast chicken with roast beef, fricassee, maccheroni and vegetables for the main course, and apple tart and blancmange for pudding. I'm going to plate it up as it would've been served in Regency times, though.'

'No Weatherby's Wonders?'

She smiled. 'Everyone's already tried them and given them the seal of approval.'

'Oh.' He looked faintly disappointed, and she relented. 'OK. Make them. You're right: they'll be nice with coffee.'

'I'll make the biscuits,' he said. 'If I get stuck at any point, I'll ask you. Just tell me what else you need and I'll do it.'

'Thank you. Apart from anything else, would you mind nipping up to my kitchen and bringing the biscuit stamper down? Plus I could do with little menus being printed for everyone.'

'Sure. Talk me through what you want and I'll sort it out.'

Why did his smile make her feel weak at the knees?

Probably, she admitted to herself, because it made her think of that kiss yesterday. She'd never reacted to anyone so strongly before.

But this was just a fake engagement and she knew that Samuel wasn't really interested in her. So they'd concentrate on work. She scribbled down the recipe for him and set to work on the soup.

Samuel reappeared with the biscuit stamper and prepared the biscuits and then the vegetables. He helped her with the apple tart and the blancmange, and she found herself relaxing with him as the day went on, to the point where she even managed to sneak in enough time to check her emails as well as answering one important call.

She'd earmarked tables in the back room of the café, putting 'reserved' signs on them, and while the vegetables were cooking and the chicken and beef were roasting she and Samuel set the table for twenty people—the house stewards, the gardening team and the café team, plus her parents.

'This isn't quite the full menu—I'm doing more dishes with each course at the ball—but I hope you'll all enjoy this,' Victoria said when everyone was seated. 'Although I'm using period recipes, I used our kitchen here.'

'It's really nice of you to do this for us all,' Nicola said.

'Samuel helped,' Victoria said, not wanting to take all the credit. 'Even though he doesn't usually set foot in a kitchen, he did lots of the prep, and he made the biscuits to go with coffee.'

'Weatherby's Wonders,' Samuel corrected her with a smile.

She rolled her eyes at him. 'Before I bring the soup through, I have good news and bad,' she said. 'The good news is that we've got the heritage funding. Not quite as much as I asked for, but it's going to pay for three-quarters of the work.'

There was a general cheer.

'The bad news,' she said, 'is that the mould damage can't be repaired. The silk's just too fragile. We need to get modern reproductions of the hangings made, and Felicity recommends we do the whole wall. The good news is that, although the timing's tight, it should all be ready just before the ball so we'll be completely up and running.' She smiled. 'And I'd like to thank all of you in advance for your support in the Christmas week fundraising. I've got a running list of who's offered to help with what and it's really, really appreciated. Anyway. Samuel and I are bringing the soup through. We'll be serving from the table behind us. I apologise in advance for not doing this proper Regency style, with the different tablecloths and everything, but it's a trial run. There's enough for everyone to have a taste of everything, and I'd welcome any feedback because I'm using recipes from the time and they might not be to modern tastes.'

'And anything that goes down really well,' said Prue, the head of the kitchen team, 'maybe we can add to the café specials board. Maybe we can produce an historical dish once a week. I reckon the visitors would love it.'

'That,' said Victoria, 'is a brilliant idea, Prue. Let's do it.'

Samuel took photographs of the two soup tureens in situ, and then of everyone sitting at the table with their soup; and he handled the photography again when he and Victoria had set out the second course.

The food went down really well, to Victoria's relief.

And then, after coffee, Patrick stood up. 'I'd like to thank my daughter for being such a trouper,' he said. 'The amount of work she's put in is amazing. And I'd like to thank Samuel, too.'

For a nasty moment, Victoria thought that her father was going to blurt out that they were engaged. She caught her father's eye and gave the tiniest, tiniest shake of her head, enough to remind him that it was meant to be a secret. For a second, he looked crestfallen, but he recovered himself quickly. 'And thank you, all of you, for your support. We couldn't do what we do here without you.'

'Hear, hear,' Diana said, standing up to join him. 'Here's to Chiverton and the ballroom restoration.'

'Chiverton and the ballroom restoration,' everyone said, and raised their coffee cups.

Afterwards, Prue and the kitchen team insisted on helping clear away, and Victoria sent Sam back to his parents' with a pile of plastic tubs, so they, too, could taste the Regency dinner.

'He's all right, our Sam,' Prue said to Victoria. 'You picked a good one there.'

'Dad knows his father, so actually I didn't pick him as my intern. He applied, and it was convenient to give him the job,' Victoria said.

Prue smiled and patted her arm. 'That isn't what I meant. Your last young man thought he was a toff and much better than everyone else. Sam doesn't. He mucks in with all of us.'

'Sam's not my—' Victoria began, panicking.

'It's all right. I won't say anything,' Prue cut in gently. 'But I think all of us see the way you look at each other.'

Oh, no. This was starting to get out of hand. The only good thing was that her father hadn't spilled the beans about the 'engagement'. 'That was a really good idea you had about using historic dishes in the café here,' she said, hoping to distract Prue.

Prue smiled at her as if to say that she knew exactly what Victoria was doing, but to Victoria's relief Prue went along with it and talked about which recipes would work where.

When everyone had gone home, although it was dark, Victoria took Humphrey for a good run in the gardens; she practically knew the layout blindfolded but took a torch with her for safety's sake.

'I'm going to have to be really careful,' she told the dog. 'Because Samuel doesn't feel the same way about me that I'm starting to feel about him. And Dad nearly slipped up about the engagement. I'm beginning to wish I'd kept my mouth shut up and just dated Donald a couple of times to keep Mum and Dad happy.'

And in a few short weeks Sam would be out of her life and he wouldn't be back.

She couldn't let herself lose her heart to him.

This whole thing was about Chiverton and the ballroom. And that would have to be enough.

The following week saw a day that made Victoria happy and sad in equal measures: Lizzie's birthday. She tried hard to concentrate on her little sister's sweetness and how lucky she'd been to have Lizzie for thirteen years. But at the same time she was sad for all they'd missed out on. Lizzie would've been twenty-five, now. Graduated, maybe married to the love of her life.

'I miss you,' she said, arranging the paper-white scented narcissi she'd always bought Lizzie for her birthday on the grave. 'What I'd give for you to be here now. You'd love all the ball stuff. And I can just see you in a sky-blue silk gown to match your eyes. You'd be the beauty of the ball.' She blinked hard. 'I know you'll be there with me in spirit. I just wish we'd had more time together.'

Humphrey nudged her and licked away the tears that slipped down her cheeks.

'You'd love Humphrey,' Victoria said. 'And I think you'd like Samuel. I'm making such a mess of this, Lizzie. He's been kind enough to agree to keep up the fake engagement until after the ball, but I...' She blew out a breath. 'I wish I was different. That I didn't keep letting Mum and Dad down, time and time again.' She grimaced. 'Sorry. It's your birthday. I shouldn't be whinging. I love you. And I so, so wish you were here.' She stood up and patted the headstone. 'Happy birthday, darling. I'm going to make Mum and Dad our special meal tonight and we'll toast you.'

When she headed back to her office, Samuel was already there.

'Are you OK?' he asked.

Obviously her eyes must still be a bit red. 'Of course,' she fibbed.

He didn't look convinced, and disappeared, returning with two mugs of coffee and two brownies. 'In my department,' he said, 'this used to fix most things. Or at least put people in a place where the tough stuff was more manageable.'

The kindness was too much for her, and the tears spilled over.

'Sorry,' she said, wiping her eyes with the back of her hand. 'Lizzie would've been twenty-five today.'

'Ah.' He took her hand, drew her to her feet, and gave her a hug.

Part of her wanted to howl even more; part of her was really grateful for the kindness; and part of her felt an inappropriate longing to hold him back, to take comfort in holding him.

But that wasn't fair.

He was her fake fiancé, not her real one.

Too late, she realised they weren't alone. Diana was standing in the doorway,

'I take it Samuel knows what today is?' Diana asked gently.

'I do now,' Samuel said. 'A tough day for all of you.'

Tears glinted in Diana's eyes. 'Almost half her lifetime ago, the last birthday we shared.' She rested her hand on Victoria's shoulder. 'But I still have my Victoria, so I know I'm lucky.'

Victoria couldn't say a word.

'Samuel, we always have a special dinner on Elizabeth's birthday. You're very welcome to join us,' Diana offered.

'Roast chicken followed by rice pudding—her favourites,' Victoria added.

'And champagne. The last of the first case Patrick laid down, the day she was born.' There was a noticeable wobble in Diana's voice. 'We celebrate having her for those thirteen years.' She stroked Victoria's hair. 'Just as we celebrate your day, darling.'

'I know, Mum.'

'I'll be there,' Samuel said. 'Thank you for inviting me. It's an honour.'

When Diana had left, Victoria said, 'You don't have to come. I'll make an excuse for you.'

'No, I'd like to be there,' Sam said. What he wanted was to be there for Victoria and support her.

'Thanks.' She dragged in a breath. 'We don't get maudlin.'

No, they'd hide their sadness to protect each other, Sam thought.

'I'm cooking, so dinner's at my flat,' Victoria said.

'Can I bring anything? Do anything?'

'It's fine. All organised,' she said.

All the same, Sam nipped out to buy seriously good chocolates and ground coffee that had been roasted locally. He knew he'd done the right thing when Victoria hugged him spontaneously.

Weirdly, even though she was his fake fiancée, having her in his arms felt more real than when he'd held Olivia. He was going to have to be really careful not to let his feelings run away with him. She was only doing this to distract her parents until after the ball.

He discovered that Victoria had been speaking the truth. It wasn't a maudlin evening, The Hamiltons smiled and remembered the good times, and Diana had photographs on her phone. Victoria was still in the shy teenage stage, but she looked happy. And Sam found himself drawn to her that little bit more.

At the end of the evening, Victoria walked him to the gate.

'Lizzie seemed lovely,' he said.

'She was.'

He rested his hand against her cheek, just for a moment. 'I know you have survivor guilt, but you don't have to make up for her. Your parents love you just as you are.'

She swallowed hard. 'I know.'

'I don't get why you don't think you're enough,' he said softly. 'Unless it's something to do with being adopted?'

She shook her head. 'I don't have abandonment issues. My biological mother was very young when she had me. She wasn't a wild child—she'd given in to pressure from her boyfriend and she was just unlucky. Her parents were taking her away for her eighteenth birthday and I was being looked after by family friends, but the three of them were killed in a car accident. There wasn't anyone else in the family who could take me on, and my mum hadn't named my dad, so I was put up for adoption. Mum and Dad chose me.'

'And I can see how much they love you.'

She nodded. 'I've been so lucky. I've always felt loved.' She lifted a shoulder. 'As you say, survivor guilt. I think I'll always feel this way.'

'Don't. Because you're loved,' he said, 'for exactly who you are. Never forget that.'

CHAPTER EIGHT

THREE WEEKS LATER, nearly everything was organised: the plan for the outdoor lights and a special menu for the café; Father Christmas; the workshops for stained-glass ornaments, wreath-making and Christmas confectionery; and the ball itself.

The only things left to put in place were the dance music and the teacher who'd hold the workshop in the afternoon before the ball and call the dances at the ball in the evening. Michael Fillion had an appointment to come and see the ballroom that morning and discuss the ball with Victoria and Samuel.

'So have you actually done Regency dancing before?' Samuel asked her.

'Yes, when I was a student. There was a group of us who loved all the Regency stuff, Jaz included. Our dance teacher died a couple of years ago, but her daughter gave me Michael's name—he apparently took over Lily's classes.' She looked at him. 'So I'm assuming you've never done any kind of formal dancing?'

'No.'

'Maybe Michael can take you through some steps today, if he has time.'

'Or you could teach me,' Samuel suggested.

Oh, help. She could just imagine teaching him to dance—and seeking a payment for her lessons in kisses…

She shook herself. 'I'm a bit rusty.'

When Michael arrived, she made coffee and showed him around the house, ending up at the ballroom.

'The room has perfect proportions,' Michael said. 'Did Lily ever come here?'

'Not for dancing,' Victoria said.

'Pity,' Michael said. 'She would've loved this. I like how you've got the room set up as it would've been in Regency times, with the seating by the wall. So you have a mirror over the mantelpiece, usually?'

Victoria swallowed hard. 'Yes. That's where we found the edge of the mould. The silk hangings—or at least the reproductions—will be back in place just before the ball. We've got a heritage grant to cover some of the costs, and the ball and other fundraising events that week will raise the rest.'

'It's a beautiful room. I'm glad it's being used for its proper purpose,' Michael said. 'We can have the quartet seated next to the piano—you did say your college has a quartet who'll play on the night?'

'Yes, so if you can let me know what music you want, they can rehearse.'

'Excellent. Will everyone be in Regency dress?' Michael asked.

'I think so,' Victoria said. 'If people prefer to stay in modern dress, that's fine, but I've asked that people don't wear stilettos, so the floor doesn't get damaged.'

'Very sensible. I have pumps in a selection of sizes, so my students can try out the classes in comfort and decide whether dancing's for them. I'll bring some along just in case anyone needs them on the night,' Michael said. 'And you mentioned you'd like a quick lesson now?'

'Is that a horrible cheek?' Victoria asked.

Michael laughed. 'In a room like this, it'll be a privilege and a pleasure.'

'I haven't danced for a long while, so I'm rusty,' she warned.

'It'll come back. How about you, Sam?'

'Never,' Sam said. 'I'm a total novice.'

'That's fine. I can lend you shoes. Victoria, do you have shoes?'

'In my office. I'll get them,' she said.

'Tell me your shoe size, Sam, and I'll get you a pair.'

Sam knew how much Victoria hated being in the ballroom right now, with the bare wall symbolising what she saw as her failure. 'Would you rather do this in another room?' he asked quietly when Michael had gone to fetch the shoes.

'It's fine,' she said.

He had a feeling that she was being brave about it; but if he made a fuss about it he knew it'd make her feel awkward.

Michael returned with shoes and a small portable speaker, which he connected to his phone. 'Obviously we'll have live music on the night,' he said, 'but this will do for now.'

Once Samuel had changed his shoes and the three of them had rolled the carpet back to give them a decent space for dancing, Michael talked them through the first steps. Everything was very measured and mannered, Samuel thought.

'It's a cotillion and reel,' Michael explained, 'and it's danced in sets. There might be four, eight, or sixteen of you, and you repeat the moves until each of you has danced with all the other partners in the set.'

'It's not quite what I was expecting,' Samuel said. 'I

thought it was going to be more like the ballroom stuff you see nowadays. But you don't seem to get close to each other. Even the one where we're crossing arms, my left arm's behind my back and my right arm's behind Victoria's, just as her left arm's behind my back and her right arm's behind hers. It's as much as we do to hold hands. There's no real touching. We're even standing beside each other rather than properly opposite each other.'

'It's the propriety of the day,' Victoria said. 'And don't forget the women would all be wearing gloves, so there'd be no skin involved at all.'

'Jude was saying something about the waltz being considered very fast,' Samuel said thoughtfully.

'In both senses of the word—it's very energetic as well as being considered very daring for the times,' Michael said. 'Victoria, have you ever done Regency waltzing?'

'Yes, though I'm a bit rusty,' she said.

Michael smiled. 'That's fine. Let's give Sam a demo.' He put on some music that sounded like a harp, or at the very least like the musical jewellery box Sam remembered from his childhood.

Sam watched, fascinated, as Michael and Victoria marched together, then turned to face each other, one arm above their heads like an old-fashioned ballerina pose and the other arm clasped round each other's waists, and turned in a circle. Then they lowered their arms so they were much closer and added in little hops as they spun round in faster and faster circles.

'I think,' Sam said, 'that would make people dizzy.'

'Fun, though. It's a bit like the modern quickstep in places,' Michael said. 'Come and have a go. I'll talk you through it.'

Having Victoria in his arms was dangerous, Sam thought. He was aware of how close they were; enough though by modern standards there was a lot of space between them, he could see a massive difference between the formal group dances where partners changed after every few steps and this, where you'd be dancing with the same person for the whole dance. How you were close enough to have a whispered conversation without everyone else hearing. How you could really flirt with your partner and break all the conventions.

Michael slowed the steps right down until Sam was confident, and then he grinned. 'Time to do it at full speed.'

The music only lasted for about three minutes, but Sam could definitely feel his pulse racing and felt very slightly dizzy when it stopped.

'Do you get it, now?' Michael asked.

'I think so. That was very different,' Sam said.

'It'll be even better in Regency dress,' Victoria said.

Apart from the fact that she'd be wearing gloves, putting another barrier between them. He'd enjoyed holding her hand through the dance and feeling the warmth of her skin against his.

Though this was crazy. She was his fake fiancée, not his real one—and the pretend engagement was purely to help her out and stop her parents matchmaking.

He really needed to get a grip.

The lesson was over all too soon. They rolled the carpet back to its usual position, and Michael promised to send an invoice and formal confirmation of the booking later that day. 'This is going to be a joy,' he said, shaking their hands.

Sam and Victoria went back to her office.

'Let's see where we are right now,' she said. 'OK. The workshops are sold out—I have a waiting list for people who want a place on the next ones. So maybe I should look at running the workshops once a month in future.'

'Good idea,' he said. 'How are the ball tickets doing?'

'Halfway,' she said.

'Looks as if we have a success on our hands, then.'

'Don't count your chickens just yet,' she said. 'There are a lot of things that could still go wrong.'

'Not with you in charge,' he said.

Three days later, Sam and Victoria headed for London, for their final costume fitting with Mrs Prinks. Victoria had agreed to do a guest lecture at Jaz's university on what it was like to run a stately home; Sam sat at the back of the lecture theatre and watched, spellbound, as she went through the presentation without a single note in front of her, and then encouraged questions from the students. She paid attention to what they were asking and didn't brush a single thing aside.

She was absolutely in her element, and she shone.

It would be so, so easy to fall in love with her. She was sweet, she was bright, she was enchanting. And he could even forgive the lying about the engagement, because he understood why she was doing it.

She was nothing like Olivia.

But he still couldn't quite trust anyone with his heart.

He was going to have to be really, really careful.

At Mrs Prinks's workshop, after Victoria's lecture, Sam stared at himself in the mirror when he was dressed up. He'd never been one for fancy dress, even as a child. And it felt weird to be wearing knee breeches, stockings, a frock coat and a fancy shirt and cravat. Not to mention the shoes; with their suede soles they'd be ruined as soon as they were worn outdoors in the rain. He looked like himself—but also not like himself. It was as if the centuries had just blurred.

Feeling slightly awkward, he pulled aside the curtain of the cubicle where he'd changed into his costume and walked out. At almost exactly the same time, Victoria did the same.

Sam had no idea how she'd managed to put her hair up so quickly, but she looked stunning in her red silk ball gown. Like a woman in a costume drama; and yet at the same time he could imagine her walking through Chiverton Hall, centuries ago.

'Wow,' he said. 'You look amazing.'

She blushed. 'So do you.'

'Fitzwilliam Darcy and Elizabeth Bennet, eat your hearts out,' Jaz said.

Sam swept into a deep bow. 'I hope you're going to save me a waltz on your dance card, Miss Hamilton.'

Jaz scoffed. 'Are you seriously telling me you can do a proper Regency waltz?'

He laughed. 'I've been doing homework, I'll have you know. And in these shoes, yes, I can waltz. Miss Hamilton, if I may presume?'

Samuel gave another courtly bow, and Victoria's knees went weak.

'We don't have any music,' she mumbled, flustered.

'That's easily fixed,' Jaz said, and flicked into the Internet on her phone. 'Here we go.'

Victoria had danced a Regency waltz with Samuel before in the ballroom at Chiverton: but here, in the middle of a historical seamstress's workshop, with both of them wearing reproduction Regency clothing, it felt different. Last time, her fingers had been bare against his. Oddly, now she was wearing gloves, the dance felt more intimate. Forbidden, almost.

For a second, the workshop and Jaz and Mrs Prinks were forgotten. It was just the two of them and the music. And it would be oh, so easy to…

His pupils were huge, his green eyes almost black. So he felt it, too, that weird pull? And at the end of the dance they were only a breath away from a kiss. She felt herself leaning towards him and could see him leaning towards her; and then she was aware of the sound of applause, shocking her into pulling back.

'Very impressive. You're a quick learner, Sam,' Jaz said.

Sam bowed first to Victoria and then to Jaz. 'Save me a dance at the ball, Jaz,' he said.

She shook her head. 'I can't. I'm supervising my students.'

'Then dance with me in your serving outfit and pretend you're Cinderella,' he suggested.

'Yeah, yeah,' Jaz said, laughing.

But then she caught Victoria's gaze, and her expression said, *I'll be grilling you later.*

'You both look fabulous,' Mrs Prinks said. 'I want to take up your hem by about two centimetres, Victoria. Sam, your outfit's fine so you can take it away now.'

Sam went back into the cubicle to change out of his costume, and Victoria waited while Mrs Prinks expertly pinned the hem.

'Right. When are you going back to Cambridge?' Mrs Prinks asked.

'Our train's in an hour,' Victoria said.

'That doesn't give me enough time to do the alterations.' Mrs Prinks looked thoughtful. 'Either I can courier the dress to you, or you can come back for another fitting.'

'Or,' Samuel said, 'we can play hooky, stay overnight, come and see you first thing tomorrow for a fitting and then get the train. If that's giving you enough time to do the hem, Mrs Prinks?'

'Absolutely,' the seamstress said with a smile.

'That's settled, then,' Samuel said. 'Are you free for dinner tonight, Jaz? And maybe we can go and watch Jude treading the boards afterwards, if I can get tickets. My treat,' he said quickly, before Victoria could say a word. 'You can't argue with Mr Darcy.'

'You're not in costume any more, so you're not Darcy,' she pointed out.

He spread his hands. 'Too late.'

'Actually, that'd be really nice,' Jaz said. 'Thank you. And do I get to meet Jude?'

'I'll see what I can do. Give me a few minutes and I'll get Victoria to text you with all the details.' He smiled at Mrs Prinks. 'You've done a fantastic job. Thank you so much. I'm almost tempted to wear this tonight, except I don't want to spill anything on it or wreck the shoes—which I assume can only be worn indoors.'

'Indeed,' she said.

And, in that outfit, he'd turn every female head in the theatre, Victoria thought.

After they'd left Jaz and Mrs Prinks, Victoria said, 'We'd originally planned to go back to Cambridge, so I haven't got any spare clothes or toiletries with me.'

'My flat has a washing machine and a dryer. We can borrow everything else from Jude; or we can go shopping now, if you'd rather.' He shrugged. 'I don't think you need any make-up.'

Because she was too plain for it to make much difference, according to her ex, Paul. 'Uh-huh,' she said.

'Because you're lovely as you are,' he said softly. He

stole a kiss—and then looked at her in utter shock. 'Um. Sorry.'

'It's OK. It's what a fiancé would do—even though we don't actually need to keep up the pretence right now, as my parents are nowhere around,' she said lightly, even though her heart rate had just sped up several notches and her mouth was tingling where his had brushed hers.

'Does Jaz know about the fake engagement?' he asked.

'No. Does Jude?'

'No.'

'Then we don't have to keep up the act.' Particularly as she couldn't trust herself not to fall for him. That moment in the dressmaker's had shaken her. She'd nearly kissed him in front of a very small audience that included her best friend. How crazy was that?

'OK. But staying overnight might also help to keep your parents convinced about our "engagement",' he said.

She nodded. 'I need to let them know where we are, so they don't worry.'

'Ditto,' Sam said.

Not wanting to hear the hope and happiness in her mother's voice at the idea of her staying at her fiancé's flat, when Victoria knew she was going to let all those dreams down so very shortly afterwards, she chickened out and sent a text.

Second dress fitting tomorrow, so it makes sense to stay over. Do you mind having Humphrey tonight as well? Having dinner with Jaz—she sends her love.

And of course her mother would expect a message from Victoria's fiancé.

So does Samuel. Love you xxx

The reply came back almost immediate.

H fine with us. Dying to see the dress. Have fun! LU xxx

'Everything OK?' Samuel asked.

She nodded. 'Just feeling guilty about lying to Mum.'

'The whole thing was your idea,' he reminded her.

'And not one of my better ones,' she admitted glumly.

'It's done now. Let's make the best of it.'

'Mmm,' she said awkwardly. 'I do need to buy stuff, Samuel. I can't just…' She grimaced and shook her head.

'Jude won't mind you using his shower gel or shampoo, or lending you a T-shirt for tonight. And I'll do the laundry when we get in tonight.'

'It still feels a cheek.'

He tipped his head on one side. 'Is that Victoria-speak for you want to go shopping? Because I would've guessed that unless it involved a book, something to do with Chiverton or a present for someone, you're not a shopper.'

She wrinkled her nose. No wonder Paul had called her boring. He'd even spitefully called her Vic-*bore*-ia, and the name had stuck in her head. 'That's a horribly accurate summary.'

For a nasty moment she thought she'd spoken her thoughts aloud, when Samuel said, 'Actually, that's so refreshing.'

She looked blankly at him. 'What is?'

'Being with someone who sees life as more than just buying stuff.'

'That sounds as if you've dated too many Miss Wrongs,' she said before she could stop the words.

A shadow passed across his face, and she wondered if he was thinking about Olivia. Then again, he didn't know that she sort of knew about Olivia. Not the details, just that the woman had hurt him. The more she was getting to know Samuel, the more she liked him; there was depth beneath his charm. She didn't understand why anyone would want to hurt him.

'Coffee, then. Or if you need to go and get girly face stuff, I'll stay outside the shop and try and get tickets for tonight.'

'Thanks, but I'm paying for the tickets,' she said.

'Nope. My idea, my bill,' he said firmly. 'I might let you buy me dinner, though.'

'Deal.'

By the time she'd bought toiletries and underwear, Samuel had booked tickets for Jude's play and a table for three in a nearby Italian restaurant. 'I hope you don't mind me being presumptuous,' he said.

'I'm not difficult about food, and neither's Jaz,' she said with a smile. 'What's more difficult is actually getting a table, so thank you for sorting it out.'

'Pleasure.'

She texted the details to Jaz, and they headed back to Samuel's flat.

Jude welcomed them warmly and seemed thrilled that they were going to see him perform that evening.

Dinner before the show was good, and they spent more time laughing than talking. Jaz gave Victoria a couple of pointed looks, as if to say that Samuel was perfect for her and she really ought to act on that; but Victoria knew that this whole thing between them was fake. OK, so there had been that kiss this afternoon, and it looked as though it had shocked him as much as it had shocked her; but this was all a business arrangement. And, after her last three disastrous relationships, she knew better than to hope that this could turn into something more.

Jude was amazing and, when they went backstage to meet him and the rest of the cast, Jaz was noticeably star-struck.

'I'm so sorry that I've already got unbreakable arrangements for tonight,' Jude said, 'or I would've suggested going out. But I might see you at breakfast—and I want to see you dressed as Darcy, Sammy.'

'He looks pretty good,' Jaz said.

But Victoria knew her best friend well and her body language said, *I think you'd look even better.*

Maybe...

Back at Samuel's flat, she asked, 'Is Jude dating anyone?'

'No.' Samuel's eyes narrowed. 'Why?'

'He and Jaz seemed to hit it off. And I was thinking...'

He gave her a wry smile. 'You and I have both been victims of matchmaking.'

'This isn't the same,' she pointed out. 'We're not our parents. Plus they've actually met and liked each other. This would be a little nudge.'

'True.' He made hot chocolate and handed her a mug. 'We could pass on their mobile phone numbers and leave it to them. But you're right—they did seem to like each other.' He smiled. 'Ironic that a real relationship might come out of our fake one.'

Her heart skipped a beat. Was he talking about them?

No, of course not. He meant their best friends.

They curled up on opposite ends of his sofa, watching the river by night—the reflection of the lights and the bridges on the water—in companionable silence.

When Victoria went to bed that night, she lay awake, thinking of Samuel. The more time she spent with him, the more she liked him. But he'd made it clear to Jude that he didn't feel the same way about her, so it was pointless wishing or hoping or even dreaming that they could make their fake engagement a real relationship. It wasn't going to happen.

Sam sat watching the lights on the river, snuggled up under his spare duvet and wishing that Victoria were still there next to him. Preferably in his arms.

He liked her. A lot. The more she came out of her shell with him, the more he was starting to wonder if maybe he could talk her into trying to make their fake engagement a real relationship. OK, so they came from different worlds, but they weren't so far apart.

Once the ball was over and the stress was off her, he'd ask.

But he was definitely looking forward to the ball. To dancing with her and seeing her shine.

Mrs Prinks was satisfied with the dress, the next day, and boxed it up for their train journey.

Outside the workshop, Victoria said quietly to Sam, 'I'm giving you the money for my dress.'

'No. I said I'd buy it for you.'

'I don't expect you to do that.'

'I'd like to,' he said. 'We're friends, aren't we?'

Her dark eyes were huge. 'I guess.'

'Well, then. Think of it as a friend doing something nice for you. An un-birthday present.'

'It feels mean and greedy, taking things from you. I'm taking advantage of you.'

How different she was from Olivia—who would've expected jewellery, shoes, and a handbag to go with the dress, and sulked if anything hadn't been expensive enough. 'Humour me,' he said. 'There aren't any strings.

Or, if you really want to do something for me, you can teach me to cook something healthy but tasty for my dad.'

'I'll do that with pleasure,' she said. 'And thank you. The dress is perfect.'

Funny how her smile warmed him all the way through.

Part of Sam wished that they were at Chiverton right now, so he'd have an excuse to hold her hand. Which was crazy.

When they did get back to Chiverton, Patrick and Diana greeted them warmly—as did Humphrey, who was ecstatic at seeing Victoria again.

'I know, I know. I've neglected you for a gazillion years.' Victoria dropped to her knees and made a huge fuss of her dog.

'So do we get to see you both in your finery?' Diana asked.

'Fine by me,' Sam said. Then he had an idea. 'Meet us in the ballroom in ten minutes? We'll get changed and come straight up.'

'The ballroom,' Victoria said, grimacing, when her parents had gone.

'It's appropriate,' Sam said.

She sighed. 'I guess. OK. We'll change in my flat.'

He followed her up to her apartment. 'Where do you want me to change?'

'The living room?' she suggested. 'Knock on my bedroom door when you're ready.'

'OK.' He paused. 'Do you need a hand with the z—the fastening of your dress?'

She grinned. 'You were going to say "zip", weren't you?'

'Then I thought it might be…'

'Anachronistic. Just a tiny bit. Good call,' she finished. He loved it when she relaxed enough to tease him.

It didn't take him long to change. Then he knocked on the door. 'Ready when you are,' he called.

She emerged, fully dressed.

'You look amazing,' he said.

'Thank you. So do you.'

He smiled at her as they walked through the house together. 'I feel as if I've just stepped back two hundred years.'

'Dressed like this, so do I.'

'Let's do what your parents expect,' he said quietly, and took her hand.

'Oh, darling,' Diana said when they entered the ballroom. 'You look…' Her voice cracked with emotion.

'You look amazing. Both of you.' Patrick said. 'I'd like to take a photograph of you both together like this.'

'Yes—for the website,' Diana agreed. 'The rest of the tickets will sell like hot cakes when people see you.'

'And we should send it with a press release to the local paper,' Sam suggested.

'I'm glad I brought my proper camera,' Patrick said. 'And if you sit at the piano, darling, and you stand this side, Samuel, I can take the shot at an angle that won't show the bare wall.'

Victoria looked totally at ease behind the piano stool. 'Do you play?' Sam asked, suddenly curious.

'She does—and very well,' Diana answered.

'Would you play something for me?' Sam asked.

'Sure. What do you want?'

'Anything.'

He'd been half expecting her to play something obscure; but he recognised the *Moonlight Sonata* instantly. 'Beethoven?'

She nodded. 'Victoria's diary talks about hearing someone play it in London.'

'It's beautiful,' he said. 'Play me some more.'

He recognised Chopin and Bach, then was totally lost when she played an incredibly fast piece.

'You're Grade Eight standard, aren't you?' he asked when she'd finished.

She gave another of those half-shrugs. 'This is a nice piano to practise on.'

Diana patted her daughter's shoulder. 'She got distinctions in all her piano exams up to Grade Eight. Our Victoria will insist on hiding her light under a bushel. And she really shouldn't.'

'Agreed,' Sam said. He took his phone out of his pocket and flicked into the piece of music he'd downloaded earlier, while Victoria was changing. 'May I have this dance, Miss Hamilton?' He pressed 'play' and bowed to her.

She went very slightly pink. 'I guess we can use that bit of the floor alongside the carpet.'

Just as they had in the dressmaker's, they waltzed together. With her in his arms, it felt as if the whole world had faded away, and there was just the two of them and the music. And it didn't matter that she'd put her gloves back on again after playing the piano; he could still feel the warmth of her skin through the silk.

When the music came to an end, it really was a wrench to stop.

'Amazing,' he said, keeping his voice low so that only she could hear him. 'You're amazing.'

Her eyes looked absolutely enormous. All he had to do was lower his mouth to hers...

He just about stopped himself kissing her stupid, the way he wanted to do. It would be inappropriate in front of her parents. And, if he embarrassed her, he knew she'd back away from him. He wanted her closer, not further away.

'Thank you for the dance, Miss Hamilton.' He gave her a formal bow, then turned to Diana. 'Mrs Hamilton, I hope you'll save me a dance at the ball.'

'It's Diana, and it will be my pleasure,' she said. 'You both look wonderful. You'll do Chiverton proud.'

'We will,' Sam promised. 'If you can let me have those photographs, I'll update the website and talk to my contacts at the local paper.'

'Perfect,' Patrick said, clapping him on the shoulder.

'I'll go and change back into my normal clothes,' Sam said. 'I need to keep these ones looking nice for the ball.'

'Me, too,' Victoria said.

Her parents watched them leave, smiling indulgently.

'OK?' Sam asked when they were back in her flat.

'Yes.'

She didn't sound OK. 'Hey. It's going to be fine,' he said. 'Everyone's rooting for you and for Chiverton.'

'Uh-huh.'

There was a sadness in her eyes, and he couldn't stop himself putting his arms round her and giving her a hug. 'I believe in you,' he said. 'You're amazing. And don't let anyone tell you otherwise.'

Oh, but they had. And it had fed into the guilt Victoria felt about being the surviving child. That she wasn't enough. That she would never be enough.

'I know you're sad about not being able to share this with Lizzie,' Samuel said. 'But maybe it's time to let the sadness go and focus on all the good memories. Maybe you can dedicate the ball and the restoration to her.'

She thought about it. 'That's a lovely idea. I'll talk to Dad.'

'You do that. I'll grab you some coffee.'

Could she let go of the sadness? Of the guilt?

It would be hard, but maybe he was right and it was time she tried.

Later that evening, Diana came to Victoria's flat.

'Everything OK, Mum?' Victoria asked.

'No,' Diana said, and enveloped her in a hug. 'Because I had no idea.'

'No idea about what?'

'That you thought it should've been you who died and not Elizabeth. That she's the real daughter, not you.'

Victoria flinched. 'How did you…?' Then she realised. 'Samuel told you.'

'Don't be angry with him. He was just worried about you. We had a little chat.'

'And he told you.' Victoria's throat thickened.

'We *chose* you, Victoria,' Diana said gently. 'You were the light of our life. You still are. And I could never, ever choose between either of my daughters. I don't care about biology. You were ours from the second we first saw you. And we both love you so much. So very much.'

'Oh, Mum.' Victoria hugged her. 'I love you, too. And it's not anything to do with biology.'

'No. It's those dreadful men you picked. I know we should let you make your own choices and your own mistakes—you've never told me what happened and I've tried very hard not to pry—but you always seemed to pick men who didn't really see you for yourself and who didn't treat your properly. Men your father wanted to horsewhip.' She grimaced. 'That Paul—I could've horsewhipped him myself.'

'So that's why you and Dad always try to fix me up with the perfect man?'

'Not perfect, but they all had good hearts. We want you to find someone who loves you as much as we do.'

'Oh, Mum.' Guilt flooded through Victoria, and she

almost told Diana the truth about Samuel, but she couldn't find the right words.

'Samuel, though—you've definitely made the right choice there. He's a keeper. I really appreciate that he told me how you'd been feeling.' Diana stroked Victoria's hair. 'Don't ever feel you're second-best. You're not. You're my eldest daughter, and I love you more than I can say. So does your father.'

'You're the best parents anyone could've wished for,' Victoria said. 'I was thinking, maybe we can dedicate the ball to Lizzie.'

'No,' Diana said. 'The ball should be dedicated to the hard-working, clever, wonderful woman who put it all together. To *you*.'

'But I…'

'You hide your light under a bushel, darling, when your father and I are desperate for you to let it shine. You have that same brightness as the woman you're named after—the Victoria Hamilton who lived here two hundred years ago,' Diana said firmly. 'Now, I want you to promise me that you won't undervalue yourself again. You're my daughter and I'm very, very proud of you. I don't just love you, I *like* the woman you've become. And every day I'm glad you're ours.'

'I love you, too, Mum,' Victoria said, wrapping her arms round Diana.

When her mother had left, she video-called Samuel.

'When did you have a chat with my mother?'

'Ah.' He looked slightly guilty. 'Interfering, I know.'

'Yes,' she said. 'But Mum and I talked about things we should've talked about a long time ago. So thank you.'

'You're not furious with me?'

'I was horrified when I realised,' she said. 'But now I'm grateful.'

'I can work with grateful.' He gave her a grin that made her feel weak at the knees, and as if this thing between them were real rather than a pretence. 'See you tomorrow.'

'Tomorrow,' she echoed.

CHAPTER NINE

THE PHOTOGRAPH MADE a whole spread in the local newspaper, along with photographs of the house.

'So are you and Victoria…?' Denise asked, looking at the photograph of Sam and Victoria together at the piano.

'We're strictly colleagues,' Sam said with a smile. That wasn't the whole truth, but he wasn't prepared to talk about it just yet. He definitely didn't want to tell his mother about the fake engagement. 'Hopefully that picture will sell the rest of the tickets to the ball.'

His mother looked faintly disappointed. 'I worry about you, Sammy. I wish—'

He cut her off by giving her a hug. 'I know, Mum, and I'm fine. Right now my priority is you and Dad—and doing a good job to help the Hamiltons.'

'I know. And I'm sure they appreciate you as much as we do,' Denise said.

Sam realised he'd definitely have to make sure that Patrick didn't bump into Alan socially for the next couple of weeks. Just in case he accidentally mentioned the 'engagement'.

'Your father and I ought to buy tickets,' Denise said ruminatively.

'Mum, that's lovely of you, but you know how much Dad would loathe dressing up in a costume and doing formal dancing,' Sam said with a smile. 'Though if you want to donate the cost of a ticket, I'm sure that would be really appreciated. And I will make cookies for you.'

'Good idea. We'll do that,' Denise said.

'Thanks. I need to go or I'll be late,' he said, and gave her another hug.

Towards the end of November, it snowed. Big, fat, fluffy flakes that settled swiftly and covered the garden in a blanket of white.

'I love this place in the snow,' Victoria said. 'It looks perfect. And it's amazing at night—with everything blanketed in snow, when you look outside it feels as bright as daylight.'

Sam looked up from the file he'd been working on. Snow. Irresistible. Would this make Victoria be less serious? 'Would the garden team mind us going out in this?'

'Provided we stay off the flowerbeds, it'll be fine,' Victoria said. 'And you can do no wrong in Bob's eyes.'

'Then I challenge you to a snowball fight,' he said. He ruffled the fur on the top of the dog's head. 'You and me versus her, right, Humph?'

Humphrey woofed, and Sam laughed. 'That's a yes. Right. Last one out gets a forfeit.'

She grabbed her coat and they tumbled outside in a rush of laughter, pelting each other with snowballs. Humphrey bounded about between them, his tail a blur, chasing snowballs that Sam threw for him.

Sam couldn't remember the last time he'd had this much fun. 'It's years since I had a decent snowball fight. This is probably the first one since I was a student,' he said.

'It's been a while for me, too. Lizzie and I used to have snowball fights—but obviously, because she was younger than me, I always made sure I didn't throw them too hard,' Victoria said. 'And we used to make snowmen.'

'I'm up for that,' Sam said. 'And we need to make a snow dog in honour of Humphrey.'

Between them, they made a massive snowman and a rather less than perfect snow dog.

'Selfie,' Sam said, and took a snap of them together in front of the snowman, and a second snap where they'd crouched down with Humphrey. Both of them had red faces from the cold, but their eyes were sparkling.

'That was fun,' he said. 'Thanks for sharing this with me. It must've been amazing growing up here as a child, with all those trees to climb.'

'We didn't really climb trees. We used to act out being knights and ladies, with pretend sword-fights and dancing across the lawn,' Victoria said.

'Did you make snow angels?'

She smiled. 'I haven't done that in years.'

Unable to resist, Sam pulled her down into the snow. She landed on top of him, and automatically his arms closed round her to steady her.

Her face was full of panic. 'I'm too heavy.'

'No, you're not.' He brushed his mouth against hers. 'Cold snow, warm you. It's a very nice contrast.' Just to prove his point, he did it again.

This time, she kissed him back. Her mouth was sweet, and the cold and wetness seeping through his clothes didn't matter. Nothing mattered apart from the way she felt, leaning into him and kissing him.

When she broke the kiss he was shocked to realise he was shaking—and not from the cold.

'Victoria.' His voice sounded cracked and hoarse to his own ears.

Panic skittered across her expression. 'You'll be soaked. Freezing. We'd better go in.'

He didn't want to move, not when she was in his arms. 'I'm fine.' He stroked her hair.

'You're cold. And wet. I don't have anything that would fit you, but I'm sure Dad can lend you some dry clothes.'

She was babbling, and they both knew it.

If he pushed her now, she'd really panic. Whoever she'd last dated had obviously really hurt her—and Sam, who'd never thought of himself as the violent type, found his fists actually clenching with the urge to punch the guy.

He let her climb off him and lead the way back to the house.

'Go up to my flat and have a hot shower,' she said. 'I'll bring you something of Dad's, and if you leave your wet stuff outside the bathroom door I'll put it in the tumble dryer.'

'Thanks.' He looked at her. 'You're as wet as I am. You have a shower and change first, and I'll make us both a coffee—if you don't mind me using your kitchen.'

'OK. Thanks.'

What had she been thinking?

Well, obviously she *hadn't* been thinking. She'd lost herself in old memories of snowball fights and making snowmen, enjoying herself with Samuel.

That kiss... It had been propinquity, that was all. Victoria knew Samuel didn't want a proper relationship. They were becoming friends, but the kiss hadn't meant anything to him, and she would be stupid to let it mean anything to her.

She showered and changed. 'Back in a tick. I've left you clean towels,' she said, not meeting his eyes.

'Thanks. I've left your mug of coffee by the kettle.'

'Great. I appreciate that.' She borrowed some dry clothes from her dad, then rapped on the bathroom door. 'The dry clothes are outside the door,' she called. 'See you back in the office.' And she fled before she could make more of a fool of herself.

When Samuel came down to her office, a few minutes later, Victoria's vision blurred for a second. She could imagine him leaning against their shared desk in forty years' time, laughing and with a mug of coffee in his hand. Just like her father had shared this office with her mother. And it put a lump in her throat.

But it was pointless wishing for something she couldn't have. Samuel had broken down some of her own barriers, but his were still in place. Whatever he'd said about her being enough, he'd meant enough for her parents—not for him.

'I put your clothes in my dryer,' she said. 'Give it half an hour and I'll go and check if they're ready.'

'Thanks. And it's kind of your dad to lend me stuff.'

'No problem,' she said lightly.

'I guess our snow break's officially over.'

He looked slightly wistful. Was it the snow he was thinking about—or when he'd kissed her?

She shook herself. Not appropriate. 'It is. And I have a pile of stuff to do.'

'We'll divvy it up between us,' he said.

Sam stuck to being professional with Victoria for the next couple of weeks. But, the week before the Christmas events, he sat on the edge of their shared desk. 'Engaged couples go out to dinner. Or dancing.'

She frowned. 'We've done dancing.'

'Regency dancing,' he said. 'Not modern.'

She spread her hands. 'Can you imagine me in a night-club?'

'Well—no,' he admitted. 'But your parents are going to start wondering why we're not going out anywhere on dates.'

'They can see we're really busy with the Christmas week preparations,' she pointed out. 'The house opens on Sunday.'

'We could,' he said, 'have a night out in London. There's a performance I thought it'd be fun to go to.'

Her eyes widened. 'Are you asking me out on a date?'

'A fake one,' he said quickly, not wanting to spook her.

'OK.'

'Friday night?' And maybe he could talk Jude into staying at a friend's for that night. 'Everything's on track and we'll be back for Saturday afternoon to deal with any last-minute trouble-shooting. Plus I think it'll do you good to take an evening off—before you burn out.'

For a moment, he thought he'd pushed her too far; but then she nodded.

'You're right. And thank you—that'd be nice to go to a show.'

On Friday, they dropped their things at Samuel's flat and went for an early dinner. When they walked to the theatre, the show name was in lights outside: *The Taming of the Shrew.*

'Really?' she asked. Did he still think she was a shrew?

'Sorry, I just couldn't resist it,' he said with a grin. 'But we do have good seats.'

'It's a while since I've seen it. And Shakespeare's always a treat.'

'"Why, there's a wench. Come on and kiss me—Vicky."'

He pronounced the 'ky' as 'Kate' and she groaned. 'That's terrible.' But she couldn't help smiling.

They walked into the foyer, and suddenly he grabbed her hand.

'What?' she asked.

'That favour? I'm calling it in, right here and right now,' he said. 'Can you please just go with whatever I say next?'

She'd done that to him without any prior warning, and he'd gone along with her; the least she could do was agree now. 'Sure.'

'You can start by kissing me. Not full-on snogging, just kind of stealing a kiss. Like a fiancée would.'

She had absolutely no idea what had spooked him like this, but she could see the wariness in his eyes. Something was definitely wrong. 'Well, sweetie,' she said softly, resting her palm lightly against his cheek. 'Let's do this.'

She reached up and brushed her mouth against his and he wrapped his arms round her, holding her tightly as if she were the only thing stopping him from drowning.

'Thank you,' he whispered against her mouth.

'Sam? Sam Weatherby? I *thought* it was you!' a voice cooed behind them.

'Olivia,' he said coolly.

Olivia? *The* Olivia? Victoria wondered.

The woman who was sashaying over to them with a man in tow was tall and willowy, with immaculate blonde hair and the kind of high-maintenance barely-there make-up that took an hour to do. Her clothes were all clearly designer labels, Victoria would bet that her shoes cost a fortune, and Olivia was wearing enough jewellery to dazzle the entire theatre.

'Good to see you, Sam.'

From the look in his eyes, Samuel didn't think it was

good to see her—or maybe it was her companion that he objected to. But he said politely, 'And you.' Though Victoria noticed that his eyes didn't crinkle at the corners when he smiled.

'This is Geoff, my fiancé,' she said. 'Darling, Sam and I are old friends.'

That wasn't quite how Victoria would describe it. That snippet of conversation she'd overheard between Samuel and Jude had told her that Olivia and Samuel had been a lot more than friends. And that it had gone badly wrong.

'Good to meet you, Geoff,' Samuel said, shaking the other man's hand. 'And may I present my fiancée, the Hon Victoria Hamilton of Chiverton Hall.'

Now Victoria realised what his favour was: the same as she'd asked of him. Except she was distracting his ex rather than his parents.

Though she didn't have time to wonder if it meant that he was still in love with Olivia, because she'd promised to go along with what he asked.

'Goodness! I didn't realise you'd got engaged.' Olivia's expression was very put out for a moment; then she looked Victoria up and down. Her gaze settled on Victoria's bare left hand, and then she made very sure to clutch her own left hand—which had the most massive diamond on her ring finger—to her chest, to accentuate the difference between them. She gave Victoria a slightly triumphant smile, as if to say that in no way could she imagine someone as attractive as her ex-fiancé wanting to settle down with someone who just wasn't pretty enough or scrubbed up well enough to compete with Olivia herself. 'Well, I do wish you the best. I take it your ring's being resized at the moment? Or is he making you wait, Vicky?'

'My name is Victoria, not Vicky,' Victoria corrected coolly. 'And, actually, we're not bothering with a ring,

Lily.' She deliberately got the other woman's name wrong, and she could see that the barb had hit home. 'Real love doesn't need the trappings and suits.' Before the other woman could make a spiteful comment, she linked her fingers through Sam's. '"My bounty is as boundless as the sea, My love as deep; the more I give to thee, The more I have, for both are infinite."' She drew Sam's hand up to her mouth and kissed the backs of his fingers. 'Which obviously is Juliet rather than Katherine, but what's a play between people who love each other?'

Olivia's expression was like thunder.

'So nice to meet you, Lily,' Victoria said, letting just a hint of patronisation into her tone. 'But I think we're being called to our seats right now. Enjoy the play.' She tugged at Sam's hand, and headed towards one of the doors. 'If this is the wrong way to our seat, it doesn't matter. We'll find another way round,' she said out of the side of her mouth.

Sam took their tickets out of his pocket. 'This is the right door, and hopefully they're not sitting anywhere near us.'

She hoped so, too. 'Are you OK?' she asked, seeing the tension in his eyes.

'Yes.' That was a lie, she knew. 'And thank you for coming to my rescue.'

'No problem.' She squeezed his hand, letting him know she was firmly on his side. If that woman thought she was going to get a second chance to hurt Samuel, she had another think coming. 'She's a festering lily.'

Samuel looked at her. 'That's Shakespeare, right?'

'Sonnet Ninety-four.' In the looks department, Victoria might be a base weed, but Olivia was most definitely a festering lily, and Victoria knew which of the two she'd rather be. 'Ask Jude.'

'Is that why you called her Lily instead of Olivia?'

'I was being petty,' she admitted. 'But it turned out to be appropriate.'

'Yeah.'

To Victoria's surprise, Samuel didn't let her hand go. He held it throughout the whole play, and all the way back to his flat. She didn't comment on it or push him to talk until they had arrived.

'Coffee, wine, or something stronger?' she asked.

'I'm fine.'

'No, you're not.' She gave him a hug. 'Look, I know it's not really any of my business, but seeing Olivia clearly threw you. I'm assuming she's your ex.' She knew that for sure but didn't want to admit to eavesdropping. And he'd helped her overcome feeling as if she was worthless. The least she could do was to be there for him. 'I'm here if you want to talk.'

'I don't really want to talk,' he said, 'but I owe you an explanation.'

'You don't have to tell me anything if you don't want to,' she said.

She thought he was going to close up on her, but then he sighed. 'Olivia was my fiancée.'

Now she understood why Samuel had wanted her to pose as his fiancée tonight. She had a feeling that the whole flashing-my-massive-diamond thing had been Olivia's way of telling him that she'd met someone who suited her better.

'We met at a party, a friend of a friend kind of thing, and...' He grimaced. 'Let's just say I wasn't very nice when I was in my early twenties. I dated a lot. I never, ever cheated on any of my girlfriends, but I never really gave any of them a chance to get close to me, either. I didn't let the relationship develop into anything deeper because I thought the world was my oyster and I had all the time in the world—or maybe my dad was right in that I was selfish and reckless and thoughtless. But somehow Olivia stuck. We'd been dating for six months when she told me she was pregnant.'

Victoria waited.

'So I did the right thing. I didn't think I was really ready to settle down—but she was my girlfriend and she was pregnant with my baby, so of course I wasn't going to abandon her. I asked her to marry me. She said yes.' He closed his eyes for a moment. 'It was only when I accidentally saw a text on her phone—it was on the lock screen,' he added quickly. 'I wasn't snooping. I just glanced casually at the screen when the light came on, as most people do, and I saw the words. It was from one of her friends. She seemed to be laughing at the fact that Olivia had pulled it off.'

Victoria frowned. 'Pulled what off?'

'The trap she'd set for me,' Samuel said. 'The massive rock on her finger, moving into a flat overlooking the river—not this one, I moved here later—and the fact she was never going to have to work again. Because that's what it was, a trap. She wasn't actually pregnant. She just knew that was what it would take for me to marry her—and, once she was married to me, that would mean either sticking with it or handing over an expensive divorce settlement.'

Victoria blinked, not quite taking it in. Olivia had pretended she was pregnant, just to make sure Samuel married her and financed her lifestyle? 'That's a horrible thing to do. What about love?'

'That's when I realised Olivia loved only herself,' he said dryly. 'And she made sure we both saw tonight how massive her new engagement ring is. Bigger than the last one. I feel sorry for the guy, because I don't think she's capable of loving anyone.'

Now Victoria understood that conversation she'd overheard. Why Samuel felt he'd been naive and gullible. But he hadn't. He'd been *decent*. 'So what happened? Did you confront her with the text?'

'I lied. I said I'd overheard her talking to her friend Hermione about the baby that didn't exist and suggested that she might like to tell me the truth. I thought she was going to tough it out, but then she crumpled and admitted it. And I ended the engagement right there and then. I gave her a month to find somewhere else to live and I moved in with Jude. I followed up with a letter from my solicitor, and I think she realised she wasn't going to get anything else out of me—so, thankfully, she left. She stripped the flat, but she left.'

No wonder he had trust issues. Olivia had treated him even more badly than Paul had treated her. 'I'm sorry. That's a horrible thing to happen.' She frowned. 'Though, as she was supposed to be pregnant, um, didn't you notice?'

'That she was still having periods? No. Hers were never regular, and her boss sent her on a couple of courses. I realised later the timing of the "courses" must've coincided with her periods. I wouldn't be surprised if she'd just taken time off and was staying with Hermione rather than going away somewhere on a real course.' He lifted a shoulder. 'I was a gullible, naive fool.'

'No, you weren't. You did your best by her,' she said. 'And we all want to be loved. It's easy to convince yourself someone loves you; it's really not very nice to realise that actually they're looking at your assets instead.'

'That,' he said, 'sounds personal.'

She inclined her head. 'Stately homes are worth a lot of

money. But, unless you've grown up with one or worked in one, you might not realise that owning a stately home means you're asset-rich and cash-poor. Or that stately homes cost an awful lot of money to run.'

'You had a guy like Olivia?' he asked.

'Yes, but we didn't get as far as an engagement, and unlike you it took me three attempts before I finally twigged why any of them wanted to date me.' She grimaced. 'I'm a slow learner. The last guy made it very clear to me that the house is the only attractive thing about me.'

'You,' he said, 'are far from being a slow learner. Your mind's first-class. And words fail me about your ex. That's a vile thing to say, and it's not true.'

She shrugged. 'I saw the way Olivia looked at me tonight. With pity. I'm not like the women in her world—well, in your real world. I don't have an expensive hairdo, expensive shoes, expensive clothes, expensive make-up or expensive jewellery.' She didn't want them, either. They weren't important.

'You don't need them.'

'Thank you for being gallant, but I'm not fishing for compliments. I'm aware of what I am.'

'I don't think you are,' he said. 'When you're talking about history, you light up. And that's *my* Victoria. The one who pays attention to detail, the one who knows obscure stuff and delights in it.' He smiled. 'The one who doesn't bat an eyelid when her muddy dog puts a paw on her knee. Yes, you can be horribly earnest and over-serious, but there's a warmth about you and you've got a huge, huge heart: and that's what I see. It's like that thing you were saying to Olivia about trappings and suits—you don't need them. You're enough as you are. Not just for your parents. For *anyone.*'

Tears pricked at her eyelids and she blinked them back. 'That's such a nice thing to say.'

'I'm not being nice. I'm being honest.' He wrapped his arms round her. 'I happen to *like* you.'

Her throat felt thick. 'I like you, too.'

'I mean I really, *really* like you.' He stole a kiss. 'And this is nothing to do with Olivia and everything to do with you.'

This time, when he bent his head to kiss her, she kissed him back. And she made no protest when he picked her up and carried her to his bed.

The next morning, Victoria woke in Samuel's arms. She was pretty sure he was awake—his breathing wasn't deep or regular—and she didn't have a clue what to say to him. This was so far outside the way she usually behaved. She had no idea of the protocols. Had this been a one-night stand, or was it the start of something else?

She still didn't have her thoughts clearly together when Samuel said softly, 'Good morning.'

'Um. Good morning.' She wanted to bury her head rather than face him, but the way she was lying meant that would mean burying her head in his bare chest. And she didn't want him thinking she was needy or would make any kinds of demands on him.

'Are you OK?' he asked.

This time, she met his gaze. 'Yes.' She wasn't—she was all over the place—but no way was she admitting that. 'Are you?'

'Yes and no.' He shifted to kiss the tip of her nose. 'I'm better for waking up with you in my arms.'

'Uh-huh,' she said, not knowing what he wanted to hear.

'Last night probably shouldn't have happened—but I'm glad it did.'

So was she. Though part of her felt antsy. She was used to everything being under control and ticked off a list. This was stepping so far away from that, it sent waves of panic through her. 'So where do we go from here?' she asked.

'I don't know,' he said. 'Maybe see how things go. Though obviously we have next week to get through, first.'

And then his internship would officially be over. 'Then you'll be busy taking over from your dad.'

'But,' he said, 'at least we'll be living near each other. And maybe we can...' He blew out a breath. 'I'm not very good at proper relationships.'

'Neither am I,' she admitted.

'Then maybe we can learn together,' he said. 'Learn to trust each other, learn to make it work.'

Was she hearing things?

'If you'd like to, that is,' he added.

He meant it. He really meant it. And her heart felt as if it would burst with joy. 'I'd like that. A lot,' she said.

He kissed her again, and by the time they got up it was way too late for breakfast. Especially as they had a train to catch.

'Maybe we should have brunch on the train while we go through our lists?' he suggested.

'Good idea.'

Even though they were officially going through all the things they needed to troubleshoot before the house opened to visitors the following afternoon, Sam found himself distracted by Victoria on the train. There was a new softness to her expression when she looked at him.

And the way she made him feel… It was a long time since he could remember being this happy. This thing between them was new and fragile, but he knew she was Olivia's opposite—she was honest and fair and *nice*.

When they reached Cambridge, he took his phone from his pocket to call them a taxi. Then he realised that he must've left his phone switched on silent from the theatre, the previous night, because there were five missed calls from his mother, and a text.

Please call me urgently, Sammy.

He felt sick. Had something happened to his dad? 'I need to call my mum,' he said to Victoria.

'Anything I can do?' she asked.

He shook his head and called his mother.

'Sammy, we're at the hospital. Your father had a stroke this morning,' Denise said.

'I'm on my way,' he said. 'I'm at the station. I'll get a taxi straight to the hospital. Text me the ward name and I'll text you when I'm nearly there.'

'Samuel? What's happened?' Victoria asked when he ended the call.

'Dad's had a stroke. I need to get to the hospital.'

'I'll come with you.'

To the hospital?

Given that she'd lost her sister to leukaemia, Sam was pretty sure that Victoria would find hospitals difficult. In her shoes, he would. OK, so she'd offered to go with him—but it wouldn't be fair to take her up on that offer.

Right now he had no idea what the situation was with his dad. The stroke might've been mild, it might've been severe, or it might've been the first of a series that would end in Alan's death. He couldn't hurt Victoria by making her face that.

He shook his head. 'You have things to do at the house.'

'They can wait.'

He dragged in a breath. 'I need to do this on my own.'

'Anything you need, just call me. *Anything,*' she said. 'It doesn't matter how big or small, or what time it is. Call me.'

Right now what he really wanted was to turn the clock back and for his dad to be OK. But that wasn't possible. 'Thanks,' he said. 'I'll call you later.'

'Give my best to your parents.'

'Thanks. I will.'

The drive in the taxi felt as if it were taking for ever. Seeing his father in a hospital bed, with Alan's mouth twisted and one eye half shut, was a shock.

'Mum. I'm so sorry.' He hugged his mother, and sat on the edge of his father's bed, taking Alan's hand. When had his father's skin become this papery—this *old*? 'Dad, I'm here. I'm sorry.'

The sounds that came out of his father's mouth didn't bear much resemblance to words.

'Don't try to talk. Just rest. I'm here now,' Sam said.

Time, at the hospital, was different. Like treacle. And, although the medical staff were kind, nobody could give any real answers about when—or if—Alan would recover his powers of speech or walk again. Sam was used to organising things, making things happen; the seven words he kept hearing drove him insane. *We'll just have to wait and see.*

How long would they have to wait?

And actually having to feed his father because Alan couldn't hold cutlery or a cup or a sandwich. Sam knew how much his father was hating this. The loss of control. The loss of his dignity.

All Sam could do was to grit his teeth and hold both his parents' hands. 'We'll get through this,' he said. 'We'll get you back on your feet and back to your normal self, Dad.'

His phone beeped several times but he ignored it, until Denise pushed him to go and get himself a mug of coffee. Then he checked his messages.

There were a couple from Victoria. Not demanding, needy, look-at-me messages like the ones Olivia had been fond of sending. Just a quiet, At Chiverton. Hope your dad's doing OK. Thinking of you all.

There wasn't much he could say to that. Because right now nobody knew how his dad was doing.

Thanks, he typed back.

He wished he hadn't pushed her away and told her to go back to Chiverton. Right now he could really do with her arms round him, His steady, quiet, *safe* Victoria.

But that wasn't fair.

Hadn't his father said he was selfish and reckless?

There was a second text, sent two hours later.

Let me know if there's anything I can do. Any time.

She was so kind and supportive: and, at the same time, it was clear she was trying to give him space and not pressure him. That she understood what it was like to be at the bedside of someone you loved, worried sick, and she wouldn't be huffy if he didn't reply within a couple of hours, let alone within seconds.

And because he knew what she'd been through, he knew he had to do the right thing. Distance himself. Protect her from having to face this nightmare all over again. So, later that evening, he sent her a text.

Sorry to let you down. I need to support my parents right now. Book a temp to help you next week and I'll pick up the bill. Hope all goes well with the ball.

Victoria stared at the text.

He'd said nothing about how his dad was. How *he* was. He'd ignored the supportive texts she'd sent him—and she hadn't flooded his phone with needy messages, either. She'd simply told him when she got back to Chiverton and asked him to let her know if there was anything she could do. She'd tried to be supportive and give him space at the same time.

She blew out a breath and tried to unpick his message.

Sorry to let you down.

Of course he wasn't letting her down. This was an emergency.

I need to support my parents right now.

Again, in his shoes, she'd feel the same. It wasn't a problem.

Book a temp to help you next week and I'll pick up the bill.

Meaning that he wasn't coming back as her intern. It would be a bit of a headache for her, but over the weeks she'd worked with him she'd discovered that they had the same attitude towards project management and she knew his files would contain all the information she'd need to keep everything ticking over. As for getting in someone to help her—she'd just pick up the slack herself. She didn't expect him to pay for a temp to replace his unpaid position.

Hope all goes well with the ball.

And that was the bit that stuck in her throat. He wasn't coming to the ball. She'd so been looking forward to it. To dancing with him in the restored room, dressed up in her Regency finery.

OK. She'd have to stop being selfish and suck it up. Samuel's dad was seriously ill. Of course he wouldn't want to come and do something so frivolous.

She had no idea whether his phone was even on, so a text was the easiest way to reach him. He'd pick it up whenever.

You're not letting me down and of course I understand your parents need you. Let me know if there's anything I can do.

She didn't quite dare add a kiss. Because now she was starting to think that what he'd said to her in London had been in the heat of the moment.

You're enough as you are. Not just for your parents. For anyone.

Maybe he'd meant it at the time. But now all her old fears came flooding back. She hadn't been enough for Paul, and Samuel was ten times the man Paul was. Whatever made her think she'd be enough for him?

And how selfish was she, putting her own feelings first when she knew how ill his father was?

She'd do what he wanted and keep her distance.

Victoria was nothing like Olivia. Of course she'd be understanding and wouldn't put pressure on him, Sam thought. She was kind. She offered help because she genuinely cared and wanted to help, not because she thought it would score points.

But everything was muddled in his head. Right now he couldn't get over the fact that his father was seriously ill.

Alan Weatherby had definitely got the measure of his son. Reckless and selfish.

So maybe it was time to be unselfish and not keep Victoria dangling on the hook. She had enough on her plate without worrying about him.

He'd do what he always did with relationships. Distance himself.

Thanks, but no need. Good luck with the future.

CHAPTER TEN

GOOD LUCK WITH the future.

That sounded pretty final, Victoria thought.

Obviously Samuel didn't plan to be part of that future.

What an idiot she was. So much for thinking she'd learned her lesson. Yet again she'd fallen in love with a charmer who didn't feel the same way about her. Though at least Samuel hadn't had his eye on the house.

She'd just have to suck it up and deal with it. The only thing she could do was to visit Alan Weatherby in hospital when he was a little better and give Samuel the glowing reference he deserved. Just because things hadn't worked out between them, she wasn't petty enough to deny the hard work he'd put in.

In the meantime, she had enough to keep her super-busy, with the house due to open for visitors, the work-shops and the ball.

She spent the day putting the finishing touches to the Christmas trees and trying not to think about how she and Samuel had collected the pine cones and the giant allium heads together and spray-painted them gold. She made a couple of kissing balls, binding the hoops together with string and covering them with greenery, adding dried or-ange slices and ribbons and mistletoe; and all the while she tried not to think about kissing Samuel. She made pomanders, pressing cloves into oranges and tying them with ribbons. Having something to do that required her attention so she didn't have time to think was really, really good.

The team who always did her flowers had gathered greenery to be spread along the windowsills and mantelpieces, and they'd done her proud with the table centrepieces.

And the one good thing about working ridiculous hours was that it meant she was physically so tired that she actually slept instead of lying awake, brooding.

The next day, Samuel's team of footmen and servants turned up—thankfully in exactly the kind of clothes they would've worn in Regency times. She set them to work with Nicola, sorted out a room for her anachronistic Santa, and made sure she was around in case any of the visitors had any questions.

Despite the fact that all their visitors seemed delighted to have the chance to talk about Regency Christmas customs and she was rushed off her feet, she still missed Samuel. Every so often she found herself turning to say something to him—and of course he wasn't there.

Stupid, stupid, stupid.

Once the house had closed, she cut some flowers from the garden, then headed for the hospital.

'Sorry, we don't allow flowers at the moment,' the receptionist on the ward told her. 'We have strict rules for controlling the spread of infection.'

'Of course. Sorry.' She bit her lip.

But at least they allowed her to visit Samuel's father. And, thankfully, Samuel wasn't there.

'Mr Weatherby? I'm Victoria Hamilton—Patrick and Diana's daughter,' she said. 'I did bring you some flowers from Chiverton, but unfortunately I'm not allowed to give them to you.'

'Thank you anyway.' Alan squinted at her.

'I'm so sorry you're ill.'

'Getting better. Words aren't...' He grimaced. 'Can't get the right ones.'

'They'll come back,' she said, wanting to reassure him.

'Got some words today, though. Getting better. You work with Sammy.'

She nodded. 'Your son is a good man. He's way over-qualified to be my intern, but he did the job anyway, with a good heart. He's easy to work with.'

Alan frowned. 'Reckless.'

'A little bit headstrong at times,' she said, 'but Samuel listens to people. He thinks about things. He's impulsive, yes, but that's not a bad thing because he has great ideas.'

'You taught him to bake.' Alan smiled. 'His mum nearly fell over.'

She smiled back. 'He was very pleased with himself about that. And he insisted on making everyone in the house try the biscuits. He's—was,' she corrected herself, 'going to make them for the ball. They're on the menu as Weatherby's Wonders.'

'Weatherby's Wonders.' Alan gave a wheezy chuckle.

'Mr Weatherby? Are you all right? Can I get you a glass of water, or would you like me to call a nurse?'

'I'm all right, love.' He patted her hand. 'Tell me. Sammy.'

There was a lot she could say about Samuel, but it wasn't appropriate. Instead, she said, 'He's kind to my dog, he makes time for everyone on the team and makes them feel valued, and our head gardener Bob—who's notorious for being grumpy—has taken a real shine to him and comes into the office for a daily cuppa with him. I miss him. We *all* miss him,' she added swiftly.

'You think he could take over?'

'From you? Yes. No hesitation. Samuel would make an excellent job of anything he decided to do.'

'You'll give him a…?' Alan frowned, clearly unable to find the right word.

'Reference?' She nodded. 'He's more than earned it. He's done everything from spray-painting pine cones, to organising a Santa and negotiating an amazing deal on Christmas trees. He learned to bake from a recipe that's centuries old, and he learned the steps to the Regency dances when he'd never done anything like that before. He never complained once. Argued with me, yes, but he had valid points.' And he'd stolen her heart in the process.

Samuel recognised that voice.

He stopped dead, not wanting Victoria to see him. What was she doing here?

Knowing that he shouldn't be eavesdropping, he listened.

She was talking to his father. And she was really giving him a glowing report.

Guilt flooded through him. He'd pushed her away—and she'd still come to give support, in a place that had to be difficult for her. She could've just ignored all this or sent a formal letter with a reference, especially as she was right in the middle of the fundraising and she was horrendously busy.

But she hadn't. She was here in person. Not to score points, but because Victoria Hamilton was a really, really good woman. Dependable. Trustworthy. Brave.

I miss him.

Yeah. He missed her, too. So much that it actually

hurt. But he didn't know what to say to her; and all the things that were in his head definitely weren't appropriate to say in front of his father. Plus he didn't want to do anything that might make his father have a relapse or a second stroke.

This was a conversation he needed to have with Victoria, on his own—and not right now. For his father's sake, he'd go and have a cup of coffee and come back in half an hour.

As for Victoria herself... He was going to have to sort that out, too. He'd let her down. Hurt her. He wasn't entirely sure how to fix it, but he'd find a way to make a start. Because hearing her voice again had crystallised everything for him. He finally knew what he wanted for the rest of his life. The question was whether she wanted that, too. But the way she spoke to his father gave him hope.

The workshops went brilliantly, including the pre-ball dance workshop. Victoria had to nip out to the supermarket and get emergency supplies for the café, because they had even more visitors than she was expecting. The reproduction silk hangings for the ballroom were so perfect that when they were up even she couldn't spot the difference; and Jaz's third years were all thoroughly enjoying the preparations for the ball supper.

And today, on the day of the ball, it was snowing. Not enough to cause problems, but a light dusting—enough to make the house look really, really pretty.

Victoria loved the house in the snow. For her, Chiverton glowed brighter than any diamond.

Her professional life was perfect, right now. The house was looking better than ever. The fundraising week had put everyone on a real high. Today ought to be one of the happiest days of her life.

Except it wasn't.

She really, really missed Samuel. So did Humphrey; he looked up hopefully every time someone walked down the corridor to her office, and every time it wasn't Samuel he put his head back dejectedly between his paws. Right now, that was what Victoria wanted to do, too. Curl up in a ball and huddle in misery.

But tonight was the high point of the fundraising week. She was expecting guests and the press any second now, and she needed to pin that smile on her face and be dazzling.

It was a week since his father's stroke. In that time Sam had done a lot of thinking. A lot of talking. A bit of persuading.

Tonight, he was hoping that the whole lot would come together. That he could fix the mess he'd made. His mother had given him wise advice; the Hamiltons had been shocked at first when he'd told them the truth about the 'engagement', but then they'd been understanding. Given him their blessing.

And now it was time to face Victoria.

He'd waited until the press had gone and the ball was in full swing. Just before supper, by his reckoning.

'Sam! I didn't think you were coming,' Jenny, the house steward stationed in the reception area, said. 'How's your dad?'

Obviously Victoria had explained his absence to everyone in terms of his father's illness, rather than pointing out that he'd let everyone down. 'He's on the mend, thanks.' He smiled at her. 'Everyone's upstairs?'

'They are. And you don't need anyone to show you the way to the ballroom, do you?'

'No. It's fine. But thanks.'

He strode up the massive curved staircase and through the Long Gallery. He could hear the music playing, and he looked through the doorway into the ballroom.

He'd seen the pictures on the website, but it hadn't prepared him for the real thing. Instead of that bare wall that made Victoria flinch, the silk hangings were back. The mirrors on the walls reflected the chandeliers, candelabra and each other, spreading the light further. And the walls actually glowed in the light.

It was stunning.

No wonder she loved this room.

The carpet had been removed temporarily; people were on the dance floor, following Michael the dancing master's instructions, and others were sitting on the *chaises longues* and chairs at the side of the room, watching them.

Victoria was dancing. In her red silk dress, she looked amazing, and his heart skipped a beat.

Please let her talk to him. Let her give him a chance.

He waited until the music had finished, then walked over to her. 'Good evening, Miss Hamilton.'

She stared at him, looking shocked. 'I thought you weren't coming tonight.'

'The night when the ballroom was back to its former glory? Wild horses wouldn't have kept me away.' Though it wasn't the room he wanted. It was her.

'Is your dad all right?' she asked.

'He's home and grumbling at my mum about not being allowed a bacon sandwich. He's got all his words back, and the physio's having to tell him not to overdo things because he's so determined he wants to be back in the swing of things. Though he's agreed to let me take over the business.'

'Is that what you want?'

'It's part of what I want.' He looked at her. 'And that's why I'm here.'

She looked him up and down. 'But—your boots!'

'I know, I know, Regency men aren't supposed to wear boots to a ball. Mrs P told me. My dancing shoes are in a bag. I can't wear them outside or they'll be ruined—especially in the snow.' He smiled at her. 'Come with me?'

She shook her head. 'I can't. It's the middle of the ball.'

'Which looks as if it's going like clockwork. Jaz and the students have the food covered, Michael and the quartet have the dancing covered, and your dad will do whatever needs to be done.'

Her eyes narrowed at him. 'How do you know that?'

'Because I've spoken to your dad.'

Her frown deepened. 'He didn't tell me.'

Because Sam had asked him not to tell.

'What did you talk about?' she asked.

'By and by,' he said. 'Come with me, Victoria. Please.'

'Outside, you mean?' She frowned. 'But I'm…' She gestured to her dress.

'That's OK—I have an anachronistic blanket.' He smiled at her. 'I was going to get you a coat, but Mrs P said even she can't make a Regency woman's coat in an afternoon.'

'Pelisse,' she corrected.

He grinned, loving the fact she was being pernickety. 'And she also said that traditionally it was trimmed with fur, and I thought you might have a problem with that.'

'I do.'

'Hence the anachronistic blanket. It's downstairs by the front door.'

She gave in and let him shepherd her downstairs, where he wrapped the blanket round her.

'I need to get some shoes.'

'No, you don't.' He swept her up into his arms.

'Samuel! You can't—'

'Yes, I can,' he said, and marched her out of the house to the waiting carriage.

'Oh, my God,' she said, seeing the horses and carriage.

He grinned. 'To me they look white, but I've been told this is a pair of matched greys. I don't care if the carriage is anachronistic, I don't want you being frozen, and an open-topped carriage on a December night in England is impossible.' He deposited her in the carriage, made sure she was settled, and then sat opposite her.

'I…' She shook her head, as if unable to think of what to say.

He grinned. 'I've got you lost for words. That's good. This is my chance to talk.' He took a deep breath. 'First off, I owe you a huge apology.'

She looked at him, her dark eyes wide.

'When Dad had his stroke, I was really unfair to you. I pushed you away—even though I know I can trust you and you're not like Olivia. I didn't know how ill Dad would get, or if he'd die, and I didn't want to put you through that. And that's why I went all cold on you and basically—' He raked a hand through his hair. 'Yeah. Stupid, I should've talked to you and told you how I feel, but I'm a bloke and I'm not very good at that sort of thing.'

'Right. So you've kidnapped me in the middle of the fundraiser ball to tell me that.'

'No, I've kidnapped you for another reason,' he said. 'By and by. Firstly, I overheard what you said to Dad in the hospital.'

'Eavesdroppers,' she said primly, 'never hear any good about themselves.'

'Oh, but I did,' he said. 'That I would make an excellent job of anything I decided to do. Which is why—'

He gestured round them. 'Technically, we don't need the suits and trappings. But I thought they'd be nice today. On a day when you've taken the house back two hundred years, it seemed appropriate to take my transport back two hundred years.'

'Only you would turn up in a landau with a pair of matched greys.'

He laughed. 'Trust you to know what the carriage is.'

She simply raised her eyebrows at him.

'Victoria. The reason I brought you out here is because I want to tell you that I love you. I've never felt like this about anyone. On paper, this shouldn't work. You're this massive history nerd and I work with figures. You live in the middle of nowhere with your parents and my house is a total bachelor pad in a very trendy bit of London.' He took a deep breath. 'But.'

'But?'

'It's you,' he said. 'Everything about you. I love that you're so serious and you pay attention to detail. I love that you pour your heart and soul into what you do. I love that you're the centre of your family—your parents adore you and your dog adores you and everyone who works in the house just lights up when you walk by because you pay attention and you listen to them and they know it.' He reached over to her and took her hand. 'But most of all I love you for you.'

'Uh-huh.'

'Which is Victoria-speak for the fact you don't know what to say.' He removed the glove from her left hand. 'I have actually done this the right way, this time. I talked to your parents about our fake engagement.'

'You did what?' She looked horrified.

'Actually, they understood. But we need to stop with the fake engagement business.'

'Agreed.'

'And the reason we need to stop with the fake one,' he said, 'is because I want it to be a real one. Let's be clear: it's *you* I want, not the house.'

'So you don't want to live here?'

'I want to live with you, whether it's here or in a—' He cast about for the most unlikely thing he could think of. 'In a yurt.'

She laughed, then. 'A yurt?'

'A yurt pitched in the middle of a swamp,' he said. 'I don't care where I live, as long as it's with you. And that's why I talked to your parents. Asking permission and stuff.' He dropped to one knee and took a velvet-covered box from his pocket. 'So this is why I kidnapped you from the ball. I love you—and, even though I haven't given you the chance to say it, I think you feel the same way about me, or you wouldn't have woken up in my arms that morning and you wouldn't have said what you did to Dad. And if Dad hadn't had that stroke, we would still have been having this conversation. Maybe not in the middle of the ball and maybe not in a carriage in the snow, but we would still definitely have been having this conversation. I've wanted to have this conversation with you for weeks.' He took a deep breath and opened the box. 'Will you marry me, Victoria?'

The ring nestled among the velvet was very simple, a single diamond set in platinum, and Victoria loved it.

And she loved the effort he'd put into this, too. That he'd clearly visited Mrs Prinks to get the right kind of boots, that he'd hired a carriage and horses, that he knew her tastes well enough to buy the perfect engagement ring—and he'd asked her parents, too, so he had their blessing before he proposed and obviously her mother had told him her ring size.

But most of all he'd said the important things.

That he loved her. Loved her for *herself.* Loved the things about her that her exes had all found annoying.

She swallowed hard. Time for her to say it. And it was different, saying it when you knew the other person felt the same way. 'I love you, too, Sammy.'

He blinked. 'Did you just call me Sammy?'

She nodded. 'And I guess you can…call me Tori.' The pet name he'd wanted to call her before, but she'd refused.

He kissed her and slid the ring onto her finger. 'I love you, Tori,' he said softly. 'And now we're going back to the ball before you freeze. How the hell did they do all this stuff in Regency times?'

'You must be freezing, too, in that frock coat.'

'Come and dance with me and we'll warm up,' he said. 'You were supposed to keep a waltz free for me.'

'I would've done, but you weren't there when they played the waltz.'

He laughed and kissed her again. 'Michael will get them to play another one for us. Especially as I have champagne on ice.'

She frowned. 'How did you manage that?'

'I had it delivered to your dad.'

'What if I'd said no?' she asked, suddenly curious.

'Then I would've written you really bad poetry and worn you down until you agreed.'

'Bad poetry.' She grinned. 'If I'd known that, I might've said no. Just to see how bad your poetry is.'

'Too late. You're wearing my ring now.' He drew her hand up to his mouth and kissed the inside of her wrist. 'Seriously, if you'd said no, then I asked your dad to give everyone champagne on my behalf to celebrate the ballroom restoration. And then I would've found myself a yurt and started writing bad poetry.' He raised an eyebrow. 'Actually, as you seem interested, I might do the poetry anyway. And I'll grow my hair out like Byron's. Be "mad and bad and dangerous to know".'

'Oh, please,' she said, laughing.

'Wait, wait. I have good, proper Regency poetry. Which I admit Jude found for me.' He coughed. '"She walks in beauty, like the night…" And you do. I love you.' He kissed her again. 'And you've just made me the happiest person in the world. Thank you.'

She felt her eyes fill with tears. 'I love you, too, Sammy.'

He carried her back to the house, then changed his boots for the dancing shoes.

'I can't believe you bought Regency boots just for tonight,' she said as they walked up the staircase together.

'Oh, I have plans for those boots.' He raised an eyebrow. 'They're the perfect footwear for whenever I want to carry my wife off somewhere and play Darcy to her Miss Bennet.'

She laughed.

'But keep your hands behind your back for now,' he said. 'Our parents need to be the first to know.'

Back in the ballroom, they went over to her parents. 'Can I borrow you both for a quick word?' Samuel asked.

Patrick and Diana looked thrilled and led them out to the Long Gallery.

'Anachronistic but necessary,' he said, taking his phone from his pocket. 'Excuse me a second. My parents need to be in this conversation as well.' He put the phone on speaker, waited while the line connected, and the call was picked up within two rings.

'Sammy?' Denise asked. 'What did she say?'

Her parents looked as if they were desperate to know the answer, too.

Victoria brought her hands from behind her back to show the engagement ring and smiled. 'I said yes.'

EPILOGUE

A year later

PATRICK STOOD BY the piano and the string quartet. 'I'm delighted to welcome you all to the second annual Chiverton Christmas ball—a tradition started by my wonderful daughter Victoria. And it's time for our first dance.'

'Well, the Hon Mrs Hamilton-Weatherby, it's all looking very festive. And oh, look, we're under the kissing ball.' Samuel stole a kiss. 'I still think we should have tinsel.'

Victoria knew he was teasing her. 'Not on your life.'

'Anachronistic,' he said with a grin. 'Come and waltz with me.'

They were in the middle of the ballroom when she said to him, 'The thing about Regency waltzes is that you were close enough to whisper secrets.'

'Oh, yes?'

'I would say that I love you, but that's not a secret.'

He laughed. 'I love it when your eyes are full of mischief. So what are you going to tell me, then?'

Demurely, she turned in a circle with him. 'Our honeymoon.' He'd taken her on a mini version of the Grand Tour, and she'd loved every second of it, sharing the museums and art galleries with him. He'd even talked the orchestra outside Florian's in Venice into playing a Regency waltz so he could dance with her through St Mark's Square.

'What about it?'

'It seems,' she said, 'it had consequences.'

'Consequences?'

'That's the thing about Regency dress,' she said, enjoying herself. 'The Empire neckline is very flattering. It hides bumps.'

'Bumps?' He sucked in a breath. 'Are you telling me we're...?'

She nodded. 'Two months. I thought I just missed a period because we were so busy. But I did a test this morning. I've been waiting for the right moment to tell you.'

'I didn't think I could be any happier, but...' He beamed at her. 'That's amazing. I really hope you're ready for this baby to be utterly spoiled by two sets of grandparents.'

'Not to mention the baby's doting papa,' she said with a smile.

'If it's a girl,' he said softly, 'maybe we can call her Lizzie.'

'I'd like that.'

'Just think,' he said. 'Last year the ball was our engagement. This year, it's our news. Next year...'

She grinned. 'Next year I'm sure the Weatherby Wonder will think of something.'

He laughed back. 'Just you wait...'

* * * * *

SECOND CHANCE IN STONECREEK

MICHELLE MAJOR

To everyone at Mills & Boon—thank you for making the stories I write into real books. I'm so grateful.

Chapter One

"It won't do for people to see you staring off into space like you're high on the wacky weed or something."

Maggie Spencer blinked, then turned to her seventy-nine-year-old grandmother. "Grammy, did you just use the term 'wacky weed'?"

"I'm not as behind the times as you seem to believe," Vivian Spencer shot back, adjusting the collar of her Jackie O–inspired tweed coat. "I know what's going on with teens today."

"I'm twenty-seven," Maggie pointed out. A gentle autumn breeze whistled across the town square in Stonecreek, Oregon, her beloved hometown. She pushed away a lock of hair that had blown into her face. "I don't smoke pot or anything else. You know that."

She waved to Rob Frisbie, who owned the local grocery store, walking past on his way to the beer booth. How Maggie would have liked to join him at the moment.

"You could eat it," her grandmother suggested tartly. "That's a thing, you know."

"I know," Maggie answered, struggling to keep her smile in place as she greeted a couple that approached her information booth, neither of whom she recognized. "Welcome to Fall Fest," she said brightly. "Are you visiting for the afternoon?"

"We drove down from Portland," the woman offered as both she and the man at her side nodded. "We're doing a wine tasting at Harvest Vineyards later this afternoon."

"We're glad you stopped by the festival," Maggie said. "I'm Maggie Spencer, Stonecreek's mayor." She picked up a tourism pamphlet and one of the flyers she'd printed for the annual festival. "Here's some information on things to do around town and a list of the activities happening today. If you have five vendors stamp your flyer, bring it back, then you'll be entered to win a weekend stay at our own local Miriam Inn."

The woman smiled and took the papers as Grammy said, "I'm Vivian Spencer, Maggie's grandmother and former mayor." She leaned forward as if imparting a great secret. "She's up for reelection next month. It's a surprisingly tight race given that she inherited the position. I held it for almost a decade with barely any opposition."

Heat rose to Maggie's cheeks as the woman's smile turned awkward. "Well, good luck, then," she said and hurried away with her husband.

"I didn't inherit the position," Maggie said through clenched teeth. "I was elected and I've done well during my first term."

"Don't take that tone with me." Vivian patted her silver hair, which was swept into a neat chignon on the back of her head. "Is it any wonder I question whether you're on drugs with how you've been acting lately?"

"I'm not taking a tone," Maggie said, making her voice gentle. "Or doing drugs. The campaign is going fine."

"Fine isn't enough to win the election." Vivian reached out a crepey hand to squeeze Maggie's arm. "I want this for you, Mary Margaret. It's your destiny."

Maggie sighed. Being the mayor of Stonecreek wasn't exactly on par with a lightning bolt scar on her forehead, but she loved her town and her role as mayor. Her grandmother meant well. Grammy had stepped in to help raise Maggie and her siblings when their mother died almost twelve years ago. Maggie's father, Jim, had struggled with being a single dad of three children. Grammy had been a constant source of love and support, and if she was a trifle overbearing and autocratic, Maggie could deal with it.

After all, she'd been content to let her grandmother steer the ship for years. It was only in the past few months that Maggie had finally wanted out from under Grammy's manicured thumb.

"I want it, too," Maggie said, wrapping an arm around Grammy's shoulders. "Plans for the debate are going well. We have lots of volunteers on the campaign."

"Debate." Vivian sniffed. "I still cannot believe Jason Stone challenged to you to a public debate. It's undignified."

Maggie stifled a laugh. "It's politics, Grammy."

"Not in Stonecreek." Her grandmother straightened the already neat stacks of pamphlets on the table in front of them. "Spencers have held the position of mayor for decades in this town. Your great-great-uncle and then your grandfather—rest his soul—and then me. For Jason to think he has a right to challenge you is preposterous."

"Why do people say 'rest his or her soul' when talking about a dead person?" Maggie asked, grasping for any way to change the subject before her grandmother latched onto—

"I have no doubt that upstart will make an issue of your wedding, or lack thereof." Grammy gave a quelling look, ignoring Maggie's off-topic question. "You wouldn't be in this predicament if you'd married Trevor Stone."

"You're right," Maggie agreed, keeping her tone even. What her grandmother didn't know was that she'd found Trevor cheating on her minutes before she was supposed to walk down the aisle. So there was a good chance she'd be in another predicament entirely. "I guess it was his loss."

Grammy sniffed again. "Stupid boy."

"He's a grown man," Maggie countered, "although I'm with you on the stupid part."

"No better than he should be," Vivian muttered.

"Another saying I don't under—"

"Although still a better option than that brother of his."

Maggie's chest tightened at the mention of Griffin Stone. The prodigal son of the Stone family had returned to Stonecreek for the wedding and ended up rescuing Maggie when she'd fled the church after discovering her fiancé's betrayal. They'd struck up an unlikely friendship and so much more from Maggie's point of view. But her romance with Griffin had been short-lived.

He was still in town, once again rebuilding the tasting room at his family's successful vineyard after fire had ravaged part of it for a second time in as many decades. Only, Maggie's sixteen-year-old sister, Morgan, had caused the fire at the beginning of summer. The fallout of that tragic accident plus the tension that existed between the Stones and Spencers, fueled by a rivalry that dated back to the founding of the town, had driven a wedge between Griffin and Maggie that she had no idea how to combat.

And Griffin hadn't even wanted to try. That was how little she'd meant to him.

Megan Roe, the town's version of a girl Friday, approached the booth. "Hey, Maggie," she called. "Hi, Mrs. Spencer. I'm here for my shift."

Megan was in her early twenties and had grown up in Stonecreek, just like Maggie. In fact, she'd babysat the three Roe sisters through most of high school. As mayor, one of Maggie's biggest concerns was attracting young people to the town. She wanted to keep things current and make sure there were good jobs to be found in Stonecreek so the town stayed relevant. Harvest Vineyards brought in tourists, but they also needed a strong foundation of other businesses to keep the local economy strong.

Grammy looked the young woman up and down. "Is that what you're wearing to represent this town?" she asked, disapproval clear in her tone.

Luckily, Megan didn't seem to notice. "Yeah." She pulled at the hem of her minidress, which looked like an overlong flannel shirt with a red-and-black-checkered pattern. Her heavily highlighted hair was down around her shoulders and she wore black ankle boots with a chunky heel. "I got it last week when my sister and I went shopping in Portland. There are so many cool stores in the city. Around here, it's online shopping or nothing."

"Next time try nothi—"

"You look great," Maggie interrupted her grandmother, gently pushing her from behind the booth. "Thanks for volunteering. We've had a steady stream of people stop by. Entries for the night on the town giveaway are starting to roll in. It should pick up before the band starts in an hour."

"No problem," Megan said with a smile. "My boyfriend is coming by to keep me company."

Maggie squeezed Grammy's elbow when the older woman tsk-tsked. "I'll be around for a bit. Text if you need anything."

The woman waved as Maggie ushered her grandma away from the booth.

"She looks like an unwashed vagrant," Vivian said, wrinkling her nose.

"She's stylish," Maggie countered.

"Dirty hobo is a style now?"

"Grammy, don't be mean. Megan is great and it was nice of her to volunteer."

"I'm not mean. I'm honest. That girl could benefit from some constructive criticism. Did you see how short her skirt was? If she bends over, everyone will see her—"

"She looks fine." Maggie shook her head. "You can't worry about every little thing, Grammy. You've retired. The town isn't your responsibility anymore."

Vivian clasped a hand to her chest, her index finger gliding up to the pearl necklace she'd worn since Maggie could remember. "You're going to break my heart with that kind of talk, Mary Margaret. You know this town means everything to me."

"I know," Maggie whispered, hugging her grandmother. She hated feeling at odds with anyone, especially Grammy, who Maggie loved with her whole heart. But Vivian Spencer was part of the old guard, with ideas and plans for the town that didn't necessarily benefit the diversity and enterprise Maggie wanted Stonecreek to be known for. She had to find a way to minimize her grandmother's influence while still showing the older woman the respect she deserved. "I love you, Grammy."

"You, too, sweetheart." Vivian drew back. "I'm going to head home. I'll see you tomorrow for Sunday dinner?"

"Of course."

Maggie watched her grandmother walk away, then turned for the bustling town square. Booths lined the perimeter with local artisans selling jewelry and gifts and local restaurants serving a variety of tasting options. Maggie had put in countless hours with the festival committee to make this year's Fall Fest a success.

Despite what she'd told her grandma, she did have concerns about the upcoming election. Jason Stone had been running a subtle smear campaign, a portion of it reflecting on her decision to walk away from her wedding without outing Trevor as the rat fink cheater he was.

But the more insidious digs at her came from her relationship with her grandmother. Her opponent was insinuating exactly what Grammy had just stated out loud: that Maggie had been elected because of nepotism and not on her own merits. She hated giving any credence to the idea, but the doubts pinging through her head made it even more essential that she win the election.

She sighed and started forward toward the bustling midway. Unfortunately right now, schmoozing and socializing seemed about as appealing as downing a bowl of cockroaches. Maggie was working overtime on the overtime she normally put in to prove her dedication to her job. She was tired, so the thought of making small talk for a couple of hours had her stomach tightening.

"You look like you're walking into a gathering of flesh-eating zombies," a voice called from behind her.

She turned to see her best friend, Brenna Apria, and Brenna's young daughter, Ellie, walking toward her.

"All zombies eat flesh," Ellie announced as they got closer.

"Aren't you too young to know that, squirt?" Maggie asked, crouching down and holding her arms wide. Ellie ran forward, wrapping her thin arms around Maggie's neck.

"I'm either going to be a zombie or a vampire cheerleader for Halloween," Ellie told her matter-of-factly, "so I'm doing research on both of them."

"She loves to be scared." Brenna gave a mock shudder. "I don't know where she gets it."

"Marcus and I watched *Gremlins* last weekend," Ellie reported. "It was PG but still Mommy had to cover her eyes for the scary parts."

"How is Marcus?" Maggie lifted a brow in Brenna's direction.

Her friend tried to hide the enamored smile that curved her mouth. "He's good. Things are getting back to normal after harvest season at the vineyard."

"Harvest season," Maggie murmured. That meant all hands on deck at the vineyard, although the winery also stayed open. Each year, Brenna coordinated grape-stomping competitions and the opportunity for the public to pick grapes in designated vineyards. But Maggie had not gone to any of the community events this year. It was too difficult to be near Griffin, which was stupid and possibly pathetic on her part.

Although she'd known him her whole life, he'd been a jerk as a kid and all through high school, three years older than her and definitely not interested in a rule follower like Maggie.

That had changed, to her great surprise, when he'd returned to Stonecreek. Even so, they'd only been friends for a few weeks and spent one blissful night together before her little fairy tale had come crashing down. Or maybe she'd just imagined their powerful connection.

The great sex had been a real thing. She hadn't made that up. Everything else… Well, she always did have a vivid imagination.

"You okay?" Brenna asked, her brow furrowing.

"Just tired." Maggie forced a smile. "Not really up for doing the mayoral thing tonight."

"You're welcome to hang with us," her friend offered.

"Come with us," Ellie shouted, grabbing her hand. "We're going to get apple cider and kettle corn and have our faces painted."

The warmth of the girl's fingers wrapped around hers made the band of tension wrapped around Maggie's stomach ease ever so slightly.

"It's a real girls' night out," Brenna added with a smile at her daughter.

"Then count me in," Maggie said.

They headed into the square, stopping at each booth. With Brenna and Ellie flanking either side of her, Maggie was able to relax, greeting old friends and various townspeople and remembering why she worked so hard at her job.

She loved this little corner of the Willamette Valley, from the terra-cotta and classical revival-style buildings to the bright yellows and golds of the leaves in the fall.

"At least I'm not getting a ton of side-eye anymore," Maggie said to Brenna as they stood a few feet from the face-painting booth, waiting for Ellie to be transformed into a Bengal tiger.

Brenna toasted her cider cup against Maggie's. "I told you all they needed was time. People were a little shocked that you walked away from the wedding, but that doesn't change what you mean to this town."

"There are still a few who haven't forgiven me." Maggie lifted a finger to touch the small butterfly one of the teenagers working the face-painting station had drawn onto her cheek. Ellie had insisted Maggie get her face done before the girl would agree to sit. "My grandmother might be one of them."

Brenna made a face. "I can't help you there. Oh, no. Don't turn around."

Maggie immediately looked over her shoulder to see Griffin walking toward them, an unfamiliar woman at his side. The woman was beautiful, with flowing, raven-colored hair, a fashion-model-thin frame and long legs tucked into vintage cowboy boots. She wore a baggy dress that just grazed her thighs, but the shape of a dress didn't matter when a woman looked like that. Griffin towered over her and was leaning close as the woman gazed up at him.

Maggie's heart stuttered.

No, they weren't heading toward her. The two of them were so engrossed in each other they could have been walking on a deserted street for all they noticed the crowd around them.

Until Griffin looked up. His green gaze caught on Maggie, the heat from it like being stabbed with a hot poker.

"What part of 'don't turn around' confused you?" Brenna muttered under her breath.

"It's fine," Maggie said, her voice weak as she faced forward again. "Who is she?"

"Maggie?"

Heat pooled low in her belly at the sound of Griffin's rich baritone. Pathetic. She was the most pathetic woman on the planet. This man had rejected her four months ago. She had no reason to be twitter-pated over him. She had no reason to feel anything for him.

To borrow from one of Maggie's favorite old-school pop songs, tell that to her heart.

But she spun around, pasting a bright smile on her face. "Hey, Griffin. How's it hang—"

She yelped when Brenna pinched the back of her arm. Hard.

"Hey," Griffin said slowly, darting a dubious glance between the two of them. "I'm…um…doing fine. How are you?"

"Hunky-dory," she said, then inwardly cringed as Brenna groaned. "I'm fine, too," she amended, her cheeks feeling like they'd just caught fire. "Fine."

"Great." Griffin nodded and she watched his throat bob as he swallowed. "I wanted to introduce you to an old friend." He indicated the woman standing next to him. "This is Cassie Barlow. Cassie's an interior designer up in Seattle. We've worked on a few projects together over the years."

Is that what the kids are calling it now? Maggie thought to herself. She held out a hand, her cheeks aching from the perma-grin plastered across her face. "Nice to meet you."

"You, too," the woman said, her eyes bright. "Great butterfly."

Seriously, could cheek muscles grow so hard they cracked? "I had my face painted," Maggie said, then sighed. Master of the obvious. How charming.

"My daughter demanded it," Brenna offered quickly. "Maggie did it for Ellie."

Griffin introduced Brenna to Cassie and then Cassie turned to Maggie again. "Grif tells me you're mayor of this town."

Grif. She called him Grif. Oh, yeah. They worked

together. Worked together on getting busy, most likely.

Maggie blinked when she realized everyone was staring at her. "Yes, mayor," she agreed like an imbecile. "I'm mayor."

Cassie tilted her head and Maggie thought the other woman must think her the biggest ninny she'd ever met. But Cassie's eyes remained kind. It was ridiculously difficult to hate someone with such kind eyes.

Ellie ran up to Brenna at that moment, her face painted in black and orange stripes. The girl held up her hands like claws and growled at her mom, then turned to Maggie and roared loudly.

"I'm ferocious," she announced.

Maggie cowered in mock fear, never so grateful for the interruption. "Oh, scary tiger," she said, making her voice tremble. "Have mercy on this little butterfly."

"You're too tiny for me to eat," Ellie said with a nod. "I better go get a corn dog."

Maggie grinned, then looked up at Griffin and Cassie. "You heard the tiger. We've got to feed her before she starves."

"It was lovely to meet you," Cassie said softly.

"You, too," Maggie agreed. She gave a casual wave. "See you around, *Grif*."

Griffin gave a sharp nod but didn't respond.

And even though Maggie wanted nothing more than to escape this awkward interaction, she couldn't quite force her legs to walk away from him until Ellie took her hand and tugged.

Chapter Two

"She thinks we're together," Cassie murmured as Maggie disappeared into the crowd milling about the town square.

"We are together." Griffin unclenched his hands, which had ended up fisted at his sides, and concentrated on keeping his expression neutral. It took every bit of willpower he possessed to watch Maggie turn away. He wanted to reach for her, to pull her close and bury his face in her hair, breathing in her flowery scent.

"As in we're dating." Cassie rolled her eyes.

"We're not dating," Griffin said as if his old friend needed clarification. "We haven't dated for years."

Cassie smacked him hard on the shoulder. "I know that, you idiot. Your Maggie doesn't."

"She's not mine," he muttered, shoving his hands into his pockets. He continued to stare in the direction Maggie had walked. Every few seconds he'd get a glimpse of her caramel-colored hair or a flash of the bright butterfly painted on her cheek as she turned to say something to Brenna. This was the first time he'd seen her since he'd ended what was between them. Ended it before it had really had a chance to start.

Stonecreek was a small town and, as mayor, Maggie was a very visible resident. He'd holed up at the vineyard for most of the summer, repairing the damage to the tasting room from the fire that Maggie's sister had accidentally started when her plans for teenage seduction had gone awry.

Cole Maren, the boy Morgan Spencer had set her sights on that night, had worked tirelessly at Griffin's side. Despite the kid's past and less-than-desirable family situation, Cole seemed determined to stay on the right track. Griffin wished he'd made that choice when he was younger. It had taken him years of running from the stupidity of his youth to straighten out his mind and soul.

A weight settled in his chest like a lead balloon as he watched Maggie and he wondered how successful he'd actually been.

"You look at each other," Cassie said, moving toward a vendor selling handmade soaps and lotions, "like you belong together."

"You don't understand how it is in Stonecreek," Griffin said with a sigh.

Cassie dabbed a sample of lemon-scented lotion on her hands, turning to Griffin as she rubbed it into her skin. "What's there to understand? You care about her. She cares about you. All that other family history stuff is just noise. It doesn't have to matter, Grif. Trust me. I'm all about cutting away things that don't matter these days."

Griffin opened his mouth to argue, then shut it again. Cassie had paid this unexpected visit to him to share that she'd been diagnosed with a brain tumor. She was due to start treatment in Seattle in a couple of days and said the doctors had given her a great prognosis. But the news had changed her—maybe for the better—as she seemed at peace in a way he hadn't ever known her to be.

"You have to try," Cassie urged.

He glanced beyond her and spotted Maggie talking to a tall guy who looked to be in his midthirties. Brenna stood a few feet away watching Ellie play in the bouncy house, like she was trying to give Maggie and the stranger space. The man handed Maggie his phone and she punched something into it. Her number, Griffin assumed, and felt adrenaline stab his gut.

"Give me a few minutes," he told his friend, earning a wide smile.

"I'll meet you in front of the stage," Cassie agreed. "The band is starting in a few minutes."

He nodded and headed in Maggie's direction, absently waving to the people who called out greetings.

"We need to talk," he told her, moving to stand between her and the man.

Her fine brows furrowed. "I don't think so."

"Come on, Maggie," he coaxed. "It won't take long."

"Everything okay?" the stranger asked.

Maggie looked around Griffin and smiled at the man. "Just a little bit of bothersome town business."

Griffin felt his eyes narrow.

"It was nice meeting you, James," she said sweetly.

"I'll call you next week," the man answered, and Griffin's hand itched to deck the guy.

Maggie held up her index finger to someone behind

Griffin—Brenna, he guessed—then looked up at him, her gray eyes cool. "So talk."

"Not here." Before she could protest, he circled her wrist with his hand and led her away from the crowd.

"Is this necessary?" she asked tartly.

"You sound like your grandma when you use that snippy tone," he said, flashing a smile at her.

She glared in return.

He continued to the edge of the park that took up one full square block in the middle of downtown Stonecreek and moved around the side of the town hall building.

"Griffin, what are you doing?" She dug in her heels and tugged her wrist from his grasp.

He turned and could see the freckles that sprinkled her nose and upper cheeks and the bits of gold around the edges of her eyes. He smelled the light scent of her shampoo and damn if he didn't want to press his face into the crook of her neck. As much as he thought he had his feelings under control, the reality of this moment still slammed through him with the force of a tornado.

Then she licked her lips and it was too much. All of it. The return to Stonecreek, the acrimony he couldn't manage to fix with Trevor, their mother's expectations and the constant undercurrent of his past mistakes that seemed to follow him everywhere, trailing behind like a child's blanket.

He did the only thing he could think of in the moment.

He pressed his lips to Maggie's mouth. It was perfect. Her softness, the sweet taste of apples, the feel of her body so close to him. All of it perfect.

Until she slapped him.

She shook out her hand, seeming as shocked by her reaction as he was. His cheek stung, although he figured he deserved that snap of pain and so much more.

"You kissed me." The words were an accusation and he had the good sense to realize how out of line he'd been.

"I'm sorry." He ran a hand through his hair. "It seemed like a good idea at the time."

She made a noise in the back of her throat that might have been a growl. "Are you crazy?"

"About you?" He flashed a smile. "Yeah. Yeah, I— Oof." He stumbled when she pushed on his chest. Hard.

"No, no, no," she said, her voice low, almost a snarl. Each exclamation was punctuated with another shove. "You don't get to do this, Griffin Stone."

He'd seen many sides of Maggie, but never had he seen her so angry. Color stained her cheeks and her breath was coming out in ragged puffs. "I'm not—"

"You rejected me." She jabbed one finger into his chest. "You said horrible things about my sister and my family."

"I was angry." He wrapped his fingers around hers, pulled it away from his body. "I'm sorry. I didn't mean—"

"I've moved on," she announced, yanking her hand from his. "Just like you."

"Like me?"

"The woman you introduced me to. The one who calls you Grif. Oh, Grif…" She gave an overly girlish laugh. "You're so handsome, Grif. So strong, Grif. Oh, Griffy-poo."

"Cassie has never called me 'Griffy-poo' in her life."

"Not the point," Maggie ground out.

Right. What was the point? Why had he pulled her away from the festival in the first place? It certainly hadn't been to kiss her. If he'd been thinking about anything other than how much he missed her, he would have known that was a horrible idea.

He'd wanted to talk to her about Cassie. She'd misinterpreted and—

"I'm dating someone."

The statement jolted him back to the present moment.

"No." The word came out as a puff of breath.

Her eyes narrowed again. "Yes. Well, not yet exactly. I'm going to date someone."

"Hypothetically?" he demanded, feeling a muscle tick in his jaw. "Or in real life?"

"Real life. The man you saw." She paused as if searching for a detail she'd forgotten. "James. He's a doctor."

"Bully for him."

"For both of us," she agreed. "I met him working on the hospital fund-raiser."

"The one I'm hosting at the tasting room?"

"Your mother is the official host," she pointed out, not very helpfully in his opinion.

"It's my vineyard."

"Your family's vin—"

"You know what I mean," he interrupted.

"I know…" She blew out a long breath. "We are

not together. Your choice, Griffin. Has something changed?"

Panic spiked through him. He wanted to say yes, but it wasn't true. He was as messed up as he'd been four months ago. Their past was messy, the present just as complicated. He'd told her he didn't do complicated. He'd hurt her. The pain he'd caused still reflected in her gaze and he hated himself for it.

He'd grown so damn tired of hating himself.

"I'm sorry," he said again, then shook his head.

She gave him a sad smile. "So many apologies between us."

"I want it to be different." As if that mattered when he was too much of a coward to do anything about it.

The smile faded from her face. "Me, too."

"Maggie—"

"I need to get back to the festival." She straightened her fitted red turtleneck sweater. The bottom edge of the butterfly on her cheek had smeared slightly where his thumb had grazed her face. "Brenna will be wondering about me."

He nodded. "Have a good night, Maggie May."

She tucked a lock of hair behind her ear, a small diamond stud glimmering in her lobe. She had beautiful ears. Every inch of her was beautiful to him.

"Have fun with Cassie," she said, then whirled and hurried away.

He wanted to call after her, to explain there was nothing between him and his ex-girlfriend. But what good would that do? Would it change everything that prevented him from committing to Maggie?

No. It felt like nothing ever changed in Stonecreek.

Cassie had told him the noise around them didn't matter, but it was all Griffin could hear, drowning out even the beat of his own heart.

Morgan Spencer shoved her phone into the top drawer of her desk when she heard her father's footsteps on the creaky staircase of the house where she'd been born. Literally born in the bathtub down the hall.

This home and town were all she'd ever known. Her perfect life and her perfect family and she didn't fit in at all.

There was a soft knock on the door and then her dad entered.

"Hey, Mo-Mo. No Fall Fest for you this year?"

She rolled her eyes. "I'm grounded. Remember?"

Her father grimaced, looking slightly sheepish. "Of course. I remember. Fire at Harvest Vineyards. You and a toppled candle."

"It was an accident," she said, shame pulsing through her at the reminder of her stupidity.

"I understand, but there are still consequences to your actions, young lady."

"I'm not so young," she shot back.

"You're sixteen."

"Duh. It's a wonder you even remember."

"Attitude isn't going to help, Morgan." Her dad's tone had turned abnormally disapproving. Jim Spencer was a big man. At fifty-one, his shoulders remained broad and only a sprinkling of silver darted his thick brown hair. Tonight he wore faded jeans and a ratty sweatshirt. From the earthy scent emanating from him, Morgan knew he'd spent the evening in his art studio. He spent most of his time there, immersed in the casts and sculptures that seemed dearer to him than his own children.

Morgan was probably the only one who cared about inattentiveness. Maggie had been fifteen when their mother died. She'd grown up quickly, stepping in to help raise Morgan and their younger brother, Ben, who was fourteen now and taller than Morgan. Ben had always been easy—'the Buddha baby,' Dad had called him. As long as he had snacks and video games, that boy was happy. Grammy had helped with all of them, but Maggie had always been the apple of Vivian Spencer's eye. Morgan's sister was smart and driven, polished and self-possessed in a way Morgan could never be.

Had never tried to be. She was the black sheep of the family, more so now that she was in high school and her inclination toward rebellion had found an outlet with the fast kids at her high school. She tended to fade into the background in the face of Maggie's perfection and Ben's affable nature. So when she'd discovered that she could get attention from the popular kids at school just by doing stupid things like playing chicken on the train tracks or toilet papering the principal's house, it had been fun. It made her feel like she belonged for the first time in her life. Who wouldn't want to belong?

But apparently she couldn't ignore her father when he decided to come out of his studio and play at being a responsible parent.

"I know," she relented with a shrug. "I'm sorry, Daddy. I'm trying."

"You are," he agreed, and she knew he meant it.

Guilt washed over her in response.

She hadn't meant to damage the building out at Harvest Vineyards. She'd been over the moon for a stupid boy, earning herself months of grounding and a one-way ticket to working the whole summer to pay for repairs to the tasting room building. She'd also lost her chance with Cole Maren, not that she'd ever really had him.

A boy like Cole wouldn't have time for a girl like her.

"Want a piece of marionberry pie before bed?" her dad asked. "Your grandmother brought one over earlier."

Morgan's stomach rumbled. Grammy's pie was her favorite. "Do we have ice cream?"

"Vanilla bean," he confirmed with his lopsided smile.

"Yum."

Maggie came home while Morgan was slicing the pie. Her sister joined them for a late-night snack, dutifully reporting on what they'd missed at Fall Fest, which wasn't much in Morgan's opinion.

Of course, she didn't ask if Cole had been there. He spent almost all his free time working at Harvest, so Morgan suspected he was behind the scenes at the winery's expansive booth. She'd seen little of him over the summer. He'd been avoiding her and now that they were back in school, he pretty much ignored her completely. It was awful.

"Are you okay?" she asked Maggie as they washed the plates after eating.

"Sure," Maggie said. "Just tired."

"Oh." Morgan studied her nearly perfect sister

from the corner of her eye. Maggie had haphazardly wiped away the butterfly painted on her cheek, and her eyes were red-rimmed, her hair mussed like she'd been running anxious fingers through it. "Was Griffin at Fall Fest?"

Maggie stilled, then flipped off the faucet. "He was there with a woman. A date, I think."

"I'm sorry." One more thing for Morgan to feel guilty about. Her sister's relationship with Griffin had gone off the rails after the fire. Apparently Griffin had said some unkind things about Morgan, most of them probably true. But Maggie was loyal, so they'd fought and that was the end of it.

"Me, too," Maggie whispered.

"Fries before guys," Morgan teased, hoping to make her sister smile. Needing Maggie to smile.

She did, and Morgan breathed a sigh of relief.

"I'm heading to bed." Maggie draped the towel she'd been using to dry the dishes over the handle of the stove. Dad had gone to the family room as soon as he'd finished his pie. He'd watch *The Tonight Show*, Morgan knew, and fall asleep in the tattered recliner he loved.

"Good night." She hugged Maggie.

"Foods before dudes," Maggie told her.

Morgan groaned. "So bad, Mags."

"'Night, Mo-Mo."

Morgan went up to her room and pulled the phone from her desk drawer. She was supposed to be grounded from it, too, but she'd placed her case upside down on the shelf in Dad's bedroom and he hadn't noticed the phone wasn't in it.

She responded to the flurry of text messages she'd

received during her family bonding time, then tucked a pillow under her covers in the shape of a sleeping body and opened the window to her second-story bedroom. A huge maple tree grew just in front of it. Trying to keep her heartbeat steady, she reached for a branch, swung onto it, then shimmied down the trunk.

A car was waiting at the end of the driveway, headlights turned off. With one look over her shoulder at her darkened house, she ran toward it through the shadows, pretending the guilt that flared inside her was excitement instead.

Chapter Three

Monday morning, Maggie turned her car up the winding drive that led to Harvest Vineyards for the first time since she and her father had brought Morgan to the Stone family home after the fire.

With less than two weeks until the hospital fundraiser, she couldn't avoid it any longer. She'd managed to hold the gala committee meetings at the hospital or at her office in town. Jana Stone, Griffin's mother, had attended all of them. She either hadn't noticed—or was polite enough not to comment—on Maggie's reluctance to make an appearance at the winery.

Today they were meeting to discuss decorations and a seating chart, so it couldn't be avoided any longer. Although that was exactly what Maggie wanted to do after her run-in with Griffin at Fall Fest. She felt branded by the unexpected kiss, all of the emotions she'd locked up tightly now spilling forth, like a dam had broken inside her.

The vineyard seemed almost fallow now that harvest season was over. As she drove closer to the heart of the operations, she could see the rows of vines spread out along acres of land, the leaves turning colors of burnished orange and yellow with the change of seasons.

In contrast to the serenity of the fields, activity bustled outside the new tasting room. Several cars and trucks were parked in front of the building, although Maggie didn't see Griffin's Land Cruiser. That wasn't a guarantee of his absence, so why did disappointment spear through her for a quick moment? It would be easier if she didn't see him today, she reminded herself. She didn't *want* to see him after the kiss. Better for both of them.

The building had a rustic farmhouse exterior with a stone veneer covering the bottom half. There were two chimneys and rough-hewn trusses that spanned the length of the building. A covered patio area took advantage of the expansive views of the vineyard below, and she could imagine tourists and locals alike enjoying long summer evenings around the built-in fire pit. The space was incredible and would definitely attract new visitors to the winery.

She took a deep breath as she exited her Volkswagen. The earthy scent of decaying leaves filled the air and although the vineyard was only twenty minutes from downtown, it felt like a world away. Had the property seemed this magical when it had been a regular farm, before Griffin's late father, Dave, had planted the first grapes that would transform the land and his family's fortunes?

"Hey, Maggie."

She turned to see her former fiancé moving toward her. It had only been four months since her runaway-bride move at the local church, where half the town had been waiting to see the powerful Spencer and Stone families united, but to her it felt like ages since she'd been with Trevor.

Well, ages wasn't too far off since the bedroom had never played a big role in their relationship. Theirs had been a union of convenience and practicality. Despite what he'd done to her and the price her reputation had paid for not revealing his betrayal, no emotion pinged through Maggie at the sight of him. Unlike with Griffin.

Trevor was safe, which was part of the reason she'd been with him in the first place.

"Hi, Trevor." She smiled and allowed him to give her a quick hug. "The building looks great."

He inclined his head. "I hate to give Griffin any credit, but he did a decent job." Trevor was a couple inches shorter than his brother and considerably leaner, with neatly trimmed hair and the kind of expensively tailored clothes that would have been more appropriate for the big city. Maggie had never quite understood what had made him return to his family's winery after college, although he was quite talented at his job as vice president of marketing for the vineyard.

In the five years since Trevor had taken over, Harvest had gone from a well-respected but relatively unknown winery to a national darling with several national and international award-winning vintages. Of course, a big part of the success was the quality of the wine, but Trevor's efforts at marketing and branding played a part, as well.

"It's more than decent," Maggie said gently. She understood the animosity that had simmered for years between the brothers: Griffin, the elder rebel, and Trevor, the golden boy and apple of his father's eye. But even though Griffin had hurt her with his rejection, she couldn't let Trevor discount what he'd done here. "It's incredible, Trev, and we both know it, especially given the setbacks he had because of—"

She broke off as Cole Maren, the former object of her sister's affection, walked out of the front of the tasting room, carrying a rolled-up set of plans under one arm. He glanced over and his steps faltered for a second as he met Maggie's gaze. His mouth curved into a ghost of a smile in greeting before he headed around the side of building.

"Yeah, incredible," Trevor admitted reluctantly. "Although I can't believe he kept that degenerate kid working here after his part in the fire."

"The fire was Morgan's fault," Maggie said clearly, "and she still feels terrible."

Trevor's eyes narrowed. "I still think she's covering for him."

"You know that's not—"

He held up a hand. "I don't want to argue with you. I know how you are when you believe in something." His mouth quirked. "A bulldog in a St. John's suit."

"It's Calvin Klein," Maggie corrected, color flooding her cheeks. In truth, she was as overdressed as Trevor for this meeting but she'd worn the chic fitted jacket and pencil skirt like a warrior might have donned his armor in medieval times. The suit made her feel braver than she knew herself to be. "Anyway, I appreciate how much your mom has done for the gala this year."

"She's enjoyed it." Trevor rocked back on his heels. "It gives her a purpose other than trying to come up with bonding experiences for Griffin and me."

"You're both dedicated to the vineyard. Isn't that something to bond over?"

"He walked away from us a decade ago." Bitterness laced Trevor's tone. "Had his own life in the army and working in construction until he deigned to once more grace us with his presence. That's not dedication. It's convenience and guilt over leaving in the first place. We'll see how long he lasts once his debt is paid."

By *debt*, Maggie knew Trevor was talking about the fire that had damaged the original tasting room, accidentally set by a teenage Griffin and several of his friends while they were partying. The careless mistake had led to a huge fight between Griffin and his dad, resulting in a rift among the Stone family that still hadn't been fully repaired.

"We'll agree to disagree," she said simply, unwilling to engage in this argument.

Trevor studied her for a long moment. "He's not here today, if you're wondering."

"I wasn't," she lied.

"He went to Seattle with his ex-girlfriend."

Maggie couldn't help but notice the note of triumph in Trevor's tone and kept her features placid. "We weren't expecting him at this meeting anyway. Is your mom around?" She glanced at the driveway. "The rest of the committee should be here shortly."

Trevor nodded. "She's finishing up a call. That's

actually why I'm here. She sent me over to tell you she'll be a few minutes late."

"No problem."

An awkward silence descended between the two of them.

"You don't have to wait with me," she told him after a moment.

His mouth tightened. "I miss our friendship."

"We're friends." She shrugged. "Just not the same kind as before."

"Want to grab a beer after work one night?"

"I…" She paused, unsure of how to answer. "Things are crazy with preparations for the gala." His mouth pulled down into a frown and she saw him sigh. "But after it's over, I'll have more time. Maybe then?"

"Great." Trevor flashed the boyish smile that was his trademark. "It's a plan."

He strode away from her and Maggie blew out a breath. Most of the time she loved living in a small town. She liked the familiarity of knowing her neighbors and the comfort that came from her routine. But some moments made her wish for the anonymity of big-city life. Like breaking up with someone and not having to worry about running into them or their mom or their brother or a dozen other mutual friends.

Her phone pinged and she pulled it from her purse. Her grandmother texting instructions on the size and placement of the centerpieces. She regretted encouraging Ben to teach Grammy how to text. It had quickly become her favorite means of lecturing Maggie.

"Ms. Spencer?"

She looked up to find Cole standing in front of her, looking like he hoped the ground would swallow him whole.

"Hey, Cole. I hear you've been a big part of keeping the tasting room renovations on track. Things look great."

"Thanks," he muttered, his gaze darting to hers before dropping again. The kid had probably grown three inches since Maggie had last seen him. He wore jeans and a Harvest Vineyards T-shirt with a small hole in the arm that looked like it came from catching it on a nail or something.

"I wanted to talk to you." His brow furrowed. "Duh. Obviously."

"What did you need?" She smiled, feeling sorry for the teen and his level of discomfort.

"It's Morgan." He looked at her, then away.

Maggie's smile froze. "What about her?"

"You need to— Your dad needs to watch her better. She's still running with the bad crowd."

"Your crowd?" she asked.

He gave a sharp shake of his head. "I'm steering clear of them, and Morgan should, too. They're not her real friends."

Maggie shrugged. "I appreciate your concern, Cole, and I'll talk to her. But we can't control who she's friends with at school. I wish—"

"What about on the weekends?"

"She's still grounded," Maggie said with a frown.

Cole took his phone from his back pocket and keyed in a code to unlock the home screen. He punched the screen again and then held up the phone to show Maggie a photo from one of the popular social media sites. Morgan had her arm around another girl, both of them wearing too much makeup and holding up red plastic cups.

The picture had been tagged "Saturday night shenanigans."

"When was this taken?" she demanded.

"Two nights ago."

After they'd had pie together and she'd gone to bed.

"Why are you showing it to me?"

He shoved the phone back into his pocket. "I'm telling you that group she's trying so hard to be a part of is bad news. Trust me, Ms. Spencer."

"I do," she murmured and Cole's gaze returned to hers, something like gratitude flashing in his eyes. Maggie knew her sister had a wild streak, but she'd thought the fire had taught her a lesson. Apparently not.

"Do you two…um… Are you friends anymore?"

He shook his head. "We never were."

"That's not what Morgan thought," Maggie told him. "I don't mean romantically, although I know she had those kinds of feelings for you until…" She glanced at the tasting room and saw Cole squirm.

"She's too good for me," he said, his voice flat, "just like she's too good for the rest of the dumba—" he cleared his throat "—the idiots she calls her friends."

"You're not an idiot," Maggie insisted, "and my sister clearly could use some friends who really care about her."

He closed his eyes, chewing on his bottom lip like

he couldn't find the words for what he wanted to say. "Yeah," he mumbled finally.

"Think about it," she told him.

"Her dad… Your dad wouldn't like that," he said suddenly.

"Our father wants what's best for Morgan. He'd get used to it."

Cole tilted his head to one side, digesting that information. "I need to get back to work," he told her as a car pulled up the driveway.

She nodded. "Thank you."

He turned and walked toward the building. Maggie pressed a hand to her stomach, feeling nauseous. She hated to think of her sister still rebelling. Morgan had been hit hard by their mother's death from ovarian cancer, somehow taking the loss to heart in a different way than Maggie or Ben. She had a lot in common with their father, actually. Dad had retreated into his art and Morgan had dealt with her grief first through acting out in little ways and now in a full-blown rebellion.

But Maggie wouldn't give up on her sister. Morgan had a huge heart and so much potential. The election, fights with Grammy and Maggie's own tattered heart weren't nearly as important as Morgan. Maggie would do anything to make sure her sister stayed safe. Anything.

"Everyone was impressed by your work here."

"Great," Griffin answered absently, nailing a strip of weathered shiplap to the wall behind the tasting room bar. Most of the big items had been checked off the list: updated lighting for the room, expanded bathrooms for customers and a newly vaulted ceiling lined with reclaimed barn wood. The bar he'd had custom built by a renowned furniture maker north of Portland was due to be delivered next week.

The rest he was handling himself, with help after school from Cole. He was good at the general contractor piece, managing all the different subs and phases of a project. But he enjoyed working with his hands most of all, the satisfaction of creating something from nothing.

"It's going to be a wonderful event," his mother continued. "We've sold close to two hundred tickets."

The hammer stilled and he turned around at that bit of news. "Really? That seems like a lot of people." His skin itched at the thought of all those bodies and the conversation he'd be expected to make. Trevor thrived on that sort of stuff. His brother could glad-hand a fish if he thought it would increase exposure for the vineyard. Griffin still preferred to work behind the scenes.

"All those people are going to raise a lot of money for the new pediatric wing at the hospital."

"Sick kids are a big draw," he muttered.

"Griffin Matthew Stone." Jana Stone could communicate more saying his full name out loud than most politicians did throughout an entire career of making stump speeches. The blatant disapproval in her tone felt familiar, if off-putting.

He ran a hand through his hair. "I'm sorry. It's a worthy cause. I know that. Today was rough."

"Cassie's doing okay?" his mother asked, her voice gentling.

"Yeah. I've never seen someone with such a great

attitude. If optimism could cure cancer, she'd be well tomorrow."

Jana frowned. "I thought her prognosis was good."

"There's no sure thing," he answered, "and I can't shake the feeling she isn't telling me the whole truth. The business about a friendly visit down here, then insisting I go back to Seattle with her for a day to meet her son? It was strange."

"People have different ways of dealing with that kind of news. You did a good thing by making time for her."

"The boy is cute…" He picked up another board from the stack piled near the wall. "If you're into kids."

"Which you aren't," his mother said with an over-dramatic sigh.

"There's time for that."

"Maggie was here yesterday," Jana said casually.

He straightened and pointed the hammer at his mom. "That was the worst transition in the history of the world."

She shrugged. "Subtlety isn't my thing."

"No doubt."

"Sass," she said, lifting one brow.

"How is she?" He went back to measuring his next board as he asked the question, knowing if his mom saw his face she'd be able to read exactly what he was thinking. She'd always had that ability. It was damn annoying.

"Efficient and capable as ever. It's thanks to the changes she made to the event registration that helped us increase ticket sales so much. There's an app for RSVPs and it even tracks the silent auction items. People are already bidding and the gala isn't for two weeks. That girl really knows her stuff."

"Since when did you become such a Spencer fan?" he asked, biting down on the edge of a nail while he lifted the shiplap into place.

"I'm a fan of Maggie," his mother corrected.

He began hammering the wood, not wanting to continue this conversation. At all.

"So is Dr. Starber," she said loudly.

Griffin cursed as the hammer slammed against his thumb. He squeezed his fingers around the throbbing digit, bending forward and trying hard not to spit out the vilest words he knew. And that was saying something thanks to his years in the army and on various construction sites around the Pacific Northwest.

His mother tutted. "You should be careful. I can grab an ice pack from the main house."

He shook out his hand. "It's fine. Who's Dr. Starber?"

"He's the chief of pediatrics at Willamette Central Hospital," she reported. "He's a member of the planning committee and drops in on some of our meetings. We wanted his input on seating hospital staff."

Griffin snorted. "What kind of doctor has time to go to gala meetings?"

"The kind," Jana said with an eye roll, "who is interested in dating our Maggie."

Your Maggie. Our Maggie.

A muscle ticked in Griffin's jaw. In truth, he'd always thought of Maggie Spencer as her own person.

"What's this Dr. Feel Good look like?" he demanded.

"Tall, with sandy-blond hair, ruddy cheeks and blue eyes."

The man he'd seen talking to Maggie at the festival.

"He's not nearly as handsome as you." His mother patted his arm.

"I wasn't aware I was competing with him."

"Aren't you?"

"Mom, you know there's nothing going on with Maggie and me."

"There was not so long ago," she countered.

"It got complicated." The word tasted like ash in his mouth. He hated that word. *Complicated.*

"It's a relationship with a woman, Griffin." Jana sniffed delicately. "Of course things got complicated. She isn't a blow-up doll."

"Mom." He groaned. "Geez."

She waved off his embarrassment. "All I'm saying is that you'd better do something if you don't want to lose her."

"She isn't mine to lose."

"She should be."

He opened his mouth to argue but couldn't find the words. "Why are you pushing this?" he asked instead. "You don't even like the Spencers."

"That's not true." Jana crossed her arms over her chest. "Vivian Spencer is a bully and always has been. I don't care for her, but the rest of the family… They're good people."

"Even Morgan?"

"Those who live in glass houses…" his mom said gently and shame winged through Griffin. He'd been the king of adolescent stupidity in his time. "Morgan is a careless teenager who made a careless mistake. I don't think it means she's a terrible person. Maggie…

Well, I'll admit I was upset with how things ended between her and your brother."

Griffin dropped the hammer to one of the saw-horses and tapped a finger on his chin, as if contemplating her words. "I'm fairly certain you had visions of tackling her to the ground and clawing out her eyes."

"Always with the sass." She shook her head. "I see now that the match never would have worked. Trevor…" She paused. "Your brother has done an amazing job with the Harvest brand. But he has bigger dreams than Stonecreek. I don't want this life to limit him."

"He made the choice to come back after college," Griffin pointed out. "Dad made him the heir apparent. Trevor loves that."

"Trevor feels loyal because of that," she corrected. "It isn't the same thing. The vines aren't in his blood."

Griffin frowned as he thought about that. He'd never considered what it meant that his brother didn't feel the same way about the vineyard as he did. He was too busy being angry that Dad had chosen Trevor as his favorite and all but told Griffin he wasn't worthy to be a part of the family legacy.

"Anyway," his mom continued, "you've done an amazing job here and—"

"Was Dad my real father?" he blurted.

Jana's face paled and her eyes widened. "What would make you ask such a thing?" she asked in a choked whisper.

He wanted to close his eyes against the pain he saw in her gaze but forced himself not to look away.

He favored his mother's family in looks, the green eyes and olive-toned skin, whereas Trevor was the spitting image of their father. Griffin hadn't thought much about it as a kid, but as he'd grown older and his relationship with Dave Stone had deteriorated, he'd begun to question why his dad had seemed so unwilling to love him.

"He never liked me," he said and his mother's eyes filled with tears. "I just thought…if there was an explanation like—"

"You were his son," she said flatly. "His biological son."

"Huh." Disappointment and relief flooded Griffin in equal measure.

"Oh, Griffin." His mom moved forward, coming around the sawhorses to wrap her arms around him. "I've made my share of mistakes in life, and it kills me that you paid the price."

"What mistakes?" He pulled back to look at her. "If there wasn't another man…"

Jana wiped at her cheeks and sniffed.

"Mom, don't cry."

"It's fine," she told him, taking a step away. "I'm fine. But there was another man. A boy, really. We were so young, and I was in love. My family had moved here the summer before my senior year so my dad could take a job as a field hand. We were struggling, and Dad tended to be a messy drunk when he got down about our situation. We weren't exactly good stock."

"That's not how I remember Pops," Griffin argued.

"He cleaned himself up," she said with a nod. "But back then, it was bad." She smiled at him. "It's why

I'm so proud of how you've taken Cole under your wing. I wish I'd had someone like you in my life."

"You had Dad."

Her smile turned wistful. "Yes, I suppose I did, but it cost both of us. I'd been in love with someone else when I first met your father. The relationship didn't work out."

She looked so sad as she spoke the words. Outrage flared in Griffin at the thought that someone had hurt his mother. "Why?"

"It was complicated," she said, laughing softly. "I started dating your dad right after we broke up. Things progressed quickly." She shook her head. "I was on the rebound and we both knew it. He didn't care because we were having fun. Then I got pregnant."

"Did Dad think I wasn't his?" Griffin asked, his mouth dry.

"No, but I'm not sure we would have lasted without a reason to get married. Your father and Trevor had a lot in common. He had big dreams. Staying in Stonecreek wasn't part of his master plan, but with a wife and a baby... I didn't leave him with a lot of options."

"He shouldn't have blamed you," Griffin argued. "I'm sure you didn't mean to get pregnant."

Her gaze, which had always been the steadiest thing in his world, faltered. "I wanted a baby," she whispered. "I wanted something that belonged to me. Someone who couldn't leave me. Like I said, I was young and selfish, not thinking beyond what would make me happy." She looked up, her eyes bright with another round of tears. "You made me so happy."

"Dad didn't feel the same way."

Her mouth tightened into a thin line. "It all worked out. He inherited the farm and planted the vines. Actually, he had you and me to thank for that."

"How do you figure?"

"Your dad had saved enough money when I met him to go backpacking through Europe before he started college in the fall. He dropped out of school to get a job when I got pregnant and used the money for a down payment on the first house we bought. But when his dad died, we sold that house and moved here. I insisted he take the money and go to Europe. He came up with the idea for converting the farm to a vineyard in Italy."

Griffin laughed without humor. "Did he ever thank you for that? Because I don't remember his gratitude."

"It was there." Jana sighed. "He loved you in his own way."

"Just not the same way he loved Trevor," Griffin said, embarrassed that even as a grown man he still felt the lack of it.

"He'd be proud of who you've become."

"Thanks, Mom," Griffin said, although he wasn't convinced. At least he understood where his dad's animosity had come from, although the reason behind it was bogus.

She hugged him again. "Maybe you should ask Maggie to the gala."

"I wasn't planning on—"

"Don't finish that sentence," she said, squeezing his arms as she narrowed her eyes at him. "You're going. You'll wear a tux. You'll dance and make nice with people. And you'll like it."

"I won't like it."

"Fine. You don't have to like it, but it would mean a lot to me if you attended."

"Fine," he agreed. "I'm glad you're having fun with this, Mom. It suits you."

"It does." She winked. "Back to work now. We're close, but the tasting room has to be perfect."

"It will be."

"I know," she said as she walked away, glancing over her shoulder at him. "I trust you."

The words made his heart lighten. Despite everything they'd been through—all the complications life had thrown at them—his mother had always believed in him. Maybe she had a point and he shouldn't worry so much about complicated. There was the distinct possibility things were only as complicated as he made them to be in his mind.

One thing was simple to understand.

He hadn't stopped wanting Maggie. It might be time to focus on that once again.

Chapter Four

"How could you do it?" Morgan demanded, slamming her hand against Cole's open locker. The metal banged shut and he pulled off his wireless headphones to stare at her.

"I didn't do anything," he said flatly.

"You ratted me out to my sister." She'd been trying to track down Cole since Maggie and their dad had laid into her on Monday night, but she knew he wouldn't respond to her texts and he hadn't been at school yesterday.

He shrugged. "I talked to her. It's not a crime."

Even though a full day had passed, she was as angry as she'd been when first confronted about sneaking out. "I was already grounded. Now I have to go to her stupid office after school."

His gray eyes flashed with anger. "You might have been grounded, but that didn't mean you were staying home."

"How would you know?" she demanded. "You've dumped all your friends this year."

"They're not my friends." He stepped closer,

looming over her like he was trying to be intimidating. "They aren't yours, either."

"My life," she snapped, "is none of your business. You made it very clear you have no interest in me."

"I never said that," he whispered and unexpectedly reached out a finger to trace the seam of her ruby-red lips. "You're prettier without all the war paint."

She glared at him. "It's makeup," she said through clenched teeth. "Way to insult me."

One side of his mouth pulled up in the closest thing to a smile she'd seen on his face in months. "I meant it as a compliment."

"Oh." Morgan dabbed at the corners of her eyes, embarrassed and angry that tears pricked the backs of them. She glanced down at her fingertips, which came away black from the heavy eyeliner she'd taken to wearing because it bothered her grandmother so much.

"I was trying to do you a favor by talking to your sister," Cole said, his tone low and rumbly. Unlike a lot of boys in her class, his voice had changed completely, deepening so that he sounded like a man. He acted more mature than most guys she knew, too, even though the trouble he'd caused with his teenage antics before moving to Stonecreek was still plastered all over social media.

He'd told her—told everyone—that he'd changed. Maybe it was true. No one really saw him other than when he was at school. Morgan knew his home life was awful and he spent most of his free time out at Harvest Vineyards, working for Griffin.

"I got in more trouble," she said, jutting out her

chin. She wasn't quite willing to forgive him so easily.

"Not as much trouble as you're going to find if you don't drop the losers."

She gritted her teeth, unable to muster a decent comeback. The friends she hung out with now were the school's wild kids, more interested in ditching class and smoking pot under the bleachers than any kind of learning. Morgan didn't do drugs. She hadn't yet anyway, and although she always accepted a cup of whatever drink they were passing around, she mostly pretended to down it.

"I'm in with them now," she whispered. She'd worked so hard to rebel. The thought almost made her laugh. What kind of poser had to make a concerted effort to do the wrong thing? But it was easier to embrace the role of family miscreant. Compared to perfect Maggie and easygoing Ben, she was the oddball out. At least that was how she felt after her mom died eleven years ago.

Her throat stung as she grasped for memories of her kind, gentle mother. Mom had always loved Morgan just the way she was. Unlike Grammy. And who knew who Dad wanted her to be? He was so preoccupied with his studio that it was a wonder he even remembered her name.

She'd tried to follow in Maggie's footsteps—but the straight and narrow had never been a great fit for Morgan. She hadn't felt like she belonged anywhere until she'd started running with the wild kids last year. Ripped clothes, a constant sneer and the right kind of makeup, and she was set.

"You're not one of them," Cole told her. His eyes

crinkled at the corners and Morgan's heart gave a little thud. "You're better than that, Mo-Mo." She glared and he held up his hands, chuckling. "Sorry. I heard your dad call you that. It's cute."

"It's a name for a little girl," she muttered. "He doesn't want me to grow up."

"You're lucky he cares what you do."

Cole's voice was hollow, and shame filled her. He had moved to Stonecreek when his mom had taken off for parts unknown. She knew his dad was a raging alcoholic and his older brother had done jail time.

Morgan had lost her mom to cancer when she was only five years old. It was terrible, but she still had a family who loved her—even Grammy in her overbearing, judgmental way.

"I know," she whispered, then someone called her name. It was Jocelyn, her so-called best friend and the one who'd posted the photo online even though Morgan had asked her not to. "I've got to go," she said. Cole's gaze had gone blank again, a slight sneer curving his mouth.

"You don't have to." His lips barely moved, the words a whisper of breath, but she felt his anger like a slap in the face.

Her stomach tightened.

"Morgan, come on!" The call was insistent now.

"See you around," she said to Cole and whirled around to hurry toward her friend through the crowded hall, hating herself more with every step.

Friday night, Maggie walked into Over Cheesy, Stonecreek's popular pizza joint, at seven on the nose, then hesitated and almost backed out again.

She'd been compulsively punctual since childhood, always the first one in line outside the classroom each morning. Now she worried she was sending the wrong impression for a first date.

Too eager? No other plans?

It was bad enough that she had to meet her date at the restaurant, embarrassed to have him pick her up at her dad's house. Twenty-seven years old and living in her childhood bedroom. In all fairness, she'd sublet her house—Grammy's old house—because she'd planned to move into Trevor's place after the wedding. So eight months from now she'd be on her own again. That moment couldn't come too soon.

"Hey, Maggie, whatcha doin'?"

She forced a smile as she met the curious gaze of Britney Parker, a woman Maggie had known since kindergarten. Britney fluffed her already puffy blond hair and adjusted the formfitting black shirt she wore as part of her hostess uniform. Adjusted by tugging it down an extra inch.

"I'm…um…meeting a friend here," Maggie said, moving forward.

"Brenna?"

"No, actually—"

"Your grandma?"

Maggie flinched. Yikes. Was she so boring that people in town considered her friends with her grandma? She loved Grammy, but the nearly half-century age gap and the fact that most of their conversations ended in a lecture weren't conducive to much girl bonding.

"I have a date," Maggie offered before Britney could suggest their second-grade teacher as a potential companion. Then she glanced around to make sure no one had heard her. Of course, now that she'd outed herself to Britney, it would be no secret. Few secrets were kept in Stonecreek. As soon as she and James were seated at a table for two, the gossip train would chug right out of the station.

She glanced at her watch. Three minutes past seven. No need to panic. He probably had trouble finding a parking space, although there had been several near her car. Or he was just running late. He'd been the one to ask for her number, after all. Plus he'd actually called to set up their date. That was a good sign.

"Griffin," Britney said, her smile brightening.

"No," Maggie corrected. "He's—"

"Hey, Brit."

Maggie stiffened at the sound of the familiar voice behind her. Then he was at her side, heat radiating from his big body. She caught the scent of cloves and mint gum and her traitorous knees went a little weak.

"You two giving it another try?" Britney's gaze swung between Maggie and Griffin.

She glanced at him, shocked to see one thick brow cock in what looked like… Was that hope on his face?

"We're not," she said quickly. "I'm meeting someone else."

"Then I don't think he's here yet," Britney said. "I'll get a table set up, though. What about you, Griffin?"

He scrubbed a hand over his face. "Trevor and I are grabbing dinner."

"Here?" Maggie squeaked.

Britney stifled a laugh. "Awk-ward."

"It's probably a sign," Griffin said, none too helpfully as far as Maggie was concerned.

"It's not a sign," she told him.

"Are you kidding?" Britney picked up her phone and started thumbing the screen. "It's bad enough that you started dating your ex-fiancé's brother. Now the two of them have to watch you on a first date?" She glanced up. "It's a first date, right?"

"Yes."

Maggie whirled around to find Dr. James Starber standing behind her. She'd been so distracted by Griffin and the mortification of this situation that she hadn't even noticed him enter the restaurant.

"You're on a date, Mags?"

Maggie thunked the heel of her palm against her forehead as Trevor appeared directly behind James, who looked back and forth between the two Stone brothers like he was afraid he'd stumbled into the middle of a kinky small-town threesome or something.

"I'm trying," she told Trevor with a tight smile, then turned back to Britney. "Could we get a table? Now."

"Sure thing." The blonde grinned, then held up her phone. Maggie blinked as the flash went off. "I just need photographic evidence of this moment. I won't tag you if that makes it easier."

Maggie inwardly cringed. "*Please* don't tag me." She looked over her shoulder and gave James what she hoped was an encouraging smile. "Nice to see you."

"Um…" He massaged the back of his neck. "You, too."

"Take care of this one," Trevor said with a hearty back slap to James. "She's something special." He wagged a finger between himself and Griffin, clearly relishing how uncomfortable this was making both Maggie and his brother. "We can vouch for that."

"Shut up, Trevor," Maggie and Griffin said at the same time.

"Right this way," Britney announced cheerily, and without looking at Griffin again, Maggie followed the other woman.

She slid into the seat, ignoring the curious gazes of the diners at the tables around them. "I'm sorry about that," she said to James when they were alone. Or as alone as they could be with half the restaurant staring at them.

He flashed a half-hearted grin. "I'm from Chicago and did my residency in Boston," he told her. "This is my first stint at small-town living. I think I got a crash course on what exactly that means tonight."

"Yeah," she agreed. "It's actually great most of the time."

"I remember hearing talk at the hospital about a runaway bride. It seemed like a big scandal."

Maggie grimaced. "Unfortunately they were talking about me. Long, boring story."

The waiter came at that moment and took their drink orders. James debated which pinot noir was the best choice from the selections offered, and without hesitation Maggie steered him toward one from Harvest. It was the same one she and Griffin had shared their first night together. Even when she got away from Griffin Stone, she couldn't seem to escape his hold on her.

She didn't notice Griffin and Trevor being seated, so either they'd chosen a table behind her or, hopefully, picked another restaurant. She couldn't help but be curious as to why they were having dinner together. Normally the brothers barely got through a casual conversation without arguing.

James was nice and interesting, obviously dedicated to his patients, but Maggie felt not an iota of a spark between them. Not even the potential for one, although when she tilted her head and squinted slightly, James bore an uncanny resemblance to a young Robert Redford. She was truly off her game if she couldn't manage a spark for a Redford look-alike. Then he explained his plan to move back to Chicago once his fellowship at Willamette Central was finished. She listened as he extolled the highlights of the Windy City, but had to admit she had no interest in discovering for herself what Chicago had to offer.

Overall the meal was pleasant and the pizza fantastic as always. James walked her to her car, the streets empty as Stonecreek tended to roll up the sidewalks early, even on weekend nights.

"Thank you for a lovely evening," she said, pasting a bright smile on her face as she pulled her keys from her purse. She hoped he wouldn't try to kiss her because that would make the next two weeks working on the hospital fund-raiser far too awkward.

His mouth quirked. "As first dates go, that was a total dud, right? You're not into me at all."

"Um…" She felt color rise to her cheeks. "You seem like such a nice guy."

"Kiss of death," he murmured.

"No," she argued. "But I'm not… Things are… It's complicated." *Ugh, that word again.*

"I get it," he told her.

She laughed softly. "Then maybe you can explain it to me."

"There was this girl I dated when I was an undergraduate," he said almost wistfully. "We met senior year. I was applying for med school and she was an elementary education major. She was beautiful and funny. When we were together I forgot all about the stress and pressure of everything else."

"I love when that happens." Maggie thought of the one blissful night she'd spent with Griffin and how everything but the two of them had faded into the background.

"She wanted to make things more serious, but I was consumed with my future. It didn't seem like a relationship had any place in it." His brow creased. "Things were too complicated."

"I'm sorry," Maggie whispered.

He shook his head. "Me, too. I should have never let her go. Now I can see that none of the excuses I gave were worth a damn."

"Maybe it's not too late," she suggested. "Things are steadier for you now. I'm sure you could track her down on social media." Even though she didn't know James well, she liked him. What she didn't like was the pain she saw in his kind eyes.

"We're Facebook friends," he confessed, then sighed. "She's married with one little boy and another baby on the way. She looks happy."

"James."

He shrugged. "I'm happy for her. I am. But I can't

help but think it should be me in those pictures. I was so focused on my future and my goals. Now that I've achieved them, it doesn't seem to matter. Not one bit."

She leaned in and hugged him. "I'm sorry. There's someone else out there for you. I know it."

"Thanks," he said when she pulled away. "I'm not trying to be Donnie Downer, but when you said *complicated* it struck a nerve. Things can seem complicated but only when we let that take over. What really matters is usually pretty simple."

Maggie's breath caught. "You're right."

"Of course." He winked. "I'm a doctor. We're always right."

She laughed, which she knew had been his intention. Lightening the moment.

"I did have a really good time tonight."

He nodded. "I'll see you at the next gala meeting," he told her and walked toward his car.

Maggie got into hers, turning it on and cranking the heat against the chill of the October night air. The cold seemed to settle in her bones. She gripped the steering wheel, the conversation with James tumbling through her mind. Seeing Trevor and Griffin. The way Griffin had looked at her in the restaurant.

Finally she backed out, but as she turned the corner a block down, her gaze snagged on a familiar blue Land Cruiser parked at the curb in front of O'Malley's Tavern.

Without thinking, she pulled in behind Griffin's SUV.

The bar was crowded with locals and a few tourists. If someone wanted a late-night drink, O'Malley's was the place to be in Stonecreek.

"Hey, Ms. Mayor," Chuck O'Malley, the tavern's gregarious owner, called from behind the bar. "Is this an official campaign stop?"

Maggie waved at the people who turned to say hello, once again finding all eyes on her. Everyone turned except Griffin, seated at the end of the bar, his broad shoulders stiff as he gazed down into the glass of brown liquor in front of him.

"I'm off the clock tonight," she told Chuck, even though she was never truly off.

"Then what can I get you?" he asked.

"My usual," she told him, moving forward.

He rolled his eyes but grinned. "You got it."

She made small talk with a few of the patrons before climbing onto the bar stool next to Griffin. "This seat taken?"

He picked up his glass and took a long drink. "Looks that way."

"You and Trevor must have had a short dinner," she said, hanging her purse on the hook next to her stool. "I didn't see you in the restaurant again."

"We ended up at The Kitchen. Over Cheesy felt a little crowded."

"Sorry," she mumbled. "Although, Friday is fish taco night at The Kitchen, so that's a plus."

Griffin gave a small laugh. "Yeah, I guess."

"Here you go, Maggie." Chuck placed a glass in front of her. "I feel like I should warn you that Jason has been canvassing the downtown business owners, offering all kinds of campaign promises about how he's going to lower taxes and add incentives to the mix if we throw our support behind him."

Maggie's chest tightened. This was why she was

never really off the clock. "I figured as much," she said. "A few people around town have been fairly conspicuous about avoiding eye contact with me in the past couple of weeks. I appreciate you confirming it."

Chuck nodded. "Can he really make that happen?"

Maggie couldn't help but hear the hope in the man's voice. "Not exactly. Any new tax breaks would have to go through council. The mayor can't arbitrarily make that kind of decision. I'm sure that's why Jason hasn't spoken publicly about it. But it sure sounds promising."

"It does," Chuck said, running a hand through his thinning brown hair.

"There's a downtown business owners' meeting next week, right?" Maggie asked.

Chuck nodded.

"Let me push some of the council members to see where they stand on things. I've also got some ideas for a new marketing campaign that I'd like to run by all of you. It would keep people coming into town even through the winter season."

"You're a gem, Maggie." Chuck reached out and patted her hand. "I'll tell Frank to put you on the agenda. I know you have our best interests at heart."

One of the waitresses called to Chuck and he headed for the other end of the bar.

"Your drink is pink," Griffin said after several moments of awkward silence.

"Cranberry juice and club soda," Maggie confirmed.

"Living on the wild side."

"I had wine with dinner."

He glanced at her, cocking an eyebrow.

"A Harvest pinot noir. The 2015 vintage. Aroma of black cherries overlaid with fennel and a smoky finish."

"One of my favorites," he said, nodding.

"I know," she whispered.

"Your date seemed nice."

"He is." She paused, then added, "Also pining over an ex-girlfriend."

"Imagine that," Griffin murmured.

"She's married now. Things were too complicated when they were together, so he let her go. He regrets it."

He swiveled on his bar stool, ice clinking in the glass as he balanced it between two fingers. "You spent the date talking about how much he misses his ex-girlfriend?"

It sounded ridiculous and Maggie laughed softly. "Not all of it."

"What's on the agenda for the second date?" Griffin asked, draining his glass. "Dissecting dysfunctional family Christmases from when he was a kid?"

Maggie sipped at her drink. "We won't have a second date."

She saw his shoulders relax slightly.

"Does that make you happy?" she asked, narrowing her eyes at him.

"Delirious with it," he confirmed with a wink.

"Why?"

The question seemed to surprise him. A muscle ticked on the side of his jaw and he looked past her, raising his glass. She assumed he was looking at

Chuck and, as expected, the bar owner appeared a moment later.

"Another Jack?" he asked.

"Please."

Chuck turned to Maggie. "More of the mayor's special?"

She shook her head. "I'm heading out. Thanks again for the intel, Chuck."

"I've owned this place for twenty-five years," he told her. "I've never seen anyone work as hard for this town as you, Mayor Spencer. That counts for a lot in my book."

A tumble of emotions clogged her throat as she nodded and pushed away from the bar. It was all too much…too… No, she wouldn't use that dreaded word again. But between her family, the campaign and her heart, Maggie felt wrung out and hung up to dry with all her vulnerable bits exposed for everyone to see. She couldn't deal with any more tonight.

As Chuck walked away to refill Griffin's glass, Maggie grabbed her purse and turned.

A warm hand on her arm stopped her. She faced him again, searching his green gaze for a clue as to how he felt about her. His eyes gave nothing away.

"Why did you come in here tonight?" he asked, his voice a low rumble.

"I saw your car."

He arched a brow. "And…?"

"No," she said, shaking her head. "I've already told you how I felt…how I feel. It's your turn, Griffin. I'm getting whiplash from your mixed signals. You don't want me to date another man, but you don't want me for yourself."

"I…" He closed his eyes. "I don't know what to say."

"That's *your* issue." She tugged her arm away from his grasp. She wasn't sure what she'd expected from him tonight. The way he'd looked at her earlier in the restaurant had given her some ridiculous hope. But if he couldn't even admit he wanted her, it left them with nothing.

Once again she was left with nothing.

She deserved more.

He stared at her and the heat in his gaze made her tingle all the way to her toes. It wasn't enough.

"Hope your friend Jack makes you happy," she told him. "At least he won't expect too much." Then she walked away, her head held high. She wouldn't break down again. Not for Griffin Stone.

Chapter Five

"How was the meeting with Trevor?" Marcus Sanchez asked Griffin on Monday morning.

"Pointless," Griffin snarled, then blew out a breath when the other man raised a brow. He didn't deserve to be on the receiving end of Griffin's bad mood. Marcus had first come to work for Harvest Vineyards as a young man. He'd quickly showed a deep understanding of the grapes as well as a knack for dealing with the business side of things, and his expertise had made him an indispensable part of the operation as the winery grew. After Griffin's father's sudden death, Jana had named Marcus CEO in a move that surprised many, including Trevor, who Griffin knew had assumed himself the heir apparent.

"Sorry," he muttered. "My brother and I can barely agree on an appetizer to order. I'm not sure what made me think he'd want my opinion on our wholesale distribution channels."

Marcus glanced around the tasting room, which was flooded with morning light. "Construction is almost complete. We need to determine what your role in the company is going to be moving forward, so you and Trevor will have to find some common ground."

"I haven't committed to staying," Griffin said.

"Harvest needs you," Marcus answered simply.

"You've been talking to my mother." Griffin picked up the can of stain he was using to deepen the color on the wood planks that covered the back wall.

"No, although I imagine she's of the same opinion."

"Oh, yeah."

"You have an affinity for the vines, Griffin. It can't be denied."

"I have other jobs in the pipeline," Griffin countered, dipping a paintbrush into the stain. "In fact, one of the developers I work with in Seattle has a new project starting next month. He needs a general contractor."

Marcus slammed his hand on the hewed wood of the top of the bar. It was a massive outburst for Marcus, who was one of the most even-tempered men Griffin had ever met. "You're a winemaker, Griffin Stone."

"I never got that chance." Griffin concentrated on applying even rows of stain to the wood, focusing so that his hand didn't tremble. Marcus's words brought up long-buried emotions. "Dad kicked me out of here and we both know he had good reason for it."

Out of the corner of his eye Griffin saw Marcus smooth his hand over the bar, as if making amends for accosting it moments earlier. "We both know you're different now. Prove it."

Something inside Griffin came to life at the challenge. It had been his dream while spending his childhood exploring the neat rows of vines his father had planted. With every expansion of the vineyard, Griffin's mind had exploded with ideas and plans for the future. Until the animosity between him and his dad had poisoned his aspirations.

And there it was. The old anger, the fear and doubt that he wasn't worthy. That he'd mess things up, as he had so many times as a kid.

He'd tagged along during every stage of the growing season, soaking in all he could about the life cycle of the vines and how the grapes were affected by nature. He'd loved both the science and the art of it, but nothing he'd done had been good enough for his father. He couldn't handle the delicate fruit. He wasn't careful enough. He got in the way.

It had been different with Trevor, who back then could have cared less about the family business. But Dad had encouraged Trevor whenever he'd showed any interest, even with Griffin standing on the sidelines, chomping at the bit to be involved.

His father's favoritism had tainted Griffin, both toward his brother and Harvest Vineyards. He still couldn't understand the point of it. As his mother had said, Dave Stone had ended up with a good life, a successful business and the respect of his peers. But he'd never left Stonecreek, other than quick business trips. Maybe that was the point. Griffin's dad hadn't been able to choose his life, while Griffin had. He'd joined the army, seen the world, served his country and become his own man. Dad had returned to the farm he'd hated growing up, and spent his days working the land, something he'd never planned for or wanted.

All that history was another set of complications, just like the obstacles keeping him and Maggie apart.

But Griffin had a choice. He could let the past define him and allow his doubts to win, or he could choose a different way. A way forward.

"Trevor doesn't want me here any more than Dad did," he said, still not quite able to let go of the past.

"Make it work," Marcus said simply.

Griffin huffed out a laugh and dipped the paintbrush into the can of stain again. "Why does this conversation feel like some kind of vintner version of a Jedi mind trick?"

Marcus leaned forward on the bar. "You belong at Harvest."

"Your confidence means a lot," Griffin admitted, drawing in a breath. "Do you think it would help if I reminded Trevor that the reason I returned here in the first place was to attend his wedding?"

Marcus shook his head but his eyes danced with amusement. "Doubtful." He straightened. "That reminds me, I'm leaving early today to attend a pre-debate rally for Maggie."

"There's an actual debate?"

"Your cousin is insisting on it to rattle her. He doesn't play fair."

"It seems strange to think of political machinations in Stonecreek." He rubbed a hand across the back of his neck. "Is there a chance Maggie could lose the election?"

Marcus shrugged. "Unfortunately yes. According

to Brenna, she's working her butt off to make sure that doesn't happen."

"Good for her," Griffin murmured.

"She needs all the support she can get," Marcus said with a pointed look.

"I need to get back to staining. I'll think about what you said and try with Trevor again. That's all I can offer." Griffin dropped his gaze, wishing he had something more to give.

Maggie brushed an invisible speck of lint from her suit jacket that evening as she stood behind the curtain of the high school's packed auditorium.

"Standing room only out there," Brenna told her.

"Slow night in town," Maggie answered with a forced laugh. It was still difficult to believe so many people cared about the mayor's race. The first time she'd been elected, after her grandmother had announced her impending retirement, Maggie had sponsored a few pancake breakfasts and met with most of the local businesses and civic organizations. Then she'd been elected, running unopposed, as if holding the office was her right.

She had no problem proving she deserved to be reelected but Jason's campaign felt weirdly personal, like he was more interested in taking her down than building himself up. Maybe it was a reflection of the state of politics on a national level, or the town's fascination with her personal life over the past few months, but Maggie didn't like it.

Marilee Haggard, the town council member who was moderating the debate, announced each of the candidates and gave a brief rundown of their respective résumés.

"You've got this," Brenna whispered, then Maggie walked out, smiling and shaking hands with Jason Stone as they met in the middle of the stage.

They took their places behind podiums that had been set up on either side of the stage, angled so that they faced both each other and the audience.

"I have to admit I'm relieved at the handshake," Jason said into the microphone, glancing between Maggie and the crowd. "I was a little afraid the mayor would expect me to bow, given that she's a Spencer and I'm just a peon member of the Stone family."

There was a smattering of laughter from the audience and Maggie felt color rise to her cheeks. "I'm not like that," she said, bending toward her microphone, "and I think everyone here knows it, Jason."

"Do they?" Jason threw up his hands in an overly dramatic gesture. Seriously, had the guy been involved in the theater department in high school? "Because you've made it clear by your actions that we're not good enough for you. Ask my cous—"

"Can we keep on point with election issues?" Maggie asked, hating the thread of annoyance she couldn't keep out of her voice. She didn't want people to see her as a shrew, but how many times did she have to defend her decision not to marry Trevor before this town let it go?

Marilee nodded. "Of course. The first issue we're going to tackle tonight involves funding for essential services and emergency management. Jason won the coin toss backstage, so he'll answer first."

As Maggie listened to Jason make his points, she scanned the audience to gauge the reaction to the patented lies he was spewing. Her opponent was good, she'd give him that much. He skirted the truth about how things were being handled currently and stayed vague on the changes he'd make to improve it.

Her dad, grandmother, Morgan and Ben were in the front row. Dad watched Jason with an unmistakable scowl, and Maggie wondered how much her father even understood the issues in town. So much of his life was spent consumed by his art, with occasional moments of parental involvement. He was getting better, she'd admit, and appreciated his efforts to stay connected with Morgan and Ben.

Grammy, on the other hand, shook her head and made little huffs of disapproval, her razor-sharp gaze snapping between Jason and Maggie. Maggie almost expected her to rush the stage and tackle Jason outright to shut him up. Morgan and Ben both looked bored out of their minds, which Maggie expected. Brenna and Marcus sat behind them and... She sucked in a sharp breath. Griffin occupied the chair next to Marcus.

How had she not seen him immediately? As if sensing her gaze, his attention shifted from his cousin to her and he flashed a quick half smile.

"Maggie?" She blinked and glanced at Marilee. "Did you want to respond to the question?" the woman asked.

"Um...yes... I—"

"Or is it beneath you to actually concern yourself with issues that matter to this town?" Jason asked, sarcasm dripping from his tone.

Maggie felt her temper flare as a disapproving murmur of voices filled the room.

"This town matters to me a great deal," she said directly to her opponent. "So much so that I returned here as soon as I graduated college to dedicate my time and energy to it."

Jason nodded. "Young and inexperienced. You admit it."

"Enough." She held up a hand. Yes, she'd been groomed to lead Stonecreek, but Maggie had never taken her place in the community for granted. "People here know me." She looked out to the audience and, while she didn't let her gaze drift to Griffin's, she saw him nodding as if encouraging her to finally stand up for herself. "I've focused on the arts as a growth factor for tourism, spearheaded the plans for a dedicated community center building and managed to hold property taxes at the current rate. Just this week I met with the owners of the local businesses to discuss a new marketing campaign to bring visitors here during winter months." She pointed a finger at Jason. "How long have you lived in Stonecreek?"

He stiffened and snorted out a disbelieving laugh. "I grew up here. You know that."

"But you left for college on the East Coast, correct?"

"So what?"

"You've been back a year now?" she demanded.

"I have vast experience in the world," he countered. "It adds to my plans for the town."

"About those plans," she said, wrinkling her nose. "You told everyone that you'd give a tax break to any business that's been established for at least five years. Actually, only the council has the power to vote on business tax laws. In my experience as mayor…" She paused, then added, "Emphasis on the word *experience* since I'm the only candidate who has experience in local government."

"That doesn't—"

She held up a hand. "Do *not* interrupt me. You had your time. This is mine. A campaign promise is only as good as your ability to follow through on it. I'm a proponent of feasible growth and realistic change…"

Jason crossed his arms over his chest. "You got the job because of your grandma and everyone knows it. There hasn't been someone strong enough to stand up to the Spencers until me."

"Being strong isn't the same as bullying people," Maggie said clearly into the microphone. "You've spent more time taking jabs at my character and personal life than understanding what makes this town work and what the residents need."

"Are we ready for the next question?" Marilee asked cheerfully.

"I understand that the mayor should have the best interests of all residents in mind," Jason said, ignoring the moderator's question. "Not just the people in her own social circles."

"I don't do that," Maggie said immediately.

"Every decision you make benefits your family and your grandmother's circle of cronies."

"That isn't true." Embarrassment washed through Maggie. She'd taken her grandmother's advice on so many aspects of the job. Only recently had she begun to question whether Grammy truly wanted to help Maggie do what was right for all facets of the town's population.

"As far as your personal life…" Jason continued. "In a place like Stonecreek, character counts for a lot. It seems to me—" he looked out to the audience "—as well as to a number of other people, that you were willing to marry into my family like some people enter into a business merger. What kind of moral compass does that exhibit?"

"Trevor and I care about each other but made the decision together that the marriage wouldn't work," Maggie said, hating that she was trotting out her dirty laundry for public consumption once again. "It had nothing to do with my position as mayor."

"Such a pat answer," Jason said. "But no one around here believes it, Maggie. Everything you do is planned and controlled, most of it by your ever-present grandmother."

"Don't bring Grammy into this," Maggie said on a hitch of breath.

Marilee stood. "I really must insist—"

"Then explain why it happened. How can we believe you won't—"

"He cheated on me," Maggie blurted and heard gasps of shock from the audience. She glanced at the front row to where her father looked furious, her grandmother incredulous. Morgan and Ben both stared at her with their mouths wide-open.

She couldn't bear to look at Griffin at that moment. Yes, he'd encouraged her to tell the truth, but she knew he hadn't meant in this kind of a public forum.

Trevor would be blindsided and Jana humiliated once again.

She wiped at her eyes and glared at Jason. "Are you happy now?" she asked into the microphone.

"I..." He shook his head. "I didn't know."

"Because it was none of your business," she told him, then turned to the audience. "It was no one's business. For the last time, I'm sorry all of you were so very disappointed that Trevor and I didn't marry. It was never my intention to let down the town. But things came to light just before the ceremony that made it impossible for me to go through with it."

Shame burned in her gut at having to relive the betrayal. She'd worn the mantle of Maggie Spencer, runaway bride, because it had seemed easier than being forever known as the cuckolded fiancée. Now she was going to get a taste of both.

She drew in a breath and addressed Marilee. "I'm afraid we've gotten quite off track this evening."

The other woman nodded, her mouth opening and closing like a fish flailing on a dock.

"I've also done all the talking I can stand for now," Maggie said quietly. "I apologize that we didn't make it through your questions. Email them to me and I'd be happy to offer my responses to be published so that everyone understands my position on things."

Without waiting for an answer, she turned and fled the auditorium.

Chapter Six

Griffin knocked on the door of Jim Spencer's house later that night, unsure of what he was doing there. Even less certain when Morgan opened it.

Her gaze dropped briefly when she saw him and pink stained her cheeks.

"Is Maggie here?" he asked.

"Morgan…" Jim's deep voice came from the hallway. "Tell whoever it is that—" He stopped when he saw Griffin and shook his head. "Not tonight. She's been through enough."

"That's why I'm here," Griffin said quickly, holding out his hand to prevent Maggie's sister from shutting the door in his face. "I want to make sure she's okay. I texted and called but—"

"She turned off her phone," Morgan reported. "About a million texts came in after the meeting. Someone posted a video on YouTube."

Griffin cursed under his breath.

"We had it taken down," Jim told him.

"She didn't do anything wrong," Griffin said, fisting his hands at his sides.

"We know that," her father answered.

"So does my family," Griffin offered, hitching his chin. "I talked to Trev and Mom after I left the high school. I didn't want them blindsided by what happened."

"You don't seem surprised at her revelation about Trevor and the wedding." Jim crossed his arms over his big chest. For a guy pushing middle age and who often had his shirt buttoned wrong, Jim Spencer looked surprisingly strong. And intimidating.

"Maggie told me a while ago."

"Did Jana know?" Jim demanded.

Griffin shook his head. "She had no idea. I wanted Trevor to tell her but…"

"What he put my daughter through was terrible," Jim said, his voice icy, "on many levels. First the betrayal—"

"On her wedding day," Morgan snarled, eyes narrowed at Griffin. "My sister didn't deserve that crap from him."

Jim put his hand on her shoulder. "Go tell her Griffin's here. Maggie will decide whether he comes in or not."

"I hope she says no," Morgan whispered, then turned and disappeared down the hall.

No, Griffin wanted to shout. *Don't let her shut me out.* He needed to see her. He needed to make her understand—

"You have to take some blame in this," Jim said.

Griffin took a step back like the older man had punched him. "What do you mean?" He shook his head. "I wasn't even here. I didn't know he was cheating. Hell, I gave him a black eye at the church after Maggie told me what he'd done."

Jim inclined his head, nodding as if he approved of that bit of retribution. "But after you found out, you still let her take the blame."

"That was Maggie's decision," Griffin argued even as guilt speared through him. He should have told someone, forced her or Trevor to reveal the truth of what had caused the breakup. He hated how people treated her because they thought she'd walked away from his brother.

"You still should have—"

"No."

They both turned as Maggie walked into the entry. She'd changed from the conservative suit she'd worn at the debate to a pair of black sweatpants and a University of Oregon T-shirt. Her face had been scrubbed of makeup, which only made her more beautiful to Griffin. Yet he couldn't stand the shadows under her eyes or the defeated slump of her shoulders.

"Griffin tried to convince me to tell people the truth. I know he pushed Trevor for the same thing." Her brow furrowed as she looked at her father, like she could will him to understand. "It was my choice and he respected it."

"I still don't understand," her dad said, throwing up his hands. "Trevor was a snake. You let him get away with it."

She winced and Griffin wanted to step between the two of them to shield Maggie from any more recrimination.

"Maybe," she admitted softly, "I was embarrassed. The choice was to be the runaway bride or the woman who couldn't keep her fiancé's attention, even on her wedding day. That option was too pathetic, Dad."

"You aren't pathetic," Jim said, enveloping her in a tight hug. "I have half a mind to drive out to the vineyard and kick Trevor's butt into next week."

"I think Mom's taking care of that," Griffin offered. "She was pretty mad."

Jim looked over his shoulder. "Your mother is a good woman."

"The best," Griffin agreed.

"Dad, I'm going to talk to Griffin for a few minutes," Maggie said, stepping away.

"You don't have to," her father told her. "You don't owe anyone with the last name Stone another minute of your time."

Griffin wanted to protest but Jim was right.

Maggie lifted a hand and pressed her palm to her dad's cheek. "Ben needs help with his science lab," she said gently.

"I'm useless at science," her dad said with an eye roll.

"He's coloring a cell diagram."

Jim perked up. "Coloring I'm good at. I'll get the oil pastels."

"That might be a little much for eighth-grade science."

"Then Ben should love it."

"Can I come in?" Griffin asked Maggie when they were finally alone.

She blinked as if she hadn't realized he was still standing on the front porch. "Of course. Sorry. Dad should have invited you in from the start."

"He was in full-stop protective mode." Griffin shut the front door behind him.

She smiled, clearly trying to make it bright, but Griffin could see a painful tightness compress the edges of her mouth. "Was that your first town meeting?" she asked.

He nodded.

"You picked a good one. Your cousin and I put on quite a performance."

"Don't do that," he whispered. "You don't need to play it off with me."

He reached for her but she shrugged away, shaking her head. "I don't know if I'm in a place where I can let you touch me."

His chest ached at the raw honesty of that admission. "I'm sorry my cousin is a goading jerk."

"I didn't mean to announce Trevor's cheating to the whole town." She ran a hand through her hair, tugging on the ends. "Did you talk to him?"

Griffin nodded.

"Is he mad?"

"Do you care?"

"I do."

The two words she would have said on her wedding day if his brother hadn't cheated. "Why?" he couldn't help but ask.

"I never wanted to hurt Trevor."

"After what he did to you…"

"Even so. I promised I'd keep his betrayal a secret, and I broke my word."

"Jason pushed you to it." Griffin moved past her, gripped the handrail of the staircase that led to the second floor. "I went to his house tonight, too. Big wimp wouldn't come to the door. All the lights went out while I was standing on the porch, like I was supposed to believe he suddenly wasn't at home."

"Do you blame him?" Maggie asked, and he heard a sad kind of amusement in her voice.

"I blame him for most of this," Griffin said, turning around to face her. "If he wants to run against you as mayor, have at it. But to try to win the election by assassinating your character is low. He always was a loser."

"I shouldn't have let him bait me."

"Stop doing that. Stop taking the blame when other people are awful. This wasn't your fault. Calling off the wedding wasn't your fault." He paused, then added softly, "The things that went wrong between us definitely weren't your fault."

"You never answered me about Trevor."

He sighed. "He's not mad at you. I imagine he's not loving the tongue lashing he's getting from Mom, but he seemed almost resolved to the truth being out there."

"I'll talk to him tomorrow."

"Talk to me right now."

Her head tilted as she studied at him. "Isn't that what we're doing?"

"You're standing a few feet from the front door," he reminded her. "I keep waiting for you to kick me out."

"I don't understand why you're here," she told him, which wasn't exactly an invitation to stay.

"I hate what happened to you tonight. I wanted to make sure you're okay."

"I'm okay," she whispered.

"Let me in, Maggie May," he coaxed. "I probably don't deserve another chance, but give me one anyway."

She closed her eyes and drew in a long breath, then blew it out. "I'm binge watching *Gilmore Girls* on Netflix," she told him when she opened her eyes again. "I needed a distraction."

He lifted an eyebrow. "I could Netflix and chill tonight."

She laughed, rolling her eyes. "How do you feel about Netflix and sitting on the couch with my dad in his bedroom down the hall?"

"That works, too." He would have agreed to anything to be near her tonight.

He followed her down the hall and into the cozy family room off the kitchen. Jim, Morgan and Ben were nowhere to be seen and Griffin wondered if Maggie's dad was purposely giving them time alone. If so, it was the most outright vote of confidence Griffin could have asked for given Jim's earlier attitude.

She lowered herself onto the couch, glancing up at him almost warily before patting the cushion next to her. "Are you sure about this? I'm not great company right now, and it isn't going to be sexy times. I can't even promise to be able to string together a decent sentence."

"Any sentence that includes the phrase 'sexy times,'" he said, sitting down, his leg grazing hers, "is way better than decent."

She laughed again and seemed to relax. She hit a button on the remote control and he leaned back against the sofa and watched the fictional lives of people who talked way too fast in a town called Stars Hollow. As far as he was concerned, Stonecreek could give the show a run for its money as far as nosy neighbors and everyone knowing everyone else's business.

"Don't let Jason or tonight derail you," he said after a few minutes.

Maggie glanced up at him. "How can I not?"

"You're strong." He put an arm around her, gathering her close, profoundly grateful that she was letting him into her life again. She was vulnerable tonight, which might have something to do with it. Maybe tomorrow her guard would be up again. Hard to say. But he'd take this and anything else she was willing to give. "Stronger than you give yourself credit for, and you're dedicated to the town."

"I wish it were that simple," she said with a sigh, leaning her head against his shoulder. He could smell her shampoo, and the warmth of her pressed against him made him want more. Want everything. But he tamped down his desire, because what Maggie needed tonight was a friend. Griffin wanted to be that for her.

"It is," he promised. "We're adding *complicated* to our banned list of words."

"We have a list?"

"*Sorry* is the only word on it so far, but it's a list. No apologies and no using complications as an excuse anymore."

"I like that," she whispered with a yawn.

I like you, he wanted to tell her but those three words seemed too simple to describe his feelings for

Maggie. And he'd just banned *complicated*. Where did that leave him?

As always, thoughts of the future made panic swell in his gut, so he buried them. Instead he focused on the feel of her in his arms. He brushed his fingers against her arm and she lifted a hand to his chest. His heartbeat sped under her touch, but this time it wasn't from lust. It was the odd sense of contentment of this moment, the satisfaction of being there for her when she needed someone.

Of how much he liked being that someone for her.

A few minutes later her breathing softened, becoming rhythmic in a way that made him know she'd fallen asleep. Griffin watched another episode of the show, finding himself craving a cup of coffee and a cheeseburger.

Finally he lifted Maggie into his arms and carried her upstairs. She snuggled against him but didn't wake as he pulled back the sheets on her bed and lowered her to the mattress. He tucked the covers around her, kissed her cheek and walked out of the room.

To his surprise, her dad was waiting at the bottom of the stairs.

"I wanted to make sure I didn't have to kick you out of the house," he said groggily, rubbing a hand across his eyes.

"No, sir," Griffin told him. "I just thought she'd sleep better in her bed than on the couch."

Jim nodded. "She had to grow up too fast after her mom died. Maggie's used to taking care of everyone else. It's not easy for her to lean on someone."

"I get that."

"It means something," Jim continued, stifling a yawn, "that she let you in tonight."

Griffin nodded, not sure how else to respond.

"Don't mess it up again," the older man told him simply.

"I'm going to try my best," Griffin promised.

Jim studied him for a long moment and then nodded. "You turned out all right, Griffin."

"Thank you, sir."

Griffin let himself out the front door, inhaling the crisp night air. For months he hadn't been able to shed the massive weight on his chest. But it suddenly vanished. He drove back to the vineyard and his room above the barn and slept better than he had in ages.

"You don't have to come out here with me," Maggie said, glancing at her sister as they drove toward Harvest Vineyards on Wednesday afternoon.

"What if Mrs. Stone is mean to you?" Morgan demanded, fiddling with the seat belt strap. "Everyone in town is talking about Trevor being a cheater. That can't make her happy."

"She's not going to be mean," Maggie said, although she wasn't exactly confident about Jana's reaction to the new revelation. Griffin had said his mom was angry with Trevor, who definitely deserved it. But it had been Maggie's choice to take the blame. She saw how wrong that was now, allowing her shame to manifest into a lie. "But I'm glad you're here. I want to spend more time with you."

Morgan gave a harsh laugh. "That should be easy since I'm grounded forever."

"Not forever," Maggie countered, turning up the winding drive. "How are things going with your friends?"

"What friends?" Morgan demanded. "I can't even text, so how am I supposed to have friends?"

"You're at school every day."

That earned an exaggerated eye roll. "Jocelyn and her crew don't exactly spend much time at school."

"Seriously?" Maggie blew out a breath. "I don't understand why you picked that group, Mo."

"It was easy," her sister admitted. "They seemed fun and cool and they let me in."

"Do you still feel that way?"

Morgan shrugged. "I take the SAT in a few weeks. I actually care about college, unlike most of them."

"I can't tell you how happy I am to hear it."

"Yeah, I know. You've been worried, but I'm okay, Maggie. I will be."

Maggie wanted to trust her sister. She loved Morgan and her independent spirit, even when it led to questionable behavior.

"Do you think Dad will unground me to go to the homecoming dance?"

"Has someone asked you?"

"No," Morgan muttered. "But if that doesn't happen, I could go with friends."

"I don't know—"

"I'm not talking about Jocelyn," Morgan interrupted. "There's a group of yearbook staff girls who are talking about going together. They don't get into trouble. You were probably one of them in high school."

"I did my time on the yearbook staff," Maggie admitted.

"Would you talk to Dad? Make a case for me?"

Maggie pulled the car to a stop in front of the tasting room and looked over at her sister. "It's hard for me to trust you. I want to but—"

"I promise, Maggie." Morgan's voice was pleading. "I'm trying to make friends with better kids but it's hard when I can't do anything."

"Fine. I'll talk to Dad."

Morgan unbuckled her seat belt and leaned over the console for a hug. "You're the best, Mags. Don't pay attention to any of the haters around here, and definitely not Grammy. You do your own thing. It's what Mom would want."

Tears sprang to Maggie's eyes and she blinked them away. "You do your own thing, too, Mo-Mo. Don't let anyone make you feel like you're not enough just the way you are." She ruffled her sister's hair, which Morgan had let fade from dyed blue back to her natural caramel color. "Especially Grammy."

They climbed out of the car and Morgan drew in a sharp breath as she looked at the restored tasting room building. "I'm still so embarrassed."

"The space is better than ever," Maggie assured her. "I think you helping with gala preparations will mean a lot to Jana."

Morgan made a noncommittal noise low in her throat.

"Plus it will help me sell the ungrounding to Dad." Maggie gave her sister an encouraging nod. "You're facing your mistakes and trying to turn things around." She draped an arm over Morgan's shoulders and led her forward. "We might be shopping for homecoming dresses in the very near future."

"What about you?" Morgan asked suddenly.

"You want me to chaperone?" Maggie grinned. "I'd be—"

"No way. I'm talking about the reunion dance. Isn't this your ten-year mark?"

Maggie dropped her arm. "Yes," she agreed slowly.

"I thought the old-school dance was a big deal for you this year."

"Um...I guess." Maggie tugged her bottom lip between her teeth. Morgan was right in theory. Each year Stonecreek High School held an alumni reunion dance the night before the homecoming football game. The event was a fund-raiser for the school and had become popular with graduates who'd stayed local or were returning for the homecoming festivities. The classes with milestone reunions made the dance the cornerstone of their celebration. "I've never gone before and wasn't planning on it this year, either."

"But you have to," Morgan argued.

Maggie laughed, trying for airy, but the sound came out more like a croak. "I didn't go to one homecoming dance in high school," she reminded her sister. "Dancing really isn't my thing."

The truth was she'd never been asked and hadn't had a group of girlfriends going without dates to join. She hadn't exactly been a social butterfly in high school. Between schoolwork, watching over a younger Morgan and Ben, and the community projects her grandmother had pushed her to volunteer for, Maggie had been way too busy for a normal teenage life. She'd wanted one, but she'd also been quiet and studious. Most of her classmates had labeled her a snob or too good for them, even though she'd never felt that way.

She'd come out of her shell during college and hoped she'd changed the town's perception of her once she'd returned to Stonecreek, despite what Jason said. But there was something about the high school, and the reunion dance in particular, that brought back all of her old insecurities.

"I bet Jason Stone will be there," Morgan said, eyes narrowed, "probably schmoozing with everyone and acting like he's so great."

Maggie pressed her fingers to her chest, which suddenly felt tight.

"Then he better not let anyone see him dance."

Maggie whirled around to find Griffin standing behind them, a smile tugging one corner of his mouth.

"Jason can't dance?" Morgan asked, grinning.

"Not unless he's taken lessons since his sister's wedding. She got hitched a few years ago in Portland. Jason looked like an uncoordinated Tasmanian devil when he hit the dance floor."

"Maggie can dance," Morgan offered. "Grammy made her take ballet classes back in the day."

"Not the same kind of dancing," Maggie muttered.

Morgan crossed her arms over her chest. "I've seen you dance. You have a surprising amount of rhythm for such a dork."

"I'm not a dork."

Griffin laughed. "Let's see those 'moves like Jagger,' Maggie May." When she only glared, he laughed harder. "Or are they moves like jaguar?" He growled and made clawing motions with his hands.

"You're a bigger dork than she is," Morgan said, pointing at Griffin.

"I'm wearing a tool belt," he pointed out, jiggling the leather encircling his waist. "I can't be considered a dork if I have a tool belt. There's some kind of rule."

"It's pretty hot."

"Eww," Morgan said, nudging her arm. "TMI for sure, Mags."

Maggie grimaced. "Sorry. I meant to think that, not say it."

Morgan plucked the seating chart out of Maggie's hands. "I'm going inside to start moving tables." She stepped in front of Griffin and her shoulders went stiff. "I need to tell you again how sorry I am, Griffin. I get that you don't have much of a reason to believe me, but I'm sorry about the tasting room and the fire and…everything."

Maggie held her breath as they both waited for his response. "Your dad told me you worked all summer to pay back some of the money he gave me for the damages."

Morgan nodded. "I couldn't cover all of it," she admitted, "but I've basically been his indentured servant for months. Every penny goes to that."

"I appreciate it," Griffin told her. "You might have heard something similar happened when I was your age."

"You and your friends were out here drinking and a cigarette caused the fire."

"Yeah," he whispered, running a hand through his hair. Maggie could tell he liked discussing his mistakes about as much as Morgan did. "I didn't stick around to make amends," he said. "That's part of why I'm back here now. It says a lot about your character that you took responsibility for what you did." He inclined his head. "Cole was willing to take the fall."

"I'd never let him do that," Morgan answered without hesitation.

"That shows character, too. I misjudged you after the fire, Morgan. I'm sorry."

"You were right about me back then," Morgan whispered and it broke Maggie's heart to see her sister wipe at her cheeks. "But I'm trying to do better."

Griffin gave her an encouraging smile. "That's all any of us can do."

"Thanks," Morgan said and headed into the tasting room.

Maggie watched her walk in and then moved toward Griffin.

"I think your sister and I are square now," he said.

Instead of answering, she placed her hands on his broad shoulders, went up on tiptoe and kissed him.

Chapter Seven

"Want some help?"

Morgan jumped at the sound of Cole's voice in the quiet space, tripping over a chair and landing on her back end on the floor.

Mortification poured through her as she scrambled to her feet. "Way to scare me half to death," she said, glaring at him as he grinned. "You think that's funny?"

"It was like you thought I was some demented clown coming after you," he said, stifling a chuckle, but not very well.

"Not the clown part," she muttered. "For sure demented."

"Sorry," he said, his voice and his gaze gentling. "Are you okay?"

Why did he have to be so darn cute that he made her heart race and all her defenses fade away? No. Morgan squeezed shut her eyes and shored up her walls. He'd pretty much told her he didn't like her. He'd given the stupid excuse of not being good enough for her. But it was only an excuse.

"I'm fine." She dusted off her palms, then winced. Turning over her hand, she noticed a small piece of wood embedded in the fleshy pad.

"What is it?" Cole took her hand before she could pull it away.

"A splinter." She tugged but he didn't let go. "I'll take care of it when I get home."

"We have a first-aid kit here," he told her, his work-roughened hand encircling her wrist. His skin was warm against hers and sent tiny sparks shooting down her spine.

"I don't need it." She yanked her arm out of his grasp and pinched the skin with her uninjured hand. It stung but the splinter didn't pop out.

"Don't be stubborn."

"I'm not stubborn."

"Afraid?"

She glanced at him sharply. His expression remained sympathetic and slightly challenging.

"No," she breathed even though she was afraid far too often. Not of a stupid splinter. But most everything else. Afraid of being alone, of not having friends, of the crowd she'd worked so hard to fit in with discovering she wasn't really as cool as she acted. Afraid of disappointing her dad and Maggie—although not Grammy. Disappointing Grammy was a given.

"Seriously, Morgan." Cole's voice was more insistent now. "You're freaking me out. Let's just take care of the splinter. Please."

"Fine," she whispered, sick of arguing for the sake of arguing.

He put a hand on the small of her back, guiding

her to the bar on one side of the tasting room. The space felt different than it had when she'd been here before, more open somehow.

"Stay here," Cole told her. "I'll be right back."

He was acting like the injury was serious and while Morgan knew a splinter was almost nothing, she couldn't help but enjoy the attention. It was the kindest he'd been to her in ages.

Maybe she should have faked a sprained ankle. That would have garnered some big-time sympathy. She swallowed back a guilty giggle at the thought. This was her turning over a new leaf, she reminded herself. Honest Morgan. Straight-as-an-arrow Morgan.

Cole returned, holding a white plastic box with red lettering. "I try to clean up the place every night, but Griffin's still working on the wall behind the bar and there's always sawdust and bits of wood flying."

"This isn't your fault." She reached for the box but he nudged her hand away.

"I've got it." He frowned, studying her. "You look pale. Do you need to sit down?"

"It's a *splinter*," she reminded him.

"Right." He took an individually wrapped antiseptic wipe from the first-aid kit, opened it and then dabbed at her palm.

She sucked in a breath at the sting.

"I'm hurting you," he whispered.

"It's fine."

He nodded, then finished cleaning the wound. He pulled tweezers from a plastic case and dabbed at the ends with the wipe. "What are you doing at the vineyard anyway?"

"Helping Maggie arrange the tables for the fundraiser this weekend."

"Your sister has been working on the event for a while. I haven't seen you in the mix before."

"I didn't really want to come back here," she admitted. "It's too embarrassing knowing I caused Griffin so much extra work."

"It was an accident," he said quietly.

"A stupid one." Morgan felt color heat her cheeks as she thought about that night and her clumsy attempts at seducing Cole. What did she know about seduction? A boy had kissed her only once in her life—Brady Rechtin in fifth grade. His teeth had clinked hers and he'd tasted like cheese puffs. Not a great memory.

"Everyone makes mistakes," Cole told her. "I'm sure Griffin understands."

"I think he does." Morgan shrugged. "So I guess it's good that I came today. I don't have to keep trying to avoid him. Plus I didn't want Maggie to be alone. Did you hear about what happened at the debate? How Jason Stone went after her so hard?"

"My brother's girlfriend was there," Cole answered. "She said Maggie freaked out and accused Trevor of cheating on her."

"It wasn't an accusation. Maggie caught him right before they were supposed to get married. That's why she walked away from the wedding."

"Harsh," Cole murmured. "You might want to look away. It's in there pretty deep, so I might have to dig around a bit."

A small groan escaped Morgan's lips. She really wished she would have waited until she got home to deal with the splinter. It felt so odd to have Cole fussing over her like this. She turned her head away from him, taking in the tasting room in its entirety.

It was cooler than she remembered from that one night. Rustic shiplap covered two of the walls while the others were painted a muted gray color. The ceilings were vaulted and a huge wrought iron chandelier made a perfect centerpiece for the airy space. Although tables filled the room, it still felt open and large. She could imagine tons of great events out here with the breathtaking view of the fields out the long bank of windows on one side.

She gritted her teeth as she felt the tweezers press against her skin but kept still. She was a lot of things but a wimp when it came to pain wasn't one of them.

"Got it," Cole said a few seconds later.

She turned back to see him holding up a short sliver of wood. "All that trouble for something so small," she said, taking the antiseptic wipe from the counter and pressing it to her palm again.

"It wasn't any trouble," he assured her, his voice warm and gentle.

She was such a sucker for gentle.

"Delilah…my brother's girlfriend," he explained, "said a couple of her friends think Maggie's just making up the business about Trevor cheating to make the Stones look bad again."

"That's not true," Morgan said, feeling her temper swell. "She'd never do something so underhanded."

"I didn't say I believed it." He put away the tweezers and snapped the box closed. "Delilah is kind of a bi—" He paused, took a breath. "She likes to gossip and can get pretty nasty."

"How are things at your house?" Morgan asked

quietly, then almost regretted the question when Cole stiffened. She knew he didn't like to talk about his family and all the trouble his dad and brother seemed to attract.

"Dad's not drinking as much lately," he said finally. "And mainly sticking to beer instead of hard liquor. That helps."

"Oh." She didn't know how to even begin responding to that.

"Sorry you asked?" He gave a harsh laugh.

"I'm not." She placed her hand on top of his and squeezed. "I'm glad things are getting better. You deserve that."

"Do I?" The notion seemed to surprise him. "What about you? How's your dad?"

"Still taking an interest in me," she said, "which is equally nice and annoying." When he gave her a pointed look, she sighed. "Okay, it's more nice than annoying. It's going pretty good, actually. Maggie said she'd help convince Dad to let me go to the homecoming dance."

He pulled his hand from hers. "So you can sneak out of it and hit the party circuit with Jocelyn and her loser group?"

"No." Morgan crossed her arms over her chest. "I just want to go the dance."

"Who's your date?" he demanded, his tone chilly. "Zach or Jonah?"

Zach and Jonah were two of the guys who ran with the wild group of juniors and seniors she pretended were her friends. Both were total meatheads and not at all potential date material as far as Morgan was concerned. She shook her head. "I wouldn't go with either of them."

"That's smart at least. Then who?"

"I don't have a date," she whispered. "No one has asked me."

"Someone will."

"I doubt it." She stepped away from the bar, glancing at the seating chart she'd taken from Maggie. She needed to act casual so Cole didn't think she was fishing for an invite. Because she wasn't. Not even a little bit. "I'll probably go with girlfriends."

"I'd ask you."

The words were spoken so quietly, Morgan wasn't even sure she'd heard them correctly.

She turned to him. "You would or you are?"

He stood on the other side of the table, staring at her like he still couldn't figure out what she was doing there.

"You already know I'm no good for you." His voice was rough and pleading, as if having this conversation was physically painful for him.

"That's not true." She gripped the edge of the table, moving it several inches to the right, needing something to distract her from the intensity of Cole's gaze. "You keep saying that, but I think it's just an excuse because you're not interested in me." She threw up her hands. "I get it, Cole. Fine. I never said I wanted you to ask me in the first place. Forget this whole conversation even happened. I'm going to find Maggie."

Swallowing back the pain from another rejection, she started for the door. Why did she keep torturing herself with a boy who was clearly not at all interested in her?

Before she took two steps, warm hands grasped her arms. Cole turned her to face him. His hands moved up until he cupped her cheeks. Then he leaned in and kissed her.

Morgan's breath caught in her throat. Although it wasn't anywhere near how she'd planned it, the kiss was the most perfect thing she'd ever experienced.

His lips were soft against hers and it felt like she was being engulfed in a tornado of butterflies. She wanted it to go on forever, but all too soon he lifted his head.

"You taste like mint gum," she murmured.

Cole tucked a strand of hair behind her ear, a half smile playing at one corner of his mouth. "Is that good?"

"Very good. Way better than cheese puffs."

His grin widened and Morgan realized she was babbling about how he tasted. She might not be super experienced, but she knew enough to understand that was not what a girl was supposed to do after a boy kissed her.

"You taste like the stars at midnight," he told her, his voice low as if he were sharing a secret.

Her heart seemed to skip a beat and she totally forgot her embarrassment. "That's not a thing."

"It's our thing," he countered and she loved the sound of that. "I know that I'm supposed to make some big production of asking, but I don't want to wait. If your dad says it's okay, will you go to homecoming with me, Morgan?"

"Yes," she whispered and then he kissed her again.

* * *

Griffin wrapped his arms around Maggie, slanting his head to deepen the kiss. As their tongues mingled, it was difficult to know where she ended and he began. He wanted to stay like this forever.

Finally she pulled away, her lips swollen and her chest rising and falling like she'd just run a marathon. From the way his heart raced in his chest, he imagined he looked much the same way.

"See how simple that was?" she asked with a laugh, and he couldn't tell whether she was talking to him or to herself.

"I was thinking more along the lines of *amazing*," he told her, "but *simple* works, too."

She laughed again.

"I missed that sound," he whispered, pulling her closer. "I missed you, Maggie May."

But before he could kiss her again, the sound of a truck engine could be heard coming up the driveway. She shifted out of his embrace, taking several steps away from him and smoothing a hand over the front of the pale gray shift dress she wore.

An older-model Chevy pulled to a stop in front of the tasting room and Thomas Helton, Harvest's cellar manager, got out. "Hey, Grif," the man called. "Marcus asked me to stop by and check the barrels they brought up here for the gala."

"No problem," Griffin shouted back, turning to Maggie as Thomas disappeared around the side of the building.

"What was that?"

She frowned. "Nothing."

"You jumped away from me like we were teenagers with your dad about to catch us in the back seat."

"Well, I don't know what this…" She waved her hand between the two of them as if fanning the flames of a bonfire. "What this is right now. Until we figure it out, I want to keep it private."

Irritation flickered along the back of his neck. "What's there to figure out?"

She chewed on her bottom lip, clearly thinking about how to answer. Overthinking, as far as Griffin was concerned. Never a good thing.

"There's going to be backlash from the debate," she said finally. "The campaign will kick into high gear in the next couple of weeks. I have the gala to get through and you're almost finished with the tasting room."

"Which means?"

"You tell me," she shot back. "The last I heard, you were heading out once the renovations were complete. You've paid your debts and all that. Has something changed?"

Yes, he wanted to shout. He'd changed. She'd changed him. But the words wouldn't form. "I don't know."

"Then we need to keep things simple," she said, almost sadly.

"Yeah," he agreed reluctantly. But his body and his heart screamed in protest. Simple was never going to be enough with Maggie, but he wasn't sure how to give more. It had been so damn long since he'd tried.

"I'm going to check on Morgan," she said after a

moment. "Thank you for coming over last night. It meant a lot to me."

"Go to the reunion dance with me," he blurted.

She stilled. "Excuse me?"

"The dance," he said slowly. "A date. You and me."

"You don't go to high school dances."

"Not in high school," he admitted. "But it's different now." He took a step closer to her. "I'm different."

"Griffin."

"Don't make me beg, Maggie." He rubbed his thumb over her bottom lip. "But I will if that's what it takes. It'll be the perfect night. You and me and some cheesy dance moves. I understand your need to keep your private life private, but it's your ten-year reunion. You have to go."

"You don't."

"I want to. I want to be with you."

She sucked in a breath, then whispered, "Okay."

"I'll get you the biggest corsage you've ever seen," he promised, unable to hide his grin.

She smiled back at him. "That might be pushing it."

"The white tux I'm already planning is pushing it." He stepped back and did a few impromptu dance moves, ending with an elaborate twirl.

"Who are you right now?" Maggie asked with a laugh.

The man trying to win your heart, he thought, but only bobbed his head again, feeling like John Travolta in his *Saturday Night Fever* days when she clapped and wolf whistled.

"Stop!" They both turned as Morgan and Cole came out of the tasting room. Morgan made a face and held up her hands to shield her eyes. "My corneas are burning," she shouted.

Cole pointed at Griffin, holding his stomach with one hand as he threw back his head and laughed. "Worst dancer ever."

"Punk kids," Griffin muttered, narrowing his eyes. "You can do better?" he asked Cole when they got closer.

"My two-year-old cousin can do better," the boy told him.

"Don't listen to them. You were great." Maggie beamed and Griffin didn't care if the whole damn world criticized his dancing. All that mattered was making her smile.

"Cole and I got the tables rearranged."

"Thank you," Maggie said, and he noticed the boy blush under her scrutiny. "We should get going," she said to Morgan. "I need to check with the florist about the centerpieces."

Morgan glanced at Cole, then gave a little wave.

He waved back, coloring a deeper shade of pink.

"I'll talk to you soon," Griffin told Maggie.

"Sure," she agreed, still grinning. "I'll have the image of you dancing in my mind for the rest of the day."

Morgan groaned.

"Lucky you," Griffin told her and watched the two sisters get into Maggie's car and drive away. "What are you smiling about?" he asked Cole when they were alone.

"I asked Morgan to homecoming."

"Nice work, buddy." Griffin gave the boy a

friendly slap on the back. "I'm taking Maggie to the reunion dance."

"Dude." Cole nudged his arm. "Right back at you."

"You own a suit?"

"Um...no. But I can—"

"We'll drive into Portland tomorrow after school. I need a tux for the gala anyway."

"You don't have to do that," Cole muttered.

"I know," Griffin agreed. "But if I offer *you* up to the salespeople, they'll hopefully ignore *me*."

"Rude."

"You dissed my dancing."

"You really suck."

"Maggie doesn't think so."

Cole snorted. "She was just being nice."

"I'll take nice," Griffin said softly and saw Cole nod.

"Me, too," the boy whispered.

Chapter Eight

"I think you should wear the black boatneck."

Maggie turned from the mirror on the back of her closet door to meet her grandmother's sharp gaze. "You look pretty," she said, pasting on a bright smile.

"That dress is suggestive," Grammy answered, ignoring the compliment. Her eyes zeroed in on the deep V of the neckline. "Are you even wearing a bra?"

"There's one built into the dress," Maggie explained, resisting the urge to roll her eyes at Grammy's disapproval. The dress was totally appropriate for the hospital fund-raiser. With no time for a shopping trip into the city, she'd ordered it online and been ridiculously pleased when it fitted. The fabric was a shimmery silver, with tiny beads sewn in intricate rows. Although it had a plunging neckline, the rest of the dress was more demure with capped sleeves and a hem that fell below her knees.

"It's scandalous for someone in your position," Vivian said, shaking her head.

"Grammy, the dress is stylish and quite conservative compared to some of them. I love it."

"Me, too," her father said, coming to stand next to Grammy in the doorway of Maggie's bedroom. "Leave her alone, Mom." He dropped a quick kiss to the top of Grammy's head, which the older woman tried to wave away. "She looks beautiful."

"Well, of course she's beautiful," Vivian said with a sniff. "She could wear a potato sack and be gorgeous. I just thought she'd want to be seen in something more modest after her most recent scandal. I don't want the haters to have any reason to talk about you, Mary Margaret."

Although couched in judgment, Maggie knew her grandmother cared about her. "I'll be fine, Grammy."

"Want me to grab a rusty knife from Dad's studio?" Ben ducked into the room between their father and grandmother. "I still haven't gotten to shank anyone."

He flopped down on the bed, arms and legs flailing like he was making a snow angel.

"You'll wrinkle your suit," Grammy warned.

"Then maybe Dad will let me change," he shot back.

"No chance." Jim tugged at his starched collar. "Misery loves company and all that."

"Who's miserable?"

Maggie heard Morgan ask the question from the hallway. Their dad stepped back to allow her sister into the room.

"Oh, my." Grammy put a hand to her chest as she stared at Morgan.

Morgan grimaced under the scrutiny. "What did I do now?"

"You look absolutely stunning," Vivian murmured. "So much like your mother."

"Um...thank you," Morgan whispered, fiddling with the material on her A-line, chiffon-lace dress in a deep midnight blue. She seemed shocked to be on the receiving end of Grammy's approval in any way.

Tears sprang to Maggie's eyes. Morgan did indeed favor their mother, with her light hair and peaches-and-cream complexion. Although it had been over a decade since their mother's death, there were times when Maggie felt the loss like a fresh wound, raw and painful.

Jim cleared his throat. "All three of my girls are gorgeous, not to mention my handsome son. That makes me a very lucky man."

"I'm hardly a girl," Vivian said with a delicate snort, if a snort could be described as delicate.

"You're a beautiful lady, then," Jim conceded.

"That's right, Grammy." Morgan wiggled her eyebrows. "You better watch the fellas tonight. Someone may try getting fresh given how hot you look."

"Don't worry," Ben added, hopping up from the bed and executing a complex series of ninja-like moves. "I can—"

"If you use the word *shank*," Grammy said, holding up a hand, "we're going to have problems, young man."

"I'll pop him in the family jewels," Ben offered instead with a cheeky grin.

Maggie laughed as Grammy rolled her eyes. As difficult as her family could be, Maggie was grateful for each one of them at the moment.

She felt far too nervous about tonight's event.

She'd kept a low profile in the past week with the excuse of needing to finalize details for the gala. But she really hadn't wanted to face the fallout from her revelation at the debate with Jason. Brenna had assured her that most people were in her corner, but Maggie wasn't convinced.

"Let's go," she told everyone, and they filed down the stairs and out to her father's Volvo station wagon.

Maggie's nerves increased as they got closer to the vineyard. They were arriving early to help with any last-minute preparations, so at least she'd be able to stay busy before the guests began to arrive.

Jana greeted them at the door of the tasting room. "This place looks even better than I imagined," she said with a smile, gesturing everyone into the building.

Maggie's breath caught as she took in the space. All of the details she'd agonized over for weeks had come together to create a magical setting. She'd chosen a scheme of autumn colors, paying tribute to both the season and the vineyard's name. The tables were covered with linens in deep shades of russet and gold, and strands of party lights had been hung above the bar, giving the space a warm glow. Light still streamed in from the picture windows onto vases arranged with sunflowers, hydrangeas and seeded eucalyptus that gave a festive look to each of the tables.

A server dressed in black offered her a glass of wine from the tray he held. "This vintage has been carefully aged in our winemaker's private cellar and opened specifically for the event," he said. She'd known Harvest had created a special label to sell tonight with the proceeds going to the hospital foundation, but she hadn't had a chance to sample it yet. She sipped the wine. The fruity flavors of ripe cherries and crushed berries exploded on her tongue.

"What do you think?" a deep voice asked from behind her.

She turned to find Griffin watching her. His gaze dipped from her face to her dress, then back up again.

"Wow," he murmured. "You take my breath away."

Pleasure bubbled up inside her at the compliment. "The space is amazing," she said. "You did such a good job."

"Thanks." He adjusted the collar of his black tux, much like her dad had earlier. "It's been a while since I climbed into a monkey suit."

"You're very handsome tonight," she said, looking at him through her lashes. His hair was combed away from his face and still damp at the ends, like he'd just showered. He was clean-shaven and filled out the tuxedo like he was auditioning for the role of a Pacific Northwest James Bond. Not that Griffin needed fancy clothes to be drop-dead gorgeous. It was a given with him. But formally dressed he looked almost out of place in Stonecreek, as if he'd just stepped out of a New York nightclub or off a movie set.

"But not as good looking as me, right?" Trevor came to stand next to Griffin, giving him a playful punch on the arm. "I mean, his tux is rented. What kind of man doesn't own his own tuxedo?"

"The kind who never wears one," Griffin ground out, clearly annoyed at his brother's intrusion.

"You look great, too," Maggie said, offering Trevor a tentative smile. They'd exchanged a few texts since she'd blurted out what he'd done, but this was her first time seeing him in person.

"It's okay, Mags," he said and leaned in to hug her. "I deserved it."

"My intention wasn't to hurt you," she said, needing him to hear the words. Needing to speak them.

Trevor nodded, but she saw Griffin's mouth thin.

"I wanted to keep my word, but Jason made me so angry. I'm—"

"Don't apologize," Griffin interrupted gruffly. "You have nothing to be sorry about." He turned to his brother. "Nothing," he repeated.

"Got it," Trevor muttered. "She also doesn't need you to defend her against me. I'm not the bad guy in this situation."

Griffin laughed without humor. "You keep telling yourself that."

"Tasting room looks great, Grif." Trevor's eyes narrowed. "When are you leaving town?" He inclined his head toward Maggie. "You know he's still planning to take off?" he asked her.

She opened her mouth, shut it again.

"Mind your own business, Trev."

"I've dedicated my career to Harvest Vineyards," Trevor shot back. "It is my business. A couple months of dipping your toes in the water around here doesn't make you committed."

Griffin glared. "Thanks for the reminder. I need to talk to Marcus." He gestured to where the CEO stood on the other side of the room, then turned and stalked away.

"Brotherly love," Trevor murmured, taking a glass

of wine from a nearby server and draining it in one gulp. "We bring out the best in one another."

Maggie could see guests beginning to arrive but she didn't move. "Does the animosity between the two of you have anything to do with me?" She colored as she asked the question. It felt ridiculous to think she had the power to have that kind of effect on either of the Stone brothers, but she couldn't help but admit they were all a part of some wonky, misshapen love triangle.

Trevor was silent for several long seconds. "I want you to be happy," he said finally. "I care about you, Mags, and I know I messed up your life pretty badly. Letting you take the fall for why we canceled the wedding was probably the worst. It was a cowardly move, and I like to think I'm better than my actions."

"You are."

He shrugged. "Apparently not. If Griffin makes you happy, I can live with that. But be careful. I know how charming my brother is. It comes easy to him. What doesn't come naturally for Grif is sticking around when things get complicated."

Maggie's mouth went dry. Griffin had admitted as much to her in the spring. She wanted to believe he'd changed. That his time in Stonecreek and the connection between them was enough to make a difference. He hadn't said the words, but she'd felt it when he'd held her...when they'd kissed.

"He's not the same as he used to be," she said, but the words rang hollow even to her own ears.

"We'll see," Trevor answered. He leaned in and brushed a kiss against her cheek. "Be happy, Mags."

She nodded, wiping under her eyes as unexpected

tears filled them. She wanted to be happy. Why did it feel like such an elusive goal? As Trevor moved away, Maggie's gaze snagged on Griffin, standing next to Marcus. He watched her with a frown and she wondered if he'd seen Trevor's friendly kiss and what it meant to him. Would they ever get past everything between them and simply focus on fostering their undeniable spark?

Grammy called to her then, and Maggie made her way to the entrance of the tasting room to help greet attendees for the night's event.

She was swept into a tide of gala business, talking to big donors and helping people find their seats. To her surprise, the few people who brought up her outburst during the debate were women. All of them seemed sympathetic to the reasons she'd chosen to hide Trevor's cheating in the first place.

It was a shock but somehow the knowledge that she'd been betrayed seemed to garner a strange kind of sympathetic connection with her. She realized that her grandmother's insistence on always presenting a perfect image in public didn't actually help Maggie. Maybe it had worked for Vivian and her generation, but in the era of social media and constant oversharing by people in the public eye, Maggie understood she'd do better just being herself.

The relief she felt realizing she could take a break from the arbitrary standards she'd set for herself was like slipping off a pair of uncomfortable heels at the end of the day. She'd always been more of a comfy shoe kind of girl anyway. It was time she stopped worrying so much about her image and started focusing on the work she wanted to get done as mayor.

She sat with her family during the dinner, happy to see that both Morgan and Ben seemed to be enjoying themselves. She hoped her younger brother held tight to his sunny disposition through his teen years. Maggie wasn't sure she could handle another recalcitrant teen, although Morgan had smiled more in the past week than she had in months. That had a lot to do with Cole, who was working as one of the busboys for the formal dinner.

"Jana tells me he's a decent kid," her dad murmured, as if reading Maggie's mind. "Your sister can't seem to stop with the cow eyes."

"I don't think they're called cow eyes anymore," Maggie told him, taking a sip of wine. "She's crushing on him."

Her dad made a noncommittal sound in the back of his throat. "And I'll crush him if he hurts her."

"Look at you being the overprotective father," Maggie said, nudging his arm.

"I'll do the same for you," he offered. "I noticed you talking to both Griffin and Trevor earlier. How was that?"

"Awkward," Maggie admitted. She leaned closer. "Speaking of noticing, you seem to be spending an awful lot of time tonight glancing in Jana Stone's direction."

"Impertinent child," her father muttered under his breath.

Maggie looked at him more closely, surprised to see that he seemed to be blushing. "Dad?"

He darted a glance at her, then trained his gaze back to his dinner plate, which appeared to hold the most fascinating piece of chicken he'd ever seen.

"Is there something between you and Griffin's mom?" Panic skittered across Maggie's neck at the thought. There were enough complications between her family and the Stones without adding one more.

"Before your engagement to Trevor, I'd barely spoken two words to Jana in the past thirty years."

Not exactly a definitive answer to her question.

"What about thirty years ago?"

"A lifetime," he whispered and stabbed at an asparagus stalk.

"Not quite. Do you have a history with her?"

He lowered his fork to the plate and sighed. "Stonecreek is a small town. I have a history with almost everyone here."

"Yes, but—"

"She's thinking of commissioning a piece for the entrance of the winery. We've been discussing ideas."

"Oh." Maggie nodded. That made more sense. "Do you have time in your schedule?" Her dad's bronze sculptures were popular, and each one took him months to complete.

"Maybe." He took a drink of wine and grimaced.

"Dad." Maggie slapped his arm, glancing around to make sure no one had seen him. "You can't make that face at the vineyard."

"Give me a cold beer any day," he told her. He put down the glass and turned fully to Maggie. "I told Jana we could talk after the election. I want to devote the next couple of weeks to you. Canvasing, making phone calls, whatever you need. Hell, I'll even make an appearance at one of your grandmother's awful Historical Society meetings if you think my presence could help."

"Thanks, Dad," Maggie whispered.

"I'm not exactly the political expert my mother is," he admitted, "but I've lived here all my life and everyone knows me. I can twist arms with the best of them."

She chuckled. "Hopefully no arm twisting will be needed, but I appreciate the support."

A hush fell over the room at that moment as Georgia Branson, the president of the hospital board, took the microphone in front of where the band had set up. "Thank you all for coming tonight," she said with a smile. "I'm so pleased to tell you we've raised sixty-five thousand dollars toward our new pediatrics wing at the hospital." There was a polite round of applause and she nodded. "I'd also like to publicly recognize the two people who have been instrumental in making this gala such a success."

She pointed toward the back of the room. "Jana Stone, your generosity in donating this beautiful location, your time and the wine is appreciated by all of us."

"Especially the wine," someone shouted and the crowed laughed.

"Maggie Spencer," Georgia continued, "your creativity, organizational skills and out-of-the-box thinking have made this the most financially successful fund-raiser we've ever had."

Maggie smiled and cupped her hands to either side of her mouth. "It was a whole committee effort," she called.

"Our esteemed mayor is too modest," Georgia told the audience. "Some of us had our doubts about a Spencer and a Stone being able to work together, but these two ladies have put aside family drama..." She tipped the wineglass she held toward Maggie, a bit of golden liquid sloshing over the side.

"Is she drunk?" Grammy hissed from across the table.

"I mean, who would have guessed Mary Margaret Spencer was such a drama queen?" Georgia tittered and then took a long swig of wine.

"Add her to the shanking list," Ben said.

"Stone for mayor," a feminine voice called from a nearby table. Maggie was pretty sure she recognized Emily Stone, Jason's wife, as the heckler.

"Shank her, too," Grammy told Ben.

Maggie felt like her cheeks might crack as Georgia waggled a finger toward the guests, more wine spilling over the side of the glass. "No politics tonight," she cautioned. "We're all here for one goal. Maggie has done a great job of getting us to that goal, despite her mess of a personal life."

Maggie sucked in a breath and felt her father squeeze her numb fingers. She looked down at where their hands were joined and was enormously grateful for the contact. Her smile remained frozen in place and her cheeks burned from the weight of the stares she could feel pointed in her direction.

Suddenly there was feedback coming from the speakers and she heard a faint grunt.

"Okay, then, folks." She glanced up to see Griffin holding the mic as Trevor led a frowning Georgia toward the edge of the room. "That was a...uh... spirited speech by our hospital board president and a great reminder that while Harvest Vineyards makes fantastic wines, enjoy them in moderation."

A few laughs greeted his words.

She could see his chest rising and falling as the room quieted once again. Griffin might have grown up in Stonecreek, but she knew he still felt like an outsider, even at the vineyard. Making himself the center of attention wasn't easy, and the fact that he was doing it for her made her heart skip a beat.

"Seriously, though," he continued, as if realizing he hadn't quite adequately defused the situation, "both Maggie and my mom have gone above and beyond for tonight." Another round of applause. He nodded, then said, "This night is particularly special to me because it marks the unofficial reopening of the Harvest Vineyards tasting room." More clapping. "Thank you. This building was special to my dad and, as most of you know, he and I didn't always have the closest relationship when I was a kid." He held the microphone closer and leaned forward, as if imparting a great secret. "Mainly because I was such an idiot."

"We love you," Jana called from the back of the room.

Griffin smiled. "Thanks, Mom. Thanks for giving me a chance to make things right here. I don't know what Dad would have thought of this, but I hope it would have made him as happy as it's made me."

He looked toward the members of the band. "It's time to let these guys do their thing, and I hope you all are wearing your dancing shoes. Although I've been told recently that I'm not exactly Fred Astaire, I'm going to kick things off." He took several steps forward and Maggie's breath caught as he pointed to her. "Maggie Spencer, may I have this dance?"

Once again she could feel all eyes on her, only this time it was easier to ignore whatever curiosity or judgment might be coming her way and focus on Griffin. It felt as if he was aligning himself with her, publicly claiming her for all to see.

Her heart soared as she stood and walked toward him. And when she slipped her hand into his, it felt like coming home.

Chapter Nine

Griffin blew out a breath as he handed the microphone to the bandleader. The strains of a Frank Sinatra song began and he pulled Maggie into his arms. For a brief, terrifying moment, he'd thought she might refuse to dance with him.

"So much for keeping things private," she whispered, smiling up at him.

"Are you mad?" He glanced around, relieved to see other couples joining them on the dance floor.

Her hand curled around the back of his neck, some of the tension easing at her gentle touch.

"I think this is another case of you rescuing me," she told him. "Now instead of people talking about my messy personal life, they can speculate on what's going on between the two of us."

"You don't need rescuing," he assured her, "and I'm done with guessing games." He leaned in and brushed his lips over hers.

She tensed and he thought she might pull away.

"Don't go," he pleaded.

"Everyone is watching."

"Let them." He splayed his hand over her back. "You're beautiful tonight, Maggie. You're also smart and funny and dedicated to this town. I get that. I also understand what's at stake for you in the next couple of weeks. But I want to be a part of your life for real, not just sneaking around when no one is looking."

"But you said—"

"Forget what I said. How I feel about you is simple. I care, more than I have for anything or anyone in a long time."

"Griffin."

"All the other stuff isn't going away. I get that. This is what matters to me. I'm not going to stand by and let people take cheap shots at you. I know you can handle it. You're stronger than most people know. But I don't want you to have to handle it alone."

She stared at him for several seconds, like she was searching for something…some kind of answer. "Okay," she said finally.

He blew out a breath and grinned. "See how simple that was?"

"Simple," she agreed and rested her head against his shoulder as they danced.

Griffin closed his eyes and swayed to the music, reveling in the feel of Maggie in his arms. It was a shockingly liberating feeling to have claimed her so publicly. Maybe tomorrow would bring real life crashing back in, but for now this was all he needed.

As the music ended, he took her hand and led her through the crowd, nodding and smiling to the people who offered words of encouragement. Support he'd take and the rest of the town could go to… Well, he had plenty of experience ignoring people who didn't support him.

The night was crisp and clear as they stepped out into it and he drew in a deep breath, feeling the band around his chest loosen now that they were away from the curious eyes of the town.

"That was intense," she said, pressing a hand to her cheek.

"Are you okay?"

She nodded. "It's strange. For years I've been in the public eye in Stonecreek. Even as a kid, my grandmother loved to trot us out for ribbon cuttings and town events, living proof of her place in the community. I don't remember how my mom felt about it, but I know Dad hated it. Morgan, too. And Ben was too little and easygoing to care. I was the one who made the effort to be the person she wanted people to see." In the moonlight she could see his brows furrow. "It was never really me. I think walking away from the wedding was the first thing I've ever done just because I wanted to."

"I'm glad you walked away," he said, unable to pretend he felt any different.

She glanced over her shoulder and flashed the faintest wisp of a smile. "Me, too, but it changed everything. I don't want to go back to being the well-behaved puppet I was before that, but discovering who I want to be now isn't the easiest thing to do in the middle of an election."

"You've said before that you followed in your grandmother's footsteps because it was expected. You were the chosen one in your family." He moved closer, reaching out and trailing one finger against her bare arm. "Is being the mayor really want you want, Maggie?"

"I want to make a difference in this community," she said, which wasn't exactly an answer to the question. "I love this town."

"There's a whole big world out there that you won't see if you're stuck here."

A shiver passed through her and she turned to face him. "I don't think of it as stuck. Do you?"

He shook his head. "Not anymore."

That answer seemed to please her because she moved forward and wound her arms around his waist. "Thank you for asking me to dance tonight."

He chuckled and kissed the tip of her nose. "Thank you for saying yes."

Voices filtered out into the darkness and he shifted so they were more fully in the shadows.

"That was well worth a check to the hospital," a male voice said, and Griffin felt Maggie stiffen in his arms.

"Vivian could only keep that girl under her thumb for so long," a woman answered. "It's about time the Spencers learned that they're human just like the rest of us."

"Seems like our oh-so-perfect mayor is not only human but also damned hot after those Stone boys. If she can't hang on to one, she'll settle for the other."

Griffin took a step forward, but Maggie held him back. "Don't," she whispered. "They aren't worth it."

He growled low in his throat instead of answering because the words he wanted to say would have made his army buddies blush. Closing his eyes, he dipped his chin until it rested on the top of Maggie's head.

He breathed in her fresh scent and flowery shampoo like it would calm him.

Car doors shut and a moment later an engine roared to life and he glanced out to see brake lights disappear down the winding drive.

"What's wrong with people?" he asked.

She shook her head. "They're petty and insensitive. But not all of them."

"Enough of them to make me want to be a hermit," he told her, smoothing the hair away from her face. "I'm sorry you had to hear that."

"No apologies." She placed a finger on his lips. "Remember?"

"Do you want to go back in?"

She shook her head. "You heard the donors. The event is a success. My work here is done."

"What about your family?"

She sighed. "I guess—"

"Maggie?" Morgan walked toward them from the entrance.

"Hey, Mo-Mo." Maggie stepped away from Griffin. "Did you need me?"

"I saw you two sneak out," the girl said, "and I thought you might need this." She held up a small black clutch.

"My purse." Maggie took it, then hugged her sister. "How's it going in there?"

"Old people dancing," Morgan reported, then glanced toward Griffin. "Some of them worse than you, which is pretty bad."

"You never even saw my best moves," he told the girl.

"Lucky me," she said with a laugh, then turned

to Maggie. "I guess you're not coming back to the party?"

"Can you tell Dad and Grammy?" Maggie asked.

Morgan nodded. "I think Mrs. Branson is already puking in the bathroom. She's going to feel real bad about her speech, especially after Grammy gets through with her."

"I can't say I feel that bad for her," Maggie said with a sniff.

"I like this new you." Morgan stepped away from Maggie with a grin. "You're all *Kill Bill* tough."

"Let's not go too far," Maggie answered and hugged the girl again.

When Morgan returned to the tasting room, Maggie held up her purse. "I'm all yours," she whispered.

"And well worth the wait," he told her, lacing his fingers with hers. "I walked over from the barn." He glanced at her strappy heels and made a face. "Do you want me to get the car and pick you up?"

She bent, pulled off her shoes and held them up as they dangled from two fingers. "I'm ready."

"Then let's make a quick trade." Griffin shrugged out of his tux jacket, draped it over Maggie's shoulders, then took the shoes from her. "I'll hold these and you stay warm in that."

He took her hand again and they made their way across the expanse of lawn that led to the barn and upstairs apartment.

"It's so peaceful out here," Maggie murmured, pausing to glance up. "The stars never cease to amaze me."

"I feel the same way about you," he said and drew her close, unable to resist kissing her again. The need and desire he'd tamped down these past few months roared to life. It was all he could do not to pull her down to the grass and strip off that sexy-as-hell dress to reveal every inch of her.

A breeze kicked up and he felt her shiver, even within the warmth of his jacket. "Inside," he told her and they almost ran the rest of the way to the barn and his apartment above.

As soon as Maggie was up the steps, Griffin lifted her into his arms, pressing her back to the wall next to the door. He fused his mouth to hers, hoping to tell her everything he still couldn't put into words. Things he barely understood about his heart and how it felt like she'd brought it back to life.

Her fingers tangled in his hair as he trailed kisses along her jaw, down her throat and then across her collarbone, tugging the delicate fabric of her dress off her shoulders. But before it fell completely, he lifted his head, his gaze zeroing in on the pale skin revealed at the center of the dress's deep V-neck.

"Did you pick this outfit just to make me crazy?" he asked gruffly.

She breathed out a husky laugh. "No, although I hoped you'd like it."

"I'm obsessed," he admitted, "with everything it revealed and the promise of what was hidden." He bent his head and licked the skin between her breasts. "I imagined kissing you here all damn night."

She moaned and pushed her head back against the wall. "Anywhere else?"

He laughed. "Oh, yes." He tugged the dress down her arms, leaving her naked from the waist up. Then he sucked one taut nipple into his mouth, making her moan again.

"More," she whispered, and he loved her willingness to take command of the moment. Of him. He kissed and nipped and sucked first one breast, then the other, wondering if he'd ever get enough of the taste and feel of her.

Her hands went to his shoulders, kneading the tight muscles there. He straightened, yanking on his bow tie. "I need you to touch me," he said as he undid the buttons of his crisp white shirt.

"I like the sound of that," she told him with a saucy smile. She shimmied out of her dress, the fabric pooling at her feet and leaving her in nothing but a pair of black lace panties.

"Going to kill me," he managed to rasp through gritted teeth, his fingers fumbling on the button of his tailored slacks, "in the best way possible."

Maggie looked up at him through her lashes. "I haven't even done anything yet."

"My point exactly." When he'd stripped down to only his boxers, he picked her up, groaning with pleasure as her legs wrapped around his waist. Her hot center pressed against his erection, sending desire rocketing through him.

"I've missed you," he said against her mouth, moving toward the bed that sat against one wall. The apartment was, in essence, a studio—a loft-type room with a small kitchen in one corner, a couch and television situated a few feet away. The bed was at the far end of the space on the opposite wall.

It wasn't exactly impressive and for the first time Griffin thought about renting his own place in town, much like Trevor did. Or buying a house. He stumbled a step, then righted himself.

"You okay?" Maggie asked, cupping his cheeks between her warm palms.

"Yeah," he whispered and kissed her again. One thing at a time, he reminded himself.

This moment—here with her—needed to be his only focus.

Not hard to do as he laid her down on the bed, stretched out across his sheets, her thick hair fanning over his pillow like he'd imagined so many times in his fantasies.

He shoved his boxers down over his hips, then leaned over her to hook his fingers in the waistband of that amazing black lace. One side of her mouth curved up and her gaze darkened, as if she liked watching him strip her down.

It was the most erotic moment of his life, his breath coming out in short pants, and there was so much more. It was difficult to believe this beautiful, intelligent, caring woman had chosen him...had risked her reputation for him. Griffin didn't know how to tell her what it meant to him, but he damn well planned to spend all night showing her.

He opened the nightstand drawer and pulled out a condom packet.

"Let me," she whispered and took it from his hands. A moment later her fingers moved down the length of him and Griffin sucked in a harsh breath.

"Killing me," he repeated, then moved over her on the bed. He claimed her mouth at the same time he drove into her in one long thrust, and he wondered how he'd ever been able to walk away from this woman. She was everything.

It was funny to Maggie that Griffin kept talking about death, because to her being in his arms, in his bed—the moment so intimate it felt as though they were one—was like coming alive in a whole new way.

Yes, she'd been with him months before and it had been amazing. But this—now—was different. She was different and Griffin... Something had changed in him, making hope spring to life inside her.

Her body tingled from head to toe as pressure built through her body. With each thrust, each kiss, passion wound around her until she was consumed by it. He whispered her name between kisses and she moaned low in her throat when he reached between them to touch her.

It was too much and everything she'd ever imagined all at once. Desire spiraled and then splintered, sending shock waves of pleasure through every cell. A few seconds later Griffin stiffened, then moaned his release, and she wrapped her arms more tightly around him, loving the gift of sharing this moment.

Loving him, although she understood at some intrinsic level that it was too soon to utter the words.

So she concentrated on breathing normally and smoothed the hair away from his forehead, beaded with sweat from his exertion. He levered himself up on his elbows, cool air rushing across her skin as he stared down at her.

"Amazing," he whispered, his gaze intense on

hers, and Maggie was grateful he felt the same way she did.

Then disappointment snaked around her gut, not at him but herself. What did it say about her that she was grateful a man thought she was decent in bed? Not much, unfortunately.

"What?" he asked, one finger skimming over the line she knew had formed between her eyes. "Tell me that was good for you."

She frowned harder at his words. "Are you joking? You have to know how good you are. I can't imagine you've made it this far without hearing it at least a thousand times."

He shifted so he was next to her on the bed, propped up on an elbow. "A thousand may be pushing it," he said with a grimace. "Besides that, what happened between us wasn't just me, Maggie. It was you, too. Both of us together. I know enough to understand how special our chemistry is. Don't you?"

"Yes," she said softly. Chemistry. Physical chemistry. Was that what he thought made this so mindblowing?

"Did I do something wrong?" he asked. "It feels like something shifted between us just now and not for the better."

She shook her head, leaned in and kissed him. "Of course not. You did everything right. More right than I realized was possible."

"Good. I'll be right back." He rolled away from her, grabbed his boxers and headed toward the far end of the studio apartment. She could see the bathroom through an open door. He closed it and she heard the sound of running water.

She stretched across the bed and reached down to grab a discarded T-shirt, pulling it over her head and then snuggling into the covers. She felt surrounded by Griffin in this bed, enveloped in his scent, her body still warm and pliant from the pleasure he'd given her. But the dull ache in her chest wouldn't ease. Fear and doubt crept in and tried to crowd out everything good about this moment.

As Griffin returned to the bed, Maggie did her best to put all of that aside. Everyone wore a mask, she told herself, and it was dangerous to let him see what was behind hers. She'd played a role for so long, how could she stop now?

"Oh, great," he murmured, wrapping his arms around her and pulling her to his chest. "You're dressed."

She snorted. Unladylike and probably the opposite of what a man wanted to hear from a woman in his bed, but she couldn't help it. "What's that supposed to mean?"

"Well, for one..." His big hands skimmed along her waist and hips, then moved under the shirt. "The sight of you in my shirt is beyond sexy." He kissed her and even though she'd thought her body completely satisfied, need and desire rose to the surface once again. "And two, I've decided my new favorite hobby is undressing you." He shifted her, gently prodding her legs open. "Now I get another chance."

She made a little noise of satisfaction, which seemed to be exactly the reaction he wanted. Within minutes they were both naked and sweaty again, and Maggie buried her fears and doubts under the satisfaction she found in Griffin's arms.

Chapter Ten

The scent of freshly brewed coffee woke Maggie the next morning. She blinked and pushed the hair out of her face, glancing at the unfamiliar ceiling above her.

"This is why I need more than one room. Sorry I woke you."

She sat up at the sound of Griffin's voice, pulling the covers with her.

"I'm naked," she whispered, then clasped a hand over her mouth when a strangled giggle escaped.

"Which is funny because?" Griffin asked the question as he approached the bed, holding out a mug of steaming coffee to her. He wore a Harvest Vineyards T-shirt and low-slung basketball shorts. His dark hair was tousled and a rough shadow covered his jaw. It was difficult to believe he could be hotter than he'd looked in the tux—or in his birthday suit for that matter—but Maggie thought he'd never been more handsome than at this moment.

Maybe it was the affection in his eyes as he looked at her. "Well?" he prompted.

She shrugged, reaching for the coffee with one

hand and using the other to keep the sheet tightly clasped above her breasts. "I don't sleep naked," she said with another giggle.

"As I remember," he told her, sitting on the edge of the bed, "there wasn't a lot of sleeping."

"Right." Maggie sipped from the coffee mug, then glanced at the clock. "I should go. It's bad enough I'm going to be doing the walk of shame into my dad's house. I don't want to be out here if anyone stops by." She rolled her eyes. "Like your mother."

Griffin leaned in and kissed her. He tasted of coffee and toothpaste and her body immediately heated. "No shame, although you're motivating me to get my own place."

"Me, too." She sighed and rested her forehead against his. "I wish we could stay in bed all day."

"That's the best idea I've heard in ages."

She shifted away when he moved closer. "Don't tempt me."

"That's what I'm here for," he told her with a laugh.

"But now you have to turn away," she said, shoving at his chest. "I need to get dressed."

"A reverse striptease." One thick brow lifted. "Sounds intriguing."

"No way." She placed the mug on the nightstand. "Thank you again for last night."

"Which part?" He tapped a finger on his chin, as if in deep contemplation mode. "When you were on to—"

"Defusing the situation at the fund-raiser. You rescued me."

He shook his head. "I've already told you I'm not

the hero type, and you're strong enough that you don't need rescuing. But I'm happy to be in your corner. Always."

"I love you," she whispered without thinking, then wished the floor would swallow her up. "I'm sorry," she added immediately. "I didn't mean it." She pressed a hand to her flaming cheek. "Well, I meant it, but I didn't mean to say it out loud. Not now. You don't have to say anything back. It's too much—"

"No apologies." Griffin leaned in for a soft kiss, then lifted his head to look at her. "You are the best thing that's happened to me in a long time, Maggie."

She returned his smile, although a sharp twinge lanced her heart when he didn't say those three words back. But he'd claimed her at the gala, in front of both their families and most of the town. That counted for something. A lot.

"I'll go start the car," he told her as he straightened. "But next time I'm holding you hostage in bed all day."

She rubbed at her chest when he walked away, then quickly got dressed. The words she'd uttered and his reaction to them replayed over and over in her mind. Was she confusing great sex with true emotion?

No.

She wouldn't believe that. Even if Griffin couldn't say the words yet, she knew he cared about her. She believed it was even more than that. It had to be. Their connection was too strong for any other explanation.

They talked about inconsequential things as he drove her to her father's house. Normally she loved their easy banter, but this morning it felt stilted, like they were filling the silence to avoid her premature declaration.

She forced another smile when he pulled to a stop at the curb.

"I'll call you later," he told her, leaning over the center console for one last kiss.

"Okay," she whispered and let herself out of the car, hurrying up the front walk in the soft light of morning. The street was empty and she said a silent prayer that none of her dad's neighbors were glancing out their windows this early.

The house remained quiet and she managed a quick shower and change of clothes before anyone woke. Her father was in the kitchen when she came back down the stairs.

"Late night?" he asked, raising a brow.

"Yeah," she agreed, reaching for the coffeepot. "You know how it goes."

He gave a noncommittal grunt in response. "I didn't see you at the event after the first dance."

"I slipped out for some air," she told him. "It got a little intense."

"I'm sure you'll be receiving a call from Georgia as soon as she remembers—"

"It's fine," Maggie lied. "At some point this town will get sick of talking about me."

"You're a Spencer," her dad said with a humorless laugh. "I doubt it."

"You manage to stay off the radar."

"Look at what it cost me." He pressed his hands to the counter. "I relied on your mother to do most of the heavy lifting as far as parenting, and when she died, a lot of that responsibility transferred to you. I didn't know how to deal with life in this town other than to hole up in my studio."

"You did the best you could," she told him.

"Which was pretty inadequate."

"Dad."

"I know." He shrugged. "I'm trying to do better. In the spirit of my more active dad role…" He picked up a flyer from the counter and held it out to her. "We're having a family fun day today."

"The pumpkin patch," she murmured, taking the slip of paper from him.

"It's got a corn maze, too," he said with a nod.

"I'm not going through a corn maze," Morgan announced as she came into the kitchen. "It freaks me out."

"Scaredy-cat," Ben said, following on her heels.

"You're both going," Jim announced, pointing between the two of them. "And you're going to like it. We're bonding."

Maggie thought about adding her two cents about how he was a decade too late for this kind of forced family fun, but at the hopeful, almost pleading look her father shot her, she couldn't manage it.

"The pumpkin farm is outside Corvallis," she told her brother and sister. "We can have breakfast at Annie's Cafe on the way."

"Seriously?" Morgan asked with an eye roll. "You think this is a good idea?"

"Sure." Maggie forced a cheery tone. "It will be a new family tradition."

Morgan snorted. "It's a little late for traditions."

"It's never too late," Maggie said with more confidence than she felt.

"And no cell phones," their father announced, earning disbelieving sounds of protest from each of them. "No arguments. We're going old-school like your old man."

"You'll survive," Maggie said, feeling like she needed to support her dad when he was trying so hard. "Cell phones in the basket on the table. You'll be reunited with them again when we're back home. Go get dressed. We leave in fifteen minutes."

Both Morgan and Ben grumbled but dutifully placed their cell phones into the wicker basket in the center of the table that held mail and other odds and ends from their daily lives.

"I'm going to change into sneakers," Maggie told her dad. "Then I'll be ready."

"Cell phone," he responded.

"Oh." She frowned, pulling the device from her back pocket. "I was hoping you didn't actually mean me."

"I mean all of us." He plucked his from the counter and put it with the others.

Maggie's fingers tightened around hers. "I'm in the middle of a campaign, Dad."

"It's Sunday."

She fidgeted under his stare. "I have to follow up with some things from last night."

"They'll wait," he said calmly.

Maggie sighed, then gingerly placed her phone on top of the others. "You're not joking about this family bonding stuff."

"It's as strange for me as it is for you," he assured

her. Then he wrapped an arm around her shoulder for a quick hug. "Getting away will be good for all of us. We need a break."

She couldn't argue so she reached up and kissed his cheek. "My goal for the day is to beat Ben through the corn maze."

He laughed. "Good luck with that."

Maggie not only failed to beat her brother through the corn maze, she'd gotten so lost that Ben had to retrieve her. She might never live down her lack of direction, but the laughs were worth the grief she took.

The day had been perfect. With no real-life distractions, the four of them had fun as a family. They took turns trading stories of Halloweens past and all the last-minute costumes Jim had put together for them.

Planning was definitely not his strong suit, although the spontaneous family outing—even though it seemed a little late in coming—had to be one of his better ideas.

They'd stopped for breakfast at one of Maggie's favorite diners on the way, then ate hot dogs and roasted s'mores over the bonfire at the pumpkin patch. There were farm animals to pet and a hayride, and Maggie had as much fun as any of the little kids milling about. Sipping apple cider, she watched the families with young children, imagining what it would be like to someday bring her own sons or daughters to the pumpkin patch. She imagined a little boy with big green eyes and rumpled hair, then sucked in a breath, choking on the juice.

Griffin hadn't even been able to say he loved her

back and already she was imagining kids who looked like him. She needed to slow down in a big way.

She concentrated on the moment and her family. The ride home in the golden light of the fall afternoon was picturesque, and it felt like weeks' worth of emotional baggage had been lifted from her shoulders.

Until they pulled up to the house.

"What's Grammy's car doing here?" Ben asked warily.

Morgan groaned. "She's on the porch waiting for us."

Maggie's stomach lurched. "I have a feeling she's waiting for me."

"I'm sure she hasn't been here long," her father said, reaching over to pat her leg. "The timing is probably a coincidence."

"We could keep driving," Morgan suggested in an overly bright tone.

"It's fine, Mo-Mo." He parked next to the white Lexus in the driveway and Vivian was already halfway across the yard by the time Maggie climbed out of the front seat.

"Where have you been?" She pointed at Maggie. "Why are none of you picking up your phones?"

"We went to a pumpkin patch," Jim said with a smile, coming to stand next to Maggie. "And left our phones at the house. Come to think of it, I should have asked you to join us on the outing. We got an extra pumpkin so you can come over for carving later this—"

"Did you know about it?" Grammy demanded,

coming to stand in front of Maggie, eyes blazing. "Did Griffin tell you first?"

"Tell me what?" Maggie forced her features to remain even.

"The planned expansion at Harvest," her grandmother said through clenched teeth. "A boutique inn and reception hall. It's a full-out assault on the Miriam Inn and our events center. They're trying to cripple our business. They're out to ruin us."

"Mom," Jim said calmly, "let's go in the house and discuss this. I'm sure it isn't as bad as you're making it seem."

"Did you know?" Vivian repeated the question to Maggie.

"No," Maggie admitted. "I have no idea what you're talking about."

Grammy studied her for several long seconds, then finally nodded. "At least you haven't betrayed me completely, despite some of the questionable decisions you've been making in town recently."

Maggie swallowed, licked her dry lips. "I've been trying to do what's right for the community," she argued, hating that her voice trembled. "The whole community."

Vivian sniffed. "You need to remember on which side your bread is buttered, young lady."

"I never understood that saying," Jim murmured.

"Grammy, don't threaten Maggie." Morgan crossed her arms over her chest and took a step forward.

"No sass from you." Grammy's focus switched to her younger granddaughter. "You're a child. You don't understand the workings of Stonecreek the way I do." She threw up her hands. "None of you get it. I've devoted my whole life to this town...to this family."

"We know that, Mom," Jim said quietly. "We appreciate everything you've done but—"

"They're trying to usurp our position," Grammy said, her voice cracking. She looked away like she needed a moment to compose herself. "I promised my father that I'd make him proud." Her gaze swung back to Maggie. "He hated that I wasn't a boy. He thought I'd never make anything of myself because I was too weak." She wiped hard at her cheeks. "But I showed him. I married your granddad and with the Spencer family's backing, the Miriam became far more than it had ever been with my father running it. I made him proud, although he was hard-pressed to admit it until the day he died."

She looked at each of them. "I won't have all of our success—my accomplishments—undone by that family of upstarts. People who forget their place."

"Grammy." Maggie placed a gentle hand on her grandmother's thin shoulder. "Everyone knows how much you've done for Stonecreek, but things aren't like they used to be. I'm sure the plan at Harvest Vineyards isn't going to ruin your business."

Vivian narrowed her eyes. "We'll be second-rate." Her chin trembled. "I'll be second-rate. Just like my father always told me."

Maggie's chest ached at the pain in her grandmother's tone.

"Mom, come in the house," Jim urged gently. "Let's talk about this. It can't be as bad as you—"

"I have to go," Vivian said with a sniff, unwilling to make eye contact with any of them. As if she was embarrassed about the tiny cracks of vulnerability in her steely tough-as-nails armor. "I have a meeting with Steve Brage from the zoning board. He owes me. Maggie, I'll call you at the office tomorrow. This is town and family business. We need to make a plan."

She stalked to her car, climbed in and drove away without a backward glance.

"That was intense," Ben said, kicking at the grass.

"I've never seen Grammy like that," Morgan added. "It's almost like she was human for a few minutes."

Their father shook his head. "Of course your grandmother is human."

"Can we have our phones back now?" Ben asked, displaying the typical empathy and focus of a teenage boy.

"Sure," Jim agreed and both Ben and Morgan took off for the house.

"I bet I missed more snaps than you," Ben said to his sister.

"In your dreams," Morgan shot back.

"You knew nothing about the plans at Harvest?" Maggie's father asked when they were alone in the front yard.

She shook her head. "Did you know Grammy had that relationship with her dad?"

"No," Jim admitted. "She's always been a force of nature, but I thought it was just family pride. My grandparents died when I was a kid, and she seemed more interested in the Spencer legacy than my dad was. I never questioned why that was."

"I need to talk to Griffin," Maggie murmured almost more to herself than her father. "I can't believe he wouldn't have shared those plans with me."

"It could be a game changer." Her dad ran a hand through his hair. "Not that I think it's as dramatic as your grandmother makes it out to be, but it will lessen the control she has over local businesses and she hates losing control."

"I know," Maggie agreed, then gave her dad a hug. "Coming home to this mess makes me even more grateful for today. Thanks, Dad."

"What the hell is this about?"

Jana, Marcus and Trevor turned in unison as Griffin stormed into the conference room in the winery's office early Monday morning.

"You're late," Trevor muttered. "As usual."

Jana sent her younger son a withering look. "Sit down, Griffin. We're just getting started."

Griffin slammed the business section from *The Portland Chronicle* onto the oak table. "Is this a joke?" He jabbed a finger at the headline Stonecreek Winery Expands Empire. "Why didn't I know about this?"

"None of us did," Marcus said tightly, his mouth set in a thin line.

"Well, I did," Trevor offered. "I wrote the press release, after all."

"This is going to directly impact the Spencers' business interests in town. You know how Vivian thinks. She'll take it as a personal attack. Are you trying to start a war with them?"

Trevor snorted. "Don't be a drama queen, Grif. This is business."

"Bad business," Griffin said, meeting his mother's worried gaze. "This came as a shock to you?"

Her brow wrinkling, she looked away with a sigh. "Not completely. We'd discussed the possibility of building a venue on the property." She held up one finger when Trevor opened his mouth to speak. "But nothing had been decided. The plan had been to meet with the Spencers and some of the other business owners in town to determine how we could complement what was already established downtown."

"My opinion," Marcus said, drumming his fingers against the table, "was that Harvest Vineyards should continue to focus on what we do best." He leveled a stony look at Trevor. "Which is making wine."

"This is about expanding the brand," Trevor argued. "And in the end, selling more wine. It's a win for all of us." He glanced at Griffin. "Except maybe those of us needing to suck up to Vivian Spencer."

"I'm not sucking up to anyone," Griffin said through clenched teeth. He paced to the far side of the room where a window framed a view of the rows of vines below. "Stonecreek is a small town and—"

"Yeah," Trevor interrupted. "We live here, Grif. None of the rest of us has the luxury of just dropping in when it suits our fancy."

"No one forced you to come back here after college." Griffin whirled around. "You made that choice all on your own."

Trevor lifted one brow. "Did I?"

Their mother rose from her chair. "Stop arguing. Both of you." She inclined her head toward Griffin. "Your brother is well aware of the vineyard's place in this community." Her gaze switched to Trevor. "You should also be aware that although you have quite a bit of autonomy in leading the marketing and branding efforts for Harvest, this is not a dictatorship. I remain sole owner of the business and Marcus is CEO."

"For now," Marcus murmured.

Griffin felt his mouth drop open at those two words. Trevor looked equally stunned, but their mother only sighed.

"Please sit down, Griffin. We have a lot to discuss."

"Are you leaving Harvest?" Trevor asked Marcus.

"We'll get to that in a minute," Jana said in the tone she'd relied on when the boys were young to put a quick end to any back talk. "Sit, Griffin."

He dropped into a seat like a puppy following the command of his human in obedience class.

His mom reached across the table and pulled the newspaper toward her. "Trevor, the next time you create a press release for the vineyard, send it through me first."

"Mom, come on. I'm not a kid."

She lifted her gaze and stared icily at him. "Then don't act like one. We'd talked about an event center that would enhance what was already available in town, not compete with it."

"I'm sick of kowtowing to the Spencers," Trevor complained. "I understood the reasoning while I was dating Maggie, but there's no connection to them now."

Trevor threw a glance toward Griffin, as if daring him to speak. Clearly, Trevor's moment of wanting Maggie to be happy had passed like a fleeting sunset.

"We have a connection," Jana said before Griffin

could respond. "This town is our connection. Our history is the connection. I won't have you using the vineyard as a way to work out personal vendettas."

"I'm not doing that," Trevor insisted. "It's good business."

"Not your call to make," Jana said simply. "As Marcus alluded to, he's decided to step back from some of his responsibilities at Harvest. He's agreed to stay on in a consulting role but as of the first of the year, he'll no longer be our CEO."

"Why?" Griffin demanded. "You love this place."

"I do," Marcus agreed. "But now I have something in my life I love more. I want time to devote to Brenna and Ellie."

Griffin shook his head. "How can it be that serious? You just started dating her a few months ago."

"I let my professional aspirations derail my personal life once before." Marcus sat back in his chair, leveling an almost challenging look toward Griffin. "I'm smarter than that now."

"Who gets the job?" Trevor asked, leaning forward.

"That's what we're here to discuss," Jana said, her voice giving away nothing. "You can see why your premature announcement comes at a difficult time, Trevor."

"That doesn't change anything." Trevor crossed his arms over his chest. "I should be the next CEO, of course."

"You've done so much for the brand," Jana agreed, "but whoever takes over needs to be able to juggle the various facets of the business."

"I can do that," Trevor told her.

"But do you truly want to?" Jana asked. "Is Harvest in your heart?"

Griffin's chest constricted at her words. Despite Marcus's encouragement, he hadn't really believed he had a place at the vineyard. Not after everything that had happened with his father and how he'd reacted. It was difficult to believe anyone would give him a chance to prove he deserved a place in the family business. But the vines were in his heart. He knew that without a doubt.

He glanced at his brother, surprised to see color tingeing Trevor's cheeks as he stared at his mother, hands clenched into tight fists on top of the table. "How can you ask me that?" he demanded. "I've made this place my life. I came back to Stonecreek, the way Dad expected. I gave up everything for him."

"I know, sweetie," Jana said gently. "Everyone knows."

Wait. What? Griffin didn't know. He could feel the undercurrent of tension at the table but had no idea where it came from. Trevor had everything Griffin had ever wanted—especially their late father's love and approval. What was his damn problem?

He met his brother's icy glare across the table. It felt as if Trevor blamed Griffin for whatever was going south right now. Impossible because Griffin hadn't been a part of any of it.

"I earned my shot," Trevor said, enunciating each word, launching them like rockets toward each person in the room. Before anyone could respond, he pushed back his chair and stalked away, slamming the door behind them.

Griffin looked between his mother and Marcus,

who exchanged worried glances with each other. "Let me repeat my original question," he said when neither of them spoke. "What the hell is this about?"

"We want you to take over the vineyard." Marcus steepled his hands and leaned forward, his warm brown eyes intense on Griffin. "Your mother and I have been making plans for this since you came home."

"Before that even," Jana added.

"Was anyone going to mention it to me?" Griffin pushed away from the table, much like his brother had minutes earlier. Instead of following Trevor out of the room, he approached the far wall to the collage of framed photos of the property over the years. There was a photo of his great-great-grandfather, who had first farmed the land, a few aerial shots of the fields and photos of the various expansions over the years.

The largest photo hung in the center of the wall and showed his dad and mom toasting each other with the first pinot noir they'd bottled. He and Trevor stood on either side of them. Griffin smiled broadly—he could still feel the excitement of that first day, but Trevor was frowning at the camera. As Griffin remembered it, they'd had to cancel a family trip to the Grand Canyon because his dad had barely left the vineyard those first couple of years. Griffin had never minded, but his brother had hated all the things they'd missed because of the family business.

"What about Trevor?" he asked, turning to his mother. "He's right about everything he sacrificed for Harvest. I got to have a life away from here. He's been tied to the vines for his whole life. Don't you think he's earned his place at the helm?"

Her mouth tightened. "Of course he has, but it isn't about that. I want him to be happy. I want both of you to be happy." Her eyes shone with unshed tears as she looked up at him. "Trevor doesn't want to leave for the same reason you don't want to come back. Your father." She sighed. "I know he did his best, but if he could have known how things would end up here—"

"He wouldn't have changed a thing," Griffin interrupted. "I'm sorry, Mom, but it's true. Dad only cared about the way he saw things. I was the screwup and Trevor was the golden child. There was no room for any middle ground in his world."

"It isn't his world any longer," she said with a sniff. "I want you to take over for Marcus. I want you to run Harvest."

Griffin ran a hand over his face. Those were the words he'd always longed to hear, but now he had such a clearer understanding of the significance of what a commitment like that meant. "I appreciate your faith in me, and I'll think about it." He wasn't sure why he couldn't just say yes, but something held him back. Something that sounded a lot like his father's doubting voice.

His mother didn't look pleased by his response but she nodded. "I'll talk to your brother," she told him.

"What about his big plan for an event center and inn?"

"We're not ready for that," Marcus answered. "I'll make sure Trevor understands why."

"It's a good idea," Griffin said quietly. "Other

vineyards have expanded to great success. It would make Harvest a destination if it's done right."

"Are you saying you support his plan?" Jana asked.

"No," Griffin admitted. "I'm saying it's smart for the business if the goal is to keep expanding." He met Marcus's knowing gaze. "But I agree that it's not where we want to be right now. Harvest needs to focus on our environmental certifications and making the best wine we can. Anyone can be the biggest. We should be the best."

"I'm glad to hear you say that." Marcus nodded. "It confirms why your mother and I believe you should be the one to take over my position."

"We'll have to find a way to pull back from Trevor's public announcement without embarrassing him."

"Of course," Jana agreed.

Griffin sighed. "I'm still not sure about this. I wasn't joking when I said I needed time to make a decision."

"You've been concentrating on rebuilding the tasting room," Marcus told him. "I know we've had a few conversations about the future of the vineyard and you were here for the harvest this year. But you need to understand the state of the business right now. Work with me for a week. Let me show you where things stand. Then you can decide how you want to proceed."

Griffin felt his heart speed up as he thought about really being a part of Harvest again, more than just making amends for his mistakes.

"Okay," he agreed. "I have some things to wrap up with my crew today. I'll report for office duty first thing tomorrow."

Both his mother and Marcus smiled.

"This is how it was always meant to be," Jana said. "You'll see."

Griffin walked out of the office, wishing he shared his mother's confidence.

Chapter Eleven

"Are they going to open a restaurant, too?"

"How many people will the venue accommodate?"

"Is the vineyard zoned for that kind of enterprise?"

"What are you going to do about this?"

Silence descended upon the room at that last question, lobbed by Vivian Spencer, of course. Maggie nodded as if acknowledging each of the inquires and forced her features to remain neutral. Her grandmother had called an emergency meeting of the Stonecreek downtown business association for Monday morning, and Maggie had cleared her schedule so she could attend.

Vivian wasn't the only one wary of Harvest Vineyards' proposed expansion. Many of the small business owners in town had concerns about what the news would mean for them. Although Harvest was officially in the town of Stonecreek, the property was an equal distance from the next town over, Molberry. And while Harvest was associated with the Stone family's namesake town, there had already been rumblings about the leaders in Molberry trying to ingratiate themselves with Trevor in order to become the preferred vendors for any items that needed to be outsourced once the Harvest event center and guest lodge opened.

"I left messages for Trevor and Jana," Maggie reported, not bothering to add that neither of the Stones had seen fit to return her calls yet. "I plan to set up a meeting with them by day's end so we can get a real understanding of the plan." She lifted the copy of Trevor's press release she'd printed earlier. "Details are limited in what Trevor sent out, so I'm guessing he doesn't have them yet."

"What about Griffin?" Russ Wileton, who ran Stonecreek Realty, demanded.

Maggie bristled at the accusation in the man's tone. "What about Griffin?" she shot back.

"He fawned all over you at the gala," restaurant owner Irma Cole added. "That has to mean something. Don't you have some influence with him?"

"As far as I know," Maggie said carefully, "Griffin isn't involved in this announcement." He'd sent her a cryptic text late last night that he was "working things out on his end"—whatever that meant. But that was the last she'd heard from him. Not exactly giving her warm and fuzzy feelings about their status as a couple, but she was probably silly for thinking he'd offer anything more.

"He had to know it was coming," Vivian said, her tone disapproving. "It reflects badly on all of them that we had to find this out at the same time as the rest of the world."

Maggie doubted the whole "rest of the world" was

interested in the future plans of an Oregon vineyard, although she understood it was big news in the regional wine industry. With the expansion, Harvest would be one of the most prominent wineries in the area.

"I don't think any of you have reason to worry," she said with more confidence than she felt. "Obviously we just had our most successful hospital fundraiser to date at the vineyard. Jana and Marcus are committed to this community."

"Trevor still has it out for you." Dora Gianelli, whose family had operated the bakery in town for more than three generations, flipped her thick gray braid over one shoulder. It was difficult to believe that the biggest gossip in Stonecreek looked like a sweet, harmless throwback to the Woodstock era. "You know…for standing him up at the altar."

"I remember," Maggie said through clenched teeth. "And in case I ever start to forget, I can always pop by the bakery for a slice of Runaway Bride Banana Bread." She smiled at Dora. "Don't you think it's time to go back to plain old banana bread?"

Dora shrugged. "The name change has been real popular. I'm trying to add more creative names to the desserts. Spice things up a bit."

"You could call one Cheater, Cheater, Pumpkin Pie Eater," Irma suggested with a wide grin. "In honor of Trevor. Display it in the case next to Maggie's bread."

"It's not my bread," Maggie said, throwing up her hands. "I doubt Trevor would appreciate that kind of attention, either."

"That's a good point," Dora said with a nod. "I

don't want to make the Stones angry. They've promised to increase their standing order of croissants and cookies now that the tasting room is open." She leaned toward Irma. "I give them a big discount, of course, because of all the tourists coming to the bakery after they try my stuff at Harvest."

Maggie resisted the urge to roll her eyes. No one in town seemed the least bit concerned about getting on *her* bad side.

"Do you think Jason has more pull with the family?" Russ asked, and Maggie bit down so hard on her cheek she could taste blood inside her mouth.

"I doubt it," Irma answered before Maggie had a chance to respond. "He was always a bit of an outsider, and I don't think anyone in Dave Stone's immediate family likes him. There was some bad blood when Dave inherited the farm and his brother got the time-share in Arizona."

"Also," Dora added, hitching a thumb in Maggie's direction, "Jason isn't sleeping with either of the brothers. That has to count for something."

"That's crass, Dora," Grammy muttered. "Even for you. To think Maggie would barter sexual favors for influence is insulting."

"Don't get on your high horse with me, Vivian," Dora shot back. "I remember when you dated Mark Kipling after Chester died. You can't tell me you were honestly interested in that onion-breathed weasel other than the fact that he owned the bank."

"Enough." Maggie rose from her chair, gripping the edge of the oak conference table. "I'm done having my private life carted out for inspection at every turn. I've worked hard during my first term as mayor.

I hope each of you will support me in this election because I'm good at this job."

She glanced at her grandmother and then away. "Not because of my family name or who I'm dating or because you think I'm a good sport about my fiancé cheating on me. I care about this town and I care about the members of the business community. I'll work things out with Harvest. While they're important to Stonecreek, so are each of you. You're important to *me*. I'm going to make sure we do the right thing for everyone."

"Don't worry, Maggie," Chuck O'Malley said in his gruff voice. "We've got your back."

"Thanks, Chuck." She smiled as the rest of the association members around the table nodded or called out their support. Her grandmother was uncharacteristically quiet and refused to make eye contact.

Maggie would worry about whatever bee had taken up residence in her grandmother's bonnet later. Right now, she was emotionally drained. "I'm going to get back to city hall while you all finish your meeting. I promise to follow up with Jana and Marcus and keep everyone updated."

With another sidelong glance at Vivian, who still appeared mesmerized by something Russ was saying next to her, Maggie waved to the rest of the business owners and then left the room. The Miriam Inn looked much as it had when Maggie was a girl. Personally, she thought the interior of the building could benefit from a bit of a face-lift—or at least a light freshening. But this was her grandmother's domain and Maggie wouldn't dare give Grammy suggestions on how to run her business.

The town square was quiet this Monday morning, with only a few people walking their dogs on the path and the local tai chi group practicing on the open expanse of lawn in the center. The day was overcast, although the brightly colored leaves and the fall decorations that adorned the businesses up and down Main Street still made downtown look cheery.

Maggie pulled out her phone again, but she had no missed calls from anyone at Harvest Vineyards. Disappointment lanced through her. Somehow she knew Jason Stone would spin this latest development in his own favor, and although she wanted to believe the members of the business association supported her, she wouldn't blame them for looking out for their own interests.

Her fingers hovered over the home screen, but then she shoved the phone back into her purse. She needed time to research other vineyards that also housed event venues before making her case to the Stones.

She breathed deeply as she entered city hall. Since her grandmother had been mayor for most of Maggie's childhood, the scent of pine and decades-old files was familiar and made the tension in her shoulders ease slightly. Her own personal version of a relaxation candle. It represented so much to her, and although the past months had been difficult, she didn't regret that she'd chosen to follow in her grandmother's footsteps. The key now was honoring that past while forging her own path.

She greeted several people but didn't stop moving. Right now she needed her own space and to recharge. Only her office wasn't empty. Griffin stood in front of the bookcase that lined one wall, holding a framed photo of Maggie as a baby in her mother's arms.

"Hey," he said with that almost smile that never failed to make her knees turn to jelly.

"Hi," she whispered, then swallowed when her voice caught on the one syllable.

"You look like her." He turned the frame toward her as if she didn't have the image memorized.

"She was prettier than me," Maggie answered. "Morgan is almost her doppelgänger."

He placed the frame back on the shelf. "Your sister has the same hair color, but I see you in her eyes and around the mouth."

Tears clogged Maggie's throat. She'd love to believe she resembled her mother, either in looks or personality. "I still miss her."

Griffin nodded, as if that was to be expected. "I miss my dad, and we didn't even like each other. I can't imagine how it must feel to lose someone you truly love."

"You don't fool me," she told him, moving forward. "I know you loved your dad." She reached out and laced her fingers with his. "I'm sure he loved you, too."

Griffin snorted. "I don't know about that part, but you're right on the first. I loved him even if I never could make him happy."

"He'd be proud of you now."

"My mom said the same thing to me."

"Great minds..."

He lifted their hands and kissed her knuckles. "You seem stressed."

"I just came from the downtown business owners'

association. It was an emergency meeting to discuss the new plans at Harvest."

Griffin grimaced. "I'm sorry for that."

"Why didn't you say anything?" She tried to tug her hand away, but he held fast.

"I didn't know. None of us did. Trevor and my mom had discussed the idea of an event venue, but she wanted to figure out what was needed based on what was already working in town."

"Like the Miriam Inn's conference center?" She raised a brow.

"Yes," Griffin answered without hesitation.

"You can understand why I find it difficult to believe Trevor didn't make the announcement on purpose."

"Believe it or not, I think him jumping the gun on the announcement had more to do with me than you."

"Because you're with me?"

He shook his head. "Marcus is stepping down as CEO."

Maggie drew in a sharp breath. "Brenna told me he'd said something about wanting more time to spend with her and Ellie, but I had no idea he wanted *that* much time."

"He'll be involved but not in the day-to-day operations." Griffin still held her hand, running his thumb along the fleshy edge of her palm. It was an absent touch but also intimate in a way that had butterflies fluttering across Maggie's chest. "He and my mom want me to take over."

"Not Trevor?"

His full mouth thinned. "I was as shocked as you are. Trevor is the obvious choice."

She moved closer, placed her free hand against

his chest and spread her fingers, feeling his steady heartbeat. "I'm not shocked that they want you, Griffin. You love the land and you have an innate gift for understanding the vines, just like your dad did."

"I've been gone for so long," he murmured, his eyes drifting shut as if in pain.

"I'm guessing it's like riding a bike."

One side of his mouth curved up as he blinked, then met her gaze. "Not exactly."

"But kind of?" she prompted.

"Kind of," he agreed.

"I asked about Trevor because he told me he expected it to happen."

"He's not the only one. He knows the business end and the branding better than anyone. His expertise is a big part of the reason Harvest is now a well-known player in the wine industry. It's not just regional anymore, either. He's expanded our reach, increased the export sales by over twenty percent the past two years and generated a ton of buzz about the vineyard's new varietals. Just listing his accomplishments makes me feel like a slacker."

"But his heart isn't in it," she said quietly, pressing her hand against his chest.

He huffed out a laugh. "It's like you and my mom are the same person."

"Ewwww." Maggie made a face and pulled away.

Griffin laughed again. "I didn't mean it like that, and you know it."

"Let's get out of here," she blurted.

He glanced around. "Out of your office or the town hall building in general?"

"Stonecreek," she clarified. "Can you sneak away for an overnight in Lychen?"

"My little coastal-town hideaway made quite an impression on you, huh?"

"I did love the town," she said, "but you made the impression." Lychen, about an hour from Stonecreek, was a picturesque town nestled against the craggy beaches of the Oregon coast. It had been the setting for their first date, a perfect night away from the pressures of family and community. An evening for just them, and Maggie wanted to recreate that magic.

"I'm supposed to meet with Marcus first thing tomorrow morning."

"We can come back tonight," she suggested, trying not to let her disappointment show.

"Or I could reschedule my meeting with Marcus." He closed the distance between them in two long strides, wrapping an arm around her waist and pulling her close. His mouth molded against hers and she hummed her pleasure as he deepened the kiss. Even though it had only been a day and a half since she'd spent the night at his apartment, it felt like ages ago.

"I like your plan better than mine," she said when he finally released her. Every fiber of her being tingled with need at the same time her stress from earlier melted away. The only thing she cared about at the moment was being with Griffin.

"What about a change of clothes?"

She grimaced and shook her head. "I can't go back to my dad's house. I'll get sucked into real life."

"No real life," he said, kissing her again.

"Too complicated," she answered, wrinkling her nose.

"The banned word." He clasped a hand to his chest in mock horror.

Maggie giggled as happiness filled her. Being with Griffin made her truly happy and she couldn't imagine a better reason to play hooky from life than the chance to spend the day—not to mention the night—with him.

They managed to sneak out of the town hall with no one seeing them. Maggie's car could remain parked in the employee lot behind the building, so they climbed into Griffin's Land Cruiser and headed for the coast. Maggie texted her dad, Brenna and her assistant, Megan, to let them know she had to take a quick trip out of town and would return tomorrow.

Then she turned off her phone and set it on the console, leaning her head against the seat to gaze out the window at the changing landscape.

"Why didn't we think of escaping before now?" Griffin asked with a smile.

"I'm not sure," she admitted. "Because already this is the most fun I've had in ages."

"It only gets better from here," he promised, and he was right. They stopped for a late lunch at a local deli in one of the towns off the main highway and pulled into Lychen just as the sun was beginning to make its way across the sky toward the horizon.

"Beach and then hotel," Griffin told her as he parked in a lot near the pier.

Maggie made a face as she looked down at her pencil skirt and modest heels. "I'm not exactly dressed for the sand."

"You look perfect to me," he told her as they climbed out, Maggie leaving her shoes inside the SUV.

She felt perfect, despite being overdressed. He took her hand and they walked down to the edge of the ocean. It was nearing low tide so a wide expanse of beach was exposed. The sand was cool under Maggie's feet. At this time of year, the temperatures near the coast were in the fifties and a strong breeze blew her hair in all directions.

She inhaled deeply of the salty air and leaned closer to Griffin. He slung an arm over her shoulder, the heat from his body warming her as they walked. A few pelicans hopped around the rock formations just offshore, foraging for food, but otherwise they had the beach to themselves.

Back in early summer when they'd had their first date, Maggie couldn't have imagined how important Griffin would become to her. They were an unlikely match—he with his devil-may-care attitude and the heart of a rebel and her always wanting to please everyone, even at the expense of her own happiness.

It was easy to be with him, natural in a way she'd never experienced with anyone else. There was no denying that she'd fallen head over heels in love with this man. And although she still wasn't certain if those feelings would ever be reciprocated, she couldn't help but believe he cherished the connection between them as much as she did. It had to be only a matter of time until he said those three words back to her.

Chapter Twelve

"Nice going, Spencer. Way to work the system."

Morgan swallowed as Zach Bryant dropped next to her on the lunch table bench. She concentrated on peeling the orange she'd packed and not looking at Cole, who sat across from her.

She didn't need to look at him to know he was angry at Zach's intrusion. Anger poured off him like heat from the old radiator in her room on a cold winter night. Cole and Zach used to be friends, last year when Cole first moved to Stonecreek. He'd immediately become the de facto leader of the wild crowd at the high school, the crazy and sometimes dangerous escapades from his previous school documented on social media to make him a legend his first day on campus.

In a way it was funny because Cole had first motivated her to change her image and become part of the hard-partying group of nonconformist kids. She'd been infatuated with him from the start but hadn't realized that while she was trying to get in with the bad kids, he'd desperately wanted out.

Now she wished she'd never gone down that path in the first place. Cole acted like it was so easy to walk away, but the fact that he hadn't outright told Zach and his crew to shove off told a different story. Stonecreek was a small town and once you were pigeonholed at the high school, it was difficult to undo a reputation.

"I don't know what you're talking about," she said quietly, glancing toward Zach, then inwardly groaning when Jonah, Jocelyn and Amanda crowded around the table.

"Homecoming," Zach said. "Jocelyn said you convinced your folks to let you go to the dance."

"My dad agreed," Morgan clarified. "My mom is dead."

"Whatever," Zach muttered, like he was mad she'd contradicted him.

She looked up through her lashes to see Cole glaring at Zach and then back at her, a muscle ticking in his jaw. Morgan gave a small shake of her head. The last thing she needed—that either of them needed—was Cole getting into trouble at school.

"So what's the plan?" Jonah asked, plucking an orange sliver out of Morgan's fingers. Jonah was the consummate lackey, following Zach wherever he went like a puppy would his owner. "Do we make an appearance at the dance first, then duck out or do a little prepartying to make it actually fun?"

"I think the dance will be fun," Morgan said, earning a disbelieving snort from Jocelyn.

"You're joking, right?" the cool blonde said with a sneer. "I say we preparty. Cole, can your brother hook us up?"

"Nope."

Jocelyn pouted and leaned into Cole's arm, making a sick pit open in Morgan's stomach. Jocelyn and Cole had dated—or at least hooked up—for a short time when he'd moved to town. Even though her self-named best girlfriend acted like she'd moved on, Morgan had a feeling she'd love another chance with Cole.

"Please," Jocelyn purred, rubbing herself all over Cole. He didn't seem to notice, but Morgan wanted to reach across the table and throat punch the girl. "Just a teensy-weensy bit of the good stuff."

Cole's gaze flicked to Morgan, then he shifted his arm away from Jocelyn. "I don't party anymore, Joce. You know that."

The girl's glossy mouth turned down at the corners. "Lame."

"I can hook us up," Zach told the group. "We'll make Boy Scout Cole our designated driver."

Jocelyn, Amanda and Jonah all laughed at that.

"I'm going to the dance," Cole said through clenched teeth. "Not to wherever you losers wind up for the night."

"Losers?" Zach's eyes narrowed. "That must make you King Loser, dude, because your list of exploits is longer than the rest of ours combined."

"Not anymore," Cole shot back.

"Well, then..." Zach hitched his chin toward Morgan. "You must be planning on going stag, because Morgan's with us." He reached out and trailed a finger along her sleeve. "Aren't you, sweetheart?"

"Of course she is," Jocelyn answered before Morgan could. "We have a plan to get ready together." She wiggled her eyebrows. "A ladies' preparty."

"Um…" Morgan licked her lips. "My dad agreed to let me go to the dance. I'm not sure I can do anything else."

She met Cole's gaze and saw something that looked like disappointment shadowed there. She knew he expected her to take a stand against their friends the way he had, but she didn't know if she was strong enough for that.

Not that she wanted to be part of their stupid antics anymore. Morgan might chafe against the expectations of her grandmother, but she wasn't into getting drunk or high every weekend. She knew she was smart enough to be accepted at a decent college if she tried. That was her ticket out of Stonecreek, and she wasn't going to blow it.

"You'll find a way," Jocelyn said, undeterred. "You always do."

"What's it going to be, Cole?" Zach arched a brow. "You giving up your date or are you going to join us for homecoming?"

"We really just want to go to the dance," Morgan offered quickly. "Maybe we can meet up with you there?"

"Why does your dad have to be so strict all of a sudden?" Jocelyn asked, her voice a high-pitched whine. "My parents barely notice me."

Morgan shrugged. "It's annoying." She felt pressured to appear that she didn't like her father taking an interest in her life, even though the opposite was true. Somehow she didn't think this group would appreciate the fact that she liked it.

Again, she could tell Cole didn't approve of how she was dealing with the situation. He grabbed his lunch tray and climbed off of the bench. "I need to stop by the library," he announced.

"Boy Scout," Zach muttered.

"I can go with you," Morgan offered, starting to stand.

Cole shook his head. "Stay here with your friends," he said and each word felt like a condemnation.

Then he turned and walked away.

"I liked him better before he went all try-hard," Amanda said, then popped her gum.

"He's not a try-hard," Morgan shot back. "Cole is who he is, and he doesn't care what anyone else thinks."

"Which makes him a total tool," Zach said, and Morgan could hear the irritation in his voice. Zach didn't like that Cole wouldn't run with their crew anymore. "Why did you agree to go to the dance with him anyway? If you'd wanted an official date, babe, I would have asked you."

Morgan bit her bottom lip. She couldn't admit her feelings for Cole to anyone at this table. They'd use it against her without a doubt.

"He works for Griffin Stone," she said finally. "My sister is dating him, so I knew if Griffin vouched for Cole, Maggie would help convince my dad to let me go to the dance."

All four of them stared at her like she was speaking Latin.

Then Zach let out a loud laugh. "Convoluted but also brilliant. I like that about you, Spencer. You don't look manipulative, but at the core, you're the same as the rest of us." He stood and patted the top of her head as if she were a dog.

I'm nothing like you, she wanted to scream, but kept her mouth shut. Jocelyn, Amanda and Jonah got up and followed Zach out of the cafeteria.

Morgan shoved her uneaten lunch into the paper sack and fisted one hand around it, dashing at her cheeks with the other. She wouldn't cry over those stupid jerks and the mess she'd gotten herself into trying to be friends with them.

She tossed her lunch into the trash bin, then headed for the library, making sure she didn't run into any of her fake friends on the way. Cole sat at a table directly in front of the librarian's counter.

Morgan waved to Mrs. Shamsi, the school librarian, then pulled out the chair next to Cole.

"I'm studying," he said tightly.

She leaned in and covered his open notebook with one hand. "I'm sorry."

"I'm not going to make you choose," he said, looking up at her, his eyes fierce. "There's no 'it's me or them.' That's a little too John Hughes for my taste."

She flashed a quick smile. "John Hughes was more about figuring out who you are and accepting yourself so other people will, too."

He shook his head but one side of his mouth curved. "You know what I mean, Morgan."

"I want to go to the dance with you," she promised. "I don't care about a preparty or a postparty or doing anything with Zach and Jocelyn."

"Are you going to let them in on that?"

She sighed. "It's not easy. They've been my friends for the past year, and I don't want to be rude."

"You don't want to be rude to the meanest people at this school." He lifted his hand to the back of her neck and drew her in for a quick kiss. "You're really something, Morgan Spencer."

She felt color flood her cheeks and she dipped her chin, darting a glance around the crowded library to see if anyone had noticed what he'd just done. "You kissed me," she whispered, her lips still tingling and sparks shooting down her spine.

He inclined his head. "Beautiful, smart and observant. A triple threat."

No one seemed to be paying any attention to the two of them, except Camryn Clarke, who sat at a far table in the corner with a couple other girls Morgan recognized from the science and technology program.

Camryn lived two doors down from Morgan and the two had been best friends until middle school. Once Morgan hit her teen years, it had been too difficult to spend time with Camryn at her perfect house with her perfect mother, who baked extra cookies to send home with Morgan. As if a batch of homemade cookies would make up for not having a mom. In fact, it had done the opposite. All Mrs. Clarke's kindness had accomplished was making Morgan miss her own mom more.

As Morgan started to rebel, she'd drifted apart from Camryn. *Drifted* wasn't actually the right word. She'd cut Camryn from her life, along with any other friend who reminded her of what her family had lost. It was easier to gravitate toward other misfits, kids who didn't ask her about not having a mom because they were too busy with their own dysfunction.

But now Camryn offered an approving smile and a nod toward Cole. To her surprise, Morgan found herself returning the smile.

"You're a lucky guy," she said, shifting her attention back to Cole.

"Damn right," he agreed, glancing at his watch. "A lucky guy who's going to be late for fifth period if I don't motor. You want to walk with me?"

She hesitated. "I need to grab a book from Mrs. Shamsi. I'll see you after seventh?"

He stood, then bent to kiss her again.

"The library is not the place for that, Mr. Maren."

Morgan pressed a hand to her cheek at the sound of the librarian's disapproving tone.

"Sorry," Cole told the older woman, then turned to face Morgan. *Not sorry*, he mouthed, making her smile again.

When he was gone, Morgan stood and walked toward the far end of the library. "Hey, Camryn," she said, her hands clenched in nervous fists at her sides.

"Hey, Morgan." Camryn rose from the table and picked up her backpack. "I'm heading to chemistry."

"Me, too," Morgan told her.

Camryn made a face. "I know. We're in the same class."

"Oh, right."

"Let's go."

"I was wondering if you'd want to hang out sometime," Morgan said in a rush of breath as they started down the hall. "Maybe go shopping for homecoming dresses? Maggie's going to take me this weekend. I'm sure you could come, too."

"Seriously?" The other girl looked dubious. "You want to hang out with me?"

"Sure."

"What happened to Jocelyn? She get sent to rehab already?"

Morgan snorted, then covered her mouth with one hand. "Wow," she breathed.

"I know. Sorry." Camryn adjusted the straps on her backpack. "But those girls, and the guys they run with, are bad news."

"I'm getting that," Morgan admitted.

"Cole's pretty cute, though." Camryn threw her a sidelong glance. "He stopped a couple of seniors from giving me grief in gym class because I was so bad at basketball. He's cool."

"Oh." Another layer of warmth unfurled inside Morgan. "Yeah, he's both those things."

"My mom wanted to take me dress shopping," Camryn said as they reached the classroom.

"That's fine," Morgan said quickly, sorrow stabbing at her chest. Mostly she was used to not having a mom, and Maggie did a great job of always being there for her. Even Grammy tried in her own way. But there were some times when she missed her mother even though it had been so many years that her memories had faded to fuzzy images. That lack of clarity hurt more than anything.

"She has horrible taste," Camryn continued. "I'd love to go with you and Maggie. I'll have a chance of buying a dress that doesn't make me look like I'm joining the convent or something."

Morgan took a deep breath as relief flooded

through her. "Awesome. I'll talk to Maggie and text you about the time."

"It's a plan," Camryn said with a smile. "Welcome back, Morgan."

"Thanks," Morgan said softly, understanding exactly what her old friend meant. "I'm glad to be back."

Nerves skittered across Maggie's skin as Griffin unlocked the door to their room in the quaint bed-and-breakfast at the end of a quiet street in Lychen.

"Not exactly the Four Seasons," he said with a grimace as he flipped on the light. The decor was vintage seventies with lace curtains and a four-poster bed with a flowery comforter covering it.

"I love it," Maggie said, then bit her bottom lip. How easy it would be to substitute the word *you* in that sentence. Now that she'd admitted her feelings once to Griffin, she wanted to blurt those three words every time she opened her mouth.

"You're easy to please," he said and drew her closer for a deep kiss. His hands wound around her waist, fingers edging up her tailored shirt until she felt his touch along the bare skin of her back.

"With you," she told him, "I might just be plain easy."

She felt his smile against her mouth. "You are precious to me, Maggie. You're beautiful and intelligent and you make me crazy with desire." He pulled back and his gaze held so much intensity it took her breath away. "I've never felt this way."

"I…" She paused and licked her lips. "Me neither." Somehow she couldn't bring herself to say the words

I love you again. They rested on the tip of her tongue but wouldn't spill over. What if she pushed him away by wanting more than he could give?

"Are you hungry now?" he asked, then hitched his chin toward the bed. "Or do you want a rest?"

She grabbed the hem of her shirt and pulled it over her head. "A rest," she whispered. "But I'm not tired."

"Then no rest for you," he answered with a wicked grin and covered her breast with one large hand. She gasped as the lace tickled her skin and the warmth of his touch made heat pool low in her belly. His finger traced her puckered nipple through the fabric and Maggie thought she'd never felt something so exquisite.

He gave the same attention to her other breast before moving closer. He claimed her mouth and the kiss made her crazy with need. Dropping to his knees in front of her, he reached around and unzipped the skirt she wore, then tugged it down over her hips.

Sensation swirled through her as she felt his breath at the apex of her thighs. He pulled her panties down, as well, but Maggie couldn't even feel nervous at being exposed to him in this way. All she could feel was desire building, and when he dipped a finger into her, she gave a yearning moan.

"So beautiful," he murmured, pushing gently on her legs, encouraging her to open more for him.

She happily gave him all the access he wanted, running her fingers through his hair as his tongue found her most sensitive spot.

"Griffin." She said his name in a hoarse breath, but he didn't pause as he lavished attention on her. She was outside her body, floating on a mounting wave of blissful pressure. Then the wave crashed over her, sending her exploding up and then spiraling back down as her whole body hummed with the electric release. Her knees gave way and she would have sank to the carpet, but Griffin was there to catch her. He looped his arms behind her knees and back to carry her to the bed.

He threw back the covers and put her down on the mattress, then efficiently shucked out of his clothes. He pulled a wallet from the pocket of his jeans and took out a condom wrapper. Maggie watched, mesmerized by the muscles that bunched with every movement and overwhelmed that this man was here with her.

Then he was on the bed, adjusting himself between her thighs. "Are you good?"

She nodded and reached up to push away the hair that fell over his forehead. "I think I'm about to be great," she said, then gasped as he filled her.

They moved together, a tangle of arms and legs, and Maggie was hard-pressed to know where she left off and he began. She could barely catch her breath in a maelstrom of kissing, touching and a rhythm that was singular to the two of them. Her muscles tensed as if anticipating the pleasure to come.

Then she was breaking apart again and only remained tethered to reality by the way Griffin whispered her name as he found his own release.

He held her close as her breathing returned to normal, and she could feel his heart pounding in his chest.

When he lifted his head to gaze at her, she smiled. "I

have a better appreciation for the 'Afternoon Delight' song."

He chuckled and kissed the tip of her nose. "There were definitely some skyrockets going off just then."

When he headed to the bathroom, Maggie pulled the sheet and comforter up to her chest. Her limbs felt like jelly, warm, pliant and totally satisfied. She could stay like this forever, she thought as her eyes drifted closed.

"Sleepy now?" Griffin asked as he climbed under the sheets and pulled her close so her back was snuggled against the warmth of his chest, the short hair there tickling her bare skin.

"Nope," she said around a yawn. "Okay, maybe."

"We have time for a nap," he told her.

"But I don't want to miss any part of this day," she said, even though it was a struggle to form a coherent sentence.

"We have all the time in the world," he promised and she drifted to sleep with a smile on her face and her heart full.

Chapter Thirteen

Griffin let himself into the room three hours later to find Maggie propped up against a pillow in the bed, wearing one of the B and B's white bathrobes.

Her hair fell in damp waves over her shoulders, so different from the polished style she usually wore. It reminded him of their night at the cabin in the woods, when she'd fallen out of the canoe and ended up soaked and sputtering.

The memory made him smile. Although things had gone horribly wrong the next morning when he'd found out the tasting room had been damaged in a fire accidentally set by Maggie's sister, it had also been the night Griffin realized he was falling in love with her.

"I woke up and you were gone. What's wrong?" she asked, inclining her head as she used the remote to mute the TV.

"Nothing." He forced a smile.

I'm in love with you, he thought silently.

Why did it terrify him so much? She'd said the words to him, so all he had to do now was reciprocate. Maggie was an amazing woman. Any man would be lucky to have her.

"I brought food, clothing and wine," he said, trying to shove down the fear that clogged his throat. He should be happy. People fell in love every day. But Griffin had never allowed himself to get that close to anyone, to open himself up to being rejected the way his father had done.

"You're like a Maslow's hierarchy of needs fulfiller." She straightened from the bed and padded toward him, reaching for the bags.

"What kind of food and what kind of clothes? I'm assuming I don't need to ask about the wine."

"Carryout from Luigi's. I hope you don't mind I didn't try something new on this visit." Luigi's Italian Inn was the restaurant where they'd had dinner their first time in Lychen. Griffin knew Maggie loved the savory northern Italian dishes and wanted to recreate everything that was good about their first date.

"I'm so hungry," Maggie told him by way of an answer. "This is perfect."

"I also have a Kiss Me I'm from Oregon T-shirt and a pair of Oregon Ducks sweatpants for you." He wiggled his eyebrows. "No undies in the gift shop around the corner, so you're going commando for the night, Ms. Spencer."

She giggled at that and gave him a saucy grin. "To be honest, I wasn't planning to spend much time dressed, so that should work out just fine."

"Killing me," he murmured and leaned in to kiss her.

"I take that as a compliment," she answered, peering into the bag with the food. "Shall we eat?"

He glanced around the room. "I forgot about a wine opener. Why don't you set up dinner and I'll borrow one from the front desk?"

She nodded and he dropped the bag of clothes to the floor, handed Maggie the bottle of wine, then let himself out of the room.

In the hallway, he bent forward, hands on knees, and drew in several deep breaths. Should he tell her he loved her? Was it real? Before Maggie he hadn't even thought he was capable of love. He'd had his share of relationships, and Cassie had been a good friend since they'd realized they were too alike to actually be a good match, but he'd always found a way to end things with the women he'd dated before they got too serious. It was easier that way, he'd told himself.

Griffin knew what it was like to love someone with your whole heart and not have those feelings reciprocated. It embarrassed him that his dysfunctional relationship with his dad had left him so deeply scarred, but that was the truth of it. And it was why he'd always kept his emotions so closely guarded.

Maggie had managed to work her way through every layer of his defenses until she filled a place in his soul he hadn't even known was empty.

He stood and moved toward the staircase, running a hand through his hair. He could make this work. She was worth making this work. Now he saw that his reaction to the fire and her sister's involvement had been a defense mechanism, an excuse to push her away because she'd been getting too close.

What a damn coward he was.

No more.

He retrieved a wine opener and took the steps to the second floor two at a time. Maggie whirled around and clasped a hand to her chest as he burst into the room.

"You scared me," she said with a breathy laugh. "You must be even hungrier than I am."

"I love you," he blurted.

Her mouth fell open, then snapped shut. She stared at him, as if trying to process his declaration.

"Sorry," he murmured. "I didn't mean to shock you."

She frowned. "Sorry you love me?"

"Not for a minute," he answered. "Falling in love with you is the smartest thing I've done in ages, even if it wasn't on purpose."

She huffed out a laugh and placed the napkins she held on the table. "You didn't want to fall in love?" She moved toward him.

"I didn't plan on it."

"Me neither," she admitted softly, placing her hands on his shoulders.

"But…"

"I love you so much," she whispered, and the happiness that rocketed through him almost drove him to his knees with its power.

He bent his head and brushed his lips over hers, and it felt like kissing her for the first time. "I love you," he said against her mouth.

"I wasn't sure," she admitted, "I was afraid I'd ruined things by saying it too soon."

"Never be afraid to tell me how you feel." He tucked her hair behind her ears, dropping kisses on her nose and then on each of her eyelids. He wanted to kiss her everywhere, to lay her out and worship every beautiful inch of her.

Then her stomach growled.

"Priorities," he said with a grin.

"Yeah," she agreed, making a face. "I wasn't joking when I said I was hungry."

He stepped back and pulled the corkscrew from where he'd stashed it in his back pocket. "Then let's eat and drink."

"Should I put on my new outfit first?" Maggie asked, eyeing the bag of clothes.

"I'd prefer if you didn't," he answered. "It will only mean I have to undress you again after dinner."

"The robe is so comfy." She turned to the small table where she'd set out the cartons of food and the paper plates the restaurant had given him.

"What were you watching?" he asked as he uncorked the wine.

"HGTV. It's my favorite thing."

He laughed. "You like remodeling shows? If I'd known, I would have put you to work on the tasting room."

"I like watching," she clarified. "Not necessarily doing." She glanced at the television. "Lucas and Megan from *Fix My Flip* are my favorites. He's the contractor and she does interior design. They help people with horror-story flipped houses make them better. At first they were just business partners but got engaged in the season finale. It's so romantic."

"That's a thing?" he asked, shaking his head. "Not much about construction is romantic in my experience."

"Have you ever gotten busy with a girl in one of your unfinished projects?"

The wine cork popped out at that moment and Griffin almost dropped the bottle onto the floor. "Um...no," he said with a laugh.

She dished out portions of chicken parmesan and Caesar salad to each of them. "What about in the rows of grapes?"

"Maggie Spencer," he said with mock shock, "do you have some sort of sex-in-public-places fantasy?"

"Maybe," she said, winking.

"Eat fast," he told her, pouring the wine. "Just imagining you naked in the vineyard is driving me wild."

"Good to know," she told him. "I'm thinking of an early Christmas present involving a bow and a trench coat."

"Already the best gift ever," he murmured, making her laugh once again.

He loved the sound of her laughter and the fact that he was the one who made her happy. He unmuted the TV so they could watch *Fix My Flip* while they ate.

There truly were no words to describe the perfection of this getaway. It was more than the physical connection they shared. Sitting in a hotel room watching some random remodeling show with Maggie was more exciting than anything he'd done in years. He had a close set of buddies from the army and other friends he'd made during his career in construction. Griffin had watched many of them get married over the years, several times as a groomsman at the front of the church.

He'd never understood the desire to bind himself to one person for his entire life before Maggie. The daily grind of marriage had seemed like a cage from where he'd stood ruthlessly guarding his freedom. He'd thought that being uncommitted made things better, but now he couldn't imagine going back to being alone.

Not when he could spend his nights with Maggie.

This was what he wanted, so much that it made his chest burn with yearning.

"Shiplap," she said between bites, nodding toward the television. "I looove shiplap."

Griffin felt his brow furrow as he watched the renovation show hosts nailing rough-sawed boards to the walls. "You say that like other women talk about diamonds or fancy shoes."

"Fancy shoes hurt my feet," she answered. "But shiplap makes me happy." She took a sip of wine. "I'm going to hire someone to install it when I move back into my house next year."

At his snort, she frowned. "Okay, fine. I'll learn to do it myself. No judgment from you."

"Your boyfriend," he said, hitching a thumb at his chest, "just happens to be an experienced contractor. I can put up shiplap or teach you how to do it yourself if you want."

"Oh." Pink colored her cheeks as she took another long drink of wine. "You're my boyfriend?"

"I just told you I love you," he explained. "I think we can safely say I'm your boyfriend."

She stared at him for a moment, then nodded. "I like the sound of that."

"Have you ever—" he leaned across the table, dropping his voice to a low whisper "—had sex on a table saw?"

Her loud cackle of laughter filled the room. "Eww...splinters."

He grinned, once again so easily charmed by her.

"I'll wipe it down first," he promised, and she laughed again. "Right. That doesn't sound much better."

"Shh." Maggie lifted a finger to her lips. "Don't talk, darling. Just sit there and look pretty."

He pushed back from the table. "Now you're poking the bear."

Her eyes widened. "Nope."

"Oh, yes," he said, moving toward her.

She shifted her chair to face him and loosened the sash on her robe. The soft fabric parted until he could almost see her breasts. God, he wanted to see her breasts.

"I hope you've had enough to eat," he said, taking her hand and pulling her to standing. "Because I need to get you back into that bed more than I need my next breath."

She undid the sash completely and opened the robe until it fell from her shoulders, a small smile playing on her gorgeous mouth. "What are you waiting for?"

Needing no further encouragement, Griffin wrapped his arms around her.

The following Saturday, Maggie drove Morgan and her friend Camryn to Portland for dress shopping. They stopped for lunch at a popular Mexican restaurant first, the two girls pulling up various photos of homecoming dress options while they ate.

Maggie couldn't remember the last time she'd seen her sister seem truly happy hanging out with a friend.

Whenever Jocelyn or anyone from that group had come to the house, there'd been sneering and sassy comebacks if the girls had been forced to interact with the family.

Today Morgan seemed more like her old self, the girl she'd been before deciding to be a wild child. They started at one of Maggie's favorite stores, Sweet Threads, where both girls tried on at least a dozen dresses each.

Maggie played the part of chaperone, steering them toward styles with which neither Grammy nor Camryn's conservative mother could find fault.

Morgan chose an open-backed, floral-print dress in shades of blue, which made her look like a fairy-tale princess, while Camryn settled on a dark pink two-piece A-line that highlighted her dark hair and olive complexion. They got shoes to match at a different boutique and Maggie bought a pair of earrings for each of them.

"What about you?" Morgan asked Maggie as the girls loaded their purchases into the back of her Volkswagen.

Maggie waved her hand, brushing aside the question. "This trip isn't about me."

"But you have the reunion dance," Morgan insisted.

"Oh, yeah," Camryn chimed in. "The old people event."

"Not quite old," Maggie objected with a smile.

The two teenagers shared a look, which Maggie chose to ignore.

"Come on, Mags." Morgan shut the trunk and tugged on Maggie's wrist. "I totally forgot about you when I was trying on dresses, but now we can focus on your dance."

Spoken like a true teenager.

"I didn't see anything I wanted for myself," Maggie lied. She'd planned to shop for a new dress but felt silly after listening to the girls discuss styles most of the morning. She wasn't a kid and the reunion dance shouldn't mean that much to her.

Except it did.

The dance would be her and Griffin's first outing as a true couple. Yes, they'd gone on dates and made tongues wag at the hospital gala, but it felt like things had changed since their night away on the coast. Attending the reunion dance together would solidify their relationship to everyone in town. There'd be no more flying under the radar after that. Maggie was ready, and she had to believe Griffin was, as well.

He'd told her he loved her and called himself her boyfriend.

They'd talked about plans for her house once her tenants' lease was up, and Griffin had seemed totally invested in helping her with her renovation projects.

That meant he was planning to stay in Stonecreek, didn't it? She mentally chided herself for not having the nerve to ask him outright. But she hadn't wanted to spoil the mood of the evening.

So she'd avoided any topics that would have caused either of them stress. Thank God for her love of remodeling shows because it would have been a pretty quiet night without that.

Griffin hadn't seemed to notice the big ole elephant in the room. He'd been loving and attentive—so attentive her toes curled remembering all the ways he'd brought her pleasure. But he had no apparent issues with avoiding difficult subjects.

That couldn't last forever, obviously, although she'd been so busy in the past week with campaign functions and the start of planning the winter carnival that she'd only managed to carve out one night with him. Because of their respective living situations, the date had ended with a hot and heavy make-out session in the Land Cruiser's back seat.

Another thing from her teenage bucket list that Maggie was finally checking off in her late twenties.

"Come on," Morgan coaxed. "That second store we went to—the one with the snobby saleslady—had some matronly dresses you'd love."

Maggie sniffed. "I don't love matronly dresses."

Morgan and Camryn shared another look.

"Then pick something for me if you think you can do better."

"We thought you'd never ask," Camryn said with a smile.

Morgan looped an arm around Maggie's waist. "Griffin isn't going to know what hit him at that reunion dance."

"I doubt that's true," Maggie said but secretly cheered as the girls led her back down the street. They insisted she try on a dizzying array of dresses, but she finally settled on a wine-colored high-low gown in a gorgeous chiffon fabric.

"It might be too much," she told Morgan even as the saleswoman—who was far friendlier when it became clear Maggie was a guaranteed sale—wrapped up the purchase.

"It's perfect," Morgan assured her as Camryn

stepped away to take a call from her mother. "I bet Mom would have loved it."

Sudden tears pricked the backs of Maggie's eyes. "I know she's watching over us," she whispered. "She'd be so proud of you, Mo-Mo."

"Then she had low expectations," Morgan said, shaking her head. "But I'm working on getting better."

"You're doing a great job, sweetie. In the end, each of us is a work in progress."

Morgan laughed. "Now you sound like Dad and his armchair philosophy nuggets."

"He's better at it."

"You do okay," Morgan said, nudging Maggie's arm.

They stopped for ice cream, then drove back to Stonecreek, dropping off Camryn before heading home. Grammy's car sat parked outside the house, eliciting a groan from Morgan.

"What a way to end the day," the girl muttered.

"We don't know why she's here," Maggie cautioned. "It could just be a friendly, grandmotherly visit."

"You keep telling yourself that."

Maggie had to admit she couldn't remember the last time her grandmother had stopped by without an agenda.

After hanging both dresses in the front closet and leaving the other shopping bags at the foot of the stairs, she found her father and Grammy sitting at the kitchen table, a photo album open between them.

"Hey, girls," Dad called when she and Morgan walked in. "Successful shopping trip?"

Morgan nodded. "It was awesome. I got this totally fantastic blue flowery dress and helped Maggie pick out one for the reunion dance. I love Portland. It's the best city."

Jim looked dumbfounded at his younger daughter's enthusiastic reply and even more so when Morgan walked to the table and gave him a quick hug, then bent to kiss Grammy's cheek.

"You need a haircut," Grammy said, tugging at the ends of Morgan's long locks.

Maggie inwardly winced but Morgan only smiled. "One step ahead of you, Grammy. I have an appointment Wednesday after school. Want to drive me?"

Vivian's eyes widened slightly but she gave a quick nod. "I'd love to. I'll pick you up at the high school. We could visit the bakery when you're finished at the salon. Marionberry is the pie flavor of the month."

"That's my favorite," Morgan told her.

Grammy patted her arm. "Yes, dear. I know."

"It's a date, then." Morgan glanced at the clock that hung on the wall next to the refrigerator. "I have homework to finish."

Their father nodded. "Ben is at Aidan's house. He's supposed to be back by six, so we'll eat then."

"Sounds good." Morgan gave Maggie another hug and a whispered thank-you, then headed upstairs.

"That must have been some shopping trip," Jim said when she'd left the room. "I haven't seen her that happy in years."

"She's excited about the dance," Maggie said, but she hoped it was more than that. She wanted to believe Morgan was truly working through her teenage demons to become the amazing young woman Maggie knew she had the potential to be.

"You found a dress, as well?" Grammy asked, lifting an eyebrow.

"It's very pretty," Maggie told her, not giving any more details. Of course she hoped her grandmother would like the dress, but at the same time had no desire to solicit her opinion.

"I assume Griffin is your date?"

Maggie took a breath, then said, "He's my boyfriend."

"Things have gotten serious with the two of you?" her dad asked.

Her first instinct was to offer a denial. It felt too new and precious to share, but she was sick of playing it safe. That had gotten her nowhere anyway. "I'm in love with him," she said in a rush of air.

Her father leaned back in his chair and whistled under his breath. Grammy only nodded. "He came to see me earlier today."

"What?" Maggie blurted. "Griffin?"

Vivian tapped a finger on the table. "He wanted to get my thoughts on the announcement about Harvest expanding."

Maggie frowned. He hadn't mentioned any plan to speak to her grandmother.

"He assured me that Trevor had released the plan prematurely and that the family will work with business owners in town before deciding how to proceed."

"Good," Maggie said, trying not to fidget under her grandmother's shrewd gaze. "That's the same thing I told you last week after talking to Jana."

"I believe it was a sign of respect," Vivian explained, "that Griffin came to me. He also mentioned his relationship with you."

Maggie edged closer, keeping her face neutral.

"His intentions are honorable," Grammy said with a nod. "Your involvement with one brother and now the other is unorthodox," she continued, making Maggie flinch, "but I approve of you and Griffin as a couple."

"Mom," Jim said, exasperation clear in his tone, "Maggie doesn't need anyone's approval."

Grammy sniffed. "I'm giving it just the same."

"Thank you," Maggie whispered, not quite sure how she felt about her grandmother's support in this case. Her father was right. She didn't need her family to sanction her relationship. But the truth was she didn't want to be at odds with her grandmother. Despite Vivian's tendency toward judgment and manipulation, Maggie loved her dearly.

"I brought over the album because I wanted you to see this photo of your mother." She touched her finger to the edge of one of the old photos. It showed Nancy Spencer holding Maggie as a baby, so she must have been in her early twenties at the time.

"It was her birthday," Jim murmured, his tone wistful.

"I gave her the necklace she was wearing as a gift," Vivian explained. "My mother had given it to me when I turned eighteen. It was the year I met your grandfather. Her mother had worn it on the boat over from Ireland. It's a family heirloom."

Maggie bent forward and peered at the amber stone set in gold. "It's beautiful. She looks so happy."

Her father nodded. "Being a mother made her happy. You, Morgan and Ben were her life."

Maggie glanced up sharply at him. "You were part of it, too. Mom loved being your wife as much as she did our mother."

His gaze took on a troubled cast but he smiled at her.

"I found this as I was clearing out my dresser," Grammy continued, pulling a small black box from her purse. "I'm not sure how I ended up with it again."

Maggie's dad blew out a long breath. "It was when I got rid of all of her belongings as part of my grieving process." He rubbed a hand over his eyes. "The anger stage, which lasted way too long in my case. You saved some things for the girls."

Sorrow pinched Maggie's chest at the thought of all the physical mementos she'd never have, and her grandmother's mouth thinned. "I remember now. Anyway, I have the necklace and I thought you might want to wear it to the reunion dance." She opened the box, revealing the delicate piece of jewelry on a cushion of black velvet. "I wore it to my senior prom."

Maggie drew in a shaky breath.

"If it's not to your taste, then you can simply keep it with your other jewelry," Grammy said in a clipped tone, obviously misinterpreting Maggie's silence.

"I'd be honored to wear it to the dance," Maggie told her. She plucked up the gold chain to examine it more closely. "I feel like I remember Mom wearing the necklace, although I suppose it could be just from seeing the photos."

"Your mom loved it," her dad said gently. "She wore it for every special occasion."

"I can't believe I didn't find it before the wedding," Grammy said. "Although now I realize that was a fortuitous bit of luck. Being able to give it to you now was meant to be."

Meant to be. Maggie's gaze darted to her grandmother and Vivian gave a small nod. Did that mean Grammy thought Maggie and Griffin were meant to be?

It seemed that way to Maggie. Despite the crazy way they'd reconnected and all the complications—dreaded word that it was—that had plagued them, Maggie's heart was certain.

"Would you like to come upstairs while I try on the dress with the necklace?" Maggie offered. "I'd love to see what you think."

Her father snorted, then covered it with a cough.

Grammy shot him a disapproving glare, then smiled at Maggie. "That would be just lovely, Mary Margaret. Thank you."

Maggie went to retrieve the dress from the front closet, her heart so filled with happiness it felt like it might overflow.

Chapter Fourteen

"Maybe I'll just have an appetizer," Morgan said quietly, closing the menu at Stonecreek Grille, the most expensive restaurant in town.

"Aren't you hungry?" Cole asked, his thick brows furrowing. "I think the steak Oscar looks good."

"It is. We eat here for Grammy's birthday every year. The food is to die for."

"Then why won't you order?"

She fingered the delicate corsage of carnations that encircled her wrist. "It's really expensive."

When Cole didn't respond for several long seconds, Morgan risked a glance up at him.

"I have the cash," he told her simply. "I made the reservation after looking at the menu."

"But you shouldn't spend your money on an extravagant dinner," she insisted. "I'd be fine at the taco truck in the grocery parking lot if we're together."

He reached across the table and took her hands in his. "This is our first real date, Morgan. I want it to be special."

"Special doesn't have to mean breaking the bank."

"Let me do this," he said and her heart skipped a beat at the intensity in his gaze. It was like it really mattered to him that they have a fancy meal before the dance.

She looked around the restaurant at the other patrons, at least half of whom were people she knew from the high school. Stonecreek Grille had always been a popular predance dinner spot. She'd just never imagined herself here with a boy she really liked.

Really liked.

"You're blushing," Cole said, amusement lacing his tone.

"I'm not." She dipped her chin so that her hair would fall forward over her face, then remembered that Maggie and Brenna had styled it into an intricate braid around the side of her head.

Cole leaned forward. "What are you thinking about?"

She kept her gaze on the menu in front of her. "Steak."

He laughed at that. "Should I ask whose steak is making you blush?"

"Yuck," she said on a giggle. "That's so gross."

She looked up but her stomach lurched as she spotted Zach, Jonah, Jocelyn and Amanda at the front window of the restaurant. They laughed and pointed, then disappeared.

"What's wrong?" Cole looked over his shoulder.

"Nothing," she said but then the door to the restaurant swung open and the group filed in, ignoring the hostess in her all-black outfit as they headed straight for Cole and Maggie.

Cole cursed and turned toward her again. "Did you tell them we were coming here?" he demanded.

"No, I promise," she whispered.

"Hey, friends." Zach clapped Cole on the shoulder a little too hard to actually be considered friendly. "We saw Cole's truck parked outside. What's the deal?" He grabbed an empty chair from the table next to them and dropped into it. "I texted that we were meeting at The Kitchen at seven."

"Yeah," Jocelyn agreed. "Where have you been, Morgan? I thought we were getting ready together but you totally ghosted me."

"I didn't ghost you," Morgan said tightly. "I told you that my sister wanted to help me get ready."

"Bo-ring," Amanda said, snapping her gum. Seriously, what was up with that girl and how she chewed gum like a cow? And why hadn't Morgan noticed it before?

"Excuse me." The waiter, a tall, thin man who was probably a few years older than Maggie, muscled his way between Jonah and Amanda. "Unfortunately, we don't have room for a larger party."

"No problem," Zach said easily. "This place smells like rotting cat throw up anyway. Cole here—" he reached out and pinched Cole's cheek "—was just telling me how he couldn't find anything on the lousy menu that even looked edible."

"He didn't say that." Morgan looked at the waiter, pleading for him to do something. "I swear he didn't say that."

"It's fine." Cole pushed back from the table, a muscle ticking in his jaw. "Let's go. This place is overpriced anyway."

"You ordered two sodas, sir," the waiter said, condemnation dripping from his tone.

Jonah snickered.

His face flushing bright pink, Cole pulled out his wallet and threw a twenty on the table. "For your trouble," he muttered.

"Big spender," Zach said, standing and nudging Cole.

"Shut up," Cole told him.

When they were all out on the sidewalk, Zach slung an arm over Cole's shoulders. "Don't be mad, bro. I save you loads of money back there. Hell, you could buy us all dinner at The Kitchen and still get off cheaper than the Grille would have cost you."

Cole kept his gaze straight ahead as he led them down the street toward the diner. "Whatever."

"I'm so glad we're all together." Jocelyn took Morgan's hand. "It's exactly how I planned tonight to go."

Unfortunately, Morgan's plan for a romantic night with Cole had been ruined in the process. He wouldn't even make eye contact with her and sat at the far end of the table during dinner. Did he really think she'd planned this? Or that she wanted to be with Jocelyn and her group?

Zach insisted that he and Jocelyn pile into Cole's truck while Jonah and Amanda follow, preventing Morgan from getting any moment in private with Cole to explain that she was as unhappy about the turn of events as he was.

The parking lot at the high school was almost full by the time they arrived, with underclassmen being dropped off by parents.

As Cole turned off the car, Zach pulled a vape

pen from the inside pocket of his jacket. "Quick hit before we head into la-la land?"

"You can't do that in here," Cole said through clenched teeth.

"Boy Scout," Zach muttered under his breath as he climbed out. As soon as the door shut, Zach took a quick hit. The others joined him while Cole remained on the other side of the vehicle, arms crossed tightly over his chest.

"I'm sorry," Morgan said as she approached him, wanting to be as far away from the illegal activity as possible.

"It's fine."

"They recognized your truck, then saw us in the window. I didn't tell them anything."

He shot her a doubtful glance. "I don't care either way."

"I do," she said, anger swelling inside her. "I was having a great time with you, and they ruined it. I hate that you think I wanted this."

His silence hurt her more than any words could have.

"Be that way. I'm here to go to the dance, not to stand out in the parking lot with them." She started forward toward the high school's main entrance.

Cole was at her side a moment later, lacing his fingers with hers. "I'm sorry, too," he whispered.

She dashed a tear from the corner of one eye, then flashed a smile. "It's not your fault."

"Morgan, I want you to know—"

"Wait up, lovebirds."

Suddenly they were surrounded again, Cole letting go of her hand when Zach tried to jump on his back.

"Knock it off," he shouted.

"Maybe you'll get crowned king of the homecoming party poopers," Amanda said, giggling obnoxiously at her own joke.

Then they were in the dance, the thumping music and lights from the DJ's table overwhelming.

Morgan pulled in a sharp breath. This had been such a mistake. She would have been better off skipping the whole thing.

"Do you want to dance?" Cole asked, eyeing the crowd jumping up and down in unison in front of them.

"Not yet," she admitted. "That looks a little intense for me."

"Jonah has a flask," Jocelyn said, leaning in to whisper in Morgan's ear.

"I'm not drinking tonight," Morgan told her.

Jocelyn groaned and put her hand to her forehead, making an L shape with her thumb and forefinger.

"She's here." Amanda rushed up to them, grabbing onto Jocelyn's arms. "On the other side of the gym by the bleachers."

"Not now," Jocelyn said on a hiss of breath.

Morgan looked to the far end of the gym and saw Camryn standing with a group of girls. She knew her friend was going to the dance with friends instead of a date, and a sliver of unease snaked its way along her spine at the thought of Jocelyn or Amanda singling out any of those girls.

Before she could ask about it, the music changed to a slow ballad. Cole tugged her hand.

"Now's our chance." He gently pulled her toward the dance floor and all Morgan could do was glance back over her shoulder at the two mean girls. They were intently watching something on Amanda's phone, so Morgan figured she was safe to ignore them for at least a few minutes.

It felt super good to be dancing with Cole, even if she was distracted. "Way better," he said, his warm hands resting on her back.

"Mmm-hmm." She shuffled her feet to get a better view of Jocelyn and Amanda.

"I'm still glad we came tonight, even if the loser crew almost ruined it."

Several couples had joined them on the dance floor, blocking Morgan's view.

"Are you happy?"

"No," she breathed, craning her neck.

"I knew it. This was a mistake. I told you I was no good for you. If you'd gone with a boy who—"

"No," Morgan shouted, whirling out of Cole's arms. She'd caught sight of Jocelyn and Amanda pulling bags of what looked like flour from their purses, like they were replaying a scene from *Carrie* or that Drew Barrymore movie where the mean boys tried to dump dog food on Leelee Sobieski at the dance.

She pushed her way through the crowd. "Camryn, move," she yelled to her friend, who glanced over, confusion in her gentle eyes.

"Shut up, Spencer," she heard Zach call from the edge of the dance floor.

"Go," she called, and Camryn took several quick steps away from the bleachers just as white powder sprayed across the floor.

"You ruined it," Jocelyn screeched, moving out

of the shadows and toward Morgan. "Our plan was perfect."

"Not my plan," Morgan clarified loudly. "And there's nothing perfect about deliberate cruelty. Find another way to amuse yourself besides bullying people, Jocelyn. I'm done with your high and mighty attitude, and I bet I'm not the only one."

A few girls standing near the edge of the dance floor clapped.

One side of Jocelyn's brightly painted mouth curled into a sneer. "Shut up, you stupid bi—"

"Enough." Cole stepped forward, placing a hand on Morgan's back. "Most of us are here to have a good time." He pointed toward Jocelyn, then turned his gaze to Zach. "If you people can't deal with that, you should leave."

"Great idea, Cole." Dr. Cuthbert, the school's stout principal, appeared behind Zach. "Zach and Jocelyn, your time at the homecoming dance is officially done."

"It sucked anyway," Zach muttered. "Come on, guys."

Jocelyn continued to glare at Morgan. "You're going to regret this."

Morgan shook her head. "I doubt that."

With another angry huff, Jocelyn turned and stalked after Zach. Amanda and Jonah followed close on their heels.

While Dr. Cuthbert called for someone to clean up the mess in front of the bleachers, Camryn approached Morgan.

"I'm sorry they were such jerks," Morgan said

softly, hating that she'd ever had any association with that group.

"You saved me," Camryn told her.

"I just stopped them from doing something really mean and stupid."

Camryn smiled. "Which happened to save me. Thanks." She hugged Morgan, then was called away by another friend.

Morgan could feel people staring at her and refused to make eye contact with any of them.

"You okay?" Cole asked, shifting closer.

"Can we get out of here?"

Without hesitation he took her hand and led her from the overheated gymnasium. Once outside, she drew in a deep breath of the cool fall air. The night was clear and stars littered the night sky, but Morgan had trouble appreciating the beauty of it.

"That was the worst homecoming dance in the history of the world." She wiped at her eyes, embarrassed when tears flowed down her cheeks. This night was supposed to be perfect and now it had been ruined from start to finish.

"Not for me," Cole said softly.

He shrugged out of his jacket and draped it over her shoulders when she shivered.

"You're done with Jocelyn," he clarified.

"Very done," she confirmed.

"Then everything is great—better than great." He drew his thumb along her cheek. "Although I'm sorry you're upset."

She sighed. "I'm mainly upset that I didn't see them for the jerks they were from the start."

"We all make mistakes." He laced their fingers together. "Trust me, I'm the poster child for mistakes."

"Are you going to take me home now?"

"No way. We've got a couple more hours until your dad expects you back, right?"

She pulled her phone from her purse and checked the time. "Yeah." Suddenly nerves skittered across her skin. Cole's gaze on her was dark and unreadable. Four months ago she'd done a really bad job of trying to seduce him but now...

How was she supposed to tell him she wasn't ready for that? She liked him so much—in fact, she was pretty sure she was falling in love with him. But that didn't mean...

"How about ice cream?"

Her gaze flicked to his. "Ice cream?"

"And a hamburger." He rubbed his stomach. "I barely ate anything earlier and I noticed you didn't, either."

"Being with Zach and them made me lose my appetite."

"Me, too." His grin was kind of goofy and totally endearing. "But now I'm starving."

"Food sounds great."

They walked to his truck and he unlocked the door and opened it for her. Before she could climb in, he turned and cupped her face in his hands. "You were amazing tonight," he whispered and then his lips grazed hers.

Heat spiraled through her as she wound her arms around his neck. It didn't matter that she was only sixteen. Morgan knew this kiss and this boy would ruin her for whatever might follow. The kiss broke her apart, then put her back together, but different, because how could she be anything else when he turned her whole world upside down?

This moment was amazing and made everything worth it. Cole was worth it. Finally Morgan realized she was, too. She thought about Maggie's words from last weekend and was happy to know that she'd finally given her mom a reason to be proud.

Maggie checked her appearance in the hallway mirror one more time, fingering the amber necklace she wore, then glancing at the clock above the mantel. Griffin was almost twenty minutes late. An uneasy feeling had settled over her and no matter how many times she tried to reassure herself about his feelings for her, she couldn't shake her anxiety.

The house was quiet thanks to her dad, who'd taken Morgan and Ben out to dinner so it wouldn't be quite such a throwback-to-high-school scene when Griffin came to get her.

Suddenly her phone chirped, vibrating almost insistently on the entry table. She rushed toward it, trying to tell herself that the panic welling inside her was just her mind playing tricks.

Her whole body went numb as she read the message.

Emergency in Seattle with Cassie. On the road now. Sorry about tonight.

Three simple sentences but they ripped through Maggie with the force of machine-gun fire. She was being stood up.

She smoothed a hand over her chiffon dress as

humiliation washed over her. What could be so urgent that he couldn't wait a few hours to start the drive north? Maggie wanted to give him the benefit of the doubt, but all her insecurities tumbled forward like the text had unlocked the Pandora's box that held each of her demons and set them free to wreak havoc on her heart.

A knock at the front door had her heart hammering in her chest. Maybe he'd changed his mind and turned around to be with her before rushing off to his another woman's side.

Drawing in a deep breath, she opened the door to find Trevor standing on the other side. He straightened his tie and gave her a lopsided smile, looking almost as uncomfortable as he had when she'd found him with another woman on their wedding day.

"What happened?" she demanded, knowing he must be there on Griffin's behest.

He shrugged. "I'm sorry, Mags. I don't know. He got a phone call and freaked out, throwing clothes into a bag and heading for his car without much of an explanation. It involves—"

"Cassie," she interrupted. "He texted that much."

"He shouted at me to check on you as he was walking out the door. I didn't have a chance to ask him anything more. Mom tried calling, but he's not answering."

"I'm fine."

"You're a horrible liar," Trevor said gently. Griffin had told her something similar and she vowed at that moment to figure out how not to show her emotions on her face. She was sick to death of people being able to read her every feeling, especially when it felt like she was regularly getting kicked in the gut.

"At least tell me this wasn't some grand plan hatched by the two of you to pay me back for walking away from the wedding."

He shook his head. "I'll admit it's still difficult for me to see you with my brother. One moment I'm okay with it because I know I couldn't have made you happy, but the next it grates under my skin because..." He huffed out a humorless laugh. "Basically, Griffin's getting everything I ever thought I wanted and he doesn't even seem to care."

"Trevor."

"This isn't about me." He waved a hand, dismissing her concern. "And it has nothing to do with the wedding. I promise you, Maggie."

She nodded but looked away, embarrassed anew by the tears that filled her eyes. Her life felt utterly ridiculous that after being betrayed by one brother, she'd been consoled by the other. Now the roles were reversed, only Trevor was little comfort against the yawning ache stretching across her heart.

"He cares about you," Trevor offered with a sigh. "If that helps at all."

She swallowed. "He told me he loved me." What a strange admission to make to her ex-fiancé, but she couldn't stop the words. "I believed him."

"I doubt he was lying, although I'm also not sure Griffin actually knows how to properly love someone. As fantastic as our mom is, both of us seem to take after Dad as far as our stunted emotions go."

"Not helping," she muttered.

"I wish I knew how to help." He shoved his hands

into his pockets. "If you still want to go to the dance, I could be your date. As friends, of course," he added when she looked at him sharply.

"Wouldn't the gossips in town love that?" She shook her head. "Thank you for the offer, but I couldn't hold it together at the dance. As soon as someone asks about Griffin—"

"Which would be five seconds after you got there," Trevor confirmed.

"Right? I'd lose it, and I'm done with my private life being fodder for the rumor mill around here."

"You can hold your head high, Mags." Trevor lifted a hand, like he might reach out to her, then shoved it back into his pocket. "You've done nothing wrong."

She pressed her lips together and nodded. "Too bad that doesn't make me feel any better right now."

"I hope it will soon, and I'm sure Griffin will call you once whatever he's rushing toward settles down."

"No."

Trevor's brows lifted. "He'll call, Maggie."

"I'm not sure I want to talk to him."

"You can't mean that."

"Yes," she said with more confidence than she felt, "I can. I don't know what happened to send him rushing to Seattle. But if I'm not important enough to share something like that, it isn't working. I'm not going to settle. I've done too much of that in my life. If he won't let me in on everything, I don't want anything."

"Is that what you want me to tell him?"

She met his gaze. "Out of respect for me, I'd ask

that you let me handle it. I need time to focus on the election next week."

"You're going to win," Trevor promised, and Maggie appreciated his confidence. "I won't say a word to Griffin. Do you want to know the details of why he left when we get them?"

Her stomach burned. "I don't. If it ends, I have to make a clean break. There's no other way."

"I'm sorry," he repeated and leaned in to give her a quick hug.

"Thanks for coming here. I know it wasn't easy."

"Anything for you, Mags." With a wave, he headed back to his car.

Maggie closed the door to the house, an odd calm settling over her. Her heart might be shattered into a million pieces, but she'd recover. Or at least she'd move forward past the heartbreak.

What other choice did she have? She went upstairs and took off her clothes, hanging the beautiful dress she'd bought for the dance in the back of her childhood closet. She kept the necklace on as she showered and washed off the makeup she'd so carefully applied.

Her family returned home, each of them shocked and supportive at the sudden turn of events. Her father got out ice-cream sundae supplies and they gathered around the kitchen table, each trying to comfort Maggie in their own individual ways.

"Seriously," Ben said, pumping his fist in the air, "why won't anyone let me shank one of the Stones?"

"Because you'd go to jail and I'd be sad," Maggie answered calmly.

"Yeah, Ben, who'd fart at the dinner table if you

weren't around?" Morgan asked with a smirk. "We'd miss it so much."

"No one farts at the dinner table," their father said, followed quickly by a loud trumpeting sound coming from Ben.

"We're not having dinner now," the boy said, taking an extra dollop of whipped cream. "It doesn't count."

"Are you sure you're okay?" Morgan asked, biting down on her bottom lip.

"I'll be fine," Maggie said and forced a smile. "Life happens but we keep moving on, right?"

Jim nodded. "You're the strongest person I know, Mags."

"Thanks, Dad." Maggie cleared her throat. "I think to help make me feel better that everyone should watch a movie of my choice tonight without complaining."

Both Morgan and Ben groaned. "Not the Hallmark channel again," Ben said in a whine.

Maggie shook her head. "I was thinking that disaster movie you were telling me about last week."

"Seriously?" Morgan asked. "You want to watch *Meteor Wave*? It's supposed to be terrible and so inappropriate."

"Sounds perfect," Maggie told her.

They all piled into the cozy family room and, indeed, the movie was as bad and as perfect for her mood as Maggie expected.

And when her phone hadn't rung by the time she went to bed, Maggie knew she'd made the right choice. If Griffin wanted her to be a real part of his life, he would have called. He would have shared with her whatever trouble he was having. That was what people in relationships did. Right?

But what had they really had other than a few special moments and a couple of idyllic nights together? Maggie wanted something real, something she could count on. She deserved that.

Or maybe love just wasn't in the cards for her. That was fine, too. She had a full life, family and friends she cared about and a job she loved. That would have to be enough.

At least for now.

Epilogue

"Congratulations, Maggie."

Maggie turned from Irma Cole and Chuck O'Malley to where Jana Stone stood with a mix of hope and regret in her eyes.

"Thank you."

"Is it okay that I stopped by your victory party?" the older woman asked, fidgeting with one of the buttons on her blouse. "I understand why you might not want anyone from my family here so—"

"I'm glad you came," Maggie said honestly, giving Jana a hug. "Your support during the campaign meant a lot to me."

"I know you'll do a great job for the town, like you always have. You're a good girl, Maggie."

"Hopefully Jason will get over his loss quickly."

Jana waved away that concern. "He'll find something else to complain about soon enough. That branch of the family is a bunch of negative Nellies."

Maggie smiled at the description. "Please have a drink or a piece of cake," she offered, hating the awkwardness that enveloped them.

"Griffin called a few days ago," Jana blurted.

Pain lanced through Maggie at the mention of his name, but she kept her features even. She'd become an expert at masking her emotions in the past week.

"I don't want to hear about it," she said, taking a step away.

"He had a good reason for—"

Maggie held up a hand. "I can't do this, Jana. Not tonight." She glanced around the crowded reception room at the Miriam Inn, filled with so many of her friends and family members. It gave her strength knowing everyone had come out to celebrate her landslide victory in the election. She wouldn't spoil the mood by having a complete breakdown in the middle of her party.

Griffin's mother took a deep breath. "But you should know—"

"How's my best girl doing?" Maggie's father was next to her suddenly, pulling her in close to his side. "You need anything, sweetheart? Hello, Jana."

Jana inclined her head. "Jim."

"I'm great, Dad," Maggie lied. She truly was happy that she'd been reelected. It was her chance to prove she deserved her position as Stonecreek's mayor.

"Your grandmother asked if you'd stop by her table. There's some inn guest she wants to introduce you to—owns a techie company of some kind."

"Let's go now," Maggie said quickly.

She glanced up to see her father's gaze lingering on Jana, who continued to finger the button of her blouse.

"Thanks again for stopping by," Maggie told her.

"Of course," Jana said tightly. "Nice to see you, Jim. Give me a call next week about that commission for the vineyard garden."

Maggie heard her father's sharp intake of breath, but then he smiled and nodded. "Will do."

They turned and headed for Grammy's table.

"Are you sure you won't talk to Griffin?" her father asked quietly. "He's left several messages in the past days asking me to have you contact him."

"I'm sorry," she said, "but no. Have you ever heard the term 'ghosting'?"

Her dad cringed. "I don't think that's what he meant to do."

"It's been almost two weeks since he left and suddenly he decides to call? Too bad. Now that the election is officially over, I have more than enough to keep me busy."

"Busy isn't the same thing as happy."

"Close enough," she told him. "I've moved on, Dad. There's no room for Griffin Stone in my life. He simply wasn't the one for me." She smiled under her father's scrutiny, keeping her eyes bright.

"I actually believe you mean that." He leaned in and kissed the top of her head. "Good for you, Mags."

Who was the master of the poker face now? "Let's go talk to Grammy's VIP guest before she grabs the mic to call me over."

"You know her so well."

Maggie moved forward, because what other choice did she have? And if the ache in her chest had become a familiar companion, no one else needed to know.

* * * * *

MILLS & BOON

Coming next month

THEIR CHRISTMAS MIRACLE
Barbara Wallace

'Can I get you lads something to drink?'

Thomas's breath caught. It happened every so often. He'd catch the hint of an inflection or the turn of the head, and his mind would trip up. This time, it was the waitress's sharp northern twang that sounded uncannily familiar. He looked up, expecting reality to slap him back to his senses the way it had with his cottage memories. Instead…

He dropped the phone.

What the…?

His eyes darted to Linus. His brother's pale expression mirrored how Thomas felt. Mouth agape, eyes wide. If Thomas had gone mad, then his brother had plunged down the rabbit hole with him. And, mad he had to be, he thought, looking back at the waitress.

How else to explain why he was staring at the face of his dead wife?

'Rosie?' The word came out a hoarse whisper; he could barely speak. Six months. Praying and searching. Mourning.

It couldn't be her.

Who else would have those brown eyes? Dark and rich, like liquid gemstones. Bee-stung lips. And there was the scar on the bridge of her nose. The one she always hated, and that he loved because it connected the smattering of freckles.

How….? When? A million questions swirled in his head, none of which mattered. Not when a miracle was standing in front of him.

'Rosie,' he said, wrapping her in his arms.

He moved to pull her closer, only for her to push him away.

He found himself staring into eyes full of confusion.

'Do I know you?' she asked.

Continue reading
THEIR CHRISTMAS MIRACLE
Barbara Wallace

Available next month
www.millsandboon.co.uk

Copyright ©2018 Barbara Wallace